D.M. Ovenden is an up and coming author from Runcorn, England. He is a graduate of Canterbury College, where he studied music for three years. He began writing *The Lightblaser Saga* in 2006. His creation, Druenn Lightblaser, stemmed from playing with a stick in the garden when he was fourteen, and over time a story developed into seven books. He lives with his wife and son.

Lightblaser

D.M. OVENDEN

The Lightblaser Saga
Book One
Lightblaser

Vanguard Press

A CIP catalogue record for this title is
available from the British Library.

ISBN 978 1 84386 952 8

*Vanguard Press is an imprint of
Pegasus Elliot MacKenzie Publishers Ltd.*
www.pegasuspublishers.com

First Published in 2014

Vanguard Press
Sheraton House Castle Park
Cambridge England

Printed & Bound in Great Britain

I dedicate this book to my wonderful wife and son – without your support I could never have achieved this.

Angela, if you hadn't endured hours of me discussing my ideas and venting my excitement I would have never been able to get this far.

Irah-Edward, thank you so much for providing me with that smile every time I felt low.

I love you both beyond words.

You both inspire me and make me a better person and for that I am forever grateful.

Acknowledgments

I am indebted to all my friends and family who took the time and effort to read my work. I love you more than you know.

A special thanks goes to Ian, Richard and Sarah who gave me some fantastic feedback and advice with my little project.

Another person I would like to thank is my mother-in-law for letting me use the conservatory for two weeks to write.

A final thank you goes to my dad who inspired me to crack on when I was losing faith.

Prologue

The Great King Gondolas placed the book back on the shelf, let out a sigh and smiled. "Our history," he said, whilst settling down for a quiet evening in front of the fire in his private chamber in the West Wing of the Palace within the walls of the capital city, Cetni. He felt he had found peace at last. The king, who had sat on the throne for fourteen years, had witnessed many wars within Tharlian and had worked very hard for democracy and for new friendships between all the races of Tharlian. He chuckled to himself, "To think, poor Draytorn had to fight for twenty-two years for peace and the forming of this great Empire... I had it easy." He paused as he spotted his cat jumping up onto his lap and curling up. He stroked her as she purred peacefully. "To think that all the races are finally friends."

He stretched and slumped into his chair that was facing the fireplace; reaching for a glass goblet on the table next to his chair he poured himself a glass of Marietta's famous grape-row garnish wine from her vineyards outside of Cetni. His eyes fell onto a portrait of his wife above the fireplace. The cat purred again, glancing down at it the king smiled and stroked her gently as he stared up at the portrait again, "Margot," he whispered. "If only you were with me to see this."

A knock on the door pulled the Great King back from his daydream. "Yes?" he replied, "What do you want?" the king turned and saw his good friend Palantine standing tall in the doorway, casting an eerie dark shadow on the carpet in front of him. Palantine was a strong, well-built man who looked well into his forties. His features were stern yet wise and his eyes were kind and radiated a peaceful aura. His gold, shining armour flickered and glistened by the fireplace as he strode into the chamber with his royal blue cloak gliding gracefully behind and his blonde hair pulled back tightly into a ponytail.

As King Gondolas gazed upon his good friend's troubled expression his peace of mind quickly evaporated into trepidation. "Palantine, my good friend, what troubles you at this hour?" he asked patiently.

Palantine fell to one knee and bowed his head, closing his eyes he started. "I'm sorry, my king, I have grave news." He paused as if what he was about to say could kill the king, Gondolas rose from his chair and placed a hand on the quivering man's shoulder. "It's your son, Lhaesnoth," said Palantine.

Gondolas fell to his knees. "No!" he gasped. "Not him too."

Palantine nodded with remorse for his king's second son, who had been assassinated that very night. Palantine felt responsible, he had sworn an oath to protect the King's children as well as the King himself.

I should have been there, he thought, before returning his thoughts to the present. "They will be coming for you next my Lord. I implore you to leave the city." Palantine rose and began pacing, whilst scratching his blond goatee. "I can't leave. I would not be able to explain my sudden departure."

The old king reached for his chair and pulled himself up off his knees, his son's sudden passing weighing heavily on his shoulders.

He dabbed a tear away with his sleeve and took a large swig of wine. "No!" he decided defiantly, "I will not run."

Palantine's expression grew pained and feared for the worst. "I understand your reasoning, sir, but with all due respect, if we lose you then the bloodline will be lost forever." He paused, leaning against the far side of the fireplace. The king stood from his chair and paced the room. He started to speak then stopped.

Palantine asked quickly, "What is it, sir?"

Gondolas took another swig of wine then returned the goblet to the table. "I'm afraid I haven't been completely honest with you, Palantine. There is another…" Their eyes locked. "Palantine, can you keep a secret and never speak of it again?"

Palantine crept towards his loyal friend and knelt at his king's feet. "Of course, my lord, I'd gladly lay down my life before I told a soul." Gondolas strode towards him with pride in each step.

And after losing his second son, Palantine thought.

Gondolas placed a hand on his friend's shoulder. "Listen, obey, and don't look back. Is that understood, my good friend?" Palantine nodded nervously. "Journey to Valmer with my last son, he was kept in hiding for such a time, he's not even a year old, his name is Tierra but that name is not safe as I know word got out of his birth. Name him…"

Gondolas turned to the fire pondering a name. "Peter," he smiled, and turned back to Palantine who still knelt in front of him.

Gondolas raised his hand towards Palantine. He stared up at the old king and took his hand. Bright lights flew around the room, Palantine's eyes followed the flitting lights that flew out of the king's ring, darting around the room then flew into Palantine's body. He began to feel weak as if his life was being sucked out of him. He closed his eyes tight and prayed he would survive this unusual feeling.

I trust Gondolas with my life, he would never let harm come to me.

When the feeling had passed he opened his eyes and stared up at Gondolas whose expression looked contorted with pain. "I am sorry my friend but this is necessary." The King began to explain his plan.

Later that evening the withered face of Palantine Albright rode off for Valmer with the last descendant to the throne held firmly to him. Gondolas watched from his window, tears welling up in his eyes. "I wish it hadn't come to this, may the divine bless and protect you Peter, and you too my good friend Palantine."

A crash from behind him sent the old king wheeling towards the door.

Assassins! Already?

A dark silhouette slowly began to fill the brick wall. Unsheathing his sword he braced himself for his final judgment.

ONE

The Descendant

As the sun blazed over the quaint village of Pinevale all that could be heard was the soft sound of the cool breeze sailing around the village. Laughter echoed gently through the houses above and the local village buzzed with life as the people bought their daily supplies of food. Birds chirped in the sky, swooping down grabbing any scraps of food that lay on the cobbled pathways.

Pinevale was renowned for its peace and tranquility. The Great Pine tree stood in the centre of the town with three shops and the Goats' Head tavern surrounding this great landmark. A girl stood by the tree, she stared at the people passing by talking with one another. Raucous laughter could be heard from within the tavern. The girl smiled as she heard her mother calling. She glanced up over the roof of the tavern; the two houses that sat behind and above the tavern were perched on a small hill that was directly behind the garden of the tavern. The little girl saw her mother leaning over the old wooden fence, waving down at her. "Dinner's ready, sweetheart!" she called down to her daughter. The girl ran towards the pathway left of the tavern, which led up and around behind the Goats' Head tavern. She followed it until she reached the two quaint thatched roof houses. She glanced over to her left, a man waved at her; he looked as if he was in his late thirties.

"Good morning, Mariko," the man said, wiping the sweat from his forehead as he placed his spade into the loose soil and leant on the wooden fence in front of his garden. "Good morning, Mr Lightblaser" Mariko politely replied. With a cheeky grin on her bright, cheerful face, she gave a small curtsy to the man, then darted into her house on the right where her father was waiting for her at the door. Little Mariko ran inside the front door and disappeared into the shadows.

Mariko's father looked up at Lightblaser waving politely "How are you, Tom?" he asked.

"Very well, Francis, thank you for asking," Tom replied. The two men stood by their gates discussing the latest news from the imperial city, Cetni. Francis began his sentences very quickly with no pauses. "Yes I heard that thief was caught finally although they said another his partner in crime is still out there he got away and is now gathering a group to pillage small towns. I heard he said it as a threat though nothing else came of it I wouldn't have thought."

"I couldn't see Pinevale becoming a target, we have nothing to offer," Tom replied anxiously. "Touch wood, of course. We don't want to jinx ourselves," he continued whilst tapping his garden fence letting out a bellow of laughter. "How's the family?" Tom asked.

"Very well, thank you, although the wife's been a bit tied down lately, the eldest went down with a rough flu, we were lucky to save her. The Mrs insisted on taking her to Cetni to speak with the mages, I thought it would be a waste of her time but apparently Mace Thendark cured her himself!" he said with enthusiasm and excitement. Tom stared at Francis for a moment incredulous.

"The Mace Thendark, as in Dark Mace the wise wizard?" he barely managed to choke out *"don't forget to breathe"* he said to himself.

"The one and only!" Francis grinned and let out a small chuckle. "Don't worry, I reacted the same way." He scratched his head. "To think, she met the greatest of wise wizards, she's a special girl."

"I know how you feel," Tom began reminiscing. Tom and his darling beautiful daughter playing catch together on the beach, the sun raining down on them; he remembered those days well, being some of his fondest memories.

That's five years ago now! he thought to himself.

"Catch me, Daddy," the beautiful girl's voice trilled a high soprano. Tom could hear his daughter laughing, her short burst of giggles.

"Well I better get in, the food's getting cold, see you, Tom."

Tom reeled from his dream "yes… yes, enjoy." Tom smiled then raised his hand to wave. The sun was directly above him; he shielded his eyes as he waved.

"One more thing before I go, Tom," Francis said as he turned back towards Tom.

"Hmm?" Tom replied. "Any word of Sarah? She's been gone a while, what's it now, seven…" He started before Tom cut him off: "Nine… nine years," Tom replied giving out a long sigh.

"Sorry to hear that, Tom, don't you worry, she'll be back soon, I know it." Francis pushed open his gate and walked over to Tom, placing his hand on Tom's broad shoulders. "Trust me Tom she'll be back, she's not the sort of girl who wouldn't return, she wouldn't be gone this long without a good reason."

In that moment Tom's mind reeled, visions of the red cloak flying out from her small body, wielding two blades smeared in blood. "Sarah!" Tom yelled as she turned away and walked into the mist.

"Tom, you still there, buddy?" Francis yelled, pulling Tom back. "Come on, snap out of it! She'll be back," Francis smiled at him and walked back to his house. "You still owe me a drink for last week, okay?" he yelled closing the gate behind him.

Tom shook his head and rubbed his eyes. "Of course... drinks... tonight!" Tom smiled and waved as Francis closed the door behind him. Tom Lightblaser let out a long sigh. "No worries, she does have a reason," he let a proud smile shoot across his face.

He propped his spade up by the fence and admired his handiwork weeding the garden and chuckled. "Wait until these plants come through," he grinned, brushing the dirt off his gloves and then wiping the sweat from his forehead. He walked towards the house, the door wide open. Resting his hand on the door he yelled inside. His eyes shot over to the little boy still sleeping in his bed. *My little ten-year-old boy Druenn*, he thought as he realised he was still sleeping at noon.

"Druenn, you lazy bum, get up, it's your sister's birthday! You do remember, right? Did you get her a gift?" The little boy's eyes shot open. He leaped out of the bed.

"I'm so sorry, Dad, I forgot!" Druenn looked around the room then at his father.

"Druenn, you are ten years old, you should be able to get your own gifts by now; do you have any gold?" his father asked, raising an eyebrow.

Druenn scratched his brown hair, turning to his shoebox he had hidden under the bed so that his sister wouldn't steal his money. *She's probably already stolen enough of my pocket money to buy herself three gifts*, he thought. After searching his box he replaced the lid and pushed it to the far end of his bed, then looked up at his father and shrugged. His father glared at him. "I'm sorry, please can I have next week's pocket money now? I will make up for it with my chores," Druenn asked timidly, wanting only to run from his father's gaze.

"Fine, but you owe me, you remember that!" his father fired back, handing Druenn a shiny gold coin from a small pouch tied to his belt. Druenn's face lit up as he cupped his hands to receive the coin.

"I will make it up to you, double, I promise," Druenn said, as if reciting for a play, then he turned and ran out the door leaving his father alone in the small house.

Cheated again! Tom thought, letting a small grin escape him as he turned to wash off the wooden table. He glanced up at the mantelpiece above the stone fireplace to realise a small stack of gold coins, gone. He turned towards the door glaring. "He's scammed me out of more money!" he grimaced now looking round the room. The window was open, the sun shining, beaming onto the bed filling the room. The curtains moving in the midsummer breeze as a butterfly flew down resting on the windowsill. He turned towards the fireplace, an empty armchair rocked back and forth creaking in the breeze, light pouring in from the open door. "I better get the supper started," the half cheerful man exclaimed as he walked out from the sunlit doorway towards the stove.

Druenn ran down the hill towards the town jumping the fence ahead. He leaped over into the back garden of the tavern.

"Good morning, Druenn," an old man yelled from his seat by the bar as the little boy entered. "Fine weather we're 'avin!"

"Yes, sir. Indeed" Druenn panted. "Sorry, sir, I can't stop; I am getting my sister a gift," and with that he was gone.

The old man looked towards the door as Druenn ran out the front door waving, running past the ancient pine tree in the centre of town he ran towards a small cottage. The young boy stopped outside glancing up at the sign above the door. ***Osphets General Goods Shop***. Druenn walked in. The room was small; he looked to his left and spotted a long counter. He had spent many years gazing at the shelves of jarred sweets. His mouth watered, shaking his head back to reality he walked up to the counter. Eyeing a small bell upon the counter, he cupped his hand and rang the bell. He heard the creaking of the floorboards on the second floor.

Druenn looked up at the ceiling, his eyes following the sound of the footsteps from the floor above. He followed the sound towards the staircase and on his right, just behind the counter, a mysterious figure stepped into view, a tall lanky middle-aged man, his clothes bright, a red lace shirt, brown-laced leather trousers and sandals. Mr Osphets lived on the second floor of the shop. Everyone knew Mr Osphets well and he was a beloved character of the village.

"Druenn, what a pleasure to see you!" A low tenor voice rang out, croaked at points.

"And to you, Mister Osphets," Druenn replied politely, placing his hands on the counter like a puppy on its hind legs holding onto a table.

"Let me take a guess, youngster, you want a gift for your older sister, am I right?"

Druenn gasped in shock. Mr Osphets grinned a mischievous and cheeky grin. He turned towards the back of the shop, Druenn watched the middle-aged man collect his ladder, placing it by one of the many shelves along the back wall behind the counter,

Druenn's eyes followed the gangly man as he placed the ladder by a large shelf, he proceeded to climb to the top and reached for a white box roughly the size of a shoe box. Collecting it he tucked it under his arm. Climbing down, he placed the box upon the counter. "There! She will love it."

Curiosity filled Druenn as he gazed at the white box. "What's in it?" Druenn's innocent lovable voice replied.

"Ahh," Mr Osphets whispered mysteriously with a mischievous smile on his face. Mr Osphets loved children; his wife had died several years before whilst giving birth to a baby girl they called Ruth; two weeks after she was born she caught the flu and died. Mr Osphets swore to never love again, knowing he couldn't bear to lose another and especially not to lose another child so he lived alone, happily entertaining children when they browsed his store. Many of the parents would hire him as a storyteller for the children and the parents for parties. He had many stories to tell, of his adventures at sea, stories of piracy, heroic stories in giant castles and mighty hunts for ancient artifacts that could sink a continent or raise an army to fight for their master. He also enjoyed telling grizzly tales of the Great Black Betrayer and his pretty wife who gave her life for him and the heroic warriors who fought for justice.

Children loved these stories and he told them so often he'd lost count of how many times and hours he had spent reciting his exciting tales. After he met Sellienia he knew he had found the love of his life, and he knew he wanted to marry her and cherish her like a husband should and live the life he had read in many stories on his long journeys at sea. He knew he was a hopeless romantic, ever since he knew how he would propose to his wife after reading a book he truly loved. *Apprentice in love*, he thought.

"Sir?" Druenn asked confused.

Mr Osphets gathered his senses and woke from his daydream "Oh… yes… Yes, sorry about that, youngster, I got lost in a daydream," he replied quickly.

"What was it about?" asked Druenn.

"My daydream?" Mr Osphets replied in shock as he pointed to himself.

"Yes, it looked like a nice daydream" Druenn said as he examined Mr Osphets' face.

Bending over the counter, resting his head on his hand as he looked at the young boy, he admired Druenn. He thought about the first time he told Druenn his stories and how he would constantly question every detail, constantly searching for more knowledge. "Yes," he said politely. "It was." He smiled in admiration at Druenn. In one swift movement he stood upright and looked at the box. Druenn jumped watching the sudden movement.

"So! To the gift," Mr Osphets bellowed out. His hands wrapped around the lid of the box, his thin gangly fingers creeping round the edges and slowly pulled upwards, the lid began to slide off. "And there we go!" Mr Osphets sang.

Druenn peered into the box and smiled. "It's perfect!" he chimed.

Inside the box was a little doll wearing a pale violet dress and matching bonnet; the doll wore a lovable smile and big twinkly eyes. "I'll take it!" Druenn whispered excitedly laying the gold coin on the counter.

Mr Osphets grinned. "I'm pleased you like her," as he recalled where he had got it *It was to be my daughter's*, he thought "Make sure your sister takes care of little Marie, that's her name, don't forget, okay?"

Druenn placed the lid on top of the box and placed the box under his arm. "I will, sir," Druenn replied as he turned for the door. "Goodbye and thank you so much!" Druenn yelled as he exited the small shop.

Mr Osphets waved politely with a small smile on his face and slowly turned with a sigh of remorse as Druenn disappeared out of view through the light that shone brightly outside.

Druenn tore down the lane, past the great pine tree, past the tavern and followed the cobblestones down towards the stream where his sister, Meredith, could be found, most days watching the water sparkle with so many colours as it trickled down the stream towards the lake further down the lane. Druenn grabbed a sign that said '**Farmer Stouts Farm 1 mile**'. Gripping the signpost tight, he spun his body around ninety degrees to face the cobblestones again as they began to angle on the hill. Continuing down the hill and leaping onto the steps, skipping a step at a time he pressed on towards the stream. Druenn loved Pinevale, the weather was always beautiful and so was the area.

The sun blazed down and the birds chirped as they flew through the peaceful blue sky and landed on the trees scattered around the perfectly green meadows as far as the eye could see; daffodils and daisies were to be seen all over the carpet of green.

The sound of the calm breeze brushing past the barley in the further golden fields whilst the birds sung in time with the crickets, leaving a beautiful natural melody. Druenn would often find himself humming in time with songs the birds sang. As Druenn reached the bottom of the steep steps he heard the sounds of flowing water, he was close. He began to walk briskly as he caught what breath he had lost, then he saw it as he came round the last hill, the stream. The stream sparkled a thousand little suns of its own, and then he saw her, his sister, sitting by the stream brushing her fingers through the cool water. Druenn smiled, his teeth glistening in the sun. "Meredith!" he yelled waving his hand in the air.

She spun round. Her beautiful smile that made Druenn's world light up even more than it already was. Druenn knew he was blessed with the perfect sister. Her long flowing, golden hair sparkled in the water's reflection, her eyes as blue as the sky; everyone loved her, she was Pinevale's sweetheart. After seeing that smile no one could help but feel happy, as if she had a gift.

"Hello, Druenn, my sweet younger brother," she sang with her melodic voice. "How are you? I noticed you slept in, you naughty little rascal!" she teased, shooting him a playful scowl. As she stood, a warm breeze rushed through the valley. Her light salmon coloured dress danced in time with the breeze.

Druenn walked over to her and wrapped his free arm around her. She embraced him; she was warm and soft, safe. No one can be hurt in her arms. "Here!" Druenn said. "Happy thirteenth birthday, my dear sister." Her face lit up and her irresistible smile came through, the smile people would die for. Druenn placed the box in her hands, arms outstretched in front of her. She looked at the box, then at Druenn, then at the box again.

"Well, open it, silly!" Druenn giggled.

She slowly lifted the lid off, revealing the doll.

"Oh, Druenn," she said, placing her hand over her heart. "It's beautiful, she's beautiful." Druenn spotted a tear well in her eye. She picked up the doll delicately and hugged her.

"I heard her name is Marie," Druenn added.

Meredith looked at Marie and kissed her forehead. "I love her, Druenn, thank you so much, you're the best brother I could have ever asked for!" and she grabbed Druenn tight, cuddling him, loving him. "You really are, I mean it!" enforcing her sentiment.

"Well I do try," Druenn replied cheekily.

"I love you," she sobbed.

"I love you too, sis" Druenn replied snuggling into her shoulder.

"Come on, father's probably got supper ready for us," Meredith said, extending a hand towards Druenn. Druenn took it soft and warm, as always, he thought to himself. They ran together up the cobbled stairs. Druenn let go and panted. "Race you to the top!"

Meredith nodded once with a grin on her face.

They sprinted upwards giggling together, Meredith held onto the side railing as they ran. Within half a second she lost her footing and slipped; she felt herself lose her balance and began to topple backwards, she yelped in terror as she realised how far up they were.

A hand as strong as a metal vice shot out, it seized her hand and she felt it and gripped tightly. "I've got you!" Druenn yelled defiantly. "Just hold on until you get your grip!"

Meredith collected herself and panted. "See," she said, sucking another deep breath of air, "you are the best."

Also panting with one hand on his hip he said, breathlessly, "I do try!" with the cheeky expression on his face again.

The two siblings walked side by side the rest of the way, approaching the corner passing Farmer Stout's signpost. Druenn searched down the road where it divided. The left path led to Pinevale and the right led out into the open plains as his father called them. Druenn had never ventured out of Pinevale before but what he had been told was the rolling hill sides of the open plains continued on for miles before reaching any towns or cities. Looking right Druenn could see hills on either side of the cobbled road and further down an archway, Druenn took three steps towards the right, taking one step at a time.

"Druenn, what do you see?" Meredith asked. She knew something had caught Druenn's eye. When something would catch his eye Meredith always compared his movement to an eagle sighting prey.

Druenn was born with very strong vision, much stronger than the average human, almost a gift. Druenn took another step forward. Meredith could make out a dark mist, way off in the distance. The sound of a deep booming horn could only just be heard. As the sound rolled over the hills towards them they both took a step back.

"Druenn?" Meredith asked, fear welling in her voice. Druenn took a step back then another then another, he gasped, his hand shooting to his mouth, his eyes wide with terror. "What?" Meredith shrieked as Druenn took a further three steps back. Druenn wheeled, his eyes finding Meredith, a new wave of terror washed over him.

Meredith! he thought. *I've got to get her to safety. I've got to warn the town, how much time?"*

Turning back to the dark mist slowly creeping towards them, Druenn began counting out loud. "One, two, three, four."

Meredith stared at him in dismay. *What is he doing?"* she thought.

"Okay, there's time," Druenn said strongly but with the hint of fear. "Meredith, I need you to run back to Pinevale and warn them." He took a breath then gritted his teeth. "Bandits are going to attack Pinevale."

Meredith shrieked but refused to open her mouth and broke into fits of tears.

"Listen, sis, I need you to do this, stay focused. Tell everyone to get out of the town," said Druenn calmly.

"What are you going to do?" she managed, her voice barely a whisper.

A lump grew in Druenn's throat. "Meredith, please do this for me; we don't have time to discuss this!"

She held Marie tightly to her chest with tears streaming down her red cheeks as she nodded twice. "I love you!" she tearfully sobbed.

"Don't say goodbye, sis, this isn't goodbye! But I love you too," Druenn's half cheeky grin returning.

Druenn turned away from his sister, and listened to her run off into the distance. Forcing back the tears of fear for the people he loved so dearly. *No time for this, Druenn, get a grip and focus, I've wished for this to happen and swore I'd know how to single handedly stop them.*

Druenn had always heard the stories about bandits destroying towns just for fun and it made him sick, so he devised a plan to stop them or at least slow them down, he thought.

"Okay, the plan!" as he ran towards a small bush under a large oak tree a few yards away from the cobbled path. His hands scrabbling round in the bush he pulled out a bow and arrows.

"Finally a good purpose," Druenn said, his voice shaky as the adrenaline began coursing its way through his blood. With the excitement of Mr Osphets' stories Druenn asked him to make a bow and arrow for him and he did. For weeks Druenn had played with it until he accidentally hurt a friend by firing an arrow into his hand. His father was furious and told him to get rid of it, as he did not want his son playing with weapons. Druenn could not part with it, so he hid it in a small bush outside the village.

Crawling up the hill in front of him he approached the top and poked his head out above the brow of the hill. His eyes were wide as fear gripped him. He began to shake *Calm down, you fool!"* he screamed to himself, getting a grip on himself. He realised they would be on the village in no time at all. He could see the bandits as clear as day now, all riding horses, brown and black. The first thing Druenn noticed was how big they all were, muscles bulging from their open tattered leather shirts, they all wielded swords, axes and maces.

Suddenly a loud clanging from the village bell rang out. Druenn jumped and his head shot up right towards Pinevale. A sound that chilled Druenn to the bone, the sound of terrified people, people Druenn knew and loved. *I should be there with them!* Druenn grasped his bow and ran towards Pinevale. The clattering of hooves closing behind him, Druenn refused to turn back, he knew it would slow him down. *Keep going, don't stop keep running, Meredith and Father need me!*

"Our first kill, boys," a deep gruff voice yelled.

"And it's a little boy," another voice crowed.

"He's mine!" a third grunted. Druenn's mind went blank. *I'm going to die!* Then something inside Druenn cracked. His mind raced, then he focused on what he had to do. Still sprinting he drew an arrow. The hooves of the third man's horse he guessed.

"No!" Druenn yelled, "I will not die today!" He glanced to his left and saw him; his huge face looking down at him, his nose stretched over his face, bald, tattoos all over his face, scars. So many scars.

"Come here, you!" the booming voice sounded again.

He saw the bandit's arm raise an axe, he began to swing letting out a loud moan from the weight. Druenn screamed in terror as he leapt to his right and fired his arrow. It sailed through the sky a second before connecting with the bandit's throat. *Blood! So much blood!* Druenn continued to fall back listening to the bandit choke and gurgle on his own blood. *Blood that is spilling because of me!* he thought.

A second later he felt an almighty crash smashing him into a spin. The boy flew through the air before hitting the cobbled path with tremendous force. He forced his eyes to open watching the black and brown horses sail past him.

The haze over his eyes gradually increased causing the world to spin, the darkness creeping around the little boy. "Father, sister, I failed you," he forced himself to get up. *Why can't I feel my arms, my hands.* Confusion settled in; the taste of blood very distinct in his mouth, he forced his eyes to look at the stones below, blood covering them. Druenn continued to force himself to at least his knees, his elbows pushed him up then finding his hands he gripped the ground for further support. All the while the horses were flying past him, he turned his heavy head. The events unfolding felt like a dream to him, then out of the corner of his eye a hammer sailed towards him.

"Say goodnight, boy!" A nasally voice sounded from the corner of Druenn's memory. As the hammer closed, Druenn said two words, "I'm sorry." With that there was a shooting pain across the side of his face then the world went black.

TWO

Legacy

Am I dead? Druenn thought. *I can't feel my arms!* The blackness surrounded him as he floated through the darkness. W*hat happened? Why can't I feel my body?*

"Druenn!" a voice screamed from the edge of his mind.

Meredith?

He turned his head in all directions only to see the black void. *Maybe I am dead*, Druenn pondered. *Should I care that I failed my family? Does it matter in this life? Is this the afterlife? Is this what we should expect for the rest of eternity?"* The questions were flowing through Druenn, and within a second he realised the truth. *I'm thinking, that means I'm alive, I must be! But where am I?* he thought while scanning the surroundings again. He began to feel something hard, something cold, like stone. *Like cobblestones!*

Then another voice came through the blackness. "Wake up, please wake up!"

Meredith! his mind screamed. *Get up; I order you, Druenn Lightblaser, get up!"* The little boy's eye's flicked, his vision blurred, as he stared upwards, a shadow emerged from the fading blackness. Druenn's heart raced as the fear gripped him again; he grabbed the cobblestones below him as he scrambled back several paces.

"Shh, it's okay," a sweet voice sang with a hint of panic.

Druenn began frantically rubbing his eyes, when he re-opened them they were clear, kneeling over him was a girl, no older than him. Her eyes a forest green colour watched him clouded with tears, her face blackened by the smoke, her white clothes now torn brown rags. *Who is she?* Druenn wondered his eyes fixed on her.

"Please, we need to get away from here," she exclaimed, scared but controlled.

Druenn slowly turned his head to his left looking over the shoulder of the little girl, he saw a man lying very still on the ground, scars and tattoos covering his bald head and face, his eyes traced down towards the arrow protruding from the man's throat. In that moment Druenn remembered, his mind reeled back to the one moment in his life where he was petrified and consumed with anger. He saw himself flying through the air screaming only this time it was slower, he saw the arrow race out from his bow and strike the bandit with such force, he remembered the sound the blood made as it reached the stones, then remembered the hammer, when his world went black.

Druenn jumped as he realised where he was, his hand automatically finding the wound on his face. He felt the pain as his hand touched the tender area, he clenched his teeth, the pain; his face felt as if it was on fire, the burning, he shook it off. *It's a scratch, I'm alive.*

"I'm alive," he whispered. The girl took his arm and helped Druenn to his feet. "I need to find my family," he said with the strongest voice he could master.

"But…"

Druenn cut her off gesturing with his hand. "I have to find my family," Druenn repeated, rubbing his face gently. He bent down and reached for his bow, it was a few yards away from him. He staggered over clutching his ribs with his right hand stretched over to the left side of his body, he picked it up only then realising the bow was in two pieces. Druenn, still dazed and confused, let the bow drop from his hands, the bow hit the stones with a clatter.

The young boy searched around the bandit, looking for anything he could defend himself with. The little girl stood and watched him in confusion, a gust of wind picked up with a whistle through the trees a few yards away; she folded her arms as a chill ran down her spine. She looked up to see dark clouds building around the village as the smoke from the burning village rose up like a giant spiraling tornado. Another gust ran down the path, kicking up dust in between the stones. The young girl shielded her eyes and shut them tightly, when she opened them Druenn had his back to her, a few yards away standing over by the dead bandit sprawled across the path.

"What are you going to do?" she asked staring at him.

I need a weapon, he thought. Then he spotted it, a sword in its scabbard around the bandit's waist, he leant over the great hulking beast and gripped his fingers slowly around the hilt of the sword, carefully he drew it from the scabbard. A wave of power rushed through the young boy as he listened to the delicate slide of the blade running past the scabbard.

He closed his eyes, breathing deeply and calmly, then raising the sword above him, he opened his eyes and watched the sun glisten off the blade. As the sun disappeared behind the stormy clouds overhead, a low rumble bellowed out from the distance as it rolled over the hills towards them, Druenn brought the sword to his side. Taking a deep breath he gathered his courage, forced back the lump in his throat as he pictured his father butchered and his sister captured and towed away on the back a black horse, he exhaled.

"It's time," he whispered. Before the little girl realised what had happened Druenn was gone, sprinting down the path towards Pinevale. He reached the archway in front of him. Looking up he studied the burnt sign. It read 'Welcome to Pinevale'. He slowly walked through into the smoke, into a world of darkness. Rain began to fall, leaving behind the last of the beautiful weather that was overhead not long before. The cold water fell heavy and fast dousing the ferocious flames from the houses he knew and remembered so well.

Everything was gone, everything had changed. Raising the sword in front of him he crept forward step by step. He passed the tavern on his right, the thatch burnt to cinders. He glanced to his left at the Great Tree he had known since he was old enough to remember, blazing, a large snap from behind him sent the little boy into a raging panic. He spun in terror, sword thrust forward in front of him. There stood the little girl from earlier. Still confused on her being there he watched her for a moment as his heart tried to slow from the rush of adrenaline. He breathed an exasperated sigh of relief. *What is she doing here and who is she?* Druenn thought. Dismissing his thoughts he refocused and began to walk up the cobbled hill to his house. Bodies lay strewn across the ground covered in blood, Druenn's legs shook violently.

"Please let me come with you, don't leave me here," the girl called.

Druenn gestured her over to him, she leapt over the bodies in front of her then ran to his side. The smoke was beginning to thin as the gusts of wind and the rain pounded the burning houses.

"What's your name?" Druenn asked forcing his voice to sound steady.

"I don't know, I don't remember," she replied almost sounding like she was asking a question.

They continued on up the hill, Druenn's heart dropped as his house came into view. He sprinted over to the burning wreck. He screamed a painful scream and fell to his knees. He felt sick.

"Everyone's dead, and it's because of me." He panted between his sniffs forcing back his overwhelming urge to lose control. Tears streamed down his face, the girl still staring at him from across the road leaning on the charred wooden fence by the other house. As Druenn collapsed to the ground his crying broke into sheer dismay, he heard a voice.

"Druenn," a faint voice groaned.

Druenn's eyes shot up, he knew that voice all too well, he crawled round a tree by his house, there sprawled across the floor was his father, clear pitchfork marks coated in blood across his chest, his breathing stressed "My son, you're alive."

Tears streaming down his face, Druenn tried to speak but nothing came out, the lump in his throat was back and worse than ever.

The sword fell out of Druenn's hands as he crawled over to his dying father; he helped support his father's head, pulling his father across his lap, he saw the agonising pain flow through his father as he moved him. Druenn looked down at his father, forcing his tears back and fixing a small smile in place. His father groaned again, a proud smile on his face as he raised his hand to Druenn's face. "Oh, Druenn, I'm proud of you, son. I did well to bring you up if I may say so myself," he chuckled in pain.

Druenn gasped; a tear fell down his face.

Tom took a deep breath. "I…" the pain cut him off.

Druenn panicked, his breathing quickened. "Father, stay with me, okay? You'll be fine!"

"No, Druenn," his father replied breathlessly, "My time here has ended, and it's time for you to continue to the next step of your life."

"No, Father," Druenn yelled out. "I can't do this on my own, I need you to guide me, Father!"

Tom stretched his other hand as if to drop something into Druenn's hand. Druenn brought his hand forward and cupped it; Tom began to unclench his hand and dropped a small necklace into Druenn's hand. "This was given to me by your mother, she told me if this situation was to arise..." The pain cut him off again, he gasped for air, Druenn quietly gestured not to talk, but he waved it off. "If this situation was to arise to give this to you, light the beacon and continue on your journey."

The Journey again, Druenn thought, his father often mentioned something about a journey that he would one day have to follow. Tom's hand fell to the ground, Druenn held his father tight as his tears began again. Druenn looked at the necklace in his hand, it was a beautiful crystal connected to a silver chain.

"Twist the crystal," his father forced out breathlessly. Obeying, Druenn gripped the top and bottom of the crystal with both his thumb and index finger and twisted, a beam of green light shot out into the black smoke filled sky. He glanced at the crystal again, the now lime green crystal blazed from within. His father searched around then back to Druenn. Where's Meredith?"

Druenn looked at the floor. "I don't know," he choked out.

"Find her, Druenn," he croaked. He arched his back in pain then pulled Druenn's head towards his. "Remember me and fulfill your mother's legacy," his father whispered to him as his eyes closed for the last time and his last breath exhaled. His father's head dropped, fell back and he was gone.

Druenn couldn't comprehend what had happened, his mind reeled and the shock settled in.

I'm alone.

His hands clenched as he wiped his tears, the lump in his throat growing as he began to hyperventilate, the sobs came faster, his suppressed groans of agony becoming more apparent. He reached for his father's hand, paused, then brought his hand back, then clenched again. He slumped his hands supporting his weight as he choked and sobbed the tears streaming down his face. The girl walked over her eyes red from the tears. "We must leave," she forced out, her voice wavering as she reached out to rest her hand on Druenn's shoulder. The distraught boy turned to her then looked down the road, his eyes blazed with hate, another tear dripped onto his hand as he shifted his body weight round then let out an agonising scream that terrified the little girl. She leapt back in fear.

"It's time for you to go, Druenn," a calm remorseful voice said from behind him. Druenn spun round, two figures stood in the middle of the road. A rough female voice began to speak; Druenn saw it was the figure on the right.

"Oh, come now, we must explain ourselves, Warren. Look, both the children are terrified." They began to walk closer through the smoke. To Druenn's surprise they were both reasonably young. The man looked quite like an adventurer, like the ones he had seen pictures of in his books, leather trousers with a linen shirt and a leather waistcoat over the top, a long grey and white robe open down the middle, his sword clearly on show, attached to his belt, with a cloak that covered most of his body.

The man's features were very much what he expected from an adventurer, rugged as if he had not shaved in a few days, his brown hair shoulder length and his eyes, so blue. *Just like Meredith's*, he thought. The man's staff looked no more than a finely carved stick. *But being an adventurer it must be a staff.* The women, however, Druenn recognised instantly. *She has to be a mage, there's no denying that.* Druenn continued to observe the woman; she wore a violet dress that covered her entire body with a staff on her back. She spoke again with a horse, raspy voice.

"I hear them coming back, they will be here to take the survivors." Her eyes fell upon the little girl. The little girl realised she was being watched and took three steps back. "It's okay, little girl, we are here to save you both," her calm voice grinded. "Warren, check Druenn, he's your responsibility now."

Druenn's tear filled eyes shot up at the man now walking towards him. He wiped his eyes and got off the floor reaching for the sword, he grasped it and held it tightly. "What do you want from me?" Druenn screamed as the man walked towards him raising his hands up in surrender.

"I am a friend, I'm not here to hurt you. I knew your father briefly." The man spoke with calm reassurance.

Druenn held the sword higher.

"Easy, please, Druenn, steady, hear me out," the man pleaded. "My name is Warren Anguish," he started. "I was a very close friend of your mother, Sarah Lightblaser."

Druenn's eyes widened. "You...you knew my mother?"

"Knew her?" Warren scoffed. "I worked with her, fought with her, but..." he stopped "I can't tell you any more, she wouldn't let me until the right time."

Voices in the distance could now be heard as well as the galloping of hooves.

"So my mother's alive?" Druenn shouted as the sword clanked to the ground.

"This is not the time for a discussion Warren, we must leave, now!" the women snapped.

"Who's the girl Sadia?" Warren asked with an edge of anticipation.

"I don't know, she has had her memory wiped, but for that reason I am quite convinced it's her, the girl we were made aware of," said the woman, exasperated.

"Really?" said Warren, with shock and surprise it seemed to Druenn.

"I'm taking her back to the university in Cetni." She swung her arm through the air and as she did so her hand ignited into a ball of colours, with a whisper of two words a black and purple circular cloud appeared. The vortex swirled inward, clouds of black sucked to the centre and disappearing, the size grew until it was the size of the mage. Druenn leapt back in fear as a gust of wind began pulling towards the Vortex.

"This portal goes directly to the university, you'll have to make your own, Warren," she turned to the little girl and took her hand. "Don't you worry, my dear. We shall get your memory back and take you to safety," she said to the little girl. The girl stared at her and then with a simple nod they both walked towards the portal.

Druenn took a step forward. "No wait… it could be a trick!" he yelled to her.

They both stopped and looked at him, the girl smiled at Druenn and replied, "I trust her."

With a beam of light they were both gone. Druenn stood, stunned, he glanced at Warren who had begun casting his own portal. Another flash of light and their portal was made.

"You ready, Druenn?" The little boy wiped his eyes for the last time, then looked at his father's body whilst listening to the swirling vortex, the voices in the distance and galloping, sounding closer every passing moment. He turned around and faced his home town. *The last time I will see this place*, he thought. Black sky, the houses burnt to the ground, the people dead and butchered and the smell of smoke and burnt wood.

"Druenn, we have no time to waste, if there was any moment in your life where you had to trust someone you don't know make it this one," Warren yelled defiantly. "This was your mother's wish; that I'd save you in this situation." Warren threw out his hand.

Druenn turned again. *Goodbye, home*, he thought as he took Warren's hand and they both began to walk towards the portal. Druenn felt the wind pull him and suck harder, he tried to break free of Warren's grasp and run but he was too strong, the portal was no more than a foot away.

Druenn closed his eyes as the swirling sound consumed him. Druenn tightened his eyes as the sound got louder, then with an almighty screech of the noise it was gone, Warren stopped walking.

THREE

Rienhold

"Druenn, open your eyes," someone whispered. Druenn slowly pulled one eye open, the other shot open with the shock. Druenn was faced with a beautiful sight, no rain, no death, no burning, just beauty. He stood at the beginning of a path leading down towards a palace. He could see the mountains off in the distance, a waterfall pouring down the side of one cascading into a mighty river below, the forests so green, the sky so blue, the lake full of so many colours.

This is the world I've been living in? Druenn thought.

"Come on, Druenn, we must press on," Warren urged. "This is to be your new home for the next few years," Warren continued as he began a steady paced walk down the cobbled path towards the palace ahead.

Druenn quickly realised he wasn't walking as he watched Warren gradually shrinking into the distance. He picked his feet up and sprinted back to Warren's side. Druenn watched a sign sail past, it looked like a stump of wood no higher than Warren carved into the shape of an arrow perched on top. Engraved on the wood were the words:

Rienhold
Warrior's Guild and hired arms ahead.

Druenn looked back at the palace and then back at the sign that was now a few metres behind him. *A warrior's guild? Why would Warren take me there?* Druenn thought. Warren began to smile as he looked down at the young boy clinging almost too close to him.

"Druenn, there is no need to fear, you are completely safe here." As they neared the palace the sun disappeared from view, the shadow bore down on them consuming them like a bed sheet covering a bed, Warren let out a sigh of relief. "Much better in the shade, don't you think, Druenn?"

"I guess so," Druenn replied with a dead voice, no emotion to be heard.

What could I expect? Warren thought. *He's watched his entire life crash down in front of him?*

"Druenn, these people will look after you, as will I and that's a promise." Warren calmly said to the frightened child. They reached a giant door, which was clearly the entrance to the palace. Druenn gazed up in shock.

"Wow it's huge!"

Warren turned to Druenn. "Quite a door, wouldn't you agree?" He grinned as he reached for the bell hanging from the right side of the door, gripping the string dangling below he shook the bell. As the haunting booming from the bell echoed around the landscape they both heard voices on the other side of the door, a small hatch in the door opened and the face of a man appeared. The man looked reasonably young, late twenties and had a moustache, a very unique style with the whiskers curled upwards. He instantly recognised Warren.

"Warren, good to see you old chum, how's things in the wild?" the man asked excitedly.

Warren chuckled. "I'll tell you all about it if you'll let me in."

The man smiled with joy as a giant bolt slammed out of its socket, then the man spotted the little boy standing two paces behind Warren, the boy was covered in ash and soot. "Who's this, then, Warren?" As he continued to gaze at the boy, he noticed his clothes torn and blackened, his eyes with water streaked marks.

He's been crying, the man thought, and something else he noticed, something reddish smeared over his clothes. *Blood?*

"The boy's covered in blood," the man continued accusingly.

"Let us in and I'll explain," Warren exclaimed raising his hands to the door.

"Okay, mate, come in." As the door's final bolt clicked out of place, it echoed round the halls behind. The door steadily creaked open and Druenn was able to peer around. He stepped forward as his eyes adjusted to the darkness. He closed his eyes and covered his face rubbing them, he opened them again, he gasped. A giant hall that continued off into the distance, a red carpet leading up to a round table further ahead. He gazed up at the roof, each beam above him hung with a sword, torches blazing from each pillar. Druenn turned to the man on his right; the man scaled him up and down.

"So," he paused, glancing over at Warren, "new recruit?"

"Dontain," Warren replied, smiled then turned to Druenn. "This is Druenn Lightblaser."

Dontain stared at the child then back at Warren. "What... you can't be serious," he said with obvious scepticism in his eyes

"Oh, I'm deadly serious," Warren grinned.

Dontain pointed at the frightened boy. "So that's the son of…"

"Not now!" Warren cut in. "He shouldn't know...not yet. I'll explain it all to you once we are alone."

"Oh. Eh, all right then." Dontain paused again. "You did understand the situation best."

Dontain reached back to a ledge just behind the open door. He picked up a large tankard of mead and took a large swig and exhaled a satisfied sigh; he placed the tankard back on the ledge and signaled Warren out of the entrance, then with a grunt of strain he began to push the giant door back into place, and return the bolts to the original place.

"Okay, you two, I suggest you'd better sign in," Dontain said as he bent down and reached out for Druenn's hand. Druenn stared at the outstretched hand then looked up at Warren.

Warren stared down at Druenn then lent down and whispered in his ear. "I believe he wishes to shake your hand and welcome you."

Druenn's eyes went wide, apologetically he threw his hand out and shook the man's, it felt rough, like stone. The young boy stared at the floor with his eyes shut. "I'm very sorry I didn't understand, it's a pleasure to meet you Mr Dontain it really is and thank you," Druenn blurted out without pause.

Dontain watched the young boys shoulders jerk. *He's crying, he must have been in something traumatic, poor little bugger*, he thought

"Whoa there, easy, kid, no need to apologise," Dontain said smiling, a comforting smile as he moved his hand to Druenn's head and ruffled his hair. Warren stepped forward and placed both hands on his shoulders, Druenn wiped his eyes and forced himself to look up and gave a weak smile to them both. Warren watched Druenn with admiration.

Only ten years old and witnessed those barbarians but still has the strength to smile; he's a brave boy."

"Come on, Druenn, let's get you set up." Turning him towards the round table, Warren took one more look at Dontain. Dontain smiled and took Warren's hand; they shook once then pulled each other close and bumped their shoulders together.

Dontain whispered something inaudible into Warren's ear; Druenn heard every word but the language was something he had never heard before, Warren nodded.

"Itel," Warren replied. They both smiled.

"It's good to have you back, Anguish," Dontain said.

"It's good to be back," Warren replied as he turned to Druenn and placed his hands on his shoulders again and began to walk down the corridor.

Dontain listened to the echo of their footsteps as they continued down the corridor, disappearing beyond the table.

"Wow!" Dontain chuckled, "a descendant of DV, this will be fascinating."

The two figures walked in silence towards the far end of the corridor. Druenn kept looking left to right, as doors on both sides sailed past them. "Warren?" Druenn said.

"Yes?" Warren replied.

"Where do all these doors go?" Druenn asked politely.

"Well…" Warren looked to his left, and saw door after door and then he looked to his right. "Well, Druenn, these are the dorm rooms."

"What's a dorm room?" Druenn asked confused.

"Well, the dorm rooms are designed for students, and all the students who live here live on campus, in this building, and at the far end of this building is the Dean's office which is where we will sign you up," Warren explained to Druenn.

The scared little boy looked up at Warren, fear in his eyes. "Are you going to leave me once I'm signed in?" A tear welled up in his eye.

"No, Druenn," Warren smiled. "I'm not going to leave you, I will be your personal trainer and ensure you're happy here."

Druenn breathed a sigh of relief. "Thank you," Druenn said, sniffing. "Sorry, I have a few more questions."

"Fire away, mate" Warren replied.

"Why did he call you Anguish?"

Warren looked down at Druenn and grinned. "Well it's my surname," he replied proudly. "It's also a nickname I was given."

"Oh… right" Druenn replied feeling let down.

"Thought it was more interesting than that, huh?"

"Yeah, kinda!" Druenn shot back also grinning. They both smiled at each other for a moment. "Second question," Druenn asked whilst waving his arm in the air.

Warren rolled his eyes with a sigh and then he looked down at Druenn and chuckled. "What's up, mate?" Warren asked

"What does 'itel' mean?" Druenn asked politely.

"Ahh…good question," Warren replied.

Druenn looked up at him intently, Warren chuckled. "Itel means 'yes' in Elvish tongue, that's the language of the elven druids in Ethalas," he explained as they approached the large last door. Warren stepped forward, he gestured Druenn to stop as they reached the door. Warren raised his fist to the door as he read the number and name. Carved on the door was number one hundred and nineteen and name ***Dean Fleeran's Office***. He knocked, the echo bounced around the long corridor.

"Well done, you made it to the other end?" a quiet voice sounded from the opposite end of the corridor.

Warren burst out with a raucous of laughter. "That Dontain!" he continued to chuckle as he knocked again.

"You may enter," an old voice sounded from the other side of the door.

Warren beckoned Druenn over and placed a hand on his shoulder. "Let's go, mate," he smiled down at him.

Druenn gave a weak smile then looked forward and took a deep breath. Warren opened the door and followed Druenn in.

Druenn looked around the room, it was different to what he expected; on the left was stacks after stacks of books piled on top of each other sprawled over a carpet in front of a roaring fire along with more books piled over a table with the chair piled up with more books. He took a glance at the Dean behind his desk, the four giant windows behind causing the light to pour in making a black silhouette of the Dean, then looking to his right he saw giant bookshelves, there was so many, he looked back to the Dean. The Dean clapped his hands and the curtains closed, *on their own?* Druenn thought.

"Magic, my dear boy…magic," the Dean said with a friendly and caring voice. Druenn stared at the Dean, he was bald apart from the thick white hair tied up in a ponytail on the back of his head, a white beard also tied up, he wore what looked like a white cloth around his top body and what looked like a red dress on the bottom.

"Welcome to Rienhold," the Dean welcomed with his arms outstretched.

Druenn took a weak bow. "Thank you, sir."

The Dean stood and grasped his cane beside him; he walked round his desk towards Druenn with a constant step, step click rhythm. As the Dean reached Druenn, he realised the Dean was not much taller than himself, the Dean's face lit up with happiness. "Yes…you are indeed her son" he cheerfully confirmed with a sweet old gentlemanly voice. "We have been waiting for you since you turned eight I'll have you know young Druenn."

"Excuse me, sir," Druenn asked politely, "how do you all know who I am?"

"Well, shockingly enough, we were all close friends of your mother," the Dean replied.

"Yep!" Warren nodded.

"But what did my mother do? I don't understand why she knew so many people I just don't."

"Well unfortunately Druenn we don't have the right to tell you, not until you have been trained and the time is right," the Dean replied.

"The best way to explain it would be that there are some people that wish to find the truth about your mother, some that would kill for this information," Warren explained.

"What?" Druenn said incredulous. "Kill? Why?"

"Like we said, Druenn, we can't tell you until you are older and trained in the art of fighting." The Dean exclaimed, "I'm sorry, my dear boy but you will have to wait."

Druenn slumped. There was a sudden bang on the door, which caused both Warren and Druenn to jump.

"Enter!" the Dean called out. The door swung open with a bang as it smacked into the wall, a broad man stepped in rushing towards the Dean.

"Sir! I must protest. I have no interest in training this…" he glanced down at Druenn, still covered in blackened soot. "Child, it's a waste of my time, get him out of my sight!" Druenn looked up at the broad man dressed in a black tunic and black tights with a black cloak and what looked to be a naked woman reclining gold earring. Warren stood and walked over to the broad man.

"How dare you speak to him like that, he's only a boy!" Warren moved in front of the confused child in a defensive stance.

"Warren, what a pleasant surprise." The man chuckled sarcastically.

"You forget yourself, Warren, you're not Anguish any more!" the man fought back with aggression in his voice. "Whether he is her son or not, I don't give a shit!" the man continued to fire back violently swinging his arms in unusual gestures.

"Calm yourself, Terribor," the Dean raised his hand.

"No!" Terribor shouted as he pointed to Druenn, the little boy taking a step back peeking out from behind Warren. "I will be doing you all a favour by doing this," Terribor growled as he whispered something under his breath. "Red Saviour you will not succeed."

The man's finger began to glow blue, the colour becoming darker and darker. Druenn stepped back again as the man's finger ignited into a ball of purple and blue, it shot towards Druenn like a bolt out of a crossbow hurtling towards the little boy. Warren yelled, "Acto-damorista!" and a blue aura encircled them both as the bolt deflected off the shield that Warren created. The Dean shot to his feet as he slammed his hand into the table creating a loud smack.

"Get out, you damn fool!" the Dean's old withered voice yelled as he charged a blue flame within his left palm. "Whether you like it or not, Druenn shall be taught at this school, Terribor."

"You're making a grave mistake, old man," Terribor growled ferociously, his sharp canine teeth glistening in the light. "Grave!" he turned and walked out slamming the door behind him.

The Dean and Warren breathed a sigh of relief turning to Druenn. Druenn stood in the centre of the room frozen and disorientated. Warren watched the little boy shiver, he turned to the Dean. The Dean stared back at Warren, gesturing him to nurture the little boy. Warren's eyes shot back to Druenn, he stepped over to him, kneeling in front of him. Druenn stared, a tear welling in his eye. Without realising what he was doing Warren shot his arms out and embraced the little boy. "Druenn, it's okay, I swear I'm here, I'll look after you." Warren spoke quietly, soothingly whilst he held Druenn close, he felt a familiar jerking in Druenn's shoulders as he heard the sniffs and the gasps.

"Why does no one want me?" Druenn sobbed. "Why has this happened to me?"

"Shh… it's okay," Warren comforted, he heard the rhythmic step-step-click as the Dean stepped over towards them.

"What did I do to deserve this… is this a punishment?"

"Shh, Druenn, this is not your fault." Warren held Druenn tight as the boy broke down in tears.

"I had a feeling that would be his reaction," the Dean said solemnly looking towards the door.

"Oh really!" Warren replied, sarcasm in his voice as he held the young boy looking towards the door. "Why let him in to the office if you knew he would cause this kind of havoc?" Warren turned towards the Dean's table as he changed his weight to hold Druenn better in his arms.

The Dean walked round his desk and sat down. "So what was with Terribor's attitude there, giving his orders in here?" Warren asked the Dean.

"Well…" the Dean started, "he's my successor."

What?" Warren yelled, "That can't be... you know what he's like, he'll destroy this guild once you and I are gone," he continued pointing towards the door.

"Now, Warren, have faith, I believe he will find his way, given the opportunity," the Dean replied politely whilst opening the bottom drawer to his desk and pulling out a map of Tharlian.

Warren stared at the Dean rendered speechless as he watched the old man walk slowly towards the windows, arms folded, with a sharp whistle the curtains shot open simultaneously. Light flooded in. Warren stood, Druenn in his arms, he turned his gaze to a chair in the far corner of the room. He tilted his head, the chair began to hover and slowly cross the room. Warren followed the chair as it settled onto the ground in the centre of the room, kneeling down he placed the drowsy boy on the chair. Druenn's body slumped as he drifted off.

"The boy is exhausted you should take him to his room," the Dean spoke quietly leaning over the desk.

"Okay, I'm going to get Druenn to bed." Warren said contently as he smiled in the direction of Druenn.

The Dean watched Druenn also for a moment then nodded at Warren with a wide smile on his face. "Aren't children adorable when sleeping?" he asked Warren.

Warren glanced back at the Dean and also smiled. He watched the Dean for a moment then nodded. "I know what you want to say, Dean, and yes I am happy he's here," Warren exclaimed with a small smile.

"I can tell," the Dean replied.

Warren turned to the Dean and bowed, the Dean turned and bowed back and Warren walked over to Druenn and scooped him up in both arms. "Speak soon, my dear friend," the Dean nodded as they left the room closing the door behind them.

Warren began to walk down the dark corridor searching for the room the Dean had selected for him. He looked down at the young boy curled up in his arms and could not help but grin.

"Finally, he's getting heavy," Warren whispered as Room 0018 came into view a few doors ahead of him. Warren opened the door as the young boy awoke.

"Hey, you," Warren whispered. "This is going to be your new room for a while, that okay?"

Druenn nodded politely as he wiped his eyes, Warren knelt down and placed him on the bed, Druenn scurried under the covers, Warren then began tucking him in. Druenn watched as Warren turned to leave the room.

"Thank you for everything, Warren."

Warren paused. "Sleep well, kid."

Druenn realised he was alone and in the dark. He searched the blackness for a distraction but found no solace. He lay back down on the bed, his head on the pillow and began to cry.

FOUR

Emily

"The room is dark, the warmth, am I dreaming? Was yesterday a dream?" Images began flashing in Druenn's memory. *I'm at home in my bed.* Druenn began snuggling up to his pillow. *Yes, this is my bed.* The warmth radiating from a nearby window convinced him it was his home. He began to look around the room, it was dark and a bit blurry but it was definitely his home. The table in the centre of the room, the fireplace, the door wide open. *Dad must be planting more seeds*, Druenn thought. Letting out a sigh of relief. The boy lay back and curled up. *It was all a dream.*

"Hey, you, wake up!" a sweet, innocent voice said.

"What?" Druenn's eyes shot open to meet a pair of eyes gazing back. Druenn yelped and crawled back across his bed slipping over the edge. The girl leaning over his bed giggled in front of him. He had never met her before, she was smiling crazily at him.

"Watcha doing down there?" she giggled.

Druenn frantically searched the room. It was small but filled with bookshelves with two beds, one being Druenn's and the other to this girl?

She giggled again. "We're roomies," she grinned, reaching down and pulling Druenn off the floor.

"Where…" he paused now getting a good look at the girl in front of him, she looked a couple of years older than him. Druenn eyed her up and down; she wore nothing but a white vest and very short linen shorts, and her golden hair flowed down her back. *She's actually kind of cute*, Druenn thought. When his eyes reached hers, he stared in amazement; she guessed exactly what he had spotted and giggled.

"Yeah, I know I have one blue eye and one green eye."

Druenn stared at her in amazement.

She watched him in confusion. "Eh, you done checking me out?" she challenged.

"Oh… I'm sorry." Druenn stared at the floor, she giggled again. Everytime she giggled Druenn's heart somersaulted and butterflies danced in the pit of his stomach. *Why?* he thought.

She thrust forward one hand to receive a handshake keeping the other behind her back. "I'm Emily!" she addressed politely.

Druenn glanced at her hand then thrust his hand forward and they shook hands. He scratched his head. "Druenn… I'm Druenn," he replied.

She giggled. "That is such a cute name!"

Druenn's mouth twitched as a grin spread over his face. The two roommates began to laugh.

"Well, well, you're up already," a familiar voice sounded from behind Druenn. The little boy spun to see Warren in the doorway smiling. "I see you are both getting acquainted?" Warren asked from the doorway.

"Yep!" Emily replied as she jumped on Druenn, wrapping an arm round him and throwing a thumb up forward to Warren, she giggled.

Warren burst out with a bellow of laughter. "You'll find her laugh quite infectious," he explained to Druenn.

"I've kind of discovered that myself," Druenn giggled, turning his head to see Emily resting her head on his shoulder gazing at him.

"Oh I love him… can I keep him?"

Warren stepped in and leant against the wall. "Well, you're fixed roommates; you two are stuck with each other so I hope you can cope, Druenn?"

Druenn nodded. *I think I can cope*, he thought.

Emily squealed with excitement, jumping up and down.

"Yey!" she squealed.

Druenn gazed at Warren and smiled. He smiled back.

"You'll be fine here, you're in good company" Warren said. "Also the Dean has seen it fit to give you both today off so you," he pointed at Emily, "can show Druenn around."

Emily grinned wildly. "Will do, sir!" she saluted. "First, bath time!" she giggled whilst she eyed the boy still covered in blackened soot and ash.

"What?" Druenn yelped his eyes open wide with the hint of panic as Emily grabbed his wrist and flew out of the room.

Warren watched them sail off down the corridor. He bellowed out another raucous of laughter, then called out to Druenn. "You'll be fine," he said, followed by another bellow of laughter.

Druenn pulled and tugged as he yelped.

She is so strong, he thought as she dragged him across the hallway and bursting through a door, Druenn read on the sign: **Bathing Quarters 10-15**.

"This is basically the kid's bathroom," she said, stopping, still holding his hand. She opened the door, steam filled the corridor and they walked in.

Druenn gazed at the room. The room was one big hot spring; steam was rising off the water, a few rocks and several bamboo shoots separating parts of the pool enclosing sections. "Come on, kid, clothes off!" Emily yelled, tugging on Druenn's shirt.

"What?" Druenn shrieked forcing his shirt back on. "Wait...you're a girl; we shouldn't be sharing," he continued.

"Oh, don't be such a baby, girls and boys share until they are sixteen." She pointed to a sign behind them next to the door, the sign read: **Bathing Area 10-15**. "See," she giggled. "Now stop squirming!"

As Druenn stood naked on the edge of the bath he slumped in embarrassment.

"Get in!" Emily laughed and thrust out her arms knocking Druenn. Druenn swung his arms in a desperate attempt to balance himself, failing; he toppled over squealing into the pool. Emily heard a mighty splash as she removed her white vest and placed it neatly on a ledge beside her; walking over to the sidewall she removed a towel from the rack, walked back and placed it along the ground.

"Okay, I'm next. Druenn glanced up at her, she was turned away from him, but he spotted her naked back. Druenn spun away, embarrassment consuming him. He swam away from her, finding a rock and hid behind it.

"Here I come," she squealed. Druenn heard a prominent splash, then a gasp as she broke the surface.

Oh no! There's a girl in the bath with me. His mind frantically searched for an escape route. *Help!* he thought. The sound of her swimming over grew louder; he ducked under the water sucking in a large gulp of air as he descended. Under the water he glimpsed Emily's arm shoot round the corner, soap and sponge and wash cloth in hand. Druenn frantically swam away shutting his eyes. He thrashed through the water tearing it violently. *I shouldn't be dealing with this at my age.*

"Hey, there you are!" Emily giggled. "You're fast, I have to admit but you're not getting away from me."

Druenn turned to Emily who stood in the bath waist deep, that was too much for Druenn; he dived again as she began to charge through the water. Druenn swam on, suddenly a strong hand shot out grabbing his foot forcing him back. He surfaced as Emily reeled in her catch.

"You can't escape a good scrubbing from me, Druenn" she continued to giggle as she wrapped her legs around him, clamping him. "No escape!" she grinned as she rubbed the soap over Druenn's body. Druenn wanted to sob with embarrassment. "Oh, grow up, you big cry baby… everyone needs to stay clean" she smiled as Druenn knelt shoulder deep in water, arms crossed.

"Hmm," Druenn grumped.

"Oh, what's up, mister grumpykins?" Emily giggled.

"I don't like baths!" Druenn sulked.

*

Warren Anguish walked through the halls of the Learning Building, the strong breeze blowing through the hall and catching his robes. Glancing side to side, the young fighters, studied their textbooks, jotting down notes as they absorbed the knowledge they craved. Some studying for upcoming exams, others learning new skills. His target was the end room. As he reached the door he glanced at the sign: **Master Terribor**. He grunted then knocked.

"Enter!" the posh, thick, gravely muffled voice reverberated through the door. The room was very much like the Dean's, only the portrait of himself above the fireplace was different.

"Warren," the voice growled. "I have nothing to say to you."

Warren calmly replied stepping carefully into Terribor's room. "I have plenty to say to you." Warren paused, picking his words carefully, frustration in his face. "What is your problem?" He paused again. "With Druenn, you've always enjoyed newcomers, you say they make you look good, that is your reason more want to study here." He took a deep breath. "What's your issue with Druenn?"

"I do not like the way he is treated like a valuable item, like he is some kind of savior," Terribor shot back.

"What if he is, what if he can reform DV?" Warren replied, hope present in his voice.

"DV is dead, your days of a saviour are over, boy!" Terribor slammed his fist into the table.

"You have always had a grudge against me for that reason, haven't you? Because I was accepted and you weren't, you want to hoard all the glory for yourself Terribor you know that, it wasn't about glory, it was about protecting the innocent." Warren stepped forward, walking up to Terribor. Terribor was a tall man who towered over Warren.

"Don't piss me off, boy!" Terribor growled throwing his arms out, his sword and staff flew over into his hands.

Warren continued to walk towards Terribor refusing to go for his weapon. He brought his hands up in surrender, "This could be our chance to rekindle those flames and once again protect our borders and retain order from chaos."

"I intend to once our numbers have grown," Terribor challenged, a devious grin on his face.

"You intend to send all our fighters to their deaths in a drastic attempt to reap your own glory." Warren began to raise his voice, he looked away to calm himself, and walking over to the bookcase he spotted a black book.

"My plan is perfect, I know how to restore peace to Tharlian I..." Terribor continued, but Warren wasn't listening.

That book, Warren thought, *it looks so familiar*. Removing it from the shelf, he searched the front for a symbol, he found it, in the top left hand corner a symbol containing a circle within the circle, an X, and over the X he found an MK+. Warren knew this symbol.

"The Mystique Knights," he whispered.

Terribor stopped his ranting, realising Warren's attention was elsewhere. Warren opened the book and scrolled the member's list.

"Don't touch that!" boomed Terribor. He strode over, snatching the book. With a violent tug he grasped it under his arm. "How dare you browse my shelves?" he roared.

Warren gazed up in shock, mortified. "You're a Cultist," Warren said deathly. That's why all the questions surrounding Terribor fell into place. "You're here to find the last members of DV."

Terribor didn't know what to say. He walked to his window turned and roared. "Arrestor-amorista!"

A torrent of purple blasts shot from Terribor's staff.

Grasping his sword Warren thrust it out in front of him screaming.

"In'thillias!"

A bright bubble shot from his sword surrounded him; the purple bolts flew into the bubble, the bubble absorbing the blasts. The bubble disappeared and Warren launched his sword towards Terribor. Terribor raised his sword whilst whispering a low chant. Warren flew against the wall with a mighty thud. Outside the students began to notice the loud noises from down the hall.

"It sounds like a fight." The students began glancing to each other.

"Let's take a look," one student whispered to another.

"Is it Master Warren and Master Terribor?" another said, grunting.

My money's on Terribor, he thought for a second. "Actually, I don't know, I think they will be evenly matched."

Some of the students began sneaking out of the class heading down to the last room at the end of the hall.

"I'm going to get the Dean," one of the younger students said, as he dashed down the hallway.

As the students began to crowd round the entrance, the two men continued to fight, slashing ferociously and swiping with spells and their staffs. With a lucky swipe of his staff Terribor flew over his desk.

Glancing round Warren spotted the students. "Get back, all of you, this is too dangerous!" he yelled to them. The students leapt back.

"Stamous-Amotosta!" Warren roared as he aimed his staff towards Terribor, who stared in horror as he heard the word "stamous" uttered as did several of the older students. Pulling the others back they gazed in wonder as Warren's staff lit up, a breeze sucking everything towards it, a ball of white energy began to hover in front of the staff. The force grew stronger, the air around them all felt lifeless, everyone felt heavier as if gravity was pushing down harder on everyone, the students gasped.

"Expel!" Warren roared. The ball ignited blasting everything in front of the staff out. Terribor flew against the windows behind, he realised too late when he heard the smash of the windows and he flew out into the school training grounds outside.

"By the Divine, he blew the bloody wall out!" one of the older students yelled.

Warren leapt outside. Terribor got himself off the ground and cast a spell, firing a small white flame towards Warren. Thrusting his hand out the flame dispersed into the air, the flame screeched into the air and ignited like a firework, the crowd whistled and cheered. Warren threw his hand out again whispering a word. Terribor spun in the air and fell, he scrambled around for his sword. Warren spotted it first, chanting again, the sword flew out of reach. Warren ran over to the scrambling man.

In one swift move he grasped his neck, holding the sword and preparing to strike, he yelled. "On your knees, traitor. Give up and I may spare your life!"

Terribor rose to his knees and the students cheered.

"That's enough. Weapons down, men!" the Dean's shrill voice sounded from the back of the crowd. "You both fought well. Follow me to my office," he said, a smile on his face as he made his way to the two fighters.

"But, sir, you need to know that…"

The Dean waved Warren off. "You can tell me in my office, back to class, children." He clapped his hands. "You all have plenty to be getting on with."

The students groaned as they trudged back to class. The Dean's bright cheerful face followed the students as they slipped out of sight, the Dean's face turned ferocious to the two men. "As for you two." He tapped his cane against the cobbled path and in a puff of smoke they were back in the Dean's office.

"Wedthorin," a strange rubbing sound began to circle them. Terribor whispered to Warren as he gulped. "What's that sound?"

Warren replied, "He's forming a sound proof barrier around us."

"Why?" Terribor replied.

"Why do you think? So he can shout at us."

"Quiet!" the Dean screeched. "How dare you both perform dangerous magic around the students, you could have hurt them!" he continued his attack.

"But, sir, you need to know that Terribor is a Cultist, part of the Mystique Knights," Warren accused.

"Yes, I know" the Dean growled back. "He left the organisation to be part of this school."

Warren stared at Terribor as he grinned at him. "Sir, I must protest, are you that naïve?"

"How dare you, Warren Anguish, how dare you test my judgment."

Warren stared at the floor, the shame flowed through him. He stepped back. "I apologise, Master."

The Dean nodded to Warren then to Terribor.

"And you?" Terribor bowed.

"Sorry." He turned then left the Dean's office. Warren also turned to leave, bewildered as to why the Dean didn't treat the matter seriously.

"Hold on, Warren, I'm not done with you."

Warren turned back to face the Dean.

"Warren, I know he was part of Mystique Knights," the Dean explained whilst walking back to his desk.

"Then you should know he shouldn't live; he's a threat to you, me and Druenn," Warren replied, worry in his voice whilst gazing at the door.

"Warren…" the Dean started, he sat grasping a cup, a steaming cauldron in the corner of the room bubbled. He passed the cup to Warren, Warren leant over the desk and took it from the Dean and walked over to the Dean's side. The Dean continued, "I intend to make him believe that I think he has changed his ways, but we can't have any more displays like today I don't want any of the students getting involved, if anyone asks it was a training exercise."

Warren nodded as he thought for a moment whilst the Dean walked over to the cauldron, picking up a ladle hung above the cauldron he dipped it into the boiling hot water. Pouring the contents into his cup he delicately collected three tealeaves from a small round wooden box on the mantelpiece above the fireplace.

"As long as he believes that we think he has turned his back on eradicating the bloodline we have access to all his information from the Mystique Knights," the Dean smiled coyly.

Warren turned. *Most intriguing*, he thought. "What if he discovers that we do know, surely we just got lucky today?" the Dean sighed.

"If he was to find out" he started, "we would be forced to kill him."

Warren walked slowly towards the Dean and joined him by the fireplace. Taking a sip the Dean breathed a sigh of relief.

"Much better," exhaling slowly.

"Master, a quick question." Warren raised his finger, representing one point.

The Dean repositioned himself on his seat and sat intently waiting for the question.

"What made you pick Emily as a roommate?" he asked confused. "Surely you should have picked a boy, not a girl."

The Dean raised his finger to Warren. "We both knew Druenn would struggle to fit in."

Warren nodded his head in agreement and the Dean continued, "I wanted to pick someone that I knew would make him feel welcome. I called Emily in to explain the situation before he arrived."

Warren folded his arms as he walked to the Dean's desk, he leant on it as he spoke.

"You called her in?"

"Yes," the Dean replied after a gulp of his tea. "Druenn will have trouble with the anti-DV members that Terribor has corrupted; he will need some strong friends, and maybe," he winked cheekily towards Warren.

Warren gazed in confusion; he unfolded his arms jumping off the table looking directly into the Dean's eyes.

"What do you mean by that?" he asked.

The Dean shrugged as he stroked his long beard. "Well who's to say they won't get," he winked again, "very close?"

Warren's eyes widened. "You mean…"

He expects Druenn to fall in love with her? Warren thought.

"Well if he does fall for her it will keep him distracted from bullies," the Dean coyly remarked."

Warren eyed up the old master. "You can't toy with people's hearts like that, sir!" Warren challenged resting his weight on the desk again.

"Oh, I'm not" the Dean shot back. "I merely paired them in a room together, the rest is up to them." He smiled, taking another gulp of tea.

Warren watched the Dean, stunned.

"Oh, grow up, Warren. He's not going to understand the idea of love for a while yet," the Dean continued. "Stop worrying, focus on your job, you need to train him…" Taking another sip he placed the cup back onto the desk. "You worry too much, Warren, it's always been your weakness, when you overcome your fears you will become a master"

"Yes, sir," Warren replied bowing his head in defeat, he turned and headed for the door.

"Warren" the frail man called after him.

He turned to face the Dean once more.

"Everything will work out."

Sure, whatever you say, Warren thought as he bowed once more and exited the office.

FIVE

Terribor Strife

Druenn Lightblaser sat up to his shoulders deep in the younger students' bathing quarters. He clung to the towel that was wrapped around his waist, glancing up at Emily, who also had her towel wrapped neatly around her. She was lying with her back against a rock, submerged in the steamy water just above her waist, her arms behind her head. She liked the bathing quarters, as one of the room's features was that it had no ceiling, it was open to the sky above. She watched the clouds above her slowly drift by, steam rose up into the atmosphere, a drop of sweat trickled its way down her face.

Druenn watched her intently. *She's so relaxed and happy*, he thought, his mind occupied by the events of yesterday, the smoke rising, the bodies, his father. *Meredith*. He closed his eyes tight; he felt a trickle of water from his eyes. *Stop it, stop it, stop it!* Quickly wiping his eyes he watched the water ripple as he lay in the warm steamy bath, his arms wrapped around his legs.

"I can't wait to show my parents how strong I have become," Emily said beaming. "They never really gave me the chance to do well at something, you know?" Emily continued without noticing the grieving boy beside her. "One day my father saw me fight off a couple of bullies with a stick." She paused for a reaction. There was no reply. "My little brother was being targeted by these two boys from his school, so one day I decided I'm going to put a stop to this." She giggled triumphantly. "So after school I saw them approaching him and I thought now's my chance." She mimicked picking up a stick. "I yelled at them, how dare you pick on my little brother." She then cut off, the rest coming back to her, she froze. "The bullies ran off and then I heard my father clapping behind me shouting well done," she said, her eyes filled with joy. "I'd never seen him so happy with me." Her mind reeled back to the present, leaning back on the rock her chirpy voice returned. "He brought me here and signed me up, and I'm not going to let him down." Her face beamed again. "What about your mother and father, Druenn?" she asked politely.

No reply.

"Druenn?" she repeated, glancing down at him. The little boy clutched at his legs tightly as the familiar jerking in his shoulders began again letting a sniff escape him. Emily saw his eyes; *he's crying*. She knelt down beside him placing a hand on his shoulder.

He shook it off.

"Druenn, what's wrong?" she asked, her voice quiet and sympathetic. His shoulder jerked more violently this time. Her hand shot back to his shoulder as she changed position in front of the little boy, her eyes fixed on his.

"Druenn, please tell me what's wrong?" she pleaded. Druenn opened his mouth but no words came out, he felt the lump in his throat again, that agonising pain he knew so well from the night before. With a shaky voice he managed. Clenching his eyes shut, he sniffed again.

"My…" he started, the lump cutting him off. "I…" he tried again.

Poor boy, Emily thought. *What has he been through?*

"My family is dead," Druenn pushed out his shoulder rattling his voice.

"What?" Emily froze. *The whole family?*

"My father was murdered yesterday and I can't find my sister." The tears rolled down his cheeks in torrents, he forced himself together. *Stop crying, Druenn.* "Stop it," he whispered.

"Stop what?" Emily replied both hands on his shoulders rubbing them soothingly.

"I have to stop crying, I can't do anything like this," he squeezed out. "I... I have no one, I'm all alone."

Emily threw her arms around him, she held him tight. "Druenn," she said tenderly óne hand stroking his soft hair. "It's okay to cry, we all need to cry, it's what we do to release stress." She gazed down at him as he broke down in her arms. "Druenn," she whispered, "You're not alone; I'm here for you."

He put his arms around her, his cries echoing off the walls, she rested her head on top of his. "Everything will be okay, I won't leave you".

*

Warren Anguish settled into his classroom. The students watching him intently, Warren walked over to a bookshelf on the far left side of the room, scrolling for a few seconds he found the book he wanted. He picked it up and slowly trudged back to the front desk.

"Okay, students, can you turn to page forty-three in our text books, please?" he asked as he scrolled through the pages. The flicker of pages floated round the room, as the students scrolled through the pages too. As Warren looked up to see his students ready and prepared to start the lesson, a couple of students in the front row spinning their pencils, several more slumped over their desks waiting. He heard a faint sound, his ear twitched, a small shrill cry erupting into pants followed by more cries. *Is that Druenn?*

The students waited oblivious to the cries.

"Sir, you okay?" a student from the front row asked. Warren refocused looking down at his student and smiled politely. "Everything's fine," he replied. He turned towards the blackboard and began the lesson.

Further down the hall Terribor Strife paced his office, only the back wall revealed the training grounds from Warren and his little scrap. He began whispering words and spells, the room sprang to life. The bookshelf lay shattered in pieces, he whispered a few more words; the bookshelf began repairing itself as it returned back to its original location, as did the wall. The books flew around the room before finding their designated homes. The room looked brand new. Terribor whispered one last word, and a familiar sound from earlier began, a sucking sound, he watched the sound barrier conceal his office. He waited for the sound to stop; as it did he smashed his fist onto his desk.

"Damn you, Warren!" he screamed. "I'll get you" he paced his room before shooting a glance to the bookcase. *How many of them still live?* he thought, dabbing his forehead. He turned to the desk, opening a drawer underneath, he pulled out a pair of black laced gloved and put them on.

"Let's see how many of you bastards still live," he seethed, spitting as he spoke. He raised a hand towards the ceiling the other outstretched towards the new windows. With a whisper and a thrust of his hand the curtains closed; clicking his fingers once the candles around the room ignited simultaneously. The room was cocooned in an eerie light. He whispered another word as a book chained to the chandelier above began to descend. The chains snapped and it floated down towards him. As it reached him he gripped it firmly. Throwing the book onto the table he raised a hand towards it as he walked around the table, the book's pages flickered, searching for a page, he continued to search. Closing his eyes, he whispered a foreign language.

"Stop!" he choked under his breath. "There." He raised his index finger and lowered it towards the book, the pages still flicking, his finger reached the book and the book stopped searching. Terribor slowly opened his eyes, his eyes now nothing more than blackness, like two lumps of coal. His lifeless eyes gazed down at the sight before him. The page title read:

Divine Victory
Members list

Name	Status
Acthorian	Terminated
Leiran	Terminated
Krona	Terminated
Henrietta	Terminated
Shreftwood	Alive
Gravland	Terminated
Anguish	Alive
Red Saviour	Terminated
Epsonstar	Alive
Amikari	Terminated

"Three still alive," Terribor said coldly. He sat down, and pondered a strategy. Sitting up, his eyes gazed over the three still alive. **Shreftwood Alive**, **Anguish Alive, Epsonstar Alive.** He grinned, his eyes ablaze. "Graduation day." He stared at his door. "Druenn, my boy, you are their lifeline."

SIX

The Scuffle

Emily led Druenn towards the canteen. "You're going to love the food they make here, this time of year the chefs are getting really good." Emily beamed fantasising about the menu list; licking her lips she dragged Druenn into the canteen. The doors swung open and she burst in towards the queue. She picked up a tray from the stack beside her and thrust one in front of Druenn. He stared at the excited girl.

"Why does this excite you so much?" Druenn asked. "It's only food."

"Only food?" she squealed. "You're in for a little treat my friend, a friend of mine, Jamee, right?" she continued, "Jamee Burger, he made this amazing food, I don't know what he called it but I hope he names it after himself I would hate to see someone steal his idea."

Druenn was shocked. *How can she talk so much without breathing?*

He jumped as the girl squealed again. "Yes, he's working today so he'll be serving them!" She jumped up and down as though she was five years old receiving a birthday present. Other students eating their dinners began turning towards them. As they glanced over realising it was Emily they turned back giggling.

I guess she does this often, Druenn wondered.

"So what did you mean when you said this time of year Emily?" Druenn asked.

Emily paused and turned to him as they both stepped forward in the queue. "Huh?" she replied.

Wow, does she love food that much she forgets everything else? Druenn chuckled to himself.

"Oh! Yes, what I mean is that there is a catering course at this academy, as well as fighting. The Dean realised there is a huge market in training chefs as they can go on to do many things."

They stepped forward another two spaces.

"Catering is needed everywhere, here and other schools, inns, taverns, even to start their own restaurants." She paused in thought. "In fact, everywhere," she giggled. A couple of older students in front began to giggle with her, unable to hold back. Emily glanced in their direction, and made a silly face, Druenn giggled too.

Within a few minutes they were at the front of the queue. Jamee stepped forward behind the counter spotting Emily.

"Emily, hey you. The usual?"

Emily beamed and nodded once. "Yes please!" she replied, her voice melodic. He scooped up a lump of rounded meat. Placing it between two wheat buns, he placed it upon a wooden plate and passed it to her. She grabbed the plate her wide eyes excited to sink her teeth into it.

"Oh, I don't recognise you little man, you new here?" Jamee asked as his eyes gazed down at Druenn then to Emily.

"Yes," Emily replied before Druenn could open his mouth "He's my roommate" Jamee nodded.

"Ah right, sounds fun," his eyes returning to Druenn. "What's your name, little man?"

Druenn looked at the young man as his broad shoulders flexed while placing a spoon to the trays full of food, He was tall but not gangly, well toned and looked like he could take down a bull. He brushed his sweaty forehead with his arm. He looked very much like someone Druenn knew back home. *He was about eighteen… he must be roughly the same age, surely.*

"I'm Druenn," he replied politely, extending a hand to shake.

Jamee brushed his silky black hair out of his eyes as he lent over the counter extending his. "Pleasure to meet ya. I'm Jamee, Jamee Burger." He smiled, Druenn smiled back.

"Hey, that reminds me," Emily burst out. "You should name your food after yourself, make sure you get no one stealing the idea from you!" she continued.

Joseph looked at her, an eyebrow raised. "Really? Call it a burger?" he replied chuckling. "Somehow I don't think that would catch on."

"Come on, hurry up I'm starving!" someone replied a few of the students chimed behind them.

"Yeah, stop holding up the queue!" another yelled

"Oops!" Emily replied turning to the queue one hand over her mouth, she giggled and waved to them all. "Sorry, guys!" she called sweetly back to them, a smile across her cute face. The queue of students, looked elsewhere, embarrassed.

"It's all right, we're sorry. We didn't mean to shout," one called out.

"Oh, you boys!" she winked playfully as she skipped out to the mess hall.

Druenn followed behind. *Wow, seems no one can resist her, quite an ability*, he thought. As he stepped into the hall, he stopped in shock. The hall was huge, and very loud, the noise of all the students and teachers talking to each other, to his left rows upon rows of dinner tables with carved chairs. As he scanned around the room he spotted Emily way off in the distance, still skipping, he could hear her singing. Druenn giggled, *what is it with this girl?* His grin grew across his face until his small giggle began to grow in to an unstoppable chuckle as he chased after her. Balancing his tray steadily he dodged and weaved through students standing to leave and outstretched feet in an attempt to trip the little boy, Druenn was smarter than them, as the feet shot out he jumped them and raced on. He chuckled to himself, *stupid bullies think they are clever, yet they can't even trip me.* He began to slow down, spotting Emily a few tables ahead.

"Hey, Emily, how are you this afternoon?" a large student said.

Druenn gazed at the boy as he slowed to a stop next to Emily *Wow, talk about a big guy,* he thought. The boy looked around nineteen or twenty; his broad shoulders and muscles made him look like a battering ram.

"I'm fine thank you, Rupert, how are you?" Emily giggled, her smile melting everyone.

"Oh, very well," he replied finishing his last mouthful of bread and washing it down with the last of his water. His eyes fell on Druenn. Rupert's eyes flickered back and forth to Emily.

"So, no introductions, Ems?" Rupert asked, his deep booming voice reverberating around the room joining the rest of the students in the hall. She gasped as she spun to Druenn and back, her face bright red.

"Oh, I'm sorry!" She took a breath then gestured her free hand to Rupert. "This is Rupert, a good friend of mine,"she said. Then, gesturing towards Druenn in the same manner, she switched the tray of food to her other hand. "And this is my new roommate, Druenn." They both smiled and nodded once politely.

"Druenn that's an uncommon name, so tell me… you a Druid?" a few of his friends turned to him and gaped.

"Don't be stupid, Rupert. He's only just got here, don't attack the poor boy in that matter," one said.

Rupert raised his hands in surrender. "Calm down, you lot, I was just curious, a friend of Emily's is a friend of mine." The friends turned back to their meals and ate.

"Sorry about them, Druenn, discussing Druids is a bit of a touchy subject, sorry if I offended you, I'm just intrigued."

Druenn shook his head. "I'm not, I don't really know much about Druids either," Druenn replied.

"I'd happily teach you sometime," said Rupert

"I'd like that, thank you," Druenn replied, bowing his head. There was something that Rupert instantly liked about Druenn. *Maybe he reminds me of myself when I first started here, a sincere thirst for knowledge. When you learn everything there is to be learnt you can't be easily surprised, and in the art of war, surprised is another word for dead,* he thought.

"So what made you ask if I was a Druid?" Druenn asked.

The question caught Rupert offguard and pulled him from his thoughts, gathering himself he answered. "Well… in the language of the Druids, which as we know is elvish druision, Druenn translates to saviour."

Emily and a few of the Rupert's friends turned in unison and gasped.

"No freaking way," one replied.

"Sit down here, I'll tell you about it." Rupert shuffled over letting the two students in. Emily launched straight into her plate of food, Druenn picked at his as Rupert started.

"You speak Druision?" a student asked, leaning forward over the table staring directly at Rupert.

"Indeed I do. I'm taking languages this year as well as ancient history."

The others stared at him impressed.

He cleared his throat then continued. "The word Druenn is much older than Druision, it pre-dates to the days of the Elvish Elders." He paused and took a swig from his cup of water. "As you guys are probably aware Ethalas wasn't only a land of Druids, there were many classes of Elves."

"There was?" someone exclaimed.

Rupert shot him a disapproving look, the young student shrunk into his seat.

"You're honestly telling me you didn't know there were more than just Druids?"

The young student shook his head in shame.

"Wow, you all seriously need to pick up a book or go to my history classes. It's really fascinating," Rupert continued, looking around the group listening to his story intently.

"Well, history never interested me," one called out challenging Rupert's remark.

"Okay, what I've just told you," Rupert began as he turned to the student three seats down from Druenn. "Would you agree that what I just said was interesting?"

"Well yes, but…"

"Then shut up!" Rupert barked.

"So why aren't there any more elves?" one called out.

"Yes, where did they go?" another joined in.

Druenn gazed over at them both. To his astonishment they both looked identical, only the colour of their eyes separating them apart. *Twins!* he thought.

Rupert's voice pulled Druenn back from the twins. "The reason is because Elves were pushed out."

"What?" the twins replied in unison.

Rupert took another swig of water and began. "Well, it began twenty years after the Elves unified all their territories under one banner, forming the entire kingdom under Ethalas."

The group stared at Rupert waiting for the next sentence.

I love teaching, he thought. Rupert was very gifted and enjoyed teaching his fellow students bits and pieces from history, to languages and even giving tips for the fighters. *I guess I just know how to capture them.* Rupert would always teach his friends in the mess hall as the chairs were old and tended to creak as the student fidgeted. At this moment in time he heard no chairs creaking as his eyes fell upon each of his friends listening to his story. *Gotcha!*

"Eighteen years later a cult of druids massed calling themselves The Threads." He paused as he scanned the group. Was anyone confused? Everyone was still captivated. "Okay! The reason for their unusual choice in name was rather simple, they had connections throughout the kingdom, to famous heroes, bank management, well regarded merchants and even the high elves within the royal guard and worse still even several of the elder council were members."

Druenn watched Rupert give his lesson, glancing at the other students around the table every eye was fixed on Rupert. Several students had even walked over to listen. *"They love him!"* Druenn thought and turned back to Rupert.

"The Threads literally had eyes and ears everywhere and wouldn't take much for a mutiny against the Elves who couldn't channel their energy and powers," Rupert exclaimed with a slight grin.

"Sorry," Druenn asked timidly half raising his hand. Some of the students close by let out small stifled laughs. Druenn's embarrassment forced his hand down and he shrank into his seat. Rupert's eyes glared at his friends who laughed. With calm eyes he returned to Druenn.

"Don't listen to them, what was you going to ask?"

Druenn took in a deep breath and gazed up at the mountain of muscles towering over him. *Yet his eyes are so calm.*

"I… I was just trying to say, what are the Druids and what's their relationship to the Elves?"

"Oh, by the Divine! We learned this in the first quarter of the first season" one of the twins laughed and the brother with him. Rupert looked at Emily who also looked very upset with their reaction, they nodded to each other both scooping some mash potato in their spoons. They both fired. Druenn watched as the mash sailed through the air and quickly connected with the twins' faces. The twin's shrieked in unison.

"What's your problem?"

"Shut up!" Rupert bellowed to the twins who were now cowering in their seats as they wiped the mash out of their eyes. The group laughed and Emily poked her tongue out at them playfully.

Turning back to a red faced Druenn, "That is a good question, Druenn. I'm sure you picked up the vibe of hatred for Druids around here." Druenn glanced around the room and watched as several of the students nodded to him. "The reason is connected with what happened to the Elves of Ethalas." He cleared his throat, stealing an icy gaze at the students that spoke mockingly earlier. The group gathered watching intently with no signs of disinterest. Rupert took one last swig on his cup of water.

"Okay, so as I said the Druids had connections around the Kingdom. The reason the organisation was formed was specifically for Druids as their abilities for channeling power were strong, even to the point of shape shifting, they could become animals and hunt and feed and be free from the bounds of their council's laws, not that they were bad rules and laws but they didn't have to follow them."

The boy next to Druenn lent over and whispered to him, "This is the good part."

Druenn turned back to Rupert.

"The Druids with their superior power began revolting in hopes that they could elect a Druid as high chancellor, but Elvin leader Tafu understood what they were planning."

Confusion filled Druenn's face. Emily leaned round Rupert and whispered to him. "Mutiny."

"Yes indeed, Ems," Rupert continued smiling at the little girl next to him, he nudged her playfully and Emily's face lit up. She let out her loving giggle again as she began to nibble on her bread loaf. "Mutiny," Rupert started. "Tafu sensed only greed within the Druids whose powers were becoming stronger through each generation."

"Got to run, my friend, got a lecture to get myself to," one boy said as he stood and reached for Rupert's hand. They smiled at one another respect present on their faces as they shook hands.

"Take care, my good friend, see you after blade practice?" Rupert asked.

"Sounds like a good plan," the boy grinned and winked as he picked up his books and turned away from the group, walking down the long row of benches. He must have been no older than eleven which puzzled Druenn.

It seems odd the two of them being good friends given the age gap.

Rupert turned back to the group finding Druenn's gaze again. "Best mate." Rupert gestured to the direction the boy walked in. "He used to live in the same village as me, that's why I know him so well… And his parents," he added.

Druenn nodded politely.

"Name's Kif… Kif is his nickname to be honest. His whole name is Kifreal Korea, nicest person you'll meet!" It was very plain to see that Rupert had a lot of respect for Kifreal.

Druenn watched the boy disappear around a pillar in the distance and out of view. "Kifreal," Druenn said. "I like that name," he smiled and looked up at Rupert. He smiled at Druenn again. Shaking his head he focused back on his lesson.

"Getting back to the story of the Druids' takeover…" he was interrupted suddenly by Emily bashing her spoon on her plate, leaning her head on her hand as she moaned.

"I'm bored, lets talk about something else," she continued to groan. Druenn giggled with the young girl's impatience. Rupert rolled his eyes.

"You're terrible, you know that Ems?" She looked up at him, a giant grin covering her face. The group all gazed at Emily and sighed in unison, instantly realising what they had all done they looked around the group, their faces instantly changing bright red.

This set off Emily's loving giggles again and she bellowed out laughing at the group of boys now shrinking into their seats in embarrassment. They went back to eating their lunch and talking amongst themselves.

"Anyway, I didn't catch your last name?" Rupert asked scooping up a spoonful of soup. He slurped loudly as he waited for the response.

"Lightblaser. My last name is Lightblaser," Druenn replied realising his voice sounded more cheerful than he would have imagined. He felt proud to say it. *I only said my last name*, he thought to himself.

Rupert's spoon fell to the table. A loud clatter of metal spoon and bowl connecting, several people looked up in the direction of the sound then turned back to their meals. "What?" Rupert growled, his voice instantly becoming sinister whilst staring directly forward. Everyone's eyes shot up, first glancing at Rupert then to Druenn. "Lightblaser?" Rupert replied gritting his teeth, his eyebrows arching.

Emily reeled in realisation of the seriousness of this turn of events. She leapt to her feet. "Druenn!" she said urgently. "Get up, we are leaving." She grabbed his arm and pulled him up, throwing herself in front of the little boy. She faced Rupert, who now began to slowly rise from his seat. His gaze slowly turned towards Druenn. Anger contorted his face.

"What's happening?" Druenn asked, his voice timid.

Emily spoke coldly and firmly, a voice Druenn had never heard from her before. "He's a Terribor supporter. Aren't you?" she spoke slowly.

"No DV descendant should be alive, you know that, Emily" Rupert replied growling through his teeth.

"I have not been twisted to believe that." The hall fell silent, everyone's eyes fixed on Rupert and Emily. Druenn edged back slowly, Emily caught his arm and whispered to him. "Don't move, honey."

Why does everyone I seem to talk to instantly hate me? What have I done? Druenn thought.

"I have a contract, this is my duty!" Rupert began to raise his voice. He turned to the hall of students. "Guess what, everyone?" he called out raising his hands up to the room.

"Don't do this, Rupert, please," Emily asked in hushed tones, her face staying as stern as possible, never letting her guard down.

I've got to get him out of here, she thought to herself. Her eyes began scanning for the closest exit.

"We have a DV descendant amongst us!" Rupert shouted. Gasps from around the room reverberated off the walls.

Thrusting his hand forward he pointed at Druenn who was poking his head round Emily. Emily held Druenn tight as she repositioned herself more protectively, as more gazes turned to scowls. *Terribor's tainted more minds than I expected,* she thought.

"Our proud leader, the master of this academy, sees fit to welcome him amongst our ranks," Rupert yelled to the crowd gathering around the three involved. Sounds of anger began whispering round the crowd. Questioning.

"Why would the Dean let him in?" some said.

"They should be killed. We don't want another DV to rise, and they are a menace and a threat to all of us," others chanted. The crowd around Rupert, Emily and Druenn began to thicken, forming a circle around them. Another broadly-built boy stepped forward.

Emily's eyes widened and she sighed in relief as seven students gathered round her. "Thank the Divine you're here, Alex," she sighed, smiling at him.

Alex grinned down at Emily as he stepped into the centre of the circle. "No worries. We have nothing more than a mere misunderstanding, *don't we*, Rupert."

Alex shot Rupert a glare that caused Rupert to shrink back a step.

Steeling himself he spoke in harsh tones, "He is a living descendant of DV; you know that's a threat," he growled at Alex, his eyes burning into him.

Druenn stared up at the two well-built teens squaring off, a fight looked inevitable. *And what is DV, what is going on?* Druenn thought. *Is this all because of me?*

"Come on, you two, break it up," a familiar voice sounded as a dark cloak appeared from the edge of Druenn's peripherals. He stepped forward towering over the young Druenn as he walked past the crowd gathered round looking for front row seats of the fight to come. The familiar voice spoke again his back still to Druenn.

"That's enough!" Rupert fumed for the interruption. The man in the cloak placed a hand on both of the boy's chests pushing them away from each other. Still eyeing Rupert he spoke calmly but sternly.

"Rupert, control your temper, there will be no blood shed in this hall. Do I make myself clear?"

"Yes, sir," Rupert replied sarcastically with dislike in his voice for the person speaking. He turned and walked away. Druenn listened to his footsteps disappear into the distance echoing around the room. The students began to whisper amongst one another. The man turned and instantly a wave of relief filled Druenn's body. He looked up into the stern eyes of Warren. Warren's eyes didn't leave Alex.

"All of you, get to class!" Warren's voice boomed with authority.

The students began to break away from the tight circle. Mutters of disappointment shot up around the room. Druenn turned his gaze to Emily. A tear welled in her eye as Druenn noticed she was shaking.

"Emily, are you okay?" Druenn asked as she sat down lowering her arms.

She glanced up at Druenn. She smiled and let out a halfhearted giggle. She wiped the tear from her eye.

"I'm good, honey, just a bit shaken." Druenn passed her some water from the table. She gulped it down hurriedly letting out a loud gasp for air as she finished. "Thanks, I needed that."

Druenn spotted Warren talking quietly to Alex. His arms crossed, his expression concerned. *What are they talking about*, Druenn thought as he turned back to a quivering Emily, his eyes filled with concern. Her eyes watched Druenn's and her face softened.

"Honey, really I'm okay, I promise," she sniffed and wiped another tear away. "I just didn't expect Rupert to act that way, I was positive I was going to be beaten up for sure."

"What? You looked so calm and ready for it," Druenn replied softly letting out his loving slanted grin. Emily had never seen Druenn smile like that and her eyes melted with adoration. She cupped her hands to her face.

"Wow!" she said half giggling. "Smile like that again."

Druenn's face glowed bright red as his eyes escaped hers. Fixing his gaze on the floor he began to grin with embarrassment as the same smile broke through his lips. Her shrill squeal made Druenn jump. His eyes shooting back to Emily. She bounced up and down like a child in a sweet shop.

"By the Divine you are so cute!" she squealed in her high soprano voice.

Druenn gave up with his embarrassment and smiled widely at her.

"Thank you, Druenn, for cheering me up," she said, her loving voice returning to her. She lent into him and kissed his cheek.

Druenn's eyes were locked on her eyes admiring the bright blue and green eyes. *She's amazing!* he thought as his body melted with her smile.

*

Warren listened to Alex as he explained what caused the fight. He watched him intently concern covering his face.

"That's basically what happened, sir," Alex explained as his eyes followed Warren's noticing his mind was elsewhere. "Sir?" he asked, "If there is anyway I am able to help I shall, there is going to be quite an uproar about this." Alex understood that Druenn's presence here would cause the entire guild to be split in two.

Warren reeled back to the present. "Thank you for that, Alex. I really appreciate it." His eyes wondered peering over Alex's shoulder down at Druenn a few yards away, his arms wrapped around Emily as her back jerked several times, obviously crying. Warren's face contorted into a wider concern. *Terribor is going to rip this guild in two*, he thought as his eyes found Alex again.

"We will all need to look out for him, okay, Alex?"

Alex saluted half playfully and at the same time hoping Warren knew he was being serious too. Warren let a halfhearted smile escape him and a small chuckle. Alex smiled back.

"Okay, I'm going to get to class if that is all," Alex said with a small bow.

"Yes," Warren replied, bowing his head to him "have a good lesson." Alex bowed to his favourite teacher, turned and walked down the long line of empty seats except for a few students, their heads engrossed in a book as they studied in their free periods.

As Alex approached Emily and Druenn he knelt down and wrapped his arms around Emily tightly as she sniffed her tears away.

"Thank you, Alex," she whispered. He drew back and looked into her eyes and winked, a smile streaking across his face.

g"No problem, Ems, we got to look out for each other while he's here," he chuckled as he knocked his head back towards Druenn.

Druenn eyed Emily and Alex, confused. *While I'm here? Why is everything to do with me?* He turned away, balling his hands up into fists. *What is all this about?* Druenn felt a hand on his shoulder as Alex walked past looking down at him.

"We'll be looking out for you, my friend," he said calmly, the smile easing Druenn's tension. He felt somewhat lighter. His body eased and his fists fell as he listened to the sound of Alex's footsteps echoed around with a final creak of the door at the end of the hall. Druenn felt a second pair around his waist. Letting out a final sniff Emily squeezed him tight. Druenn smelt her perfume seep into his nose and he inhaled deeply, his eyes closing losing himself in the warm smell.

"Thank you," she said, adoration in her voice as she squeezed him to her. He patted her arm as she released him and he turned to face her. She smiled at him as a voice from behind her made her turn to Warren. He walked over to them.

"I think, Emily, you should go back to class, and I need some time alone with Druenn."

"Really?" she whimpered her smile fading.

Warren took her and gestured for Druenn to sit down letting a small sigh escape him. *Why won't anyone explain to me what is going on!* he thought. He sat and watched the two talking quietly a few yards away. Emily took a seat on the bench as she looked up at Warren. Her hands shook from the adrenalin of the earlier argument. Warren lent down bringing his head level with Emily's.

"I think it will be best if I begin training with Druenn right away, I don't want him to be defenceless because we both know he will be picked on every day and we won't always be around for him." Emily nodded glancing over at Druenn who was straining to hear the conversation.

Her eyes fell to her hand as she realised she was no longer shaking. She closed her eyes and took a deep breath. *I'm calm now,* she thought, refocusing on Warren.

Warren gazed back smiling at her. "You'll be okay, now run along to class."

She politely smiled back, nodding her head at him as she leapt up from the bench. *Okay, everything's okay,* she thought. *Nothing will be much different just a few enemies instead of all friends.* She looked at Druenn again and her eyes melted. *He's so cute!* Her smile returned to her face. Druenn's eyes lit up as he saw the smile he loved so much. She passed his seat and as she did she winked coyly.

"See you after lesson, cutie." She spun back to the direction she was walking. Her hair glinted in the sunlight that now began pouring through the windows above, creating an upside down pyramid on the centre floor where Emily was walking.

Druenn sat on the bench looking down at his clean white silk shirt and his brown linen trousers. He began playing with the lace that tied his shirt. Flashbacks of the night before were starting to come back in torrents. His father dying, clothes drenched in his own blood, the burning houses. Friends dead, the great pine tree burning. His sister, Meredith. *Oh, Meredith, I must find her*, he thought.

In that moment he realised he missed something else. Clutching his chest he stared off in the direction that Emily had walked to class in. As his heart felt a new kind of pain. *Wow, I miss Emily so much already*, the little boy thought. *I guess she makes me forget everything that happened yesterday.*

The silence broke when Druenn heard Warren's footsteps approaching. He looked up at the young teacher and let out a small grin that looked no more than a twitch in the side of his mouth. Warren sat uncomfortably next to Druenn.

"Warren," he started. "Tell me straight, why have certain people got a problem with… what do they call it?"

"Come on, shall we get started?" Warren said trying desperately to keep Druenn's spirits up. "Let's head towards the archery range."

SEVEN

Rickarus Diaz

Warren escorted Druenn outside. The sun blazed down on the fighting grounds outside the west wing of Reinhold. Druenn squinted in the bright light. Shielding his eyes he stared up at the sun and listened to the quiet hum of crickets in the grass and the light breeze cooling him from the bright sun.

"Follow me," Warren called to Druenn who was now a few feet ahead and turned to him gesturing Druenn to follow him with his hand. The confused boy followed at an easy pace towards a short dirt track path, which steadily dipped to a lower section of the field. He trudged through the dirt under his feet as he walked, dust clouds drifted along with him as he picked up his feet.

Druenn looked to his right as he walked down the path seeing a small tent fitting no more than two people in at a time. Next to that five archery targets paced no more than eighty yards further down the field stood awaiting its next archer to step forward for practice. Druenn noticed two people next to the furthest range from them, slowly walking back across the field, arrows in hand. Warren gestured to the two boys and they began to jog over. By the time the two groups met they were at the end of the final range.

Druenn eyed them; both wore similar clothing to him. The only differences Druenn could see was that one boy who stood head and shoulders over Druenn wore a green linen shirt and brown leather trousers with a single leather shoulder pad on his left shoulder which further connected to a leather sleeve that ran the length of his whole arm. He lent on his large longbow, which stood a foot higher than Druenn. Druenn gazed up at the golden embroidered phoenix that curved and twisted round the bow until his eye caught the other boy to the right of them.

The other boy who must have been no more than a foot shorter to the one in green was identical except he was in blue and held a large crossbow in his hand.

"Ah, Rick Diaz and brother Joseph, how are you this morning?" Warren greeted. "How are you finding your new bow Rick?" Druenn watched the one in green as he tested his bow, stretching and knocking an arrow for a test shot. The arrow sailed through the air with a quiet whistle as it began to make its decent toward the target. The arrow fell and hit the target with a muted thud. Druenn stared at the target. The arrow wasn't quite a bull's-eye, but not far off the arrow sat within the third ring from the centre.

"Good shot," Druenn said quietly to himself without the intention of anyone hearing him. Rick turned to him and knelt down bringing his eyes level to Druenn's.

"So who might you be?" Rick asked with a wide smile on his face. His voice was a soft soothing tenor that rippled through the sound of the birds and the hum of the bees.

Warren stepped forward placing a reassuring hand on Druenn's shoulder. "This is Druenn," Warren replied with a smile on his face.

"Druenn Lightblaser," Druenn said sheepishly, expecting another dining room uproar.

Rick's jaw dropped. He stared at Druenn for a moment. "I am in the presence of a descendant?" Rick looked up at Warren, who had a smile on his face, half chuckling. Rick looked back at Druenn with a mixture of smiles on his face.

Druenn could see adoration, fascination and joy. Druenn was stunned. *He likes me?*

A hand flew out in front of him and Druenn jumped back in shock, looking at Rick's hand extended to him he realised he only meant to shake hands. Druenn gathered himself and shook Rick's hand

"It's an honour to meet you Druenn Lightblaser, I am very grateful for what your mother did for us," Rick said half bowing his head to him.

Druenn couldn't hide his shocked expression. *What my mother did?* He turned to Warren who lent down to him and whispered in his ear.

"You will be learning about your mother and what she did for all of us in my class about the history of Divine Victory."

Divine Victory? His mind reeled back to Rupert's shouts:

"We have a DV descendant amongst us!" he heard Rupert calling from the corners of his memory. "They should be killed, we don't want another DV to rise, and they are a menace and a threat to all of us," the voice continued.

As the two boys returned to their positions the second boy, the one in blue, Druenn grimaced. "Fan-bloody-tastic!" he snidely remarked. "A bloody descendant," he whispered as he turned away from the group in an attempt to avoid greeting the little boy.

As Druenn focused on the two brothers again the soft crack made him jump as Rick's open palm smacked his younger brother round the back of the head causing him to stumble.

Rick turned back to Warren and Druenn. "Please excuse my brother; we both have different views when it comes to DV."

Warren nodded carefully eyeing Joseph wearily as he aimed crossbow, looked over his shoulder at them and back again staring down the bolt.

He angled his feet carefully and took a deep breath then he fired. The bolt shot out with a thud and flew towards the target like a stone thrown by a child towards the sea. A muted crack sounded a second later as the bolt landed in the third ring. The boy cursed out loud as he kicked his foot and prepared to cock the crossbow.

"Joe!" Rick yelled back at his brother.

"Oh, shut up, Rick. I'm not in the mood any more." Gripping the crossbow tightly Joseph glared at his brother and threw the crossbow to the ground with a loud crack as the wood impacted with gravel on the ground. Turning, he stormed off, his leather boots crackling below his feet as he trudged through the gravel up towards the south wing of Rienhold.

Druenn stared after the boy his face covered in confusion. *Everyone here is crazy.* It seemed to Druenn that the only two types of people there were in Rienhold were either friendly or hateful; there didn't seem to be any middle ground. The young boy pondered over the matter trying to comprehend why these people only seemed to like him or hate him due to what his mother had done many years ago. *And it always seems to be linked with something called Divine Victory.*

There was too much running through Druenn's mind to be worrying about doing some archery at the range a few yards ahead of him. His head was beginning to ache from the constant bombardments of information people were giving to him. *And it always leads to what my mother did.* Reassuring himself, Druenn watched ahead at Rick picking up an arrow placed neatly in a quiver which hung on the fence divider next to him. Knocking the arrow he slowly raised the bow taking steady aim; he breathed deeply and exhaled, pulling the string back to his chin he breathed deeply again. A second later the arrow ripped past him and flew towards the target landing with a *thud*.

"Nice shot!" Warren called out as he walked over to Rick's side. Rick stared down the line at his target, the arrow protruding from the second circle. Warren placed his hand under Rick's elbow and his other hand on his shoulder he pushed his elbow upwards until it was completely vertical.

"You've got to keep your arm completely straight, see?" Warren demonstrated. Rick concentrated as he listened to Warren's advice then tried. He nodded in thought as he knocked a new arrow and took aim once again. Keenly staring straight down the line, correcting his previous mistake he straightened his arm. Druenn began walking over. Rick fired; this time as the arrow left it flew faster than before leaving a whistling sound behind it and connected with the bullseye.

"Perfect shot!" Warren clapped unable to conceal his excitement and shook Rick by the hand. Rick could not stop smiling. Druenn could plainly see the joy on Rick's face, smiling up at him.

"Great shot indeed. Keep it up and you'll be an expert in no time," Warren continued.

Rick turned to Druenn looking down at him and passed him the bow. "Your turn, Druenn," he said his arm outstretched towards the timid little boy. "I want to see you hit the bullseye."

Druenn stared at the bow in front of him, dangling in Rick's hand. It had only been a day since the young boy had used his own bow to kill a bandit attacking his home, "and I'm in no hurry to use one again," he whispered. Sheepishly he took the bow from Rick gripping the wood tightly in both hands.

"Go on, Druenn, I have a feeling about you with bows." Warren coaxed him toward the range.

Druenn stared down the long range. Already he was calculating the distance. *Seventy? Maybe eighty yards, yes I make it eighty.* He nodded his head in reassurance.

Warren and Rick stared at one another, Rick confused with the hushed tones the little boy spoke, Warren on the other hand was nodding, his arms crossed, waiting for the first shot.

"Okay, now thinking of wind resistance and drop ratios," Druenn picked up an arrow and bounced it in his hand. "I'd say about twenty-five percent drop rate," he continued to whisper. Druenn always enjoyed the bow and arrow. He enjoyed the thrill of the arrow reaching the exact point he would want to hit.

But this was the real thing. He was holding a real bow and a real arrow. Not saying his previous one was a fake but it had been made and carved from an oak tree along the outskirts of Pinevale with no intention of killing people with. *I've got to be careful of what I may become within these walls*, Druenn thought to himself.

He told himself he wouldn't kill again, but the fact that he had enemies within Reinhold for what his mother did he knew deep down he was not likely to escape the fact that he will need to defend himself. Naturally his fingers curled around the string, testing the strength. He eyed the target and knocked the arrow. He felt the cool breeze dance around him rustling the trees. Taking a deep breath he drew back the string the tension building, as he pulled back further; when the string was brushing his cheek he focused on the aim, raised the bow high, eyeing the target once more his eyes followed the arrow again.

Taking another deep breath he whispered, "I will not miss."

Angling the bow slightly to the right, he fired. The whistle that ripped through the sky caused Warren and Rick's hairs on the back of their necks to stand on end. The arrow sailed through the air at a tremendous speed landing in the bulls-eye with a soft *thud*.

"Perfect shot!" Warren roared, teeth glistening in the sunlight with his wide smile as he clapped ferociously. Druenn looked back at Warren and smiled his one sided grin. Turning back to the range he saw from the corner of his eye Rick passing another arrow.

"Beginner's luck, I say," Rick teased with a grin.

"Come now, it's his first shot. Give the boy some credit," Warren argued back as he stepped forward assertively. Rick waved him off.

"Trust me, Warren. I think it is just beginner's luck. I want to see it again." He stepped back as Druenn took the arrow and knocked it staring down the range. Rick crossed his arms and eyed Warren. He stared back at him confusion across his face. Rick stared back and winked.

He's pumping him up, Warren thought as he stepped forward until he was a few feet behind the little boy.

"Maybe, Rick, it could have been beginner's luck," he joined in.

"Beginner's luck!" Druenn scoffed. Without a pause Druenn searched, aimed and fired and same as before the arrow whistled through the air before slicing right through the previous arrow cutting it in two. The two men stared their mouths gaped.

Druenn turned to them, a grin on his face. "You want to see that again?" Druenn said, the cockiness in his voice palpable.

Before Warren could reply, Druenn picked up another arrow knocking it and turned to the range once more aimed and fired. The same result, the arrow ripped through the previous one.

"That's incredible, Druenn," Rick finally replied "Where did you learn these skills. I... I mean, not even our best archer can top that!" Rick stammered tripping on his words as he spoke.

Druenn was unable to reply to Rick's remark. He was not sure he knew either. He believed it could have been due to the fact that his eyes were sharper than the average human's but even then it could not explain why he could perfectly align himself.

"Well, my boy." Warren spoke in hushed tones as he walked over to him patting his shoulder. "I think we found your weapon of choice."

Finding Rick's gaze he pulled him aside as Druenn continued his training. "Rick, I'm going to need a favour from you."

"A favour?" Rick replied arching an eyebrow.

Warren took a deep breath and continued. "Druenn almost got into a fight this afternoon with Rupert." Exhaling again he folded his arms. "Terribor seems to have a large grip over half the students in this school and I don't know how I'm going to keep the boy safe."

Rick listened intently resting his arms on his longbow.

"I need a friend that can be with him as much as possible, I've asked Alex and Emily to look after him and I want you as well."

Rick's face grew more concerned as Warren continued to reveal the corruption over the students with their views on Divine Victory. He listened incredulous to Druenn's misfortune the day before and his entire ordeal, *then to come here and have the likes of Rupert starting a fight for what Druenn's mother did to save the people of this Kingdom. That must have been hard.*

"I'll do it, I'm more than happy to help."

"Thank you, Rick. I appreciate this." Warren smiled, placing a solid hand on Rick's shoulder. Rick smiled back. Both the men walked back to Druenn admiring his fine archery skills.

Druenn smirked up at them both. "Thought I'd make a face," and sure enough when they glanced back down the range a distinct smile gazed back at them, the bullseye clearly being the nose.

Warren shook his head in astonishment. "Druenn, you're just setting yourself up for greatness, aren't you?" He chuckled as Druenn passed the bow back to Rick.

"Thanks, Rick, I really appreciate borrowing your bow." Rick looked down at the boy and smiled widely. *After everything that's happening he's still so polite!*

"No trouble whatsoever. Just remember if you ever need help with anything come find me."

"Thank you, Rick." Druenn thrust out a hand and they shook.

Warren gestured Druenn to follow as he began making his way back up the steady dirt track hill. Druenn waved down to Rick, he waved back as they disappeared over the edge and out of sight. He let out a sigh of concern as he picked up an arrow. Glancing back up the dirt track he thought about his own past when he lived back in his village.

"Yes, Druenn," he said quietly to himself letting the words get lost in the breeze. "You're not the first boy to be picked up because bandits destroyed your home." He closed his eyes. The village was ablaze, *my mother screaming.*

"Get out, get out now, boy, while you still can," she screamed, an axe keeping her leg pinned to the blazing house wall. He remembered the burning heat on his thirteen-year-old face. *I was young* he thought. *Far too young.*

He remembered gripping his father's pitchfork and leaping out the window. Staring up at the spiraling black smoke as the wind picked up and the storm raged overhead, the thatched roof collapsing on top of his mother's head as the last of her burning agonizing screams began to die. He saw in front of him a bandit dismounting a horse to grab a young girl.

"Get off my Neena!" he screamed as the broad armed bandit turned to him throwing the bruised girl to the floor. As the bandit turned to him Rick saw the tattoos plastered down his face and arms. The bandit licked his lips as he approached unsheathing his sword. Rick ran towards him launching himself upwards his foot shooting out as the bandit raised his arm to swipe, his foot coming into contact with the bandit's knee. An almighty crack rippled through the chaos around them. The bandit let out an agonizing scream as his other leg buckled and he toppled over.

Rick raised the pitchfork high and rammed it home deep inside the man's eye. Leaving the pitchfork to stand proudly over its kill he watched it sway for a moment catching his breath. He searched for the sword the bandit had dropped, gripping it tightly he ran to Neena's side, reaching his hand out.

"Come on, Neena, we have to leave," before she could take his hand another bandit was on him.

"I'm gonna carve your face for a new mask!" the bandit grunted.

"Let's see you try!" Rick roared back. His father had taught him well in the art of fighting, he hoped one day Rick could fight in Reinhold picking up contracts for work and bring some money into the family. His father's words still rang strongly in his ear.

"One day, son," his father would say his broken accent very apparent from the south-western areas of Tharlian. "One day you'll make the Diazes rich." He faced the bandit now stealing a glance at his father's torn body strewn across the street a few feet away.

"Fight me, you pathetic excuse for a human, fight me!" Rick's rattled croaky voice sounded, the smoke in his lungs wearing him down, his desperate cries for his parents he wanted to spew out in mourning, but now was not the time – he knew that. The time for mourning was later. The time for revenge was now. The gangly bandit in black leather swiped as Rick dodged under to the left, his sword connecting with the bandit's a second later pushing the bandit further over and taking him off balance, Rick swung his sword back slashing the bandit's leg.

"A downed enemy is a dead enemy," his father used to say. "Just dance the dance, every dance has to end at some point," Rick liked that one. His father used to say it with an evil smirk in his eye as if to say "I've won this fight already," so he danced with the words of his father ringing in his ear.

The Viper snags the mouse, as the bandit moved a step back to gain his composure only to be seized back as Rick cut down another two spaces with a downward side slash. The off balanced bandit desperately swiped ferociously. His father also taught him this one. "The prowling cat pounces the angry dog." Rick watched the sword slash the air.

"Now, my son." He saw the gap and he pounced the sword aiming for his heart just missing the bandit's swipe, he felt the air rush by as it passed his ear. The sword slid deep into the bandit's chest. The man looked down at the blood trickling down the sword. Everything went silent.

The bandit fell to his knees, his eyes already dead sliding back he went limp and he was gone. Rick pulled the sword out of the body now laying on the cobbled ground the blood still flowing, filling the cracks in between the cobblestones. Rick turned back to Neena, she gazed up at him as he extended his hand to her. The wind unnaturally strong now, Neena stared into the sky as she climbed to her feet. Rick saw her eyes grow wide with fear.

She pointed up and screamed, Rick turned as the wind pulled harder, the dust rising faster. Rick searched around him for anything to hold onto. The wind was pulling on them.

Rick struggled to stay on the ground. "We need to find something to hold on to!"

The wind ripped at their ears as they searched for an escape, the wind continued ripping the roofs and burning buildings upwards into the swirling black vortex. Rick saw his house rip away into the blackness before it disappeared. *The dust! I can't see a thing!*

Panic washed over Rick as everything went black, the vortex covering the entire village. The wind struck and blew them both off their feet pulling them upwards.

Neena screamed.

"Don't let me go, Rick. Please, I beg you, don't let me go!" she screamed. She was terrified and Rick knew it, her eyes filled with tears, blood smeared across her sky blue dress gripping his hand tightly as they flew ever upwards.

"Hang on, I'm here. I won't let go!" Rick screamed back forcing the fear back; they saw bodies and rubble flying round them and darting back into the blackness. Rick saw a large house still intact, he braced for the mighty stone structure to kill them. He held Neena tightly behind him so he'd receive the full force of the blow.

He closed his eyes. He was back in the archery range, eighteen again. "Yes, Druenn. Don't worry." He aimed the bow at the target feeling the fresh breeze in his nostrils. "You're not the only one."

He fired.

EIGHT

Memories

Emily twiddled her thumbs with boredom as she unconsciously watched the teacher at the front of the class giving his lesson on the creatures of Tharlian. She did not care for this lesson it was just a waste of time in her eyes. She'd much rather have stayed with Druenn and continued the tour around Rienhold but she knew the fight had got out of hand. *Lucky thing that Warren was around to hear it*, she thought to herself. A bell tolled in the corner of her memory as she watched on silently, paying no attention to the lesson.

Stealing a glance at her open book she was shocked to see Druenn's name written multiple times over her page. Before she could begin to rub the names out she saw the class packing their books, quills and pencils into their satchels. *The lesson's over*, she mused. With a wide grin she leapt to her feet quickly grabbing her book and pencil from the table and throwing them in her satchel, she swung the bag across her right shoulder and ran for the door. As she reached the front row Mr Burnsley blocked her way.

Towering over her his arms folded, his long green and blue robes flowing gently in the open window breeze. He was a very broad man, not overweight but chubby and the muscles to define his shape, his hair tied back into a tight ponytail almost pulling his hair out by the looks. Emily always believed he pulled his hair back so tightly it would pull all his wrinkles back, which was also a reason Emily struggled to conceal her laughter.

"You didn't listen to a word I said, did you, Emily?"

Emily forced back a stifled giggle. Mr Burnsley's voice always made her laugh.

The forty-nine year old had a high pitched weedy, whining voice that at the beginning of the year he would have to let the students laugh at his voice until they got it out of their system and became accustomed to it. It was a degrading experience but he got used to it, the students got over his voice and then were able to continue the lesson. Now Mr Burnsley stood over the only exception of the class.

"Emily!" he squealed, the sound a piglet makes as you pick it up. Emily doubled over, a giggling wreck. Mr Burnsley snorted in disgust tapping his foot waiting for her to calm down. The giggles slowed, Emily's friends Ruby and Precious waited by the door holding back their laughter. Emily was the funny one of the group and she loved being the one that cheered them up when one of them was upset. Ruby and Precious knew they needed to get her out of there before she was given another detention for this. Emily looked up at the scowling man looking down at her, his greasy hair shining in the sunlight.

"Are you finished, Miss Fletcher?"

The bellows of laughter that came next was astounding to all of them. Mr Burnsley threw up his arms in defeat, a tear trickling down his cheek, 'Why, why do I have to put up with this? I shouldn't have to deal with this kind of pressure." He broke down in to fits of tears as Emily's laughter only increased into panted screeches still rolling on the floor, Mr Burnsley's distorted squeals he made as he cried only fuelling her laughter further.

It wasn't that she found it funny she made him cry, far from it. She just found his voice funny. Panting rapidly in an attempt to stop the laughing she broke out in more fits of laughter with every squeal their teacher made. Running in, Precious and Ruby grabbed her. They dragged Emily out of the room, Ruby curtsying deeply as she appologised and darted out of the room leaving the broken man in his seat behind the desk rubbing his eyes as he cried.

"By the divine, Emily! What did you do?" Precious giggled as she supported her friend down the long hall heading for the dorms. It was the last lesson of the day and the students were heading off to their after school activities or dorm rooms. Emily's face streamed with tears, her eyes red. She caught her breath and began to wipe her eyes.

"Oh wow, that was funny," she replied to Precious, giggling again.

"It was funny but you really upset him this time, I think you should apologise."

The girls looked at one another and giggled again.

"Okay, girls, I'VE got to run. I'm going to meet a friend."

The girls stopped and watched her for a sign of a joke.

"Meeting... a friend, after school?" Ruby asked

"But you never meet people after lesson," Precious chimed in "you always come to practice our sword fighting"

"Yeah but... not today." Emily glanced at the pair of them with a cheerful grin and slipped around, darting down a dark corridor. "I'll catch up with you later, okay?" she called back to the girls waving to them as she disappeared into the darkness of the corridor. Precious stared at Ruby, one eyebrow raised. She rolled eyes and smiled as Ruby gestured toward a corridor that led outside to the training grounds.

Emily sprinted through the crowds of students leaving their lessons. Darting and weaving in and out of the students she darted out a side door leading towards the archery courtyard. As she ran she covered her eyes until they began to adjust to the bright light. Big dust clouds puffed gently in the wind behind her as she kicked up the dust and gravel on the pathway.

She began down another pathway that connected further down to the Archery range when she glimpsed Warren with… "Druenn," she said breathlessly, stopping and watching as she ran her hand behind her long flowing hair blowing gently in the summer breeze and tucked it behind her ear. She sprinted towards them.

Emily noticed Warren's outstretched arm across the Reinhold grounds, she presumed Warren had continued the tour in the end after all. As Emily approached Warren looked up eyeing her and smiled as she darted the last few yards. Druenn spotted her and his face lit up.

"Emily!" he called to her walking towards her. The force of the impact was unexpected, Druenn jumped with the mighty blow to the chest as she embraced him in a big hug.

"Druenn, I missed you!" Emily chimed with a giggle. Druenn attempted to put his arms around her but the fact she had winded him made it very difficult to master the energy.

"Can't… breathe," he managed with a croaky voice, he heard Warren chuckle to himself listening to the winded boy. Emily let go instantly and Druenn fell to the ground, sat up and attempted to catch his breath, taking in big gulps of air.

"Oh, I'm sorry!" she squealed in her high soprano voice. She knelt down in front of Druenn stroking back his brown hair. Warren shifted uncomfortably as he eyed the two children.

"Okay I'm… eh." Warren paused, he smiled a reassuring smile at them both and continued. "Okay, that sound you just heard Druenn was the schoolbell so when you hear that one it is the end of school so it's your own time, feel free to do what you like."

Druenn looked up at Warren smiling down on him as the sun slowly disappeared past Warren's shoulder causing him to look spectacular in colours, pinks and yellows shining over his head and shoulders. He looked somewhat regal to Druenn. The little boy nodded and bowed slightly thanking Warren as he did.

"Okay, Druenn, I have signed you up to study the sword, the axe." Warren pointed to each of his fingers as he mentioned the weapon. "Eh… the spear, the mace." Emily and Druenn looked on in astonishment.

"Why must he master all of those weapons?" Emily asked aggressively. "That will take him years surely to do them all."

Warren smiled at her, placing his hands behind his back he bent down to her. "Druenn has already saved himself a year of training with a bow, I think he could be a master bowman by tomorrow."

"Re—eally?" Emily stammered and she gazed over at Druenn with an eyebrow raised and a cheeky grin. "Check you out Mr Smarty-pants," she teased. Druenn blushed and returned his gaze to the ground.

Turning back to Warren she asked, "How long do you think he'll be training at Rienhold?"

Warren estimated, counting on his fingers. "I wouldn't be surprised if about eight years."

Druenn's eyes shot up. "Eight years!" he screamed. "I can't wait that long. I have to find Meredith!" he said, his memory wandering back to only yesterday to his beautiful perfect sister, her golden hair dancing in the pleasant breeze that Pinevale always created, the beautiful sounds of the fresh water in the stream and the grass in the long tumbling fields.

Her laugh! Oh, how I miss her laugh. Her bright blue eyes gazing back at him, the twinkles only making her smile more magical. *I love you, sis, and I will find you.*

Warren gripped the boy's shoulders. "Druenn, are you listening to me?" He spoke hushed but harsh tones.

Druenn's eyes shot back to the present and stared Warren in the face his eyes strong as steel.

"There is nothing you can do for her, not in your situation" studying him head to toe. "In this state you'll do no one any good, I need to train you before you can become a great warrior and by that time she'll be long gone and that is if she is still alive."

The unexpected last words caught Druenn offguard. *If she is still alive, she could be dead*, the poor boy thought. *Oh, sis, please don't be dead.*

The tears Druenn felt also caught him offguard, he dabbed his cheeks with his sleeve.

Emily wrapped her arms around him. "Warren, I understand you mean to help but the wound is still too fresh. I'll look after him, you get back to your duties."

Warren folded his arms as he realised the pain he must have caused Druenn, he nodded to Emily's remark and bent down to Druenn. His eyes remorseful, Druenn stole a glance at his eyes spotting a tear in the corner.

"I'm sorry, Druenn, I didn't mean to upset…" He cut off, unable to finish his sentence. His eyes fell to the ground.

Frustrated with himself he cursed under his breath. *Fire consume you, Warren Anguish. Why did you have to make the poor boy cry, what is your problem!* he argued with himself. Closing his eyes he stood, bowed and walked away.

Emily watched as he left, holding Druenn she listened to him sob into her shoulder, feeling his tears drip through her white linen shirt.

"It's okay, Druenn, I'm here." She pulled away and wiped his tears away and guided him back to their dorm room.

Terribor strode through the halls, books under his arm, a soft clanging from his belt buckle echoed round the empty space as he walked back to his private quarters. He wore a smug grin under his black goatee. Entering his quarters he placed the lesson books on the table, swishing his hand the books began to levitate towards the bookshelves, aligning themselves with the gaps and slotting into them.

Terribor then swished his hand again eyeing a book in particular. The book began to edge out of its spot and float towards the table. As the book landed on the table he threw out his arm. The book trembled and flung open the pages spinning leaving an eerie fluttering sound in the room. As fast as it begun it stopped as the book's pages halted and landed on a page that Terribor was very interested about. He eyed the title:

Possessing Human Enchantment.

He read the title again. This was indeed the enchantment he wanted. He scanned his finger over the enchantment then returned the book to the shelf.

Leaving his quarters he strode towards the southeastern end of Rienhold, his black cloak flowing out behind him creating a terrifying silhouette on the candlelit stone wall. He turned into a dark corridor towards the far end of Rienhold leading outside to a spear training ground. He knew he could find a few students he knew were easily manipulated. He could plant his next plan and set the motion of things to come.

Reaching the end of the final corridor he opened the wooden door leading outside, the door creaking loudly as it opened. Gazing out over the sunset seeing the bright colours in the sky, the pinks and yellows clashing with the blues and dark blues as night closed in. *The best time of the day*, he thought. Placing a hand on the hilt of his sword he began to descend the steps. Rupert and the twins fought in the dirt ring which was no more than a horse riding practice area.

The twins fought with their quarterstaffs fending back the strength of Rupert alone. As the twins spotted Terribor they stopped and bowed to him.

"Good evening, sir," they both chimed politely.

Rupert turned as Terribor closed on them.

"Good evening, young students, I do trust your training is going well?" he replied with a mischievous grin, his voice low and raspy.

Rupert bowed, replying, "Very well, sir. How may we help you?"

The breeze picked up as Terribor's black cloak began to flap violently in the wind, he raised his hand. "Help me?" Terribor chuckled. "How can you help me indeed!"

Warren sat in his private quarters. He gazed around the dark room; running his hand over a candle with three wicks in, he lit them, and his hand igniting for a second then the candles were lit.

He stared at the flames dancing, he breathed out toying with the flames as they clung to the wick as though holding on to life. He pulled himself away from the candles, running a hand through his shaggy shoulder length brown hair and searched for a book on his desk. Finding it, he opened it up and turning to the page he had turned to every night since the book was written, he flicked through reaching page eighteen. He gazed at the picture; he remembered the original being painted twelve years ago and now only a replica existed in this book. Warren hated the people of Cetni for burning that painting.

He eyed the girl in the painting, her proud face standing alongside the ten greatest warriors in Tharlian. His vision became misty as a tear slipped down his cheek. He poured himself a goblet of red wine. Taking a swig he returned the goblet to the desk and brushed his hand over the beautiful girl. *She was only nineteen when she was in this picture*, he thought. The silence that filled the room spooked Warren, he was not used to this kind of deadly silence.

Within Rienhold there was always something going on whether it was the younger students playing tag around the grounds or the older or more disciplined students would be practice and exercise the skills they had learnt that day. Not tonight. Tonight was silent, the only noise being the low calm breeze outside. Rubbing his eyes he looked around the room, gazing off into the pitch black.

Something caught his attention. Not something within the room but something from a distant memory. Pulling himself up from the chair he re-wrapped his long flowing grey and white patterned robe around him; grasping his grey, white and orange scarf he wrapped it around his neck. His eyes focused back on the book, the pages flickering in the candlelight, the words dancing in and out of the blackness.

He gazed back into the picture of the eleven great fighters that had made this Kingdom a proud one; he thought of how they were betrayed by their own people and cast out. His eyes scanning the eleven fighters carefully his eyes fell to a young lad no older than the young girl, he remembers his age very well. *He was twenty, I remember that much.* Warren eyed the man's clothes and looked at his own. They were the same, the scarf also correctly wrapped around his neck and the tails falling to his mid chest and the robe tightly clung to him by a multicoloured cord. Pushing away from the desk he slowly paced into the centre of the room, the blackness surrounding him, the memories rushing back.

The crowd roared as Gondolas announced the arrival of a great force of fighters. The blackness began to take shape, shapes he knew, shapes he missed.

Looking into the blackness he could see the crowd around as Warren proudly strode down the steps from the great Palace of Cetni. The crowd parted into two, leaving long lines leading out of the palace courtyard. Alongside him he could see a proud Warrior wielding a great broadsword in one hand, his shield ornately patterned with a tower in its centre and a sun rising above it, slung on his back, and his shining silver armour glistening in the sunlight blinded Warren. He saw the warrior look back at him and wink with a wide grin. Next to him he saw the girl, that beautiful girl that he loved from the start. Her brown flowing hair danced in the breeze, her scent caught fluttering around him, a stone caught him off guard and he stumbled. The young girl stifled a laugh as her eyes captured him, her beautiful eyes as blue as the sky. Her smile dazzled him and he could no longer remember anything around him, all he could see was her. As hard as Warren tried to remember the scene he could not, only her.

"Warren, is that right?" she asked him her voice a soft and gentle cream sounding soprano voice melodically flowed out.

"I'm… eh… oh… Ma'am, my name is… eh." Warren tripped and stumbled on his words, completely taken aback that this beautiful princess spoke to him. *Well with beauty like that she must be a princess, surely?*

She laughed out loud as several of the older fighters glanced back, disgust on their faces. Warren stumbled on another stone and his eyes caught her thin and nimble thighs under her brown leather greaves. Her brown boots came halfway up her leg, not quite to the knee, but not far off. Her blue cloak flapped around her green linen shirt protected by a brown leather chest pad cutting off below her breasts and also protecting her shoulders. His eyes gazed back into hers and lost himself again. The blackness consumed him again.

"No!" the memories fading. "Come back!" he called. Blackness. The memory shifted to a blue and red stream of light spiraling round each other only just missing his head and igniting into a ball of flames. Warren remembered this nightmare well, haunting his dreams more often than he'd wish it to. The picture slowed to a crawl as the spiraling ball of blue and red flames hurtled towards the king beyond Warren.

Warren spun, his face contorted in trepidation, he saw Durroc Epsonstar from the corner of his eye, his steel armour gleaming in the hurtling colours, throw his shield to block the blast. The spinning colours rippled into the finely crafted shield smashing it and melting it. The screeching crunch that followed was defining like scratching on a chalkboard and a ship scraping across the edge of docks. Warren covered his ears as the shield ripped into pieces leaving only a melted piece of metal strewn across the stonework pavement. The fireball hurtled towards Gondolas. Warren gazed over with incredulity then he saw her. His angel, his world, his love *my whole* he thought. The girl flew out of the corners of his memory.

"No, don't!" Warren screamed, thrusting his hand forward, his palms flat as if to say halt, unaware he was shouting aloud in his dark room. His angel darted into the line of sight throwing herself in front of the balling inferno striking her body, she ignited, the flames engulfed her. She didn't scream, Warren will never forget that, as her body convulsed in agony. Warren ran towards the shadow that had caused the flame ball. Blackness. Another memory washed over him.

Inside the palace, his angel still burning on a stone table, everyone unable to distinguish the flames, she screamed in agony. Before he could reach her he cast a spell throwing his hand out in front of him.

"Hydroll!" he screamed. His hand began to glow blue as a torrent of water shot from his palm dowsing the flames, kneeling by her side. She quivered from the burns. Warren's eyes clouded by the tears, she raised a trembling hand to his cheek and mouthed three words. The blackness engulfed him. Warren clamped his hands around his head almost clawing at himself trying to kill the memory. The tears broke out in torrents as he collapsed to the floor as the last candle burnt out leaving him in total darkness.

NINE

Training

Druenn began to stir from his sleep, a dreamless night. He was relieved, as he knew the dreams would be of one thing and he knew there was nothing that could be done. He had lost his family and his village, everyone he'd ever loved gone, snuffed out in an instant. He rolled over, his eyes still closed keeping his father and his sister in his memory but not to mourn, there was no time to mourn he had to train to avenge them.

He saw Meredith's face. That giant smile he knew and loved. "Druenn, Druenn, Druenn, Druenn, Druenn, Druenn, Druenn, Druenn."

A voice chimed, *Meredith? You're never this annoying!*

"Druenn, Druenn, Druenn, Druenn, Druenn, Druenn," it continued.

He began swatting the voice in all directions until he felt a soft *thud* on the back of his hand and a soft crack of a bone. His eyes shot open. Emily stood by his bed in the same garments as the night before, shorts and vest, but this time instead of the friendly smile she covered her cheek, wincing. Druenn's eyes went wide as realisation hit him.

She breathed heavily. "So you want to play that game, do ya!" she scowled with the hint of a smirk.

"No! I didn't mean to, it was an accident, I swear!" Druenn squealed as he leapt out of bed the opposite side to avoid a direct confrontation. Her eyes blazed through him as she pointed towards him the other hand placed firmly on his bed.

"You're mine, Lightblaser!" Emily poised herself like a cat, she coiled like a viper then she sprang. Druenn screeched in terror as she chased him around the room. Druenn leapt over Emily's bed, running to the bookcase he scurried up the shelves two at a time. Emily watched him scurry up and giggled.

"As if I'd let you get away with this one." She walked over to her bed and jumped bouncing higher with each bounce. Druenn watched her, his eyes following her up and down, he realised there was no escape but he clung to the high bookcase for dear life until he felt a hand shoot out and grip his ankle.

"Oh, crap!" he said plainly as he lost his grip and plummeted to Emily's bed. With a small *thud* they bounced on the bed as she began to knuckle his forehead. Druenn squealed in pain but before he could scream for help she had stopped giggling her loving giggle, she dressed, donning leather trousers and a clean linen shirt. Grabbing her brown leather belt hung up above her bed, slipping her scabbard onto her belt she ran towards the door and picked up a wooden training sword. She slipped it into her scabbard quickly and with ease. She dashed back over to Druenn still recovering from his severe rubbing and entangled in Emily's bed sheets.

She reached him as she tied a red ribbon around her long golden flowing hair, pulling it back into a ponytail. She bent down and sneaked him a peck on the cheek as she dashed off calling back to him. "Have a good day, cutie!" before she disappeared around the corner of the doorway she stole him a quick wink. Druenn blinked and she was gone.

He rolled over and out of the covers, shooting the doorway another glance.

Warren stood in the doorway eyeing him up. Like yesterday he lent on the doorway. "Get ready!" he said coldly. "We have a long day ahead of us."

"We do?" Druenn replied rolling onto his feet just in time to receive a pair of leather trousers and a brown linen shirt in his face.

"Put them on quickly we start practice in five minutes, I want you to be down in the sword training grounds by the time the bell tolls. We were there briefly yesterday, do you remember how to get there? If you are not there in five minutes I will have you scrubbing floors and dishes for a week, do I make myself clear?" Warren blurted out without taking a breath. The little boy nodded as he danced around the room one-legged attempting to put his trousers on. Warren disappeared too.

"Make sure you pick up your training sword and scabbard at the door will you? I have already taken the liberty of tying it onto your belt so put the belt straight on," he heard Warren calling from outside the door.

Warren left the little boy to change as he made his way down the corridor. Before he reached the door at the end of the corridor the little boy shrieked, followed by an abrupt clang. *Obviously he had no luck with the trousers*, Warren thought.

Druenn scrambled to his feet searching for his shirt, his eyes caught an unfamiliar hourglass sitting on top of his bedside table. *Warren must have put it there so I'm not...*

"Late!" he yelled seeing the sand slip away faster than he could move. He donned his shirt and grasped his belt dashing out of the room tying his belt on as he went, the sword and scabbard catching his inner thigh causing him to stumble each time his other leg caught in-between. Racing down the long corridor and through the open doorway he reached the great hall.

Druenn recognised the area and knew he had to take the door on the far left, *second*, he reminded himself. *The second door*. Reaching the training ground he saw Warren his hands behind his back staring up at the morning sun, spilling its colours halfway up in the eastern sky. Honey yellow blending into a deep orange. The bell tolled behind Druenn. Warren didn't turn.

"Defend yourself, your training begins… now!" Warren turned in one swift motion, his training sword unsheathed and in his hand. He launched himself at Druenn, the boy blinked and leapt back, his sword shooting instinctively into his hand and blocked the first blow.

"That's good, Druenn. Again!" Warren encouraged forcing the boy back with a stab for the chest. Druenn leapt again swooping his sword under and around Warren's, throwing a slanted up cut slash. Warren dodged it easily. Warren lowered his sword and took a step towards Druenn.

"Well done, Druenn. That is very impressive, being only instinct."

Druenn lowered his and smiled up at Warren.

Warren raised his sword again and slashed, Druenn again jumped back followed by a flail of slashes. Warren weaved in and out like a viper. It frustrated Druenn that he couldn't land a blow. Warren began coaxing him.

Landing blows and taps each time being told to concentrate harder. After half an hour had passed he lowered his sword, Druenn held his composure his sword held firmly in front of him, his hands creaking as he re-gripped the sword due to the sweat. Warren paced back and forth in front of the composed boy.

"You must without fail stand firm, this." He pointed to Druenn's sword tapping it with his index and middle finger throwing it aside, Druenn watched the sword flap in his hands as he took in Warren's lesson.

"Lock your wrists, allow enough leeway as not to damage your wrists, but they must be locked firmly."

Re-gripping his sword Druenn nodded. Warren tried again. The sword did not move.

"Better, now be steadfast!" Warren launched another attack landing multiple blows.

Frustrated, Druenn attempted over and over trying to land a blow never succeeding.

"Okay!" Warren breathed heavily hocking up phlegm and spitting it onto the grass just outside the circle shaped dirt ring. "Let's go again, faster."

Druenn realised with the intensive training the days quickly turned into weeks, which turned into months. Over time Druenn began to feel more at home in Reinhold. Rick Diaz spent many hours with him teaching him about tactics he had picked up in his time at Reinhold.

"If you ever find yourself in danger and only having either a sword or a shield to choose from, go with the shield it has multiple uses," Rick told him.

At night Emily would sneak into his bed and snuggle up with him, her head resting on his chest. Druenn appreciated it when she did and would hold her tightly to him. The night time was a lonely time only the sound of the crickets to be heard bringing no solace to him, so when Emily asked to join him one night because she couldn't sleep, tears in her eyes, a month after arriving at Reinhold he raised the covers and let her in, holding her cold body to his, warming her, her shivering slowing as Druenn's heat began to warm her.

"I have to admit something Druenn," she whispered to him.

"Hmm?" Druenn asked, his eyes closed and arms around her holding her tight.

"I can't sleep because I'm lonely, I miss my family, Druenn," she sniffed.

Druenn feeling a tear drip onto his white linen shirt and seep through to his skin.

"How can you say that, Emmy?" Druenn asked. She looked up at him, his face pale from the moonlight. He opened his eyes and looked at her, his eyes glinting in the faint moonlight, his cheeky smile on his face. "I'm family, aren't I?" She kissed his cheek, and they fell asleep.

Druenn was also never far away from confrontation. Another DV hater as the DV supporters would call them. He found himself talking his way out of fights but Alex was never far behind yelling back off or letting them walk away with a black eye. Druenn's wit and skills with the sword began to help and it wasn't long before word got out that a ten-year-old had fought a twenty-year-old and was being sent to the hospital wing for stitches.

Druenn was sent to the Dean for that one and explained what happened. The Dean listened intently, showing great sympathy for Druenn's situation, he let him off.

"You must be careful in the future, Druenn, you can't go around giving everyone stitches, it's not the way to deal with bullies," he told Druenn, a polite tone in his voice. When he wasn't in training or lessons he would be in the library on his free time researching everything he could.

Druenn watched his eleventh and twelfth birthday sail by. Every birthday Warren left a new weapon outside his door, which they would be studying and training over the year. For Druenn's eleventh birthday he found a pair of daggers on his bedside table and for his twelfth a quarterstaff. Memories of his father and sister began to fade but never lost. The pain began to ease, which made focusing a lot easier.

After a heated argument talking about families with Rick, Druenn found himself learning about Rick's past. He no longer felt alone. Rick and Druenn's friendship grew after that day and they began to train, study and eat together. Emily began to grow jealous of their friendship. Emily watched Druenn grow, slowly watching the young boy she knew and loved grow into a young handsome man. She began to realise her own changes from a young girl into a young woman. She found herself having to cover up or ask Druenn to leave the room to change. She did not like these changes.

For Emily's seventeenth birthday they had been asked to put a sheet up to split the room in two. Emily hated this but Druenn had no quarrel so she allowed it, hiding her emotions. She wanted to be able to snuggle up with her best friend at night. There was nothing romantic about them but it was just comforting knowing someone cared and that's what they both agreed on one night. She feared tomorrow, it was Druenn's sixteenth birthday and he would have to leave the dorm room and join another male student.

She tossed and turned in her bed knowing her best friend will have to leave. Tears welled in her eyes and she fought the urge to try something she missed so much. Pulling the covers off her flustered body she looked over in the dark, a small beam of light trickling through the window from the moon. She lowered her feet onto the cold wooden floor and she slowly tiptoed towards

Druenn's bed, her heart pounding. She stared up at the white bed sheet separating the room and scowled as she wrapped her arms tightly around her, folding them under her breasts, the cold causing her to shiver. Pulling aside the bed sheet she stepped over to his bed and gently tapped him on the shoulder, he stirred but did not wake

"Psst! Druenn," he stirred again. "Druenn!" she whispered loudly and nudged him. This time he opened his eyes, he looked up at his best friend, Emily. He could see she was crying.

"What's wrong?" he asked his voice concerned.

She sniffed. "Can I please come in?" her voice slightly panicked

"Of course," Druenn said pulling the bed covers open for her. She almost leapt in her heart skipping for joy and he wrapped the cover around the two of them. She snuggled into his chest, she could feel the change; his muscles were bigger.

"Wow, check out the muscles, Dru!"

Druenn hated that nickname and she knew it. She giggled whilst squeezing his right bicep, he scoffed, a wide grin on his face.

"They aren't that big."

She snuggled her cold feet up against his and he flinched from the cold, she giggled again and slipped a cold hand up his shirt. He flinched again, she bit her bottom lip as she looked up at him.

"How's that?"

Druenn could tell she was in a playful mood. She always bit her bottom lip when she was in a playful mood.

He laughed as he wrapped his arms tightly around her. "You know it would take a lot more than that to get me to..." He paused.

"Make that noise," she giggled that loving laugh as she lay her head back down on his chest. Druenn held her. He had missed this a lot more than he expected. She sniffed and he felt a tear on his chest.

"I have to admit something, Druenn," she whispered to him

"Hmm?" Druenn asked, his eyes closed and arms around her holding her tight with a smile on his face, feeling this felt very familiar a few years earlier.

"I can't sleep because I'm lonely, I miss my family, Druenn," she sniffed half upset but half overjoyed as well that he joined in the reminiscence, Druenn feeling another tear drip onto his white linen shirt and seep through to his skin.

"How can you say that Emmy?" Druenn asked. She looked up at him, his face pale from the moonlight. He opened his eyes and looked at her, his eyes glistening in the faint moonlight his cheeky smile on his face.

"I'm family, aren't I?" Her heart pounded as an unusual overwhelming torrent of emotions gushed through her like a river, tears flowed down her rosy cheeks. She took his cheek in the palm of her hand and pulled her lips to his. Druenn wasn't sure whether it was the kiss that made him light headed or the shock. His heart skipped and jumped as a tear reached his eye. They kissed passionately over and over as they experienced something they both could never have dreamed of feeling. She lay on top of him feeling his sweet tender lips trace around hers before finding them and placing a passionate kiss upon him.

"I love you, Druenn Lightblaser," she whispered as he held her

"I love you, Emily Fletcher, so much," he replied between overwhelming feelings cutting him off. As they lay in bed together Druenn lay behind her one arm resting her head and the other wrapped around her chest, she clung to his arm.

"I don't want you to go tomorrow, Druenn. Please stay," she said, serenely kissing the palm of his hand.

"I don't know what we can do but I will ask."

She wrapped Druenn's arm around her tightly wearing a sweet smile as her eyes closed, kissing his hand again she wished him a good night and fell asleep.

TEN

Sixteen

Druenn awoke to the usual sound of the great bell clanging high above the highest tower of Rienhold representing ten minutes before the start of lessons. It was the beginning of year seven and Druenn was excited to finally learn the history of Divine Victory in Warren's lessons. **The History of Divine Victory**. That was the name of the class.

Druenn had waited patiently for six years for this lesson and had been in many arguments with Warren because of it. He lay on his bed looking up at the ceiling, the dark oak wood staring back at him. He remembered the last time he argued with Warren. He remembered landing his first blow on Warren with the training sword as Warren struck he dove and rolled under Warren striking him in the crutch as he rolled. He remembered the wincing guttural sound that bellowed out of Warren as he fell to his knees writhing in agony.

He received a large round of applause for that one, *I was only eleven* he chuckled quietly to himself. Looking to his left Emily was fast asleep her head lay snugly into his shoulder. Leaning over he gently kissed her forehead. She began to stir, her morning groans breaking the silence as she awoke, pulling herself up and opening and closing her eyes. She rubbed them and yawned.

"What's the time?" she asked, another large yawn rippling out of her.

"Don't worry, the bell has only just rung," Druenn replied before a yawn shot out past his lips. He always seemed to yawn when others yawned or even mentioned it.

"Okay, sweetie, I'm getting up" kissing him on the forehead she dragged her dreary body out of bed and began dressing. Emily watched him for a second then turned back to change. She knew why he wasn't getting ready.

She knew he loved to torment Warren. It was always the same, Druenn asked many questions which Warren refused to answer.

She had to admit of all the things she loved about Druenn, his cheeky wit enjoyment of irritating people was her favoutite. Not in a nasty way, he only meant to have fun, but it was fun to watch all the same. She remembered his last birthday – Druenn and his friends along with Warren, the Dean and several other teachers – gathered round a birthday cake, when one of the students, *Warrick*, her memory told her made one of his biggest mistakes. He challenged him. She knew to embarrass him on his birthday.

Druenn watched her intrigued propping his head up on one arm, his eyes studying her. She shot him a playful look, arching an eyebrow as she winked and turned away. She grinned remembering once again that Warrick fought him in the training grounds, he couldn't touch him while Druenn toyed with him, giving the students a lesson on fighting skills during a battle, she thought. *He's too cheeky for his own good.*

Winding her belt round her, she tied on her scabbard. Students would have their training swords replaced with real swords once they reach key skills level three in sword fighting, and also when they reach fifteen years of age. She wrapped her hand around the hilt as she picked up her sword. Swinging it around for a second she carefully slid it into the scabbard.

"Okay, I'm off, sweetie, thank you for last night, it was perfect," her voice purred out a beautiful soprano. That dreamy voice Druenn loved and she knew it. "Try not to piss Warren off too much today, for me. Please, sweetie?"

Half jokingly Druenn agreed. He exhaled. "Okay," he said, followed by a playful tut and a rolling of the eyes.

"Thank you, sweetie, and happy birthday!" she cooed, giving him a quick romantic kiss on the lips as she left the room. Before disappearing round the corner she winked at him giving him a quick kiss and blowing it to him. He smiled his one sided grin and watched her disappear behind the door. He lay back on the bed as the bell tolled again representing five minutes before lesson. The first lesson of the day was the same as every day for the last seven years.

"*Combat Skills: A Fighter's Tale* by Warren Anguish," he said with a mocking tone and rolling his eyes. He scoffed. Warren, or as he should say, "master", was really getting on his nerves holding so much information from him.

He liked him everyone could see that, they were like best friends but it didn't stop the fact that he found him so irritating at the same time. His fighting lessons were seriously intensive and it annoyed him why he had to work so hard compared to everyone else. He tried a fighting lesson with another teacher and class to try it out and it frustrated him that he had beaten five students at once sending them all crashing to the ground in no more than three moves each.

Surely they can't be that bad, he remembered thinking, but when he took the whole class down without little more than a burst of energy. *I need a challenge more than anything right now.*

When he confronted Warren that he was ready for the fighter's exam, fighting Warren was the challenge but once again he was told he was not ready. *I am ready, Warren. Why can't you see that!* Druenn thought. Druenn turned to the hourglass on the wall, he stared at it, the hourglass almost empty of sand. It was a clever design, he watched one turn automatically so the sand was on top again, and he remembered asking the Dean about it.

"Oh, the hourglass magic," he winked playfully. "It's magic that turns the hourglass as it empties at the end of an hour then starts again for the next hour. The sand changes colour each hour of the day so that way we know which hour of the day it is for example." He pointed to the hourglass closest to them. "As you can see its green sand." The sand trickled through silently a quarter of the sand already through into the bottom. "It's representing that the time is three fifteen in the afternoon."

Druenn realised how scattered his thoughts were today as he refocused on Warren, remembering the arguments they have had since being told he is not ready. The arguments escalated further to almost physical violence when he thought he was ready again a few weeks ago and planned to set out to find Meredith but Warren said otherwise.

"You're too reckless, you don't stand a chance out in the wild," Druenn thought differently which resorted in the next few lessons to be very intense and tiring as Druenn resulted in earning cleaning duties and scrubbing pots for evenings on end was not how he wanted to spend his free time. Druenn smiled in bed reminiscing.

He enjoyed being defiant, more *than* he enjoyed a challenge. By the time he was fifteen no one dare not attack him, students who didn't like DV or Divine Victory felt they could pick on him and push him around with names like 'descendant scum' or 'hero's son' and 'betrayers brat' Druenn quickly knew enough to put them in their place. He had become strong even though he didn't look it.

He wasn't small as in short. He was an average size for his age but for the strength mentally and physically *which* he emitted in battle surpassed his years, by many years. They knew he would win. He became a formidable foe. Druenn made and lost many friends through this. Younglings that joined Rienhold later looked up to him as he was a defender of the weak, or so many said. Enemies respected Druenn and friends alike and he could walk the grounds of Rienhold proudly. He could see whether he liked it or not he was to become a worthy hero. Looking up at the hourglass, the last few grains of sand trickling through, he pulled himself out of bed.

Well I better get up, he thought.

Warren paced back and forth in the Dean's office, his left arm folded round him and his right elbow rested over the left, his right hand resting on his chin.

"I can't do this, Master. He's getting out of control, I'm losing him."

The Dean studied him a concerned expression masking his face. "You're losing him?" he replied, carefully trying to understand the situation. "I see no problem, he has improved tremendously, you have done a fine job," he said, pointing a finger towards him.

"Master, he challenges me on everything I say, he has so many questions I can't and won't answer I…" He stopped pacing as he paused, then continued. "He wants to take the exam."

"Then let him," the Dean replied,

"But he's not ready! He's too reckless and to be honest, Sir Arrogant, he is always contradicting me!" Warren argued,

"And is he right?" the Dean asked, seeming to already know the answer.

"Yes, but that's not the point, is it!" Warren fired back as the Dean rose out of his seat and made his way over to a large cauldron boiling over a fireplace in the corner of his office, taking a mug from the shelf above and a tealeaf from a small orange clay bowl next to the row of mugs. He dropped the tealeaf into the mug, he scooped a ladle from out of the cauldron, holding the mug over the bubbling boiling water he poured the boiling liquid into his mug. Warren watched as the Dean sipped it and slowly walked back over to his seat stroking his long white beard with his free hand.

"You need to understand Warren, he is a fine growing boy who will become defiant, with the skills and knowledge he possesses, have you noticed how often he is in the library?" Warren hadn't thought of that, he was extremely well educated, even out of lessons his thirst for knowledge was endless.

I guess that's what happens when you live in a small village such as Pinevale, they never leave.

"He has passed all of his other exams – history, literacy, religion, mathematics, and even all his weapons training, he just needs his leadership skills exam from me and I'm putting him in for it tomorrow, we are just waiting on you to let him try for the final battle exam. Only Druenn will know when he is ready to take the exam and he sounds more than capable. Remember, Warren, a bird can only teach its offspring how to fly it can't stop them from leaving once they know."

"But I…"

"You need to have more faith in your student, and I think Druenn can see that; the more chains you hold him with the more he'll want to break free". Warren paused again in thought.

"I'll try it, Master, I'll put him in for this week's examinations." The Dean nodded a smile on his face. "I am positive he knows what he is doing."

ELEVEN

The Final Test

Warren walked into the fighting arena, the wintry cold finding the cracks in his long robe. Sliding the warmth off it revealed his fancy brown leather trousers and greaves, his black boots reaching halfway to his knees the buckles glinting in the early winter sunlight. His blue and red embroidered shirt covered by a well cut leather chest piece except for the sleeves protruding from the sides, off he dropped it on the fence which surrounded the perimeter of the ring. Druenn waited patiently. As he turned Druenn stood incredulous as half the school followed him.

"What's going on Warren?" Druenn asked stammering on his words. Warren strode towards the training circle, sword in hand.

"Its exam day, Druenn. You fight me!" Warren rared defiantly in the hopes Druenn would back down and say he is not ready.

Druenn leapt in the air screaming words of joy. The students watched shocked at the reply.

Emily watched from the crowd listening to some students muttering. "Is he mad?"

Come on, Druenn. You can do it! she prayed twiddling her thumbs in anticipation.

Druenn kitted up donning leather greaves and chest piece.

"Is that all you're wearing, Druenn?" Warren called out from the other side of the ring. "You are aware we are using real weapons"

"Don't need 'em," Druenn called back. "They'll slow me down."

That was the hope, Warren thought. *He's not ready for this.*

Druenn stepped forward long blade on his left and short blade on his right. "Ready when you are, old man!" Druenn taunted. He heard a faint muffled grumble from Warren. He only made out the echo of the old man. He chuckled. Emily's concern grew, he's too confident. The crowd went silent as Warren stepped forward.

The Dean stepped forward calling out, his old croaky voice echoing around the crowd. "This battle is for the examination of Druenn Lightblaser for the title of Grandmaster in weaponry." The words of the Dean faded into the background as his heart pounded with the anticipation of the fight, his mind racing.

Okay, Druenn, don't forget keep moving keep weaving, like the snake and the cat stay poised and strike, composure, poise, strike. You read all those fighting books for this.

"Let the battle begin!" The Dean threw his hand in the air and the crowd roared.

The two of them stood waiting for one another to strike, they both knew the first to strike was the dead man. Warren watched Druenn bounce on his heels waiting for him to make the first blow.

He remembered that? Warren thought, shocked that Druenn took it in.

"Okay," Warren started, "let's walk to the centre together and begin."

Druenn nodded once and began to walk. As soon as Warren saw him walking he walked too; he noticed the crowd had become very quiet, maybe getting bored. The two of them reached the centre. Warren struck his sword out towards him. Druenn leapt back throwing his long blade in its path and retaliating with his short blade. The sound of the clashing of the swords was exciting, for the students this was like some kind of clash of the titans. Quickly gambling, students began collecting bets.

"Who'll win the fight?"

"Five silver pieces on Warren."

"Ha! Not a chance, two gold on Druenn."

Whispers scattered round the crowd.

The fight grew more intense as Druenn and Warren began throwing everything they knew into the fight. Druenn thrust his sword forward as Warren would weave so fluently, like trying to slash a linen cloth caught in a morning breeze. Warren would then strike Druenn having to spin to avoid the blow. Each time Warren noticed a pattern in his fighting style.

Each time he spins he tries to take me off guard with his short sword on the back slash, Warren thought and decided to try this theory.

Lunging at Druenn he spun again, Warren's eyes locked on the short sword swinging towards him. Thrusting his hand forward it ignited in a ball of flames, the fireball crashed into the sword the sound of screeching metal and a bubbling sound as the sword began to melt. Druenn threw the sword down, shaking the burns away, the sound of the sword sizzled on the floor, steam rising off it. Druenn dove out the way from Warren's next blow. Warren began leaping and jumping through the air, front flips and sideways flips as he began to approach Druenn.

Exhaustion began to rack Druenn's body as Warren raised his sword, his other hand seeming to ignite again as he lowered his hand from the tip of the blade down, Druenn stood catching his breath as he looked on incredulous. The sword was ablaze now, a fiery weapon with only one purpose, *to make me fail.* Druenn's sixteen-year-old body shook violently with anticipation and exhaustion waiting for Warren's next attack.

Warren swung and missed Druenn side stepping with a spin, his sword striking first blow with a tap on Warren's back. He backed off a few steps forcing himself to control his breathing. *If I don't take him down soon I'm done, by the divine I can't breathe!*

"Getting tired, boy?" Warren growled.

Druenn was stunned and recoiled at Warren aggression in his voice.

Warren approached again.

Druenn wanted to run but he couldn't move. *No!* he thought. *I can't be that exhausted. I mustn't, not yet!*

"I told you, you're not ready," Warren almost spat "You arrogant little child!" This time Warren did spit landing a few feet short of striking him.

Anger racked Druenn's body, his shuddered violently. "I... am... not... a child!" Druenn roared. His body felt lighter, anger festering and settling on him. His eyes narrowed and he scoped his target. His eyes locked on Warren. Druenn exploded with energy, he felt replenished and stronger. He all but leapt forward running at Warren, he roared as his sword struck Warren's and they clashed, each of Druenn's slashes coming faster and faster, blow after blow. The crowd watched on as a beam of light from the sky began to focus on Druenn.

Warren stepped back further and further unable to keep up with Druenn's oncoming attacks. The sound of Druenn's heart pounding uncontrollably and his pants were the only sounds he could hear.

Breathe, Druenn. Breathe left, right, right, left, strike forward again.

Warren's sword clattered and he began taking hits on his arms and legs as the sword whirled fluently like a gale in Druenn's hand. Druenn blocked the sword and punched Warren in the cheek. Druenn lent down grasping his half charred short sword and continued to whirl the two blades with tremendous force.

The crowd roared.

"Come on, Druenn!" Emily heard Rick cry out

"Go on, mate!"

"Kick him in the knads," another cried.

Emily spotted the Dean's face, awestruck over the heads of other screaming fans. She also noticed Terribor's glare in horror as the events began to unfold. Turning his back and flinging his long black cloak out behind him he stocked off back to the school. Emily's gaze went back to Druenn, her smile growing with excitement.

He might actually beat him! she thought, a little laugh outburst of overwhelming happiness shoot past her lips.

Druenn leapt off Warren's sword.

How can he do that! It's too thin!

Druenn's foot kicked Warren square in the face as he flew back. "Druenn!" he roared, leaping back into the fray.

Druenn steady as a flower blowing in the breeze, just like back in Pinevale playing with his bow and arrow, he said his favourite line before making his final and perfect shot that would finish game set and match. Warren hurtled towards him. Druenn never flinched.

"Target confirmed," he murmured quietly, his swords slowly rising. Warren's sword struck steel the short sword flying forward, Druenn spun as the hilt smashed into Warren's palm, his sword flying into the air. The sword whirled as it glistened in the sunlight casting an aura around Druenn as it fell towards the earth again.

Throwing his short sword to the ground Warren lost his balance. He attempted to weave past the long sword, unable to hold himself any longer Warren toppled back collapsing on the floor. Druenn quickly placing both feet on Warren's hands, the long sword held to his throat, Warren's sword fell towards him as Druenn caught it and crisscrossed the swords to Warren's throat.

"Druenn is the winner!" The Dean's croaky voice cried, flinging his arm high in the air. The crowd erupted in cheers. As Druenn panted, the feeling he felt, this feeling that made him feel so alive, no one can hurt him, this heightened feeling of focus and awareness, his eyes gazing round the crowd, listening to every person cheer

He could hear the twins Sam and Bram cheering saying, "Nice one, Druenn. You were amazing," in unison. Their voices didn't stand out above everyone else's he just knew, Emily weeping and the sound of her dabbing her eyes and the sniffles.

I can hear all of that? Every individual clap vibrating he could tell who they belonged to. Druenn pulled the swords away slowly. Warren rose from the ground, his sweat smearing his forehead. Breathing heavily he raised a hand to place it on Druenn's shoulder.

"Well… done, my boy" he panted. Druenn still panting sensed the hand coming towards him. Rage filled him like a waterfall crashing on the rocks. His sword flew up to Warren's throat.

"Back off!" he growled.

Warren stared at him incredulous. "What?" He stepped back as he saw Druenn's eyes blaze a golden honey colour.

"I will kill you!" Druenn screamed, his sword flying through the air as he attempted to land a blow.

The Dean flew through the crowd like a cheetah into the ring throwing himself between Warren and Druenn, the crowd stepping back unsure of the situation. The Dean harnessed the magic that flowed within him, throwing Druenn back in a torrent of light blazing from the Dean's palms.

"Warren, stun him!" the Dean wailed as Druenn thrashed through the light to reach the Dean, anger forcing the strength within him. Warren pulled himself from the daze surrounding him. Embracing the magic he weaved his arms back and forth, the Dean raising Druenn off the ground, the boy still thrashing.

"Now!" the Dean screeched, the small black smoke that swirled in Warren's palm shot out with a crack like thunder towards the possessed boy faster than a bolt leaving a crossbow. It hit the boy knocking him out of the sky. He flew a couple of feet further down the ring. The crowd's whispered words of astonishment ran round the students.

"Everyone, back inside!" the Dean's voice crackled, breaking mid sentence. Warren collapsed on the ground in a cloud of dust exhausted from the fight and the shocking event. Druenn lay unconscious as the Dean watched him, the students being guided back indoors by the other teachers, Emily and Rick being caught in the crowd of students unable to break free. Within minutes the crowd was gone and just Warren and the Dean remained.

"Warren, come give me your hand."

Warren reached over and took the Dean's hand. The Dean touched his other hand to Druenn's forehead. In a second they appeared in the Dean's office. The Dean placed his hand over Druenn's unconscious body and he began to levitate. The Dean guided him onto the table. Swishing his arms around the room the blinds began to close and candles floated in mid air hovering around the motionless body on the table.

Gasping for air Warren shakily rose from the ground wiping his mouth of the blood seeping out of a split lip. Reaching into his leather trousers he pulled out a handkerchief, dabbing at the open wound vigorously.

"Okay... what just happened?" Warren panted his voice broken and croaky. The Dean raised his arm again. A mug from the shelf over the large cauldron teetered and fell, abruptly the mug stopped in mid air, it began floating towards the bubbling water, the ladle serving itself poured the hot water into the mug as well as a tea leaf dropping in, the mug began to float over to Warren.

He took the mug, taking a sip he placed it down on the chair behind him. The Dean flew his arm in the other direction making unusual symbols with his fingers with each swish. He began weaving the flows of magic surrounding him, his hand melodically swiping at the air as if conducting an orchestra. Warren had never seen the Dean use this much magic at one time before.

"Master, why did he try and kill me?"

The Dean refused to speak.

A book was floating towards Warren, the book opening and the pages spinning already finding the page. The book fell into Warren's outstretched arms landing on a page. Warren read the title. "The Overdrive ability?" Warren asked, raising his head, face filled with trepidation.

"Yes, Warren" The Dean answered slowly, his voice crackled like wood on a fire. He paced placing his hands behind his back, a dark silhouette casting over the boy on the table in the flickering candlelight.

"But, Master, is that possible?" Warren began to stammer his eyes fixed on Druenn.

"His mother possessed the power of the Overdrive, why not him?" His eyes washed over Warren, icy and concerned as he nodded in the direction of Druenn. The shock gripped him like a vice as realisation hit him.

By the Divine, Sarah could use the Overdrive.

"The Overdrive, what is it?" Warren asked, his breathing steady now, forcing his hands to hold the book steady.

"The Overdrive power is an ancient one, one that has lasted since the old blood. The blood of the heroes, this Overdrive power sends the user into a state of perfect awareness, all senses are heightened, taste, smell, touch, hearing, sight," the Dean coughed, taking the book off Warren.

"It sounds good but I'm guessing there is a downside to this," Warren replied, awaiting the worst.

"Yes, without keeping a steady control of the power it can drive the user mad with rage as you saw Druenn do today. He needs to learn to control it."

"What will happen to my…" Warren swallowed hard. "What will happen to my apprentice?"

The Dean eyed him coldly, his eyes boring through Warren, he recoiled as the Dean turned fully to him. "He can use the Overdrive power so he is dangerous!" The Dean's voice snapped like a whip. They both turned to Druenn, the young boy's eyes twitching as he began to regain consciousness.

Warren reached for the great magic, the Dean quickly waved him off.

"He's safe. He won't harm us, as far as he is aware he fell unconscious during the fight."

The boy stared and his eyes fluttered open, groaning he pulled himself up off the table looking around him. "How did I get here," he said rubbing his eyes, his eyes gazed over at the Dean, refocusing he saw Warren behind him, shocked, he realised he was fighting him before everything went black.

"What happened to the fight, who won?"

The Dean placed a gentle hand on the boy's shoulder, eyes filled with sympathy he smiled a reassuring smile. "You're safe in my office, young Druenn. You lost control of yourself during the fight." The Dean went on to explain the Overdrive ability and how he must learn to control his emotions in the heat of battle otherwise the Overdrive can be deadly. "Overdrive," the Dean continued, "can be an essential ability to use."

Warren kept his distance as if at any moment he could pounce on the boy, his eyes blazed into him. Not hatred, but fear.

Why is he looking at me like that? Druenn thought. Refocusing on the Dean he listened to his instructions. He learnt that the Overdrive ability was the same strength dragons used to form the earth and it was passed on to humans, which the dragons had preordained to have bright futures. Druenn scratched his head.

"So my mother had this Overdrive in her blood?"

The Dean nodded slowly, his hands grasping a mug of tea. In fact so was Druenn; he quickly realized looking down at the mug he held in his lap as he sat on the desk with the Dean sat on a chair in front of him. Warren arms folded at the back of the room refusing to take his eyes off the boy.

"I know it's a lot of information to take in, my boy," the Dean continued, "but this is something you need to learn quickly." The Dean had gone on to explain that he must practice to hold the Overdrive until he feels the way he felt fighting Warren and hold it until he felt that sense of rage. Druenn remembered that well, a hateful feeling of the world around him. He shuddered at the thought.

The Dean stood. "Okay, Druenn, let's try it."

Druenn coughed on his tea.

"What? Right now?" Druenn's eyes wide open with fear. *I never want to feel that power again,* he thought as the Dean hurled a shock wave through his body.

Rick Diaz and Emily Fletcher paced precariously in front of the fireplace within the far wing of the northeast tower. It was the students' common room where they could come and relax after lessons or study with friends. Two girls played hacky sack by the far window and three boys in the right corner fenced, two against one.

Emily sat down on the leather sofa behind her, her nerves getting the better of her. She breathed out heavily, her thoughts on Druenn.

What could have happened to him? she thought to herself.

Rick sat down next to her. "Come on, Em, everything will be fine"

Wrapping his big arms around her she held him, resting her head on his shoulder, his arms like tree trunks locked around her.

"I just don't understand. Druenn wouldn't do that to Warren; they argue a lot, yes, but Druenn looks up to Warren like a father more than a master."

"That's because your boyfriend's gone crazy!" a girl chimed behind them pronouncing the last word 'crazy' sarcastic and melodically.

"Shut up, Shiele!" Rick called back to the girl.

Shiele let out a sigh of exasperation as she turned back to her book.

Emily and Rick listened to the soft crack of the fireplace as the flames danced with the twilight sky on the carpet below them. Rick heard a soft clunk of a book closing behind them and the soft footsteps come closer. Rick sighed whispering in Emily's ear. "Shiele's coming, goodbye peace." He let out a forced grin as the young girl trotted over.

"Hey, kids, watcha doing?" Shiele's high soprano voice chimed.

"Go away, Shiele, I'm not in the mood for talking," Emily said, desperation in her voice, her eyes lazily turning to the girl. Emily studied the youngster up and down.

She was wearing the regular garb for a fourteen-year-old brown leather trousers and white training vest, her long flowing blonde hair pulled back in to two pig tails, a long blue ribbon from both curling loosely around her arms.

Her hands on her hips she bent down to Emily as she slunk back further into Rick's arm. "Ahh, come on, Em, don't be like that. I'll cheer you up."

Rick could see Emily didn't know how to get Shiele to back off. Rick wasn't one for confrontation, he avoided it when possible, but he knew he needed to get Shiele away from Emily.

"Shiele, back off," she cursed something under her lips something like peanuts for brains. She kept coming, putting less distance between Emily's and her own face.

Emily looked away as Shiele eyed her closely.

"Surely this moodiness isn't because of that descendant boy, is it?"

Emily's nostrils flared. "Don't talk about him like that, I swear to the divine, Shiele!" Emily barked back.

It dawned on Rick. *She's looking for a fight, but why?* Rick knew that students liked to strike up fights as an excuse to practice their new

143

skills they had learnt. Shiele had learnt how to use arcane spells such as fire and lightning as of late and had got herself a place at the Mages University in Cetni. *She's showing off before she leaves.*

"Back off, Shiele!" Rick growled his hackles rising.

"Oh, mister tough boy, barking at a little girl, is he?" she cooed, a cheeky childish grin to her whilst her eyes blazed.

Rick released Emily as she pleaded him not to. He rose from the sofa standing head and shoulders higher than her, twenty-four-year-old Rick had grown his well-toned muscles, apparent now, towered over the young Shiele as his eyes bored into her. He opened his mouth to speak when a bark from the back of the room caused Rick to jump.

"You causing trouble, Shiele?" as the room turned to find Druenn Lightblaser breezing into the room, they turned back cowering away trying to avoid his gaze; all turned back except Rick and Emily.

"Druenn!" Emily called relief in her shrill exasperated voice. She all but flew into his arms, in to her comfort zone.

Rick's bulky body walked over to Druenn, Druenn's head coming level with his shoulders. Patting him on the shoulder the two stood around him, Shiele slipping away into the crowd of students her eyes darting back and forth to the three stood by the door and finding her book.

"Druenn, what happened?" Rick asked a second before Emily shot out the same question.

"It's…" He broke off eyeing everyone in the room. No one seemed to be paying any of them attention although he knew his display in the training ground would have put an unclear reputation on his head; rumours would be escalating by tomorrow.

"Can we go back to my dorm and talk?" Druenn asked as he turned for the door, the other two hot on his heels.

Shiele eyed the door waiting for the click. As the door clicked shut behind them she spoke. "So, everyone!" She addressed the room, leaning back on her chair her arms outstretched. "Are we just going to avoid the fact that Druenn tried to kill Warren?" she called around the room in the hopes she'd grab someone's attention.

"Oh, come on! You all saw what happened! What should we do?"

"What can we do, Shiele?" a graceful voice spoke.

Ruby slowly glided over, her body flowing like a river, melodically and with purpose towards the table placing her hands, fingers outstretched in front of Shiele as she leant down bringing her eyes level with hers. Shiele eyed the girl carefully.

Ruby had been raised to the higher degree of her training program, she wore the same brown leather trousers but now she had a green linen shirt and a brown leather chest piece over the top, her brown locks tied back. Shiele looked up to Ruby; she had a secret blaze in her hazel eyes that showed her dominance.

"I personally am not getting involved with a descendant," Shiele scowled at Ruby as she eyed her back carefully, giving a flicker with her eyebrow as Shiele began to pout. Ruby let out a soft laugh as she walked back to Precious. Shiele just about heard the words 'such a child'.

Shiele began to think of what she felt needed to be done. She gazed over to the entrance again and saw a young boy panting in the doorway searching the room. She recognised him to be a friend of hers, Elias. A young fourteen-year-old student with a love for insects, she found his fascination with them creepy but also unique and that's why she liked him. Like all children under sixteen they all wore the basic training garments, a white linen shirt and brown leather trousers, his black curly thinning hair looked a mess as his gaze found hers.

"Shiele, Warren... wants to see... you," he barely managed in between large gulps of air.

She looked at him confused. *Warren wants to see me?*

TWELVE

The Explanation

Druenn stepped into his dorm room. The Dean felt he should be the one to remain in his old dorm room and Emily move instead. Rick followed after then Emily entered, a cool feeling swept over her. Memories rushed back, like a cool breeze on a summer's day.
I really miss this room, she thought as her eyes slowly studied the shelves of books and sweeping over where her bed used to be, at the far end of the room.

Her hand brushed against the shelves as they walked through to take a seat on a table Druenn had obviously put in place of Emily's bed. Emily wasn't offended but just felt, it was odd. Druenn sat on his bed, the straw mattress making a soft crunch as he made himself comfortable.

The cool wintry breeze filtered through the cracks between the windows, a dim gleam from the faded sunlight hiding between the clouds. Druenn scratched the back of head, his voice unsure on how to proceed.

Rick eyed him intently unsure of how to approach the conversation, as if Druenn was a vicious wolf, waiting to pounce any second. So he chose silence and waited. Emily continued to browse the room she loved, her eyes constantly moving.

"Okay." Druenn started clapping his hands together and holding to them tight. Rick seemed to recoil from the clap, his eyes shooting widening for an instant then he composed himself. "Once again, it's to do with my mother," he began slowly. He knew he owed these two an explanation for what happened and he must tread carefully because one word out of context could send them running. "My mother had this…" he paused his face creasing. "This… power that was the source of her strength and ability."

Emily and Rick studied him, unsure whether to run in case he lashed out at them. Druenn could see they weren't scared, not fear, more concern on whether he was worth the trouble.

He cleared his throat, the air feeling particularly dry, feeling his cheeks become red, his heart pumped harder, his breathing quickened, his palms grew sweaty.

By the divine, I'm panicking, he realised. His face of reassurance grew to a face of concern then pleading.

"Please," he whispered hoarsely. "Don't run away. You're my best friends, I need you guys." He held his hands clamped together so hard they began to ache. He didn't care, his friends were at stake, and in a flurry of words everything came out almost tripping on his words unable to get them out fast enough.

"Listen, please. I didn't mean to do what I did it was an accident, the power within me is called Overdrive and it's an essential ability I have been told and with training I can harness it so please just hear me out and…"

Emily cut him short. "You have the overdrive?" she asked concern holding her still keeping her hands in her lap. Druenn nodded his pleading eyes imprinting in her memory, she could see he was holding back tears.

This is something he can't control. Oh, bloody havens, he wont hurt me I know that why am I acting so cautiously around him?

Leaping out of her chair she threw herself at him, her arms flying around him, Druenn held her. Rick stood to grab her arm but was too late.

"Rick, why are we being this way? We know he won't hurt us." She wiped his tears away with her sleeve. She turned back to Rick.

"Overdrive is an ability of total awareness in which the user can create the feeling that they have slowed down time in order for them to react faster. In reality Druenn appears to move faster and smoother." She poured her knowledge on to Rick as he took his seat again. "The only downside to this power is, if uncontrolled by the user, it can fester into a corruptive rage."

Rick took in every word apart from getting his head round how she came by this information.

"Obviously he must have discovered it in the field." She turned back to Druenn as he nodded ferociously.

"Yes. I've been told all I need to do is learn how to harness the power without getting taken in by its corruptive nature, I'm training with the Dean all week to harness this." Druenn was starting to sink back into the mattress finally beginning to feel at ease around his friends.

"So… you… won't… snap?" Rick asked, brokenly.

"He can't."

Emily jumped in before Druenn could speak. "He's not like a wild animal, nothing will send him over the edge. Overdrive can only be wielded when emotions take over," she barked at Rick, her eyes cold as ice.

"Yes," Druenn agreed with Emily, who was now sitting on Druenn's lap.

"As you saw, anger and aggression seems to be my strongest emotion so the Overdrive has latched on to that."

Rick only looked half convinced, he continued to study Druenn's face.

"Rick, do you honestly think I'd *kill* Warren?"

"I know, Druenn. I do know, but you need to understand from my point of view that I saw you win an incredible victory out there then saw you almost take his head as a prize, how can I be sure that won't happen to me or Em?"

Rick's eyes were cold and Druenn knew this wasn't easy for him to accept.

"That won't happen," Druenn continued, his eyes unable to face Rick's stare. "I can have this skill harnessed in a week; that's what the Dean says and I believe him," Druenn went on. "And I trust him."

"I'm sure you're right, Druenn, and I'll see it throughout this week." Rick spoke hushed in hopes he would not hear but the glare he received told him otherwise, "I'm sorry, Druenn. I don't mean to be like this," Rick began to apologise, his eyes now sincere in regret.

Druenn breathed deeply. "I'm relieved you listened to me, I'm honestly no different it's literally a state of heightened awareness."

"Well I believe you," Emily said, wrapping her arms around him tightly and planting a kiss on his forehead.

Druenn smiled and held her tightly his arms linked around her waist.

Rick breathed heavily and stood. "Okay, I trust you, Druenn. We've been friends for six years and I know it wouldn't be like you to consider the idea." Rick smiled at him although Druenn still saw the hint of concern in his friend's eyes.

He nodded back his one-sided grin. "Thank you"

A bell tolled in the distance. Lessons were beginning in ten minutes. Druenn turned to the hourglass on the wall as it turned over for the next hour, the sand dye a blue green colour.

Druenn breathed heavily, nerves getting the better of him, butterflies rattled in the pit of his stomach bringing him closer to nausea.

This is it, the lesson you have been waiting six years for, the history of Divine Victory.

Emily held him tight before releasing him. "It will be okay," she said, calm only present in her voice as she shot him a reassuring look. They both stood as they left the room making their way down the corridor, Rick falling behind. Walking down the same hallway they were so used to, there was no solace within those walls. Druenn knew what he had to face.

An hour lesson that's all it was, a single lesson explaining the history and purpose of Divine Victory, *and my mother's purpose and what she did.* His mind raced over the idea of what she did, *did she become bad? Or stay good? Or most importantly, what sacrifice?*

His vision became blurry as he teetered on the edge of consciousness, he stumbled as bile rose in his stomach, Emily caught him, her hand shooting out and gripped his arm; she took his hand and held it tight.

"Druenn, calm down, my love. Everything will be fine I promise you." Her smile brought little relief but it brought some and he appreciated it.

Reaching the classroom, Warren waited at the far end of the room in front of the blackboard. The classroom was no different to the others. The walls decorated with pieces of art, fighting skills, tactics, the alphabet, but instead of twenty to thirty wooden desks with nicely ornate carving oak chairs, there were only seven chairs placed perfectly in a semi-circle. All the seats were full except three. Warren spotted them as they walked through the doorway.

"Ahh, Druenn, Emily and Rick, good to see you three. Come in," Warren greeted, flicking his chalk in the air and catching it with ease. He threw his arm out gesturing for the three of them to take the three spare seats.

The students turned on the welcome. Druenn was surprised to see the twins Sam and Bram their bows by their sides. Their identical black hair tightly pulled back into ponytails, they were both rather beautiful boys, not handsome but beautiful, they looked rather feminine boys, *Rupert's friends*. They both smiled at him so he didn't worry they obviously bore no grudge against him. Alex was there too which he couldn't help but smile, he didn't see much of Alex as he was of the age to leave the grounds and follow out contracts whenever he pleased, in fact the only reason he stayed was for the bed. He sat waiting for the lesson to begin his bulging muscled arms tightly folded.

He smiled and nodded as he saw the three walk in. The biggest shock for Druenn came when a little girl with blond pigtails with blue ribbons turned to see them.

"Shiele?" Emily said, almost accusingly, or at least it sounded accusing to Druenn.

"Yes, I've been dragged to this lesson too," she said, rolling her eyes and turning back to Warren.

"Come on, you three. Sit down and I can begin the lecture." Warren spoke hastily as he returned the chalk to the board and sat on the desk at the far end of the room placing his feet on the chair in front of it. "Okay, everyone settled?" he spoke calmly swishing his arm once as mugs of tea flew over to the students. All taking their mugs they listened, intrigued after the drink. They were not allowed to drink in lessons.

Warren smiled his hands clasped together. "You're wondering about the tea, aren't you?" Shiele made her surprise most obviously arching her eyebrow and nodding.

"Okay I don't want this to be a lesson but a lecture as you are to learn the whole truth about Divine Victory for," pointing to Druenn. "Druenn's sake, he needs to know everything and as you'll learn in this lecture there is a lot more to Divine Victory than we can mention but I have selected you six, plus Druenn, to know as I feel you can help each other and maybe some day do Tharlian a big favour." He eyed the group to search for confused faces. They all sat sipping their tea listening and waiting patiently, except Druenn. He could see that he was nervous, he could just make out the trembling in his knees.

Poor boy, knowing that your about to learn how you're mum died.

"Okay," he clapped. "Let's begin."

THIRTEEN

The Truth about Divine Victory

Warren placed his mug of steaming hot tea down as he settled into his spot on the desk. "Okay, let's get a show of hands, who knows about the purpose of Divine Victory?"

Alex, Rick, Emily and Shiele raised their hands. Warren guessed that the twins and Druenn knew this question but he had a feeling the twins were afraid to get the answer wrong and Druenn not know enough.

Pointing to Shiele, she looked around the room quickly then proceeded with the answer. "Divine Victory were protectors of the king, like royal guards." The group eyed her.

Warren folded his arms as he stood and returned to a leaning position. "Okay, it's a basic start." He paused with the suppression of agitation. "Yes I guess they could be seen like royal guards, yes." Turning back to the group he looked in Alex's direction. "Alex, share your wisdom," he said, calm returning to his voice.

"Divine Victory served the king, as Shiele said, personal guards, but they were hired for a more important purpose, to protect the royal bloodline."

"Yes!" Warren said. "That's what I was looking for, to protect the royal *bloodline*." Beginning to pace, one arm folded with his elbow resting on the folded arm, resting his fingers on his chin.

"Okay, so we know they protected the royal bloodline, what was the reason to protect the royal bloodline?"

No hands went up as Warren studied the group except a sheepish Emily, her arm half raised, eyeing the others for support.

"Emily? Don't be shy, give it a go," Warren said reassuringly.

She began sounding timid. "Wasn't there a group of people, like a cult or something, trying to kill them?" Emily asked, her voice half rattled with making a mistake.

"Yes, Emily. Very good, there was," Warren replied, his smile raining joy down on her. Emily's smile was magical everyone could see she was proud of herself as she lay back into her chair, a cocky smile printed on her face.

"Emily is right, there was a cult that wanted the bloodline destroyed," he said, his eyes constantly scanning the room for confused faces. "Over time more groups began to show themselves, anyone heard of the Mystique Knights?"

Alex raised his hand.

"Care to share more wisdom on the group?" Warren gestured with his hand to the group.

"Okay, the Mystique Knights were a group of mages within the Mages University in Cetni, when in public and in the university they were the keepers of the colours of magic but their secret identity was the organisation Mystique Knights, their duty was to destroy the royal bloodline. Not to mention there were many other groups we don't know trying to kill the king."

"But why?" Shiele asked. "Why would so many groups want the king dead? Was he a bad king?"

"No, in fact far from it," Warren replied. "The king of the time was Eldarth Thorian, second king of Tharlian. He was a fine king as great as they came, but he had some knowledge passed on to him by his father Draytorn that would assist him to live by, that would help make him a great and powerful king."

"What was this knowledge, what was it?" the twins chanted.

"Listen, you seven, this is what we are not allowed to tell you because it is dangerous, okay?"

The group nodded.

Warren breathed deeply closing his eyes. "Okay, hear me out before you question me."

They nodded again, Alex and Rick leaning forward.

"In the scripture of the old religion they say that the living could contact the Divine, and in turn the Divine could contact the living. It is said that Okarta, King of the Divine, visited Draytorn. It is said that Okarta told Draytorn Thorian to lead the people of Tharlian to great heights, and if he serves the people well and becomes respected, loved and cherished, in other words if he proves himself worthy he can ascend to the Eternal Light and join Okarta's side as an ascended Divine."

"That's insane!" Shiele squawked. "I've heard of Divine interventions but that can't be possible!"

"Really, Shiele? You are banishing ideas that are beyond your understanding and even beyond what we can possibly learn, all we know is Draytorn was visited and every king to follow," Warren shot back. "But there was a catch, they must live to see death come to them, they must die of old age. If they are killed or assassinated they will not ascend."

"Oh!" Realisation covering Rick's face. "That's when the assassinations began!"

"Precisely, Rick," Warren called over to him his hand rose clicking his finger before smashing his hand down on the table making a mighty bang! "That is why the assassinations started. So someone within the walls of the palace who had access to the chambers was in the right place at the right time, overheard this and began the killing."

The group all exchanged puzzled looks then realisation.

Druenn watched on listening intently. *Can there really be something beyond death? Even the Divine? If they really have an effect on this world why did I have to lose my friends and family?* he thought, resting his head on his hands as he leaned forward.

Warren continued and began to pace again. "Okay, so far we have the King's Divine interventions, all of a sudden the kings are dropping like flies, Tharlian sees the end of six kings in the space of two years, they know something has to be done, but they continued to drop until Gondolas, our proud King at the moment."

The group's eyes were were drawn to a picture of the king hanging on the wall behind Warren.

"He was the first king to make a stand against these cults, groups and organizations or as DV called them C.O.G. They didn't want to name each one there were so many, so they named them the COG. Although as we know one very well, the Mystique Knights. The reasons the Mystique Knights were the most famous is because they were led by a group of very influential people within Cetni and all over Tharlian. They were the group with people in high places, the first manager of the royal bank of Cetni was a member, one of the three councillors to King Gondolas himself was a leader."

Taking a sip of tea Warren moved over to the blackboard facing back to the group. "But the leader behind this group was the high lord of the Mages University as well, earned himself the title The Black Betrayer."

"Tharlandrial," Emily and Alex said not really thinking about what they said. The atmosphere in the room went cold. Druenn could see this was a very dangerous subject. His eyes scanned the group, all their eyes to the ground.

Warren nodded. "Yes, Tharlandrial," he said, his eyes cold as his eyes touched each student, he saw Druenn looking back at him confused.

"Who was this Tharlandrial?" Druenn asked wondering why this person caused everyone to feel so much grief.

Shiele scoffed. "Really? You don't know?" she said snidely eyeing Druenn leaning back on her chair. "He's the guy that killed your mum!" she almost barked back.

Druenn felt his heart pound uncontrollably as bile rose in his throat, chills shooting down his spine. He turned to Warren again, his face dismayed.

Warren scowled at Shiele.

"What? He was going to find out anyway," she replied casually, shrugging as though she could have just mentioned that she was telling them she had finished her homework. Hopping off her seat Shiele walked over to a desk that had been pushed aside to make the space for the seats, jumping up on the desk she sat crossed legged back at Warren.

Warren's gaze returned to Druenn. Taking a breath his face contorted in grief for no more than a second, he then composed himself. "Yes he is, I will get to that soon," he said, turning his back for a moment. Druenn thought he heard him say how ever much I don't want to as he turned away but he couldn't be sure. "Anyway where were we?" Warren asked turning back to them his voice and face composed once more.

158

"So far kings have been assassinated for generations and Gondolas was the only one to take a stand then you told us by this point many groups were wanting to kill the bloodline," Alex said his deep booming voice reverberating around the walls.

"Ahh, yes!" Warren said taking the chalk and beginning to write names on the board. "Yes, so Gondolas needed protection from more than guards, he needed the best fighters in Tharlian. So he held a tournament." He paused then rephrased his words

"A fighting tournament to find his group of fighters. The winners would have a personal meeting with the King who would be entrusted with the knowledge of the Divine and becoming the greatest knights the kingdom had seen. The first to join the ranks of the group was Acthorian Richeck, Leiran Almsleed, Shreftwood Swiftrunner, Krona Overa, Henrietta Overa and Durroc Epsonstar. They were the first generation. They would lead the armies to battle, protect the King at all costs, locate and find the COG and end their reign of tyranny. They became Divine Victory, protectors of the King and fighters for the Divine. After two years a few more moved up to become second generation Divine Victory members.

He returned to the chalkboard and continued to write more names down. "We have Gravland Petture, Amikari Marie, The Anguish and Red Saviour." He almost chocked on the name when he mentioned Red Saviour, not out of anger, more remorse.

"Why do the last two have no names just titles?" Rick asked, biting his thumbnail.

"Those two wanted to protect their identity in case something went wrong," Warren replied, now sounding if he was struggling to finish his sentences.

"Well, to be honest we know one of them don't we," Shiele replied once again not sounding at all respectful or bothered, shooting a bored look at Druenn.

"I guess you do," Warren said even more remorseful. Druenn studied Warren, something was causing him grief but he was sure it couldn't be because the group disappeared sixteen years ago.

It could be, he thought. *These emotions he's showing are too big for just a group disappearing.*

Druenn looked around the group all their eyes trained on Warren listening intently. No one seemed to notice. *How can that be, something is getting to him.* Druenn began scanning through the strongest emotions.

Warren continued. "Okay, after four years of Divine Victory protecting Tharlian only peace reigned. They stopped bandits, solved petty crimes, and fought wars. Formed alliances with other nations. Destroyed many of the COG's until…" he paused.

Everyone leaned forward.

"Go on," Shiele gestured with a nod of her head.

Warren collected his thoughts. Visions and memories came back in a torrent like a waterfall crashing down on him throwing him off the lecture, leaning for the table at his side he sat down and shook the memories away. He wiped his forehead as he began again.

"This is where you would learn different in Terribor's lecture. He would tell you that Divine Victory sought power and plotted to overthrow the King. The truth is that rumours started by the COG themselves and having people in high places got the word out like wild fire, people soaked up the news and passed it on, before long the public, the people Divine Victory had helped for so long were beginning to hate them for what they believed they were plotting.

To keep the people from revolting against him, the king had no choice and with much regret exiled Divine Victory."

The group watched Warren as his expression sank lower.

"The Depression," Alex said. "The point when everything went wrong," Warren nodded forcing himself on.

"After they were exiled the COG moved in revealing Tharlandrial as their leader; he attempted to take the throne forcing all the COG out to battle. The armies of Tharlian fought with the COG. Tharlandrial ordered his men back, and built a fortress high in the western parts of Tharlian. Anyone heard of the Great Tower of Drialthendal?"

Everyone but Druenn nodded.

"Okay, from there they launched a war to destroy Tharlian and take it for their own. The people living in fear prayed for Divine Victory's return. They did and the armies of Tharlian formed under one banner, the banner of Divine Victory. They pushed back the armies and struck at the tower of Drialthendal" The group listened mesmerized with the story of these great fighters.

"I heard at one point the dead came back from the graves to fight?" Alex asked, walking over to a black cauldron in the corner to make a new round of teas for the group.

Warren nodded. "Yes they did, it sounds insane, I know," he said mockingly in Shiele's direction. Shiele didn't appreciate that and folded her arms as she huffed looking in a different direction.

"This in my eyes is a sad story in itself, Tharlandrial loved the Queen of Valmorgen, which is two days ride south of here; she did not return his love so he cast as spell on her. He enchanted her to be infatuated with him."

"That's wrong," Emily said her voice sorrowful. "People should be entitled to fall in love with the ones they love."

The group agreed nodding.

Warren continued. "Yes, the great Queen Morrandier was the last Necromancer in Tharlian."

Everyone's eyes including Druenn's shot up in horror. Even Druenn knew what a necromancer was.

"So you mean under his instruction..." Alex started before being cut off by Warren.

"Yes indeed, my friend. She summoned an army of the dead, in fact the great heroes that had died from previous wars," Warren said solemnly.

"So with that in mind," Druenn started, "that means Cetni was fighting a battle on both sides."

The group eyed Druenn surprised he was contributing to the lecture. Emily eyed him carefully. *To be honest I thought he'd be too upset to be talking.*

"That's right, Druenn. It was a battle on both sides," Warren replied, receiving a new full mug of tea from Alex as he passed them around the group.

Thanking Alex he continued. "After no more than two weeks of holding the armies back Divine Victory knew they had to strike. Parting the group, sending Red Saviour, Anguish, Gravland, Amikari and Epsonstar to destroy one of the greatest queens of the age," he said mournfully again. "The other five went to Drialthendal in Tholaria to bring down the Black Betrayer.

"After a long and arduous battle the Necromancer was killed and her army fell, the people of Cetni insisted that Tharlandrial had a fair trial and would be burned at the stake."

"And the people got that?" Druenn demanded. "He was too dangerous he should have been killed right there."

"But what you need to understand, Druenn, is that the people had lost respect for the King, to be able to ascend he needed the people to love him," Warren retaliated.

"That's no excuse. Who was killed in the fights?" Druenn once again threw back at Warren. Rick could see another argument building between the two, more than anything it was because he knew the truth was coming about his mother.

"Gravland and Amikari in the fight with the Death Queen and Henrietta at the battle of Drialthendal," Warren replied all anger gone only remorse.

"Exactly. The others did the right thing, eliminate the danger! Why couldn't the others follow safety over orders."

"It was their duty to carry out their king's wishes, Druenn, and I will not take your tone of voice!" Warren barked back.

Druenn calmed himself. He needed to know the whole story before throwing himself into a half understood argument.

"I should have asked this earlier," Alex replied. "Why do you know so much?"

"Because, my friends," Warren began. "I have deceived you all. You all wonder why I ask everyone to call me by my first name. I said it was so everyone feels more at ease and like a friend more than teacher and student."

The group nodded.

He took a final breath. "I am Warren Anguish of Divine Victory second generation, Lord Captain Commander of army seven-five-one and defeater of the Lady Morrandia and Death Queen."

The group stared at him incredulous.

"So why did these… COG," Alex started, "want the King dead? What difference would it make if no one ascended?"

163

Warren placed his hands behind his back and paced. "Divine have a life span, all Divine have a life span and they need to be ascended to continue bringing peace to the land, if they all died out, then there would be chaos, the Divine do a lot more for us than anyone can possibly imagine."

The twins went on to say, "What happened next, Warren? What happened after Tharlandrial was captured?"

Warren sipped his tea and continued. "Sixteen years ago, Divine Victory brought in to the city centre the black betrayer, bound in chains and placed at the stake to be burnt." As Warren spoke each memory was strong as if it had happened yesterday.

"The crowd gathered round in a ring, the whole of Cetni was there, cheering Divine Victory and the King. The Great King Gondolas stood on a large wooden platform with Lord Palantine both clad in golden shining armour and their blue cloaks flapping gloriously in the late afternoon breeze standing over the city centre. With them stood the proud fighters of Divine Victory all standing in their silver armour except Acthorian who also stood in gold representing his leadership. He remembered Divine Victory all to be racked with guilt and sorrow for their fallen comrades, Krona in particular, his neck long brown shaggy hair trying to cover his tearful eyes for the loss of his wife. Tharlandrial tugged and writhed as he was placed upon the stake.

"'Tharlandrial, I hereby find you guilty of treason, heresy and a threat to Tharlian and the King,' Palantine cried out in defiance as he read the parchment in his hand. 'You shall be burned alive at the stake for your crimes, how do you plead?' Silence befell the city as they awaited the response.

"Tharlandrial continued to tug as he roared a terrifying demented cry of agony, distress and hatred. Eying the king his body shook violently.

"'You shall die!' A black and purple shadow shot out from his chest and hurled itself towards Gondolas. No one reacted fast enough, they watched the events unfold, and suddenly one reacted. Warren turned in terror as Sarah Lightblaser launched herself in front of the shadow screaming in agony as the shadow enveloped her."

Warren remembered the feeling all too well, his distraught body trembled, feelings of loss and hate filled him. He felt his body burning, a raging fire within him. Leaping from the stand as Shreftwood fired his arrow at Tharlandrial, Acthorian threw his sword, Leiran fired a ball of flame; they all attacked. Tharlandrial laughed hysterically as the arrow imbedded in his shoulder, the sword slammed into his chest and his body ignited, dark shadows flying out of him in streams floating into the crowd. The crowd ran in all directions. Warren seized him with his magic; Tharlandrial floated in the air still laughing hysterically, madness taking him.

"'I will kill you all,' he screeched in agony as he continued to cackle the sky turning black and purple as his power gripped Tharlian." Warren threw his hand down and Tharlandrial slammed into the ground, the dark crimson blood seeping in between the cracks in the stone carved path. The wind picked up, the King being pulled away by Palantine covering his eyes from the dust.

Warren's tear filled eyes blazed gold as he forced the path upward his left hand clenching causing the pavement to crumble and the right forcing the ground up. Divine Victory holding Sarah Lightblaser and escorting the King back into the palace.

Shreftwood stayed protecting his eyes from the wind as he listened to the clink, clink on his mail silver shoulder pads encrusted with a large tiger of Cetni on left and the great eagle of Valmorgen on the right, dent as stone after stone was hurled into the air catching everything around the area. Shreftwood gaped as he watched Warren force the ground up until he had burrowed deep into the ground, slipping down the hole pulling Tharlandrial with him.

The wind stopped, Shreftwood looked up, the black and purple clouds dispersing, holding a tight grip on his phoenix encrusted bow. Leaping off the stand he ran towards the hole, looking down into the black abyss. He could hear the laughing still reverberating upwards.

Warren found himself deep under Cetni in a room of blackness, igniting his hand a flame appeared, throwing the flame ball up as if to bounce the ball it hung in the air and followed his eyes fell upon seven graves, his hackles rose as realisation took him *in in the catacombs under Cetni, the tomb of the kings.*

Quickly seizing the power he dug deeper, the laughter of the insane Tharlandrial followed causing Warren to slowly be over come by fear rather than hate. Harnessing the purple magic he forced the hole out that he had made, creating a four-walled chamber in which no one could get in or out. Warren knew from a young boy he had too much power for his own good. Forcing the stone up he forced together a table, iron chains slithered their way down the hole like snakes finding a new victim.

Clamping his hands and feet he harnessed enough power to force him onto the table, finally stretching the Black Betrayer to the point of ripping the man in two. The man shrieked in agony, as he stared down as his shirt ripped and saw flesh stretched to its limit peel and snap in places, his dark crimson blood pouring from gaping wounds. His breathing becoming more labored he stared up at Warren's eyes now moved from the beautiful gold to a dark crimson red.

"That will stop you laughing, won't it?" Warren spoke mockingly. And with that he flew back up into the hole leaving Tharlandrial to scream until death. Warren filled in the holes behind him as if no one had ever made them.

The group sat around Warren their mouths gaped.

"Warren, how heartless can you be?" Emily said, barely suppressing the sorrow she had for both Tharlandrial and Warren. "Even after he did that what made him deserve that?"

Warren turned away from the group, "Yeah... well... I sealed him away in a place he can't harm anyone again."

Druenn still could see that pain in Warren's eyes.

"After that the group divided off into pairs; Acthorian and Leiran, Krona and Epsonstar. Shreftwood went off on his own and Red Saviour and Anguish went into hiding after assassins came for Shreftwood and Acthorian. They stayed low until one by one they were found and killed.

"Anyway, you better go, the bell will go in ten minutes so you might as well leave early."

The twins were the first to leave, finding the lecture most fascinating. Rick and Alex followed, concerned on knowing the truth and the implications, the danger to Warren.

Emily stayed by Druenn's side, Shiele left next constantly looking over her shoulder at Druenn and Warren, and she could see that Warren was upset too. Shaking her head she left the room.

"Come on, Druenn, let's go," Emily's safe, loving voice said. Her view of Warren had been changed forever. Druenn was rather convinced that she would never like Warren in the same way again.

"I'll be with you shortly, I'm just going to talk to Warren," he said, placing a tender kiss on her hand. She looked at him with the most adorable face he had seen, her smile was radiant, he felt the butterflies in his chest again he had felt the night before.

She left him shooting him a cheeky wink as she turned out of the door. Druenn turned to face Warren who still had his back to him watching out the window.

Slowly moving towards him he shot a glance outside. "A lovely day, isn't it?" he said, trying to the get the conversation flowing.

"How do you do it?" Warren said, his voice croaky from holding back the tears.

"Do what?" Druenn asked.

"I was positive that you couldn't defeat me yet you did, you excel in every class and you passed all your exams, not to mention you learned to control your feelings."

"I don't know what to say, Warren. I just like to know what I'm doing I guess."

Warren turned to him and smiled, a tear rolling down his cheek, ruffling Druenn's hair. He chuckled and said, "You turned out well, son." His eyes gaped and he rephrased himself, "Sonny boy."

Druenn gave him a confused look. Brushing the odd comment aside Druenn refocused. "Warren, that unusual display of emotion, that wasn't just loss of a comrade, there's a lot more to this than you're letting on."

Warren began walking round the room heading for the door. "I don't know what you're talking about," he said, levelling with him, wiping his eyes and concealing the emotions in his face.

"Warren, I want to understand, you put Tharlandrial to death in a seriously harsh way; you would not do that without a significant reason. You're like me in many ways/its shocking! I know you Warren and you wouldn't do that."

Warren realised that he had let Druenn in too much recently and it's led to a direct confrontation about him. Of all the people Druenn could lecture it was he, and lecturing him like he was a student.

"Druenn, I have nothing else to say to you, so please leave me," he said, holding the door for Druenn while keeping his eyes trained on the floor.

"You were in love with my mother weren't you, Warren Anguish. You were in love with my mother, Sarah Lightblaser!" there he'd said it, now all he had to do was wait for the truth.

"Out!" Warren roared, eyeing Druenn his eyes searing with rage. Druenn recoiled at that, he stepped out and the door slammed behind him.

Druenn's frustration grew as he stormed down the corridor. *That's got to be it, he fell in love with my mum and either knew he couldn't have her because she was with my father or, maybe he didn't get round to telling her in time.*

Druenn pondered over the possibilities as he made his way to the next class.

FOURTEEN

What Now?

"Seven eras have passed since the first emperor came to power. When the kingdom of Tharlian was first formed into a Kingdom three hundred and twenty-three years ago.

Tharlian had been a battleground for centuries. The two kingdoms either side were constantly at war with each other. **Razosanas Jauda**, east of Tharlian, dwelled the realm of men along with Dwarf communities.

To the west of Tharlian was the realm of Druids, Elves with a strong understanding of the world around them. Men have always desired power and development, which is why the dwarves settled with them. Dwarves have always looked for development and ways to improve their living qualities. Both races desired one thing more than anything else, wealth.

Ethalas, the kingdom in the west where the druids dwell, were a race of elf with the ability to transform into any beast they see fit. The druids lived in harmony with the world around them and did not intend to harm the trees and beautiful world they lived in. It was not until one day one hundred and two years before the forming of the kingdom of Tharlian a famous explorer called Serleiclass ordered an exploration team to the far regions.

170

With a group of three hunters, a warrior and an artist they scaled together the land of Tharlian calling it **Threepthus**; this later became the name they gave to Tharlian. They continued over the borderline into Razosanas Jauda.

On their arrival they were horrified to see the landscape bare and stripped of all its life sources. Outraged with the humans they encountered in Razosanas Jauda and with the destruction they had inflicted on the once beautiful landscape. Serleiclass ordered the sketch artist to draw everything she saw and return them to their leader Tafu. The others fought and died.

When Tafu saw the images she was disgusted with the way they had destroyed their lands and ordered the druids to destroy the earth killers, and so began the great Life-war" The students took down the notes in their books. Only the voice of the teacher and the quills scratching on the paper could be heard

Many families on both sides were against the wars that broke out throughout their lands and left for Threepthus in the hopes for a more peaceful life.

Humans, Dwarves, Druids and Elves found themselves wandering in small groups, setting up small camps and housing two to three families. As the war became more serious the troops on both sides began setting their own camps within Threepthus, forcing the families further into the kingdom.

Draytorn Thorian, a wise and inspirational warrior led the free people deep into the heart of Threepthus. Many families began meeting different races, all agreeing on taking no part in the war. They grouped together in larger camps. Over time these larger camps grew bigger as more people flocked in after hearing about a war free utopia.

The group grew and began to create their town. They named it Tharlia, which in the old dwarfish tongue meant peace. The war became greater still and word got out of another force growing within the centre of Threepthus.

Both sides grew concerned and ventured in to see these rivals. The leaders on both sides received messages daily on their troops not returning. Both factions learned of this group known only as the Tharlianians intent on eradicating war. They began to wage siege but the Tharlianians fought back the waves. Their skills in warfare were remarkable.

The reasons for their skills were through simple discussions and combining their known skills with the skills of others and fighting side by side. As men, elves, druids and dwarves began abandoning their campaigns to side with these rogues, they forced all forces of druids and men out of the Tharlia border and past their own borders. Quickly after the borders were formed so were many fortresses and cities.

The Kingdom flourished. The people of Tharlia knew they had claimed a Kingdom and needed a wise leader. The people all agreed."

Pretending to voice the people he spoke the next sentence with a peasant like voice. "Draytorn Thorian should become the Emperor of the Kingdom."

The people discussed. The students liked it when Mrs Fortaga did her voices. Weeks after the war was won the people chose Draytorn to become Emperor.

"This is a proud day for all the free people who have fought for many years," Draytorn yelled down to his people from his palace balcony in the capital city known as Cetni. "This kingdom has grown strong through all our efforts." He took a breath.

"Men, women, children have fought for freedom, we have made peace with other races, elves, dwarves, you are most welcome here." Now shouting defiantly, he said, "Our nation stands for one thing, freedom, our Kingdom… our Empire will stand for generations with these same motives, to eradicate war from this kingdom. We shall live in peace and be open to all who wish to live here."

Raising his hands to the sky he called down to his followers, "No more war!"

The crowd cheered hysterically.

"No more hate!"

The crowd cheered again.

"Respect those you hold dear."

The crowd continued to cheer.

"This isn't just my land; this is your land, love it as I do and share in my vision to make this Empire great, live and prosper my friends hold true and we shall be a great asset to the planet and progression combined."

The crowd's cheers bellowed out like a horn to the world.

Draytorn raised his hands high. "I give to you people, the new Empire our Kingdom." He paused. "I give you Tharlian!"

The crowd's triumphant screams ripped through the Kingdom. The world could hear them.

"From that day the ideals of Tharlian were born"

The pupils cheered and praised her theatrical display as Druenn sat in the back row his head resting in his hands, thoughts elsewhere staring out the window.

What was Warren to my mother? A friend? Or more?

The classroom began to disperse as the last bell of the day rang out over Reinhold.

Mrs Fortaga stepped in front of Druenn's table, reeling back to reality he stared up at the forty-three-year-old gazing down at him. "Did you listen to the lesson, Druenn?" she asked him flashing him a quick glance with her eyebrow arched, her arms folded looking down her spectacles.

Druenn dismissed her going on to explain everything she had said within her lesson as he packed his bag and went to leave. He didn't need to be in that class, he had learnt everything he needed to know by spending night after night in the library. The final result was he taking the exam half a year early.

Druenn left the bright room taking a final glance back at Mrs Fortaga who stood in the centre of the classroom her hands tightly folded under her breasts staring at him, her figure looking radiant as the evening colours of orange and pink that glowed brightly through the windows. Shooting her a grin he left down the hallway. Meeting up with Rick in the common room he sat on the brown leather sofa in front of the fireplace watching the flames.

"What a lesson, ah, Dru?" People were starting to call him Dru for short, he didn't like that at all.

Druenn shot him a quick scowl as if to say I've told you once, don't do it again! Rick appologised and rephrased his question.

A lot of people thought Druenn to be mad the way he joked about with Rick, toying with him sometimes with his cheeky nature. Rick was a big lad, not fat or podgy but broad shouldered and with arms like tree trunks. No one would want to get into a fight with Rick, or Alex for that matter. They both stood like bodyguards too, and Emily was like a trophy on his arm. Now people will start suggesting Shiele and the twins, Sam and Bram, have been dragged into Druenn's web of lies and deceit, but that was the fine line between DV supporters and haters within Reinhold.

There was Terribor's Team and Warren's Team, red versus blue in a manner of speaking. Rick now threw a punch at Druenn's shoulder. The pain seethed through his body, his mouth open wide and clutching his shoulder he looked at Rick in shock.

"Oow!" he winced. "That really hurt!"

"You weren't listening," Rick chortled as his grin grew wider with satisfaction of his pain.

Druenn rubbed his arm ferociously, grimacing. "What?"

"How did you find the lecture it was fascinating, do you think it could be true… I mean, all of it?"

"Most likely," Druenn replied. "I know Warren and I'm convinced he has nothing to gain by lying, Divine Victory have already been hunted down and exiled, what would he have to gain by lying?" Druenn replied his eyes returning to the fire as it danced and leapt. The sound of crackling flames was peaceful.

His thoughts returned to Warren clamping Tharlandrial to the stone table. *My mother meant something to him, but what?*

"Oh, also!" Rick started making Druenn jump in fright. "What's the matter with you, Druenn? You seem on edge today."

"A lot has happened today if you think about it, the fight, Overdrive, my mum's death."

And the unusual feelings he showed towards talking about my mother.

"Of course I'm going to be on edge, it's a lot of information to take in." Druenn rearranged himself on the sofa, as Rick stuck his hands out towards the fire to warm them.

"Yes. As I was saying, Terribor has asked permission to have the week off, something about going to take care of business outside of Reinhold, so he won't be teaching us throughout next week."

Druenn and Rick both knew that with Terribor gone their last week before completing all their exams and graduating will be easy, Terribor was never far away to make their day harder, giving them additional work to do, cleaning duties, detentions for no reason apart from looking at him. *Not to mention using magic pathetically like tripping me up in the corridor.* Druenn thought about this. *Terribor has always seemed he is planning a lot more than he lets on, I mean my first day of arrival he tried to kill me.*

"I wonder what he's planning," Druenn said absently

"Who cares as long as he isn't here," Rick guffawed, standing to make some tea over the large stove in the far right hand corner where a large cauldron stood over a roaring fire.

Druenn looked at Rick as he dipped the ladle in and scooped out boiling hot water for both mugs, returning the ladle he reached for two tea leaves and dropped them in. Druenn realised how many rooms have those cauldrons in them, most classrooms, in all common rooms, in fact every room which would be used for a social meeting. Returning to the sofa Rick handed Druenn his mug of tea as he took his seat again.

"Have you seen Emily?" Rick asked Druenn surprised not to see the two of them together, they always seemed to come as a package deal, get one friend get a second free.

"She's with the Dean doing her leadership exam. I have mine tomorrow."

"Aah," Rick replied, nodding as he registered her absence, his eyes landing on the tea. "How long is the exam?"

"Three hours," Druenn replied again, his voice a drone. Rick knew he had a lot on his mind, he knew there was nothing he could do, he had to let Druenn just figure it out for himself. A thought popped into Rick's head *if Druenn is most aware when he's fighting, I could help him by practising the sword with him.*

"Druenn, can you teach me some of those moves you performed when you fought Warren, you know before you... you know," he gestured in a monster growling and clawing manner.

Druenn looked at him, his eyebrows creased into a shocked look. "Sorry, what? Are you saying before I became a monster?"

"Well I didn't want to say it." Rick teased rolling his eyes, his teeth shining as he began to chuckle. Druenn knew deep down he was only messing with him. At the end of the day he wanted to practice fighting. Druenn's eyes sharpened as they always did when he got excited. The look that he gave put Rick on edge, he knew that was Druenn's excited face but he could see the hint of a smirk too, *he's up to something I know it!*

"Let's go!" Druenn said, dashing out of the common room, Rick trailing behind feeling the hint of regret.

What have I let myself in for? Rick thought as he walked out of the common room to join Druenn.

FIFTEEN

Epsonstar

The Great City of Cetni was constantly alive, the people buying their usual supplies in the trade district, the young couples enjoying picnics and walks in the garden district, the sound of battle clashing with giant cheers as gladiators battle for fame and glory in the great arena. The blue sky towered above the large white stone walls, the sun beating down its beautiful rays of heat leaving no shadows within this blessed city.

Durroc Epsonstar, clad in his Royal guard regalia, the silver armour glinting proudly in the sunlight, his great blue with gold trimming cloak flapped like a flag in the morning breeze, realigning his brown shaggy hair into a neat ponytail with his red ribbon, strode into the Palace courtyard.

At his side, his son only just turned nineteen, Drykator Epsonstar, clad in his father's old training leather chest piece, and red linen shirt underneath, silver plate greaves and bracers, shield and two blades on his back which used to be his father's but had been passed down. Each sword bore a name carved into the blade. On his left Justice, and his right Destiny.

Drykator stared at his father's two-handed broadsword on his back and mighty shield, which was almost the same size as him. Drykator was told a lot about Divine Victory and the days his father served within their ranks. He continued to stare at his father's large broadsword, of which the pommel stood above his head, the hilt riding down the distance of his head and neck with his guard reaching his shoulders and the blade travelling the length to his knees. He struggled to comprehend a story his father told him. His memory wandered, bringing back the moment he was told.

"Wow, you should have seen it!" his father's bellows of laughter crackled over the noise of the tavern as he downed another pint of ale, his arm of muscle like steel slapping his eighteen-year-old son on the back. It felt like he had just been smacked into a brick wall. "Acthorian's blade... Divine! Was huge!" Divine was the name of his blade.

"No joke really!" his father continued to bellow standing up on shaky drunk legs as he stretched his arms out symbolising the sword stretched from the floor to the height of his broad muscle filled shoulders. "Not to mention the hilt," he steamed on gesturing to his arm, the hilt measuring the length of his wrist to his elbow. "And the width of the blade was the most fascinating feature." He lowered his finger to roughly three quarters of the length between wrist and elbow.

How is that possible? Drykator remembered thinking. *How could someone carry that, it would weigh a ton!* His memory faded and his mind reeled back to the present as the two proud warriors reached the palace gates.

The sounds of the guards calling back and forth to each other: "Open the gates, open the gates," and, "It's Epsonstar!"

The large doors towered over them as they creaked open into the palace. As they entered Drykator stared around him in amazement. The grand halls stretching out, the large room was

179

garbed with expensive pennants hanging from the ceiling draping down in reds, blues and greens of each nation that had made peace with Cetni.

Their footsteps echoed around the great stone hall, walking on a long red carpet leading up stone steps into the king's public meeting chamber. Durroc gazed down at his son smiling, the boy was almost the same height as him now, not quite but almost. He was a very attractive young man, his neatly cut blond hair seemed to gleam in the bright palace torchlight, his deep blue eyes, keen and always alert. He could see his son was nervous about meeting the king finally but he kept his face composed, as still and perfect as a painting.

Entering the main chamber at the far end of the room were two thrones, clearly for the king and queen. The thrones were empty as expected. From the corner of the room, a woman watched. Obviously she was one of the servants, spying them as they walked in she left the newly placed flowers in the vase she had just placed on a small podium. Walking over she kept her hands cupped together and gracefully strode over to them. Durroc eyed her as she smiled at them, her usual servant's garments, a long green flowing dress, cheaply cut, white linen apron tied around her waist.

"May I help you my lords?" she asked politely her voice a high whispery alto, her voice contained the common accent of Cetni, a formal voice with every word well pronounced. She curtsied to them, raising her skirts as high as her ankles before lowering them and returning to her original position.

"We are here to see King Gondolas," Durroc replied, his booming voice dwarfing the young servant's voice.

"Of course, my lord. I shall be but one moment," she replied, her eyes shifting to Drykator. She battered her eyelids at his handsome features.

Drykator watched her, his eyes surprised at the sigh that followed as she spun on her heels and disappeared down a side corridor, her footsteps disappearing into the distance. Durroc chuckled quietly.

"What is it, Father?" Drykator sounded exasperated as he keenly eyed the painting behind the Throne of the late Queen Margot of Cetni who had passed away during childbirth, refusing to let his father's chuckles draw his gaze.

"I think it's easy to see she liked you." He continued to chuckle. Drykator continued to roll his eyes when a thin and frail voice caught his attention.

"Ah, my good friend, Durroc Epsonstar. How good it is to see you!" the voice sounded overjoyed.

Drykator turned and saw a well dressed man, his gold and purple robes were the garments of royalty, threads of gold created the image of the battle between Draytorn Thorian and the armies of both Razosanas Jauda and Ethalas fighting from either side of him, the image above Draytorn the great tiger of Cetni floating above his head.

Drykator's eyes were drawn to the crown upon this man's head. *He's the king!* His mind reeled and he begged himself not to panic, his body controlled and his expression never changing except for joy and honour to be in the presence of the king. He watched his father stride towards the old king, taking his hand, he fell to one knee kissing the great King Gondolas's ring.

"Oh it is so good to see you, my friend," the great king said, his hair thinning and grey, waving under his crown.

"It is an honour to be in your presence, my lord," Durroc replied, standing and following the king to his throne. As Gondolas walked over he gestured to his servants to fetch chairs for the two guests. Drykator stood stunned. *My father is a friend of the king, not just acquaintances?* This surprised Drykator, he didn't expect such a warm welcome. As Gondolas sat upon his thrown his eyes shot to Drykator standing still watching and waiting, his eyes shifted to a concerned look.

"And who are you, my fine fellow?" Gondolas asked.

Durroc turned and threw his arms out gesturing him to come closer. Drykator slowly walked forward, his body swaying in a formal manner.

"This, my lord, is my son, Drykator."

Drykator reached to where his father was standing. Placing a hand over his heart he bowed stooping low. "An honour to meet you, my king."

The king waved off the formality with a wide smile and gestured for them both to sit.

"No need for the formalities, my dear boy. It is an honour to meet such a pristine lad such as yourself," Gondolas replied as the two Epsonstars sat. "So what do I owe this honour to be in the presence of two great warriors such as yourselves?" the king continued in his raspy booming voice of authority.

Drykator listened in surprise, the king was very old and at least in his seventies, yet his voice was strong and influential.

"My lord, just to see how you are this time?" Durroc's voice boomed.

The king was thrilled except Drykator noticed there was a hint of disappointment in his old features.

"Ah, that's good to hear, no news of movement within the city?"

"No, sir, nothing," Durroc replied.

The two began discussing rumours from beggars and the people of Cetni, something about a possible invasion of COG, but there have always been rumours speculating that the mystique knights could return, even the Dark Assassins. Drykator knew too many groups to remember.

What he did know was that each group had a specific purpose and style of fighting, some magic based and others melee based, all with the same purpose.

"I remember sixteen years ago," the king began to reminisce. "It was the night Palantine told me about my second son's death, the night he disappeared, assassins had made it to my bed chambers and you flew in at the last moment and saved me, from that day I will always be in your debt, Durroc."

"Sir, the honour is mine." Drykator listened to his father's passionate words. Gondolas turned to Drykator sitting quietly waiting.

"So, my young boy, do you intend to take up Divine Victory once more to continue where your father left off?"

"Yes, sir, I am currently searching the lands for men willing to join me in this quest," Drykator replied formally, sitting erect in his chair.

"I wish you the best of luck with that, you only need three more members to start Divine Victory, Tharlian needs heroes Drykator, and they need loyal men they can depend on," the old king replied solemnly. Divine Victory played a large role in the protection of Tharlian, keeping peace and justice throughout the land.

Drykator and his father strode out of the royal gates of the palace, his expression concerned. Looking up at his father he said,

"We need to reform Divine Victory soon, it's too unsafe for the king."

Reaching the north gates of the Cetni walls they exited the city striding over to the stables just outside.

Joadin the stable boy ran out to greet them. "You're heading out, both of you?" he asked politely, his eyes shifting between the two men. Durroc nodded to the young boy.

"Yes. I want our horses ready and saddled by the time I finish my drink."

Durroc strode past him, his cloak flapping in the cool breeze slapping the young boy's face as a gust caught under the long cloak. The young boy watched Durroc enter the tavern across the road, Drykator bent down and ruffled the young boy's hair. He guessed he must've been about nine or ten.

"I apologise for my father's arrogance." He smiled widely as he looked at the little boy trying not to cry.

"It's okay, Mr Epsonstar, I get it all the time. My master hits me when I do things wrong." Drykator's eyes flew up to the stabled horses where a fat man stumbled out of the small cottage attached too the stables and pen.

"Oi, boy! Get back 'ere! I need you't work," the drunken man slurred as he threw his tankard to the ground, making a loud clank around the countryside outside the walls.

Drykator stood and strode towards the man.

He was well into his fifties, his black hair showing streaks of gray, his white shirt no longer white with grime and his trousers too; he wore a filthy black apron which Drykator presumed was white once upon a time. He staggered back and forth as Drykator walked towards him. The man eyed him. Recollection began to shine across his face.

"You be Epsonstar's boy, hmm?" He tried to point but unsuccessfully in the right direction, his words slurring. "Ahh, tiz-tiz a pleasure." He began to bow before losing his balance and forced him self steady. Leaning on a barrel next to the door of the cottage he eyed the boy again. "Boy, get back 'ere."

Drykator strode up to him, his face contorted with fury.

"How dare you speak to a boy as young as him like that, you maggot!" he roared defiantly. Seemingly out of nowhere a whistle, a sound like an arrow being fired, flew towards him. Wheeling he leapt out of the way diving into a roll. Unsheathing Destiny and his shield he prepared for an attack but stopped in surprise when he saw the boy, a boy looking like a hero from the stories his father used to tell him when he was a young child.

Riding a white stallion he pulled back his brown leather stitched hat, the boy's lopsided grin stared down at the drunken man. "Don't you think you are treating this child inappropriately?" He held on to the last word his voice a middle range tenor voice.

Drykator stared up in adoration at this character, his bright blue embroided linen shirt and chest piece, two belts crisscrossing his chest, filled with small throwing knives. At his side a long knife. *Or a short-short sword?*

Drykator wasn't sure but the hilt and pommel was well carved, the guard being a dragon's wings leading into the handle being the neck and the pommel the head of a dragon.

The boy hopped off his horse with elegance, his long teal coloured cloak flapping out behind him as he landed. His brown leather boots and trousers completed his outfit with a belt filled with brown, green and red leather pouches with God only knows what. He also noticed what looked like a small oak box on the back of his belt constantly being hidden by the flapping cloak no bigger than knuckle to waist length. As the boy strode past Drykator the boy eyed him carefully, that lopsided grin never leaving his face. The boy was almost the same size as Drykator and looked about the same age.

On his left arm was a crest of a dragon breathing fire with a single person plunging a knife through its heart. Drykator clicked. *I think I know who this might be, I didn't know he was a real person though.* For the first time Drykator turned to the man now pinned to the wooden wall of the cottage, four daggers holding his shirtsleeves to the wall and his trousers, *he threw four at the same time?* Drykator couldn't believe who he was watching. *It's a hero a real life hero.*

He walked straight up to the man pinned to the wall, pulling the knives out and flicking them back into his pouch. He sniffed the man's breath and recoiled instantly.

"Blood on the Divine what crawled in your mouth and died?" He turned away from the man as he collapsed on the floor unconscious, obviously the drink being too much for him. He turned to the little boy still standing where Drykator had left him. Bending down he wiped a tear away.

"Hey, little guy, if this disgusting heap of cow crap hurts you, you tell me, okay?" The boy giggled and nodded as he ran inside.

"Kids huh?" the boy said standing and pulling his cloak over his shoulders, the cool breeze getting to him.

"Yeah, indeed," Drykator stammered. Flipping out a knife he flicked around his fingers, the blade never touching his fingers.

"You're Drykator Epsonstar, aren't you?" the boy asked, reaching round for a belt pouch he had hidden behind his cloak. Pulling out a pipe he stuffed the chamber with, from what Drykator could smell, Morttis leaves.

Drykator knew about morttis leaves, they were an expensive leaf to buy and rare to find, having all the effect of regular Tarbocaring without the threat of damaging the lungs. The boy lit the pipe and began to smoke, leaning on his horse, which stood steady, and unwavering, the morttis giving off the sweet scent of jasmine, cinnamon and ginger.

"May I ask for your name?" Drykator asked still staring in awe at this fascinating character who feels as if he's stepped off a page.

The boy pulled his hat back again making eye contact. Pointing to the symbol on his shoulder, the symbol of the dragon and the lone fighter, his face incredulous. "You mean you don't know by looking at this?" tapping his shoulder repeatedly.

"I have an idea but I'd rather not jump to conclusions." Drykator let out a nervous laugh. *Why am I so intimidated by him?* Drykator was beginning to feel like a child in the presence of their biggest hero.

"I'm Drago Dragonslayer, also known as…" He flapped his cloak out behind him, standing erect and taking a heroic pose. "Drago the Dragonslayer."

Drykator's first thoughts were right; he was in the presence of the famous Drago Dragonslayer, famous around Tharlian but more for his efforts in the land of Razosanas Jauda, according to the rumours that he and his father had heard walking through the Cities of Valmorgen, Chaydle and Cetni. Drago had made his fame and fortune by killing dragons as his name so rightfully says.

"So what brings you to Cetni, Drago?" Drykator asked, taking his hand for a handshake. "Any dragons causing trouble in Tharlian?"

"Nah!" Drago replied leaning back on his white stallion, patting his chest. "Me and Strike were heading in for a little relaxation, and to make a lot more money." When he mentioned money his eyes lit up menacingly.

"Gambling man, then?"

"Oh yes!" Drago replied with a chuckle. The little boy flew back out of the cottage, a clipboard in his hand.

"Would you like us to take your stallion sir?" Drago eyed Strike and turned back to the boy, impressed with getting the correct breed.

"Yes, his name is Strike, look after him well," Drago replied placing seven gold coins in the boy's palm. The little boy stared up at him incredulous. His smile that followed filled his face as he leapt up and down.

"Thank you thank you thank you," he chimed over and over. "Don't worry I'll take good care of Strike for you, Mr." He paused, realising he hadn't taken a name.

"Drago Dragonslayer," Drago replied, his voice strong and confident. The boy's eyes grew wider when he heard his first name.

"Oh wow!" the boy screeched. "I'm your biggest fan, Mr Dragonslayer."

"Oh really?" Drago replied, his lopsided grin holding, his hazel eyes were dazzling as he watched the little boy jump in excitement. "I have a little gift for you then my friend." He reached to the back of his chest belt for a small throwing knife, flipping it in his hand he passed it to the young boy. "This is yours, may it protect you," Drago said quietly, bending to place the small blade in the boy's hand.

The boy looked up at him in awe. "Thank you so much! I'll treasure it forever!" The boy held the blade forward in his hand, gazing at it. He then pretended to fight an invisible foe slashing and lunging.

Drago chuckled. "If that evil master of yours tries to hurt you, threaten him, if it still doesn't work, find me"

"I will, sir. Thank you, sir!" He took Strike by the reins, he resisted at first before Drago placed his tender hand upon his muzzle.

"Shh, it's okay, he will take good care of you." Quickly realising he didn't know the boy's name his expression changed to intrigue.

"Kid, what's your name?"

"Joadin," the boy replied. "Joadin Fletcher."

"Okay." Drago eyed his beautiful white stallion "Be nice for Joadin, okay?"

Strike watched Drago carefully; he lowered his head to the young boy and rested his muzzle on his shoulder.

The boy eyed Drago, confused.

"Don't worry, he's picking out your scent, resting his head on your shoulder is a sign that he will give you no grief," Drago said giving Strike a final pat before turning to leave.

Drykator watched as Drago unloaded a large brown stitched leather rucksack and a box shaped like a lute. "You play the lute?" he asked, turning to follow Drago.

"Yeah, and the harp, flute and the Valmorgen horn… Oh and violin."

Drykator nodded impressed by Drago's knowledge. "You want to play tonight? I'm going to find myself a nice inn and get myself a free room and food for the night, all I got to do is pull in a good crowd and that's what I do best." Drago winked at Drykator cockily.

"I don't play," Drykator defended.

"All right then, sing?"

"Sorry, Drago, I am on a reconnaissance mission with my father but we will be back early tomorrow, I would quite like to ask if you'd like to join me on this mission to find new members to begin Divine Victory, I think you may be a potential candidate once I've seen you fight of course."

Drago eyed Drykator incredulity staining his face raising his eyebrow.

"Me? Divine Victory?" Drykator smiled knowing he had caught his interest. "No, sorry. Not a chance!" Drago shot back, shaking his head in refusal. He began his sentence again carefully returning to his cocky voiced self, almost sounding patronizing.

"Besides my life is too hustle-and-bustle to be caught up in a silly attempt to protect an old man."

"Excuse me?" Drykator now arched an eyebrow in shock placing his hands on his hips. "Old man? That's the king you're talking about."

"Yeah, whatever," Drago replied, feeling very smug, he flung his rucksack over his shoulder and walked off.

Drykator felt frozen to the spot in shock. *He refused the opportunity to join the new Divine Victory?* He couldn't believe it.

Drago walked towards the great gates of the Imperial city Cetni. Giving one last turn, he looked back at Drykator and waved. "Don't forget, the most expensive inn, that's where I'm heading."

Drykator watched Drago disappear through the gates before his eyes were drawn back to the groggily drunk owner of the stables, attempting to pull himself off the ground. Drykator whistled to the two guards standing by the open gates to Cetni. Hearing the whistle they dashed over, their steel garb consisting of a red and yellow tunic reaching down to their knees, steel greaves, wrists, helmet and chest piece clanking and glistening in the midday sunlight as they ran, using their pikes like staves as they dashed across to Drykator.

Everyone within the walls of Cetni was very aware of the important status of Durroc Epsonstar which gave his son instant respect.

"How may we be helping you, Mr Epsonstar?" the taller guard asked in his raspy accented voice saluting as they both arrived. Drykator explained the cruelness the man on the ground showed to the young boy and he wanted him locked up. The guards quickly jumped at the opportunity to help the son of a DV member and dragged the man away.

Drykator called out, "And I want you to find someone equally qualified to run the stable and take care of the little boy."

"Yes, sir!" the two guards called back in unison as they hurried away. Durroc Epsonstar stepped out of the tavern calling to Drykator. The boy dashed out with the two horses. Meram, Durroc's faithful white and black spotted Appaloosa and Runner, Drykator's mahogany brown palomino, trotted out with the young lad.

"All saddled and ready to go, Mr Epsonstar," the little boy said politely.

"Thank you," Durroc said, sounding very drone and flicking Joadin a silver coin as he leapt up onto Meram's back.

Joadin stared appreciatively at the silver coin in his hand. Thanking Durroc he watched him ride past leaving Drykator saddling himself. Drykator knew that a silver coin would barely buy the boy a loaf of bread. *His family must be poor to send a child of eight or nine out to work.* Pulling a pouch from his belt he opened it and gave him seventeen gold coins, which would feed him and his family for four months. Seventeen gold coins were roughly four months' pay on a decent Cetni wage.

Joadin looked at the coins glinting in his hand as the sun's rays rained down on them. "Oh thank you, thank you so, so much Mr Epsonstar!" Joadin squealed in delight.

"Get back to your family and give them the money and look after yourselves." He flicked Runner's reins and the brown Palomino took off. Young Joadin placed the coins in a leather pouch on his belt and ran into Cetni to his parents.

SIXTEEN

Luck of the Dragonslayer

Drago strode proudly through the city, his eyes catching on almost everything they rested on. The birds flew low grabbing and picking at the crumbs of food caught in between the stone brick paths leading and weaving off into multiple routes, the giant white stone buildings towering over ~~through~~ the districts, the people of Cetni called to young ones or friends spotting each other, laughing and discussing recent news, laughing children pushing wooden wheels with sticks down the streets, the old folk sitting on benches and fountain edges playing cards or stone totems and elders watching over their shoulders. Cetni was a truly magnificent capital city. Drago couldn't help but smile with all the happiness that this city was so enveloped in.

Turning down a side passage he found himself staring up at a sign pointing in his direction saying **Trade District**. Following the large crowds of people all coming from different backgrounds, lords and ladies buying their finely cut garments and food, peasant and farmer folk mingling around searching for supplies on the cheap or setting up their own stalls in hope of selling their own crops for coin. He watched all the traders standing alert on their stalls holding out all sorts of goods from fresh fish to well cut jewellery, Drago passed through the crowds listening to calls and cries of the traders alike.

"Fresh fish, half price, half a gold shimry and a silver dimo," and, "step up and roll forward, check out these fine scarves and cloaks buy one get a second free."

Eyeing a guard clad in the usual town's guard wear standing patiently in front of a large wooden door he walked over holding himself erect, bowing he said.

"I say, old bean," Drago started in a fancy upper class voice. "I do be looking for one of your most spiffing expensive inns." The guard stared at him. "You're a Valmer boy, aren't you?" a deep rumbling voice began.

"Nah, just messing with ya," Drago continued in his own town voice "Just looking for a posh place to stay."

The guard stared incredulous eyeing the eighteen year old up and down. "Move along, kid, you couldn't afford it, I don't have time for your games."

Drago dipped his hand into his pocket retrieving five shiny gold coins and taking the guard's hand let them gently clink into his palm. The guard fixed his eyes on the glinting gold.

"These gold coins say I can," Drago sneered with his own arrogance, his eyebrow curling upwards and his lips turning into a cocky lopsided grin.

"Right away, sir." The guard quickly lifted his quarterstaff and walked briskly forward clanking with each step towards the grand district. Along the way the guard explained that the grand district was for the more wealthy customers. Drago reached an intricately designed white stone building, stone vines and what Drago guessed must be ivy weaving up the building.

"Welcome to the Dragon's Demise," the guard announced before bowing and turning away back in the direction of the trade district.

"Hmm, this looks like my kinda place," Drago grinned, eyeing the inn's name on a small board gently flapping in the breeze. Opening the door Drago eyed the spacious room.

To his left he looked over at the many seats and tables as all normal inns and taverns have, also to be expected, in the far corner was four tables all with different gambling games, two of which were cards. Drago could see, most likely, one game was four houses and the other could be any gambling card game. On the other two tables was a board. Drago once again knew they must be stone totems boards.

As he turned his head forward he looked up at the oak beams overhead. Returning his eyes to the far end of the room he could see a small raised platform, of course this would be for the dancers or live entertainment. Drago gave his lute bag a cheerful tap. He listened to the fireplace roaring in the far right end of the room and also as expected in the right, next to the fireplace, the bar.

This inn did not look any different than any other Inn, the tavern on the bottom floor and once you received a key you would have access to the upstairs, which is where you would find your beautiful art work displayed on the white brick walls, possibly a fountain and a violinist or a harpist playing peacefully in the corner of the room, before ascending another flight of stairs to find your room. Drago knew if could determine lords and ladies wearing peasant garments so as to avoid thieves and bandits at night, or as many landlord and tavern owners would say, determine friend from foe and keeping the riff raff on the lower level. distinguish

Drago stepped forward towards the bar, the floorboards creaking under his feet. He felt right at home here, quickly glancing and then turning towards the onlooking lords, raising their gazes from their drinks and games to see the newcomer causing the creaking.

Well they are in for a treat, Drago thought as he lay his lute on the floor resting his arm on the counter.

The middle age bartender glanced round at him giving his large belly a tap. Turning to him his double chin bounced as he scrubbed down the counter. He wore a proud smile scratching his thinning comb over hair. His smile broadened before speaking. His voice was proud and booming like a circus ringmaster announcing the start of the show.

"Welcome traveler to the Dragon's Demise," the man bellowed out with authority. "If you need food, drink or a room to sleep the night just give ole George a shout." It sounded like a line he had rehearsed many times in the past.

Drago lent towards the fat man, eyeing his ridiculous moustache, which curled up and around his cheeks like two hooks awaiting a fish to bite them. Drago held his tongue; he knew making fun of this man would get him thrown out faster than he could say bless you.

"Well, George," Drago began, "I'm in need of a room and some of your finest ale please, my good man."

George looked him up and down; he sniffed loudly wiping his nose with his arm and wiping his snotty arm on his grubby once white but now more of a black stained grey colour apron.

"Can you afford it?" Drago displayed seventeen gold coins on the counter. George licked his lips eyeing them; his mouth began to water, reaching out a hand creeping towards the coins. Drago snatched them back up slipping them into a brown leather pouch in one swift movement. He had to learn to move money quickly as a gambler before someone planted a knife through your hand because they think that you were cheating.

"Nah-ah-ahh," Drago said mockingly. "This is gambling money, hiding the pouch of coins up his sleeve. Pulling out his pipe again and retrieving his green pouch he retrieved several leaves. The smell was enticing, elderflower, jasmine and something George couldn't quite place, but it was magnificent. He knew what leaves they were.

"That's greenword, isn't it?"

"Hang on," Drago replied, also pulling two Morrtis leaves out and adding them to the pipe stuffing them deep. "Smell that," Drago requested, George lent over the counter and smelt the sweet aroma that flowed out of the pipe. He breathed deeply taking the sweet scent in deep into his lungs and exhaled.

"That smells beautiful!" the innkeeper replied, his eyes closed and grinning. Passing him a few leaves, George collected them up stuffing them into his own pipe.

"Green Morrtis, this is," Drago mumbled the holding the pipe in his mouth as he struck a match also held in the green pouch, then passing the flame to George they both began to smoke. Slipping off his blue coat with the crest of the Dragonslayer on it, he lent back on the counter and gave his proposition. "Okay, George, listen up. I will do a four hour set with your band including all the classic songs you know, if I can have a bed and a meal for the night."

Drago felt quite chuffed with himself being able to talk to innkeepers this way, many would normally cower or be as polite as possible to get a room for a cheap deal.

Decent inns such as the Dragon's Demise were normally ridiculously expensive as the Innkeepers were all competing these days so they will try to provide the best services for the higher charge. Once you reveal a large amount of coin it would be the innkeeper grovelling at their feet.

"No deal!" George replied sounding none too concerned. "That's a pathetic bargain for a room in the Dragon's Demise." George wiped down the counter again before lowering the pint of ale in front of Drago. Drago was stunned. *A pathetic bargain? Who is this wise guy? Who does he think he's talking to?*

Drago collected himself, forcing back the stammer. "W… well," he thought for a second. "With my skills I could fill this room in an hour." Pulling himself back to George he spoke, his cockiness returning to his voice.

"All right then, I wager that room for the *week*." He stressed the word week while he watched George's eyes widen.

"Yes… a week," he said again. "And two meals a day if I can not just double your daily income but triple it in two days the rest are free."

George loved to gamble. *He'll never do it and I at least double my money, the odds are in my favour*, he thought cruelly as he thought about throwing him out of the door with his own pockets full to bursting.

"All right, sir, you have yourself a deal."

They shook hands, smoke beginning to fill the small area.

"You start at seven and no later."

"Yes, sir." Drago's expression grew deeper with self-satisfaction. *I always get my way*, he thought.

Hauling his lute bag, rucksack and tankard of ale over to one of the far tables where three men were playing cards, he eyed the cards in their hands and what was on the table and realised they were playing Royalties.

Drago remembered learning this game shortly after running away from home. The idea was to collect the king, queen, and jester followed by the knight. His memories wondered to a half drunk man in Razosanas Jauda.

"This is how it works." The man knew he had won the game so he laid out his final attack, placing the king halfway on an opponent's, jester on queen which in turn are moved to the player placing the cards next to the knight then knight sits on top of queen then knight moves over to the Jester laying on top of him then finally knight sits over the half of the king underneath still showing. The cards that have been covered were then removed from the table back to the player that lost.

"The player that has lost the cards must now make exactly fifteen before he can regain a royalty card, so the idea is to take all four players royalty cards before they gain theirs back," Drago nodded listening. Looking now at the drunk man's Royalty cards in the centre he guessed it must mean the royalty cards have taken the throne.

"How do you protect your title?" he asked

"If someone challenges you, you must be able to make fifteen in your number card pile," he said, pointing to a small deck next to him. "If you both get fifteen then you keep the throne."

"How were you able to take the throne straight away, pointing to the last four cards he was returning to the table's deck," he said.

"I had my fifteen sitting next to me ready, once you use a fifteen card number you must return them back to the deck, also each turn you pick up a card."

"I think I get it," Drago replied.

Reeling back to the present he watched the game and sat down to join them. The group eyed him. All three wore fancy multi coloured clothes, silks and linens, blues, greens, reds and gold. It was clear these three were lords.

"Ahh so ye be wanting to play, would ya?" a strong Chaidlyi voice gruffly rang out from the man directly in front of him. The main feature that stuck out from this character was his big bushy black eyebrows and his deep brown eyes, his nose seemed out of proportion to his face which led down to his drooping lips with a bushy black beard and no moustache. A large gold earring was dangling down his right ear. He looked a bit what he'd imagine a sea trader would look like and sounds like for that matter but his clothes seemed too posh for that.

"Don't mind if I do," Drago replied sounding enthused as he dumped his bags on the chair next to him. As he lent down to arrange them accordingly, he fastened the two bags to his left boot with a steal chain already wrapped around his boot, as to ensure no thieves ran off with his belongings.

Returning to the table he eyed his opponents. "Okay, let's say a wager of hmm…" He hummed and hawed, scratching his chin before throwing his hand up and throwing a brown leather pouch on the table, the clank of the falling coins drew the three opponents in, eyeing the leather pouch.

"A hundred gold pieces," Drago spoke slowly, he grinned widely taking a long drag on his pipe and blowing the smoke around the three men. The game began with the man to Drago's left dealing the cards. Drago watched the men carefully, watching for their tells, waiting for his moment.

After what seemed like an hour but spying the hourglass in the corner of the room still on the colour he had seen on entering it must have been forty-five minutes roughly. He had lost every hand letting the contents of the leather pouch deplete by around forty gold pieces. He didn't care he had a plan. He always had a plan. The man in front of him who had said his name was Biare, it sounded like a sea trader's name to him.

He must be a sea trader, Drago thought.

"Did ye be hearing they say that there be Divine Victory members old and new on the move?" the dark coloured man on the right barked suddenly causing the group to jump, this character looked unusual, with his skin tone he could only presume he had come over from one of the partnering isles or in fact maybe The Crack. The Crack was an interesting feature Drago had heard about within Tharlian.

Along the coastline towards the west a chunk of land had broken off from the mainland. No one knew why until investigators entered Ethalas along their coastline and were incredulous on the discovery of a maelstrom that had been created during the wars between the elves and druids. The maelstrom was ripping their kingdom apart and now was pulling part of Tharlian's land in too.

The Curse the druids called it and the idea that it was ripping apart an entire kingdom scared Drago.

If that thing got any bigger it could destroy Tharlian too.

Pulling himself back to the game, he watched Biare as he cackled with joy of his win pulling the coins towards him.

"And I'm afraid that is my win," Drago said, seizing the throne in one fluid movement.

"What?" Biare replied as he watched him, shock slowly creasing across his face.

"Yep, that's all mine," he replied, pulling the gold towards him and sliding the cards to the centre of the table.

"Nice win, kid," the dark coloured man replied. This routine then went on for another hour, money sliding into Drago's pocket.

By this point he had heard all their names, to the left, Lord Beeran of house Seabrook in Valmer, Biare opposite and the dark coloured man on the right was Chin Carney, a respected master in chief Guardsmen from Teelan, the fortress on the isle The Crack. As the hours continued to roll by and the pockets of the gentlemen growing lighter and Drago's heavier, they grew to questions.

"You seem to have the luck of the Dragonslayer," Beeran said with the hint of questioning as he stared down at his hand.

Drago shrugged it off with a grin. "Maybe, seems to be the case," he said pulling another five gold pieces his way.

"I do be hearing that, that Dragonslayer is coming to Cetni at some point," Chin said.

"Dragonslayer?" Drago asked stifling a chuckle under his breath. He loved hearing people talk about him.

"Well people been saying he's come down here to fight dragons, but I don't know bout you lot but I not been seeing many dragons round here, I wonder if he comes for other motives. I be hearing the boy's been fighting and killing dragons for a living, it's what has made him famous; his fighting skills must be something like out of a story book. Dragonslayer do be becoming legend around here. Ye know why they say luck of the Dragonslayer boy?" Chin asked Drago pointing his pipe at him reorganising his sitting position. Drago shrugged and shook his head whilst reorganising his cards.

"He be the luckiest man alive it seems to be, you could play him at cards for a week and you won't win a single hand."

"Really?" Drago replied sarcastically but no one seemed to pick up on it. Beeran's expression was slowly becoming concerned with each hand he lost to Drago, his eyes fixed on him. He knew no one can win seven hands in a row they all knew it.

"I hear that Drykator chap is looking for some darn good fighters," the well-spoken Valmer Lord Beeran said, reorganising his next hand. Drago listened intently although not paying much attention to him directly.

"I heard the word is he plans to get Divine Victory together again and protect the King," Beeran chuckled.

"But from what I might dare say, or from whom? There's no enemies around here until reaching Razosanas Jauda."

"Ahy unless those attacks be still happening, don't ye be forgetting that Durroc Epsonstar is his personal bodyguard," Chin replied.

The three men immediately scoffed as Drago moved his royalty cards yet again to the centre of the table, showing his fifteen of hearts he claimed the throne. Biare scowled and threw his cards down; kicking back the chair he stood erect.

"You lying cheating son of a bitch! I'll have your hide on a spit." He towered over Drago as he stared down at the smiling eighteen-year-old. "After the first hour it's been nothing but wins, I say you're cheating!"

Drago lent over the table his grin remaining on his face. "What do you think I was doing in that first hour, huh? I was learning your tells, incidentally you always scratch your neck with a good hand so I know it's quickly I need to strike."

Biare leapt over the table grasping Drago by the scruff of his neck. The two other men pushed away from the table escaping the enraged Biare.

Drago realised he was in trouble. All his weapons were under his chair. Biare lifted Drago up. Drago searched the room, anything to get the large hulking man off him. His muscles were now apparent as Biare held a solid grip like a vice around Drago as he backed him up against the far back wall.

Oh, if ever I needed a Dragon to slay it would be…

Suddenly a screech rippled over Cetni, the sound of a cat screeching at its enemy, like metal scratching against metal. The next sound that followed was all too familiar.

"Dragon!" the people screamed from outside. Cries, screams and running footsteps filled the streets as the people of the town took cover and ran for their homes. A peasant man burst into the inn yelling in terror.

"Dragon! Run or arm yourselves, it's a dragon," Drago grinned and shoved Biare's grip on him aside and he fell to his feet, running over to his equipment he strapped himself up.

My time to shine, Drago thought.

The people within the tavern were frantically looking to George, the innkeeper to take them down to the cellar, out of the way from the fire yet to come.

Biare stared at Drago watching the young cheat throw his blue jacket on. He eyed a symbol on the left shoulder, the emblem of the Dragonslayer. Drago donned his knife belts around his shoulders, crisscrossing them over his chest.

"Where do you think you're going, boy? We aren't done yet!" Biare growled, his eyes blazing into Drago whilst he watched him place all the gold and silver coins into his rucksack. Drago didn't reply, he had a job to do. Who did he think he was with a dragon outside terrorising the city and wanting to fight?

Pulling the small wooden box off the back of his belt he opened it whilst placing it on the table, the cards scattering with the clunk and rush of air as the box hit the table. Biare looked over Drago's shoulder, keeping a safe distance as Drago further armed himself with more weapons. He watched the young man pull a small metallic object, which looked very much like a small crossbow, only missing half of its parts.

Drago quickly pulled his right sleeve up to his elbow revealing his plate bracer, it glinted in the candlelight above the table. Biare saw markings with the Dragon being slain by the lone warrior just like on his jacket. *Who is he?* Biare realised there was a small hole in the centre of the bracer, then it came clear as he looked at the crossbow again. The crossbow included the lath and string, what looked like a quick winch, which was pulled down for quick cocking and at the end the stock, mounted on it was a small wheel with a thin rope wrapped around it, below the stick was a large bolt. *It connects to his bracer!* Biare realized. *How damn clever, it has to be a Razosanas Jauda invention.*

Drago aligned the bolt with the hole, the crossbow facing towards the left he slipped it straight in, turning the contraption ninety degrees to the right. The crossbow was now facing forwards and attached firmly to his bracer. Slipping a bolt from out of another pouch, this one was blue, unravelling the rope connected to the wheel at the rear of this fancy contraption he slid it into a small hole in the bolt itself. Tying it he placed the bolt in the crossbow and pulled the winch down firmly the weapon was cocked. Once it was cocked a trigger flipped out from underneath the bracer. The trigger looked like an upside down metal stirrup that he could grasp and Biare guessed push down on to fire.

Pulling his left sleeve up he pulled his cloak off the back of his chair and flung it around him, the colour of teal consuming him as the wind got under it. Striding towards the door he fastened his belt again and placed his left hand over his mini crossbow checking if everything was in order.

"Where are you going kid? I'm not done with you!" Biare roared trying to hold his anger from letting fear settle in about the dragon.

Drago walked out the door. The sun was low now, twilight was laying over Tharlian and there was a chilly breeze tonight. Drago could see the moon in the dark blue sky as the sun was disappearing over the horizon.

The people of Cetni ran all around him, knocking into him searching for cover and safety. Drago didn't care about the people. *All a bunch of wimps*, he thought whilst searching the sky. Biare reached the door and stood at the threshold preparing to shout as a screech rippled overhead again. Biare stared up as a black silhouette appeared over the moon. A giant black monster flapped its scaly wings over them. The wingspan looked at least the length of a small trading ship's sails. The creature's long snake like neck coiled round searching for victims. Letting out an agonizing scream it flapped profusely and fire streamed out of its mouth like a volcano.

His eyes filled with terror as he backed into the Dragon's Demise again. Drago watched the creature calmly. At that moment the beast's dark crimson eyes locked onto him. Even from there Drago could see the pupils of the creature as yellow as the sun. He had been through this routine so many times he was guaranteed he could do it blindfold.

The beast flew down like a stone being thrown off a cliff. Choosing the right moment Drago kicked a foot forward throwing himself into a run forwards, as the beast changed its direction to grab Drago with its talons, he darted to the right. As the beast flew down low enough to grasp him, everyone left in the street fell to the floor screaming and holding their heads down. He thrust his right arm out towards the beast as it flew past him and down the street. As it began to ascend for a second run Drago fired his crossbow. The bolt sailed through the air, a soft whistle cutting through the screams of panic.

The soft thud that followed made Drago smile, a pained scream ripped the sky overhead. The bolt hit the dragon, Drago couldn't see where but it was a hit. The wheel on the back of the crossbow began unwinding, the reel of rope shooting out of the wheel down the street and into the air as the dragon continued to ascend.

Drago began running down the street as the latch caught, it was the end of the reel and the wheel stopped with an almighty crack. A second later and Drago was airborne, Cetni shrinking into the distance as the dragon continued to climb.

Drago wasn't afraid, he had done this too many times to care. Biare and the people of Cetni looked up into the sky as the dragon and the unusual boy disappeared into the dark clouds above with the coming night. The sound of footsteps marched down the high street, the king's guard and a few soldiers of Cetni arrived unsheathing their swords and asking the people what was going on.

"Where's the dragon?" one asked. The man looked blankly at the soldier and pointed up slowly. The soldier looked up into a large cloud overhead, the moon now shining brighter left an eerie silhouette, the dragon behind the clouds in a struggle, shooting flames in short intervals, the screeches and wails rippling out of it as it struggled for survival.

Drago swung left and right on his rope as he propelled himself from under the dragon and onto its back, the dragon tossed and twisted in the attempt to shake Drago off.

Drago drew his long blade dagger, spinning it around his fingers as he held the rope like reins around the dragon's neck, he plunged the dagger deep into its back, an agonising wail of pain ripped through the dragon as it jerked its back against the dagger.

The purple and blue blood began to flow freely from the beast. Drago didn't pull the blade out until he found what he was looking for.

Jab the blade into its spine and twist till it goes rigid paralysing the beast.

He twisted the blade, pulling harder on the reins forcing the dragon's neck further back causing it to arch its back further for him. The dragon flicked its wing around clipping the back of Drago's head. He tumbled forwards into the dragon's left wing. He bounced over the thin tissue and quickly dug his blade in to stop him falling off the dragon completely. Again the dragon screeched. This time it flicked its tail round, Drago knew to fear the tail most, at its tip there was a sharp blade like talon no more than the length of a sword.

Drago forced himself back onto the dragon's back as the tail whipped round for a strike just missing his right boot. Balancing himself again he grasped the reins tightly again to help with his balance as the tail whipped round again and again. He dodged and weaved, blocking with his blade against the tail until he remembered the gaping hole now in the dragon's back. Backing up to the hole, the tail whipped around again like a scorpion strike. The blade came down and he leapt back again as the blade like tail struck the hole and plunged deep into the dragon's nerve system. A loud crack rippled through the beast's back as the dragon arched its back and went limp.

The dragon began to descend, falling faster and faster. Drago's job wasn't done yet, the beast wasn't dead, he needed to get under it and pierce its heart. As it fell Drago swung on the rope, swinging himself under the mighty beast. Quickly locating the dragon's chest, he plunged the dagger deep and forced it down ripping another gaping hole in the dragon. Blood poured over Drago's face as he stared at the heart, as he swung freely he reached for the heart.

Damn, I can't reach! he thought. Quickly assessing his situation, how high he was, how fast he was falling, sheathing his dagger he grabbed for one of his throwing knives. One good placed shot could pierce the heart.

He swung back and forth uncontrollably. He stayed calm. Holding the blade between his thumb, index and middle finger he threw his arm out. The knife flew as straight as an arrow into the dragon's heart. Taking another look down, he was now level with the tallest tower of the citadel of Cetni. He let the rope guide him back to the dragon's back as he gripped the reins and held on tightly to the dragon's back. The ground came closer and faster. With a split second to think he jumped as the beast crashed into the brickwork path, dust and rubble flying high as Drago landed back on the dragon's back, helping reduce the impact.

Now for the triumphant finale, Drago thought. As the dust began to clear and the crash faded into the past, the people began crowding around the slain beast. Torches began being lit for the night and handed out around the people moving in for a closer look. Drago knelt for a second before anyone saw him there, before standing and throwing his cloak back letting the wind catch it. He waited for the dust to dissipate a second longer then he stepped forward, holding his shaken body still and erect. The people saw him through the dust and stared incredulous. And the moment Drago had been waiting all day for.

"It's… it's Drago… the Dragonslayer," someone called out. Realisation settled around the crowd. Drago watched them, unable to wipe the grin off his face.

"It's the Dragonslayer," another called, Chin appeared at the door of the Dragon's Demise.

Very appropriate, Drago thought.

"Why I don't believe what me eyes be telling me, it be that Dragonslayer," Chin called. The crowd roared with cheers and praise. Drago took each step slowly giving his legs time to recover from the impact. The growing crowd crowded around him shaking his hand and shouting.

"Three cheers for the Dragonslayer. Hip – hip –" was followed by a loud "hazaar" after each "hip – hip".

Also other people would shake his hand saying, "Nice kill, sir. Congratulations," and, "it's such an honour to meet a real hero, Mr Dragonslayer."

As Drago reached the entrance to the Dragon's Demise he met Chin's gaze, he looked torn. It looked like sheer joy to meet him but at the same time Chin knew he had been beaten by the Dragonslayer at cards many times that day so he decided to back into the Dragon's Demise with a half happy grin and gave him a polite nod.

Drago turned to the crowd and called to them all. "I'm playing music and we have pretty girls dancing all night and everyone is invited" The crowd cheered and followed him into the tavern.

Walking up to the bar Drago placed his hands on the counter. "George my man get all these people a nice strong brew, on me," he called back to the crowd and George. The crowd cheered again as Drago pulled a brown pouch off his belt and let the contents clink loudly into his open palm. He piled up the large stack of gold coins on the counter and stared at George with his cheeky lopsided grin. Grabbing George's bar cloth he wiped his face pulling all the purple blood off his face and linen shirt collar. George beamed at the money and the people crowding round the bar and bustling in through the front door filling all his seats, sitting and talking amongst one another.

"Oh, it is a pleasure, Mr Dragonslayer. It really is, please take a seat and enjoy the serving girls, would you like a meal? One for a dance perhaps, anything you need let me know!" George said without a pause.

Oh, he is going to make me rich, he thought whilst licking his large lips.

Drago nodded to George once and picked up his lute from the far table where he sat playing cards. Biare was gathering his belongings and looked exhausted and defeated. Gazing over at Drago pulling his lute out of its case he scowled quickly hoping Drago wouldn't spot him.

Drago's eyes flickered up at him and spotted the scowl before Biare could wipe it off his face and look away. He grinned an evil looking grin, letting out a quick chuckle under his breath. *A cheat he thinks of me huh? Well I'll show him, I'll make him crap himself.* He dropped the lute down on the table letting the crack of the lute reverberate around the room. The room went silent with that and they all looked over at Drago watching him eye the uncomfortable Biare.

"You called me a cheating son of a bitch, didn't you?" he asked defiantly letting his words become louder with irritation.

Intimidation is the key, he thought carefully. Biare raised his hands in surrender letting Drago back him slowly into the far corner.

"I… I… I didn't mean what I said," Biare stammered out, as he bumped into the back wall. "What…what I meant was that you be a cheating loser"

"A cheat… a cheat!" Drago spat. Drago was shorter than Biare, standing shoulder height to the towering man yet Drago seemed to be towering over him rather than the other way around.

"I… be only joking with ya," Biare tried to keep his voice level and friendly. Drago's expression instantaneously changed into a joking but mocking expression.

"Aah, right, well that's okay, of course I can take a joke," and he laughed, the crowd laughing with him. Biare grinned unsure whether to laugh along with him or keep his mouth shut, he grinned wildly and nodded his head with a chuckle.

Drago's expression instantly changed back to serious. "I don't like being joked about."

The room fell silent once more.

Biare forced a smile though serious to avoid further insult. Holding a sheepish friendly smile he replied, "I'm… I'm really sorry, I didn't mean what I said."

Drago stared at him for almost an entire minute with a look of hatred.

Biare jumped as Drago bellowed out in raucous laughter. He tried to speak but the laughter continued to come, his eyes watered as the crowd also laughed on how pathetic Biare looked against an eighteen-year-old boy.

Drago dabbed the tears away as he walked back up to his lute and picked it up. "Oh… you are a hoot and a half, Biare. Oh, you make me chuckle." Turning to the crowd he called for musicians. "Okay, guys, I need a violin, harmonica, tambourine and cello come on!" He threw up his hands ordering them to follow him to the stage. The crowd cheered as people picked out their instruments and headed over to the stage.

The hustle and bustle that Drago loved about taverns began to come to life. Serving girls pushed tables and chairs aside making room for a dance floor. Lords and ladies, peasant folk and lovers made their way to the floor.

Biare sank to the floor in shock and embarrassment. *I is going to be the laughing stock of Cetni by sunrise.* Pulling himself up whilst everyone's attention was fixed on Drago he grabbed his belongings and left the tavern, ducking under the people keeping out of sight.

Slipping out of the front door he pulled his arms through his brown and blue leather coat, donning his silk purple cloak he raised the hood over his head covering his face.

"Mind yourself, sir, and stay back from the dragon please," a guard called over to him clearly showing his authority as he held the large spear up in front of him. He carefully stepped around the guards as they discussed a strategy for removing the large dragon from the street.

As Biare sank into the black night he looked over his shoulder as Cetni disappeared behind him. Breathing into his hand it ignited in a bright ball of flame. Holding his hand up he looked out on to the cobbled road that turned steadily southwest towards Valmer and beyond that the capital city Valmorgen. It was a peaceful night, chilly but pleasant, the moon shone down providing a lot of light but Biare knew wolves and any other creatures tend to avoid torches.

Stick to the road and I be fine, he told himself. Biare always found his powers rather amusing. He had seen many wars in his time, so many fights he had lost count, he thought about how he had found himself in this position. *Fighting in the army for so long does pay off once you get paid.*

Biare reached back and felt his large pouch of money.

*Captain General Biare Toman, King Leonidis Leanadon of palace Stonar to a lord, a common lord of the crack and simply because I could afford it, h*e thought to himself glancing up at the sign disappearing behind him. He didn't practically enjoy keeping a low profile and back down to fights but against Drago the Dragonslayer, that was a different matter.

Everyone knew of his efforts in and around Tharlian and Razosanas Jauda. It wasn't a fight worth getting involved in. *Best to back down and keep a low profile for now, it'll make later on much easier,* he thought. His lips slowly curling into a smirk, he chuckled to himself. "You haven't seen the last of me Drago, not yet!"

The people sang and clapped to the song. If they weren't singing or clapping they were stamping their feet in time with the music. Beer tankards clanking together as the people cheered Drago and the musicians on for a brilliant rendition of one of the sea folk's songs up and behind, under and over the sea. Laughter rolled round the tavern, old folks laughing at youngsters dance poorly to the old dance of this song, boys dancing with pretty barmaids and serving girls. In the corner George passed customers large tankards of ale watching Drago yelling at the top of his voice.

"Divine blesses you Drago I'm rich, divine bless you!" His bellowing laughter blended into the crowd as the song built up into a crescendo of raucous cheers.

Drago called a barmaid over signaling her by clicking his fingers. She glided gracefully across the dance floor a tray full of tankards of beer and ale. The people waiting intently for the next song, titles of songs called out around the tavern. Drago took a tankard from the tray and flicked a coin onto the barmaid's tray the clang of the coin landing lost in the shouts of the people. He shot the young girl an enticing cheeky grin and shooting a wink in her direction.

She was a very pretty girl, looking about eighteen or nineteen, her brown hair tied back tight extenuating her smile. She was slim and held her head high, her long radiant white blouse complemented her perfect body.

Oh, I will dance with her all night tonight, Drago thought as she smiled at him, her teeth gleaming. The screams overwhelmed the moment and he was pulled back to the crowd; quickly locking eyes with the young barmaid he blew her a kiss as she disappeared behind the people flooding on to the dance floor.

"Okay, people, let's do a classic!" Drago called. The crowd quietened for a moment, enough to hear Drago cue the other musicians. "Okay, you all know 'Folks Welcome to the Mother Land'?"

The musicians nodded and the crowd cheered as the violin struck up the first chord followed by Drago on the lute then the harmonica then the cello and the tambourine. The people stamped their feet and the dances began again. George watched whilst frantically taking more gold coins yelling at barmaids and serving girls to get the empty tankards washed and refilled. Drago stepped forward searching for the young girl he spotted a moment ago.

Sing this song to her then she's mine, with no fail.

She peeped around an old lord, he guessed it was a lord by the brightly coloured clothes, talking to another lord. He jumped off the small stage leaping into the crowd to start singing to the young girl.

Her bright green eyes watched him carefully, admiration filling her, he spotted her catch her breath as she placed a hand over her heart.

Yep, she's mine, he grinned his lopsided grin at her as he winked again standing no more than two paces apart in the centre of the dance floor, the young and old couples dancing with their partners. He played the lute and danced around her as he began to sing. The crowd joined in as he began.

Allow me to take you from here to another land
It's possible to live like a king and better with your band
And better to dig your feet in and feel the soft, grainy sand
We can be together in Tharlian
You'll never feel lips as sweet
Than the ones you've placed on mine
With the loving warm embrace from your man
And by the time you've lived like a king for longer than our one
Then I'm kitting up in a guardsman suit and I'm sending you back home

He looked deep into her eyes, her cheeks began to glow as a tear glimpsed in an eye. Drago smiled openly and picked up for the second chorus:

If I've forgotten how to love before I leave this land
I'll leave my heart in a silver box for my lover in Tharlian
And insist she never takes it out for the contraband
So please respect my choice and let me run
You'll never see the Divine unless you prove yourself to him
And let us live together for good
And you'll be my sweetheart in this pure and existent foreign land
And we'll leave the suit behind and find our way back home.

The crowd roared, Drago knew that one would pull in loads of people off the streets not to mention the girl now running her arms around him. Placing the lute down on the table next to them, he slowly brought his lips towards hers. Their kiss brought on another series of cheers around the tavern.

He whispered in the young girl's ear. "Wait for me, okay?" she nodded, her smile making Drago's heart thump wildly. Running back to the stage he whispered under his breath, "Gotcha!"

Leaping back onto the stage a lord called to him. "Drago, here!"

Drago spun to see his lute flying towards him. Catching it with ease at the last second he called back. "Thanks, man!"

Turning to the band he chose the next song and turned back to the audience. "Okay, here we go!"

SEVENTEEN

An Unfortunate Turn of Events

The bright moon gazed down on the lonely cobbled path, the small stones shining tiny moons back into the sky. The pale green grass and trees cast eerie shadows along the ground, crickets chirped in the tall grass and the soft cries of the frogs could be heard from a distance by the streams nearby.

A clap of hooves sounded in the distance as Durroc paced slowly down the path, Drykator followed at his side, one hand on the reins and the other holding his torch up in front of him. He looked out into the thick forests either side of the path, looking up the sky was quickly being absorbed by the trees and before long the trees overhead covered the night sky, the moon only appearing for brief moments a time in between the leaves and branches. Looking back down the path the darkness seemed to creep inward towards them.

Drykator moved in his saddle warily shining his torch left and right, the darkness making him feel uneasy. A rustling in nearby bushes sent him wheeling back to scanning the woodlands again.

It was not the silence and the darkness that had him on edge tonight. He was never spooked like this normally. This was something entirely different, more primitive.

Something is going to happen, I can feel it.

"So where are we heading father?" Drykator asked, hoping this mission wouldn't take them any further into the forest.

"Pinevale," Durroc replied instinctively whilst brushing away the low lying branches out of his face.

"So Dray, my boy" Drykator hated it when his father used his nickname. "You found yourself a nice... uh."

He listened to his father stumble on his words obviously embarrassed to bring this conversation up about girls.

"You... uh... found... hmm... yourself... a young lady?"

"Oh, Father, please. Do we really have to talk about this?" Drykator fired back, his cheeks feeling flushed and rosy. The only thing easing his embarrassment was that is was too dark to see his features, even with their torches.

"No I haven't, all right. Please, let's change the subject." He let out an exasperated sigh before his father continued.

Entering a clearing in the trees, Durroc pulled on the reins and turned towards Drykator.

"No. Son, it is important we have these sorts of discussions, I know I haven't always been the best father and more of a teacher but I want to make it up to you son, you see when..."

"Oh, by the divine, no! Please not this!" Drykator began searching in a direction to run before his father could continue.

"Listen, Dray, it's all completely natural."

He buried his head down on the reins and covered his ears, his eyes tightly shut.

"You see, a mummy horse and a daddy horse, who love each other a lot begin to get certain urges which leads to..." a voice from the trees cut him off.

"It's been a while, Epsonstar! It's good to see you're still in good health and with your little boy, I see." The voice echoed around the forest, the voice sounded breathy but powerful.

Durroc wheeled in fright scanning the forest pulling his reins left and right. Drawing his sword he called out to the voice. "Who said that?"

"Oh, I see, so you don't recognise my voice, hmm? Well think, Epsonstar, think!" the voice continued becoming agitated with Durroc's failure to recollect his voice.

Drykator drew his sword slowly letting the tender sound of the blade sliding out of its scabbard echo around the forest in hopes to ward off the voice.

"Playing fair as usual, I see!" the voice mocked.

"Two against one? It'll only make my victory bigger." A fireball ignited behind Drykator. Durroc spotted the blast too late, the ball of burning magma hurtled towards the young warrior causing the green landscape to have a yellow tint to it. The fireball smashed into Drykator's shield on his back, the shield splintered as a mighty crack ripped out of it. He groaned with the blast arching his back as he flew off Runner.

He flew into a spin his face hitting the ground with tremendous force. Runner reared and backed off into the trees.

"Dray, no!" his father roared defiantly leaping off Meram he pulled off his dark Titanium shield from his back and held it up towards the direction of the blast.

The rectangular shield would have concealed his entire back, but now it was held out securely in front of him facing whatever evil stepped forward. The white crest of the Epsonstar family beamed in the moonlight, the picture of an eclipsed sun and moon with a sword hanging in front with an eagle flying overhead. He backed towards his son sprawled out on the ground.

"Son, you okay?" Durroc asked quietly and hurried, his

breathing quickened as he frantically searched the darkness for the figure.

Drykator heard a voice in the blackness.

"Son, can you hear me?" the voice said again. He forced his eyes to open. *Come on Drykator wake up don't leave your father to do this alone!* His back throbbed, a burning sensation running up and down his spine. His eyes slowly began to open, his vision blurred. He saw a bright object in front of him. *Stay focused Dray and don't panic, that's your torch over there, I need to locate my sword and shield,* he forced himself to stay focused, dragging himself on to his knees and elbows. Holding his head, ears still ringing from the impact he shook the throbs away and searched for his sword and shield. He heard his father again.

"Come on, coward, show yourself!"

"Coward? That's a big word for scum like you," the voice spat, and echoed around the clearing.

Drykator pulled himself up grasping his sword and his round shield now with quarter charred and broken off the once bright red now smeared with black burns and marks.

"Who are you and what do you want?" Drykator called out trying to keep his voice level.

"I was once a friend to your father before you all turned against me. Some called me the right hand of the black betrayer!" the voice spoke calmly.

Drykator watched his father's face turn to recollection then to incredulity.

"Oh no," Durroc looked at Drykator his face a picture of fear.

"Dray! Run!" Durroc said his voice dismayed.

"Get out of here!" Durroc began pushing his son away from the clearing before another fire blast ignited and hurtled towards them.

221

Durroc gripped his shield and twisted a bolt next to his wrist, the shield doubled in size, two large panels shooting out one above and one below. He stood as the blast crashed into the shield, fire spewing on every side, the sound of the metal slowly melting left a soft growling sound as it sizzled and bubbled.

Drykator crouched behind his father. "Who is it!? Drykator called over the noise.

"It's t——!" The noise overpowered Durroc.

The flames stopped.

Durroc lowered the shield, the shield now standing as high as his neckline as he peered over the top. A man clad in black floated out of the trees.

"Now you remember me, scum! Now you remember!" the man growled ferociously, beginning to pace like a caged lion back and forth waiting for a fight, his fingers igniting into little flames no more than the size of a candle flame. His fingers constantly toyed with the fire, blending the flames into a small sphere shaped fireball that sat precariously in his palm, flitting and sparking in and out of existence.

"What are you doing here?" Durroc called to him, still shocked.

"I've come to finish what I started Epsonstar, you know as well as the others did, it is your turn to fall along with your fellow comrades."

Durroc angled his sword in the direction of the man dressed in black.

"So it was you who issued the attacks on the others?" he choked, dismay in his voice as realisation settled in as all the pieces of the puzzle were slowly slotting into place.

"Of course, who else would have done it? Tharlandrial? Oh no, Anguish stuck him in his prison under the catacombs!"

"You know he's there?"

"Of course I do scum, many people saw him and documented it and Anguish will get his comeuppance, but you're first."

Drykator's heart thumped frantically, his knees shook violently. He knew he wouldn't stand a chance of defeating this man without being strong.

Compose yourself, Drykator, you can do this.

Drykator stepped out from behind his father and stared at the man.

"Not before you meet your own," Drykator replied calmly, his face stern and composed. He stood tall like a hero out of legend.

The man flew his black cloak out behind him and rearranged his black and silver embroidered gloves. He smiled at the young boy as the warm breeze around them began to grow.

The wind howled around them, the trees waving violently inwards towards the clearing.

Durroc stared at his son shaking his head. "No, son, don't do this, run!" he called over the violent winds.

Drykator eyed his father and smiled, reciting:

"We are Divine Victory
We stand side by side
Through divine's touch
No evil shall hide
Till we find death or we find pride
We shall stand as one with no divide."

Durroc watched his son, a sense of pride ran through the man as he raised his sword once more and charged at the man clad in black.

"Dray, all you need to know his dodge and strike, side step, dodge and strike with this one," Durroc called as he began assembling his own weaving pattern.

"Yes, sir!" Drykator called as a soldier would to his superior.

Durroc had fought this man, this enemy many times throughout the threat of Tharlandrial. He'd learned how to beat this one before he would flee was to weave in and out of his fire blasts, blocking direct hits with the shield and rolling side to side before landing a blow.

The fight began quickly fireballs hurtling towards them, Durroc instantly felt as if he was fighting with his great and loyal team again, this foe was evil and should have been killed years ago and not allowed to start this new war of tyranny.

Where has he been hiding all these years? he thought before raising his shield as another fireball crashed into it. Durroc didn't anticipate the force of this blast. Anyone who had spent time around the realm of magic and mages will know and understand that the longer a mage holds the magic, the larger and more powerful the blast will be. But this man, this new Black Betrayer fired them instantaneously, he gazed over the shield and watched the man in black dance and weave, his hands creating peculiar patterns.

Many styles of fighting with magic were known. Many used staffs, pole arms and even wands to strengthen their powers by focusing their energies on a single object. Others would fight using words and ancient languages, ancient scripture. This one fought with the movement and flows with body movements and creating intriguing patterns. His form of fighting was known as magic dancing as the way they moved looked like a dance.

"Father! Get up!" Drykator roared his eyes never wavering from the man in black.

Durroc wheeled back to the present, realising he was on the

floor he gazed up at his son. *Get up, you old fool!* His mind screamed at him, seeing his son attempting to get close to this beast he felt anger take him, he clenched his teeth tight, his fist clenched around his shield to the point of pain.

He gripped his sword and jumped up, Drykator stepped back as he watched his father sprint at the man spinning and leaping and anticipating every blast. Finally reaching the man Durroc thrust forward his shield clattering into the black clad man, knocking him off his feet. They flew through the air before crashing into the ground, fire spewed around the shield as Durroc attempted to hold the hand still in flame down on the ground in trying to pin the man.

"Dray, now!" Drykator watched incredulous, thoughts unable to process.

"Stab him! Kill him, Dray!" Drykator registered, glancing at his sword he ran towards the two men struggling on the ground.

"Drykator reached them, Durroc arched his back sideways to the left giving Drykator enough room for a perfect kill.

Drykator raised the sword high and brought it down. A large clink as if he had hit metal echoed around the clearing and the sword stopped, no more than an inch from the man's chest.

Durroc stopped struggling with the man as he realised rule number two of Divine Victory.

When engaging magic users, never let your guard down with an easy kill.

Magic users will let you take the bait if they can create barriers.

This was a powerful mage and he was a powerful warrior. Durroc walked straight into his plan.

"My turn, scum," the man whispered in Durroc's ear. His eyes opened wide. *Oh, no! Stupid, stupid Durroc, you've killed your son!*

With a jolt of air, which to Durroc and Drykator felt like riding headfirst into a brick wall, they flew back, a purple bubble dispelling around them. Durroc landed first, crashing into the soil, dust and grass flying up. Drykator fell a few feet further away. Drykator teetered on the edge of consciousness as he forced his eyes open.

Don't give in, please body you can do this! His mind focused as a wave of calm raced through him. *I know his attacks and I know his movements.*

His memory played back the fight they both had as his father picked himself up from the fire blast. He searched for a weak point in the man's movements. The black cloak wisped through the torrents of wind now gusting in towards them. He paced closer to Drykator's father, standing over his prey like a vulture waiting for the perfect moment to end the suffering of its meal. Durroc groaned as he realised he couldn't move. *My back! It's gone, I can't move!* A wave of panic washed over him. Durroc searched for his shield and sword both out of arm's reach. The black clad man drew his sword and placed his spare hand to it, the blade ignited in a blade of flames and something else, a purple sphere danced around the blade also. Drykator knew his father would die now. Mastering the energy he still had, Drykator lunged at the beast of evil. The man's sword of flame came down. The clash of metal on metal, Durroc gazed up at the sword of Drykator Epsonstar holding back the blade of flame, his eyes turned to his son and smiled.

"Drykator, you can defeat him." A wave of hope rippled through the old hero up at his successor, *Drykator Epsonstar member of Divine Victory and fighter for the king.*

"Let's dance, scum!" Drykator said, an eerie calm and an evil glint in his eye. The two warriors' blades rose and the dance began.

"Go on, my... boy you can win... you can... stop... the evil that... dwells in this man," Durroc whispered exhaustion setting in as he panted.

Drykator's eyes held on the sword, the flames heating his face and singing his clothes as the blade came too close to him, he blocked and dodged, weaving in and out of the strikes.

"You can't defeat me, boy!" The man spat as another blow crashed down on Drykator's shield, the force pushing Drykator to the ground, held on one knee he swiped for a hit at the man's leg, he weaved out as Drykator rolled back to his feet.

Drykator knew exhaustion would consume him soon. He was now struggling to hold himself up, his legs couldn't hold him up much longer. *It's now or never.* Drykator knew he needed to use all his energy for this final attempt and either kill or flee.

He held himself poised waiting for the opening as the onslaught of swipes started again. He saw him swipe and dodged correctly and saw it, the man's left chest exposed for a quick jab. He knew now was the time. He jabbed the sword forward, he hit flesh and the blade went in but not enough to kill him. *No! That was just a scratch! Nowhere near deep enough to do any sort of damage.* Fury racked at Drykator.

"Why don't you just die!" he roared striking up his final assault as anger took him.

He pushed the black clad man back further and further with every swipe getting closer to striking flesh.

"Die. Die. Just die!" he roared defiantly, the man dropped the sword and clapped his hands. Once again Drykator flew back, balancing himself. As he landed he fell to his knee and held himself on his fingers. Watching the man ignite his hand once more "You've had your fun now it's time for you to die the both of you!" The black dressed man screeched. A fireball ripped towards Drykator.

Everything seemed to slow, the fireball gracefully drifted

towards him, he turned his head but he couldn't move it fast enough, *what's happening why can't I move? Why is everything so slow?* he thought.

"No!" A voice, slow and pained, echoed from the corners of his memory,

"Father?" his eyes reached his father gliding through the air in front of him. As his father reached him the light around the fireball disappeared as it enveloped his father.

Time caught up and everything was as it was, his father flew back as Drykator realised what happened, his breathing quickened, he began to pant as he watched the fire burn his father, Durroc screeched in agony.

"Father... No!" he heard his voice, it was panicked; it was scared.

Fear set in. *My father!*

He shook his head violently and roared as the body landed in front of him, as he hit the ground the flames flew out of existence leaving Durroc Epsonstar wriggling and writhing in agony. Drykator crawled over to the smoking body of his father, the sound of sizzling and the smell of charred flesh still very strong. He forgot all about the man in black slowly walking towards them, he gazed into his father's eyes. His father's charred features gazed back at him.

A cackle began to echo from the dark figure walking towards them.

"Run... my son," he choked out in barely a whisper, a trickle of blood streaked down his lips. Drykator only wanting to cry knew it wasn't the time. Feeling as if he was in a daze or some form of a nightmare Drykator forced his breathing to a normal pace.

Think of a plan, I am not dying here! Eyeing the man walking towards them he formulated a plan. *Live today, fight tomorrow.*

Grasping his sword he stood and launched at the black figure, quickly grasping Justice from his back scabbard he threw it following his sword, frantically grasping his shield he picked his father from off the ground and all but threw him on Runner's back. The mighty crack that ripped through the night caused Drykator to jump, turning towards the black clad man he watched his sword ripped into scrap metal, followed by his short sword Justice he checked his father was on Runner's back slumped over the saddle. Taking one final glance back he turned and threw his shield at the black beast ever walking forward. With a final rushed thought he leapt for Durroc's shield and pulled the mighty slab of metal onto his back.

Leaping on to Runner's back he jerked the reins and fled the clearing.

The man smashed the shield with another blast, he spotted Drykator on Runner, he fired endlessly towards them.

"You aren't escaping me! I am the betrayer reborn!" the man roared, the colours flying out of his hands and fingers, yellows, pinks, purples, blacks and whites.

Drykator weaved and jumped through the trees. "To Cetni, boy," Drykator whispered to Runner.

Runner forced himself faster through the trees and bushes until they were lost in the blackness.

The man in black who called himself the betrayer reborn stepped into the centre of the clearing observing the patch of blood where Durroc fell, and chuckled.

"Durroc Epsonstar terminated," glancing down at the sword protruding upright in the loose soil at a slight tilt with the Epsonstar crest woven into the grip and the pommel.

The betrayer ignited his palm once more and fired at the sword, the sound of melting metal sizzled and bubbled until the sword was no more than a patch of metal on the ground.

He turned, wrapping the cloak around him, and turned into the forest.

EIGHTEEN

Revenge

Drago's eyes shot open as he heard the young barmaid he had slept with that night begin to snore.

Brilliant, now's the time to leg it! he forced back a chuckle.

Slipping out of the bed he tiptoed towards his things, sliding silently into his gear, brown leather trousers, black leather boots white linen laced shirt he slipped on followed by his blue shirt over the top. Belting up he slipped his pouch belt on silently, threw his knife belts in his rucksack and belted on his long dagger. Finally grabbing his lute there was a bang at the door. Drago wheeled around.

Shit! Not now!

"Hey, Lavender, you in there? It's your husband, Joe!"

Drago's eyes grew wide

Oh shit, shit, shit! Drago stared at the window as Lavender shot upright in bed her eyes instantly landing on Drago in mid stride for the window.

"Where are you going?" she asked, clearly not phased by her husband's raucous bangs at the door.

"You... husband... you... I... hmm... you... what?" Drago whispered, his eyes flashing between her and the door then at the window then at her and back to the door. He bit his fist in panic.

"It doesn't matter, me and him are finished, and he's nothing to me any more. You're my strong handsome sexy future hunk," Lavender replied shooting him an enticing grin.

Drago's eyes grew wider as he heard the sound of a child outside.

"Mummy? It's Suzie, can we come in please… Mummy, are you awake?"

Pointing to the door Drago gave an exasperated scoff of horror, his eyebrow raised and right side of his lip too.

Lavender shrugged. Gesturing frantically with his hands Drago forced himself to whisper.

"What's the matter with you, woman! You're, like, eighteen? Wife and mother?" he continued to whisper his arms creating many peculiar shapes.

A mighty bang at the door sent Drago eying the window again. Taking a step closer to the window he gestured forms of politeness, which looked like a form of I'm off.

He smiled widely in attempts to distract her as he walked another two steps, opened the window, fanned himself as if he was hot, threw his rucksack and lute on his back and jumped out of the window. Landing with a clatter from the second story he picked himself up and began running down the street towards the Trade District and towards the front gates of Cetni.

By the bloody Divine, Cetni women are crazy! he thought as he slowed to a walk. Cetni was peaceful at night, the only people out at this time were the guardsmen, which was understandable really, it must have been around two Drago thought. Turning into the main street from the Cetni gates he realised to his surprise guards running towards the front gate.

Drago began running with them.

"Open the gates, open the gates!" the guards yelled back and forth.

"Hey, what's the commotion?" Drago called up to a guard placed up on top of the wall.

"It's Epsonstar! One of them is injured," the guard called back down to him, whilst assisting two other guards placed on the wall gates with a large turn wheel which opened the large iron gates to the city.

A large clank, clank, clank as the doors slowly creaked open for Drykator and Durroc.

Dismounting Runner, Drykator pulled his father off the panting horse with him and held him, slinging his dying father's arm around his shoulder. Holding Durroc's chest he dragged the both of them into the city, Drago watched Drykator struggle with the largely built man hanging limp by his side. Drykator stumbled over the path. The guards watched him struggle instead of reacting and helping, which shocked Drago.

They must be in shock to lose someone so dear to this capital.

Drykator fell to the ground with his father creating a soft thud like a pile of cloth landing on a concrete floor. Drykator searched the small group gathered around them.

"Help! Can't you see he's dying! Help me with him?" Drykator's pained shouts sounded exhausted and agonized. His eyes were watery and red, no longer the calm and focused Drykator Drago knew from the first time he saw him the morning before by the stables. This was the face of a terrified child losing his father.

Drykator's eyes fell upon Drago.

"Drago, help me. Please! I need your help, my father is dying."

Drago ran over to him, dropping to his knees as he reached Drykator and the body of his father.

"He's... he's still breathing... but... he won't last long! I don't know what to do."

The guards gasped in horror as their eyes fell upon the charred face of Durroc Epsonstar.

"Who could have done this to him?" a guard whispered.

The captain of the guard stepped past them, barging the guards aside the man's hulking body plated in shining silver Cetni armour from head to toe, the royal blue cloak gently gliding in the breeze behind.

"Move aside, you dog hustlers," his commanding voice yelled gruff and low over the commotion beginning to get larger as the people of Cetni were venturing out to find the cause of the noise.

Drago turned to the giant, the man's black hair was thinning on top, a prominent eye patch on his left eye the scar traveling from his forehead down under his eye patch and continuing down his cheek and stopping at his top lip, his lips puckered into a half grimace and sorrow.

"Renwein!" Drykator called to the captain of the guard. "It's my father! He's dying!"

Renwein's expression grew pained with remorse, shaking his head and muttering to himself.

"Get him to the king quickly," he said quietly. Turning to the crowd he pointed to seven guards. "Set up a perimeter around this case, no word gets out till we know more, any questions, don't answer reply with any story, that's an order!"

The guards saluted and marched themselves into place.

"What about the dragon case on the other side of Cetni?" a short guard asked, Drago shot a glance at him.

Woops! he thought.

"Make it an attraction or an exhibit or something until we have this one wrapped up!" Renwein replied absently waving the young guard away.

Before Renwein, Drago and Drykator could pick up the great hero a soft croaking came from Durroc.

"Son." His breathing was laboured. Drykator brought his head down to him.

"What is it father?" Drykator replied, forcing his voice to remain steady. Holding back the lump growing in his throat he absently wiped a tear appearing from the edge of his eye.

Durroc looked up at his son, pride and admiration filled the hero with great joy. He smiled widely up at his son.

"Look at you, you're all grown up I—" the pain cut him off and he winced, Drykator grabbed his father's hand.

"You're not dying! Father you... you're stronger than that and you know it," Drykator tried to convince his father.

Durroc slowly shook his head and brought his other hand to Drykator's cheek.

"No son, even you know, I'm not surviving this..." the pain caused him to stop again.

Drykator opened his mouth to protest but Durroc waved him off. "I go... to you're mother's side, I... you have grown up so strong, you will bring great honour to our family Drykator Epsonstar. I love you, my son."

"I love you father!"

Gesturing with two fingers to come closer, Drykator lowered his ear to his father's mouth. His voice barely a whisper he took his final breath.

"To... start Divine Victory you... need the boy I was searching for, find him Drykator as my final request."

"I shall, Father, I promise," Drykator whispered, his father gripped his hand tightly and Drykator held his.

Durroc's body convulsed violently. "Find Druenn Lightblaser."

Durroc Epsonstar's body became limp and his eyes stared into the night sky.

Drykator lowered his head as the tears came. *I will not whimper!* He refused to whimper, tears for his father were enough. His father's grip fell and his hands fell to the ground. Drykator placed a hand on the body of his father, his voice low and a whisper.

"Be at peace father, Durroc Epsonstar of Divine Victory.

The great King Gondolas with his large fur robes wrapped around him ran into the courtyard, after hearing the news about his fallen hero. He gazed towards the distance as they came over the top of the stairs leading into the palace courtyard the faces of Renwein, and Drykator, a well-dressed lord maybe and three guards carried the body of the great Durroc Epsonstar on a stretcher placed on their shoulders.

"By the divine, no!" a croaked voice broke out of the king.

Reaching the procession he gazed down the stairs to the city, a large gathering with candles and torches lit to honour the death of the hero.

King Gondolas placed a hand on Drykator's shoulder.

"I am so sorry for your loss, my boy, what happened?"

"We were attacked by a man in black, that's all I know," Drykator replied absently, his eyes fixed on the palace ahead.

"Follow me," the king said remorse filling his voice.

Reaching out for a torch hanging on the stone wall either side of the pathway leading from the stairs to the palace gates, he called down to the people he gestured with his hand for them to join them.

"Come, my friends, let us pay our respects to this loyal hero of Cetni."

Gondolas lead the procession through the palace and out in the gardens out the back. At the far end of the gardens a large stone white building with intricate designs sat carved into the cliff behind the palace.

The old king with the assistance of five guards opened the two large stone doors and slowly descended into what Drago guessed must have been a crypt.

"This is the tomb of the members of Divine Victory," the king explained to the group. The people stopped at the crypt doors, the guards holding them back.

Drago looked back up the stairwell listening to the guards voices echoing down the small chamber.

"Stay back no one else is allowed past this point."

Drago realised he had been very lucky to have met Drykator by that simple chance. He watched Drykator to the side of him, his eyes fixed on the ground, determined and focused. Drago knew if someone was crying whether they showed it or not and although Drykator refused to let his sorrow surface he could see it.

Drago opened his mouth to say some words of comfort, and then closed again.

What words of comfort could I have for him? He's just lost his dad. I mean how would I feel if I lost my... father?

His thoughts wandered to memories of his father. A loud voice booming down at him, Drago stared up into his father's eyes the hulking man stood tall and broad like an almighty statue of a warrior.

"You will learn this! We taught you and brought you up to continue the family's cause Drago, you will obey me," the man roared reaching for his belt.

"Dad, I just don't believe in the cause, what you're doing is evil! Do you really want to kill all those people? What have they done to deserve this?" Drago shouted back knowing he wouldn't stand a chance.

Drago remembered that belt cracking his arm that day leaving the mark that never healed. He remembered that burning pain. He looked down at his arm.

His mind reeled back to his escape of the city. Stealthily weaving through tables and chairs leading to a long hall, a maid cleaning some clothes in the kitchen. Escaping the room he reached a window, leaping from the fourth story he scaled his way down the wall, using two knives to dig into the brick and slow his fall.

Finally reaching the dragon stable he saddled his green and brown coloured scaled dragon, he took off weaving and diving in and out of arrows. A screech rippled through the night sky as he eyed a large pole protruding from his dragon's back, he plummeted into the ground below and blackness brought Drago back from his daydream. Nearing the end of the staircase they came out onto a semi circle ledge that stood openly on the side of a cliff. Ten pillars followed the semi circle around and in between them the night sky could be seen and the calm dark blue sea below, the low moon shimmering on the waves.

Drago realised on each pillar he could see carvings, on the inner side a statue of members of Divine Victory.

Amikari on the far left next to her was Anguish then Shreftwood followed by Krona and in the Acthorian, by his side Leiran next to her was Henrietta, next to her was Epsonstar then Gravland and finally was Saviour, also Drago knew her to be known as Red Saviour. Many theories on the true identity of Saviour went around, some believed her second name must have been in fact Saviour, and others say she may have been Lightblaser, which annoyed Drago.

Lightblaser is such a fantastic second name for being part of a second using group.

The group placed the body of Durroc upon a stone rectangular slab that stood as high as Drago's waist in the centre of the semi circle. The three guards began collecting wood and twigs from a stone that looked like a coffin in the far left corner, placing them around the body. The guards took torches up and placed them on each Divine Victory member that had died. Only Warren and Shreftwood's statue remained dark.

"Let us begin the ceremony," the old king said, pain and sorrow clear in his voice.

Gondolas reached for a spare torch Renwein held out to him.

Raising the torch high he began. "We commend this body back to the realm of the Divine, may he return with honour and dignity. We leave behind a true hero, but more than that, a friend, a husband, a father." Drykator lowered his head forcing the tears back, Drago stood halfway in the doorway, a feeling of unwelcome here.

Not that anyone gave him any hints that he shouldn't but it was by chance he had been given this honour and he had no friends or connections with anyone that was there.

"Although the body will burn and disappear, his memory will last a lifetime, an age," Gondolas continued lowering the torch to the firewood, the crackling of burning branches began, the members of the procession that were wearing helmets or hats removed them in respect.

"This loyal valiant hero will become legend as have his friends, brothers and sisters in arms, rest in peace our fallen hero"

The crowd continued to repeat the last line all bowing their heads.

"Our fallen hero, be at peace."

Drykator's body shook violently. Gripping his hands tightly together he forced himself to watch the body of his father burn into memory. Tears streaming down his cheek he watched. *Be at peace father; watch over mother I can look after myself I'm... alone.*

His throat caught and he almost gagged.

The procession began to slowly leave, men showing encouragement by raising a friendly hand to each other's shoulder. As they passed Drykator standing erect, his arms folded, they placed a hand on his shoulder repeating.

"I'm sorry for your loss," followed by an absent nod from Drykator. Gondolas stepped forward placing his hand upon Drykator's shoulder. Drykator's lips trembled, another tear streaked down his face.

"Im sorry my son, I wish there was more I could have done to help, I wish you great luck on your quest to reform Divine Victory, I have full faith in you, you will do your father proud."

Drykator stole a glance at the old king, his blue eyes hazy just like his; this was a great loss to both of them.

Drykator nodded forcing his voice steady. "Thank you, my lord," his voice croaked uncontrollable.

The king turned and made for the stairway.

The sun began to shine brightly over the sacred ledge of Divine Victory.

Drykator sat on the cold stone floor gazing up at the stone table where his father once was, now only ash. Drago remained still in the stairway entrance. He slowly crept to Drykator's side, he heard a sniff from Drykator and stared forward out over the water whilst Drykator pulled himself off the ground.

"What's your next plan?" Drago asked calmly. He turned and eyed Drykator staring out over the water, an unsettled focused glint in his eye.

"First I'm going to find Druenn Lightblaser, then I'm going to find and kill the man in black." Stealing one last look at the black ash and dust upon the stone table he turned and walked towards the stairway. "You're coming with me, Drago," he said, leaving nothing for choice or compromise.

"I am?" Drago replied, shrugging to himself he turned and made for the stairs. "Why not, sounds like a laugh."

The two disappeared into the dark stairwell.

NINETEEN

The Final Morning

"You have done well, Druenn, very well," the Dean's voice croaked as he returned to his place behind the desk after making two cups of tea and pushing one towards Druenn, the small white cup floated through the air over to Druenn's outstretched hand.

Druenn gripped the cup and stood in front of the Dean's desk. The Dean glimpsed a smirk in the corner of his mouth.

Well, he deserves to be pleased with himself. He passed flawlessly.

"You've passed all the exams with flying colours," Druenn nodded, the smirk leaving his face now.

The Dean reached for a notebook in the top left corner of his desk; it looked like a diary to Druenn. The Dean placed the book flat down in his palms; the book began to float up towards Druenn along with a quill beside it. The book stopped in mid air less than a foot away from Druenn.

"Sign the book Druenn, these is your graduation papers from Reinhold"

Druenn's heart began to race. *I'm finished, after all this time, I'm done. I can finally leave and find Meredith… if she is somehow still alive.*

He signed his name in a flowing italic style.

"Now," the Dean started, "you are able to leave the school grounds and carry out contracts. Just to ensure you understand the formality of a contract, they are jobs for people outside of Reinhold that need assistance, they pay us in which we pay you to do them for us, they can range from working fields to cooking dinners or even sent on a quest for bandits," the Dean's voice became more stressed on the last job.

Searching for bandits? I wouldn't mind that, Druenn thought.

Druenn knew he was coming to the end of his time at Reinhold, which left him more time to think about what his plans were for after Reinhold. *I have to find Meredith.*

"Do you understand that Druenn?" the Dean finished. That brought Druenn wheeling back to the present. He shook his thoughts violently away and his eyes fell on the Dean once again.

"Sorry what was that?" he asked, confused.

The Dean let out a soft sigh. "I knew you weren't listening." He grinned and chortled to himself.

"I guess you're thinking about what's next for you, aren't you, Druenn?"

He nodded.

"Well, you're welcome to stay for the bed and food for as long as you need till you get yourself on your feet, now off you go and don't forget to be out in the fighting ring, that's where the graduation party shall be taking place," the Dean replied as he ran his fingers through his long white beard.

"Thank you, sir. I'm truly grateful." Druenn bowed and turned for the door.

After the door clicked shut the Dean turned to the window

behind him. Letting out an exasperated sigh, he took a final sip of tea then stretched his right hand out, the morning's paper gently glided over to his outstretched hand, catching it he read the title: *The Cetni Courier*. The headline read: 'An Unfortunate Turn of Events, Epsonstar's Death'.

The Dean read the article and shook his head.

"Why do I have a feeling that I know who's done this," he aid quietly to himself.

"The enemy is on the move."

The morning sun shone over the training grounds, the sun slowly making its assent into the blue sky. Druenn stepped out from his dorm room wearing the clothes of a graduate. Now he had completed his training he was free to wear what he liked and no longer bound by Reinhold rules. He checked himself in a window as he passed.

"Much better," he said quietly to himself, a smile growing on his face.

He had chosen to go with the black training boots that reached mid way up his shin, brown leather training trousers, a white laced linen shirt and an olive green tunic and a long olive green cloak spanning Druenn's entire body.

He strode into the courtyard and breathed in the morning air. The sky was shining a beautiful array of colours starting with bright pinks nearest the low sun, then slowly changing into orange which slowly turned into the perfect blue sky, the beautiful array of colours left a tint of pink in the green grass below Druenn's feet.

Heading towards the training grounds he scanned the area for rising students who had awoken up early for morning practice. His eyes fell upon a young girl as he stared off to his left, Reinhold's lake stood no more than ten paces away. He watched the young girl stood on a rock which stuck out of the water in the centre of the lake, her back was to him, her long blonde flowing hair whisked around her in the cool morning breeze, and two very distinctive blue ribbons.

"Shiele?" Druenn said quietly, confused. "She's up early."

His sharp eyes keyed in on her. His face became incredulous, his eyes widening as the truth became clear.

There isn't a rock in the centre of that lake, I've spent years looking out over that lake and I've never seen a rock sticking out of the water.

He watched her slowly dancing as water sprayed out of the lake like fountains dancing with her.

She's floating on the water. How? Druenn thought, still watching her.

Shiele gracefully danced in a circle until she was facing Druenn, her eyes tightly clamped shut, and he could see she was concentrating very hard on what she was doing.

Druenn shifted his weight onto his left foot; a twig snapped under his foot, Sheile's eyes shot open. She spotted Druenn instantly, her eyes turned into a picture of horror. Before Druenn was aware of what had happened she was screaming in terror as her body fell into the lake, the splash echoing round the open space, the ducks quacked and flapped wildly to be airborn.

Druenn stood watching the ripples. *Did I just dream that?* he thought squinting and blinking his eyes. The ripples slowly made their way over to him.

A light from beneath the surface began to glow before Shiele broke the surface in front of him. Her soaking hair and clothes dripped onto the fresh grass.

"Druenn! What are you doing here?" she squeaked, suppressing her anger to ensure no one overheard the two of them.

"Well I could ask you the same question," Druenn fired back. "What was that? Magic?"

Shiele nodded. "Yes, now would you please keep quiet!" she spat back speaking hurriedly as to shut Druenn up faster.

"I found out I am a mage about five weeks ago when my powers were really kicking in, the Dean told me to keep it quiet so please do the same, the only person who knows apart from the teachers is Rick, he saw me finishing up a lesson I had with the Dean, so please… please just keep it to yourself!" she replied her voice wavering with worry.

"But…that was magic, your magic, that's… that's incredible Shiele" The grin on Druenn's face grew wider wonder filling his eyes. "I'll keep it to myself it was just a shock as you can imagine."

Shiele nodded and mouthed the words 'thank you'. She closed her eyes once again, she raised her arms up, flows of air began to fly around her, Druenn backed up several paces as he watched in awe, and Shiele's training garb began to dry.

Her hair also began to dry her ribbons flying to-and-fro like a tornado. A few minutes later and she was dry, her eyes opened again and her gentle eyes fell on Druenn.

"I'm leaving Reinhold today, I am being moved to the Mages University in Cetni."

Incredulity returned to Druenn. "No! Seriously? Why?" he all but squawked back.

The young girl threw her index finger over his lips. "Shh, be quiet! I don't want anyone to know, all right?"

Druenn nodded and drew himself away from her finger.

She brushed herself down from the dried pondweed that was stuck to her now dry clothes.

"I'm being moved to the Mages University because the Dean

feels it will be wiser and safer for me to train with them. He also said something about they can discover my full potential being there in the right place, so I'm leaving in about ten minutes, a cart is on its way, I want to be gone before everyone gets up, that way there aren't any awkward goodbyes," Shiele explained.

For some reason this upset Druenn, not just a little bit, but a lot.

Why does it bother me that she's leaving? We were never really friends at all.

He began reminiscing. Shiele had joined Reinhold two years after Druenn and like Druenn she was ten when she joined. Shiele was only fourteen now but she didn't seem it, she had always been on the wavelength of the older students, she fitted in happily with the eighteen-year-olds talking in the common room than playing outside with the younger students. Druenn remembered a time when she had two students in her year picking on her. Druenn hated kids picking on other kids, backing the two bullies up against the wall, Emily and Rick watched from across the hall as he spoke to the two of them, he remembered Shiele watching him carefully. To him it looked as though she was unsure why he was showing her kindness.

After the bullies ran away promising never to harm her again he stared back at Shiele. She stared back at him, eyes of stone. Druenn blinked in shock and before he could open his mouth she was gone. There were many encounters very similar.

"Eh… Druenn?" Shiele asked suspiciously, her eyebrow curling up as she eyed Druenn's blank expression.

"Hey, come on, don't sulk on me. I don't really want to go either," she said as to comfort him.

Druenn reeled back from the distant memories, shaking his head he glanced back at Shiele.

"I'm sorry," he whispered

"What? What for?" Shiele went on. She took a step closer and looked deep into his eyes, their noses an inch apart. Druenn hated when she did this, her looking deep into other people's eyes as if she could read words off their eyes. She did that a lot and found herself being pushed back many a time because she'd break through the other person's personal bubble, a lot of people didn't like her for it.

Druenn didn't understand why people didn't like it, for a fourteen-year-old she had beautiful eyes.

Druenn gazed down at the ground and shuffled his feet before taking a long breath. "I'm sorry, I didn't get to know you better, I feel…" He paused, more thoughts rushing back. "I wish we had time to become better friends."

Shiele looked taken aback, she smiled at Druenn, running a strand of loose hair back behind her ear.

"Druenn, it was an honour to meet you, I will be back, you'll come and see me though right? You graduate from Rienhold today, your time here has ended, and you can go wherever you want. You haven't seen the last of me, Mr Lightblaser," she teased, as she let out a soft giggle.

Her giggle was sweet but still nothing in comparison to Emily's.

A whistle from behind her sent the two wheeling towards the south building directly behind Druenn.

The Dean, Warren and another teacher Druenn didn't recognise stood outside a gate which led round the side of Reinhold and out towards Cetni. This entrance was only used by traders selling their goods to the chefs and new or repaired swords, the list was endless when Druenn thought about the amount of goods he saw come through that gate whilst training.

The Dean was waving Shiele over.

With a final look back at Druenn her face became mournful.

"Goodbye, Druenn." She wrapped her arms around him for a final hug.

"Take care of yourself," she whispered.

"I will," Druenn replied. Then as if she wasn't in his arms at all she was gone gliding towards the three men.

Druenn stood fixed to the ground watching her leave.

As Shiele ran up to the Dean she gazed back at Druenn, he stood exactly where he was before, the rising sun created an eerie silhouette of his shadow on the green grass in front of him. He looked alone.

Doesn't matter anyway, Shiele thought. *He's a top celebrity in this place not to mention his two bodyguards Rick and Emily.*

The Dean's voice brought her back from her thoughts.

"Shiele," the Dean's soft voice radiated an aura of calm through the little girl.

A woman stepped from the cart, her purple robe covering her entire body, her hand poked out of one sleeve and her staff which she used as a walking stick stood taller than her. The staff was a simple design from what Shiele could make out; it was completely silver, with two blue orbs at either end of it.

The Dean took a breath then continued as he stretched his arm to his left. "This will be your new teacher."

The woman stepped forward alongside Warren; she brushed her hand across Warren's shoulder as she gracefully nodded at him. He nodded back, placing his hands behind him.

The woman turned to the young girl. She began to speak in her high tenor though her voice was raspy and hoarse. "Hello, young Shiele Massery, my name is Sadia O'Skreeva. Are you ready to go?"

Shiele's heart began to race. She wrapped her blue ribbons tightly around her arms, holding back a tear welling in her eyes she took a final glance back at Druenn and Reinhold.

"Goodbye, everyone," she whispered, then in a single motion glided towards the cart.

Druenn watched Shiele turn back for no more than a second then turned back for the cart.

"Goodbye, Shiele Massery, take care," Druenn whispered, his eyes now keyed in on the woman, he thought he heard the name Sadia and that familiar raspy voice, something echoed back from his past. He recognised the face.

But from where?

She turned to bow to the Dean, Warren and the teacher he didn't know. They bowed back and then it hit him, like a building crashing down on him, the voices from a past he had spent many a year trying to forget came back like a torrent.

His memory could hear the woman speaking again with a hoarse, raspy voice. Memories of Pinevale coated in ash and flame danced around Druenn as a woman gazed down at a young frightened girl.

"I hear them coming back, they will be here to take the survivors." Her eyes fell upon the little girl. The little girl realised she was being watched and took three steps back.

"It's okay, little girl, we are here to save you both," her calm voice sang.

It's her! Druenn knew who she was. *The one who took that little girl.* Fixating on the woman he went to take a step forward only to discover he couldn't move, he was frozen in place. Forcing his feet to move he searched around for the cause, shock setting in his eyes fell on Warren. Warren stared back at him with eyes of stone.

"Let her go, Druenn," Druenn heard in his head, it was Warren's voice but his lips did not move. The voice came again sounding as if Warren was right next to him.

"This is her path, do not intervene let her go in peace."

He knew he stood no chance against Warren's magic, gritting his teeth he submitted and watched the last events of Shiele Massery at Reinhold unfold.

Shiele looked up at the cart. The chestnut-coloured cart stood tall about twice the size of Miss O'Skreeva, the purple canvas pulled over the top flapped gently with the cool morning breeze, two large bulking horses pulled on their reins and bucked their heads. With a quiet gesture from Miss O'Skreeva the two horses stopped and stood patiently waiting quietly for the two of them to board.

Shiele hopped up into the back of the cart. The small space was shadowed by the canvas above her, which made a gentle rustle as ripples danced along the canvas roof.

Shiele's eyes fell upon a girl; her cloak covered her. The robe she wore was a similar purple to O'Skreeva's, it covered her entire body from head to toe.

"Emm, hi!" Shiele said as she suppressed a nervous stammer, she shivered openly.

The girl looked up at her.

Shiele was stunned into silence only letting a small gasp escape her lips. *She's… she's beautiful*, Shiele thought, a wave of affection and jealousy stabbed at her as she stared into the girls bright green eyes.

"Oh, hello," a radiant high soprano voice danced out of her

"You must be Shiele, it is a pleasure to meet you," the girl continued.

Shiele's awestruck face managed a small abrupt curtsy as she fought with urges to weep. She began to hyperventilate as the cart jolted forward. Shiele toppled over onto a small wooden box.

"Oh dear, you okay?" the girl giggled as she reached over to grab Shiele's trembling hand.

Shiele gasped for air. *Why am I feeling this way, I'm so confused; do I want to cry? Am I angry?*

Another small giggle escaped the girl's lips as she lowered her cloak hood; her brown flowing hair fell down just passed her shoulders.

"You're okay, young one. Don't fear how you feel, you're stressed from leaving your home, that's all."

Shiele sniffed ferociously, forcing back the tears. She dabbed at her cheeks

"Shh, it's okay, eahmaa," the girl whispered whilst stroking her hand.

A cool wave seemed to seep into her as her shoulders relaxed; she took a deep breath and the air tasted sweet, her heart slowed and she began to gather herself.

"What did you do?" she asked.

"I cast a relaxant spell, just to take the edge off, now you will be able to calmly work all your feelings out." The girl's smile was dazzling, her white teeth glistened in the opening of the cart.

"My name is Nathuni Albright," she said, her calm sweet voice resonating safety and peace throughout Shiele's body, she felt her muscles relax.

After a long breath she turned to the open back. Dust clouds danced in the bright space as the wheels kicked up the loose dry dirt leaving a dusty haze on the view behind them but she could make out a dirt road, trees either side of her and Rienhold disappearing behind the hills.

Warren slowly walked towards Druenn, his hands still behind his back.

"How are you feeling, Druenn?" Warren asked the young man, as he stood frozen in place.

"A little confused really, War. Why did she have to leave?" Druenn replied, confusion painting his face.

"Well, Dru," Warren started, a smirk tracing round his mouth as he used Druenn's hated nickname as Druenn had his, "she has magical abilities that we can't unlock here, she needs to be in an environment where she can study with people who share her abilities."

Rolling his eyes with irritation after the name Dru he shook it aside and replied again. "But you know magic, so does the Dean, why aren't you both training her?"

"Well, lets just say... to keep it simple." He paused again, struggling for a way to word his statement. "She harnesses abilities beyond me and the Dean."

Druenn's eyes shot to Warren's, searching for a hint of some kind of stupid joke but his stare was only met with a blank silent expression which said to Druenn, Yes a lot stronger.

Druenn's eyes went back to the gate as the last of the dust settled again.

"Druenn? Druenn?" a familiar sweet high soprano voice echoed from behind him.

With a tut Warren patted Druenn on the shoulder and began to walk away. "I must get going before your team gets here."

Druenn turned and Warren was gone, looking across the training grounds his eyes locked with who the voice belonged. His one sided grin grew and he ran towards her. Her beautiful smile shot right back and she ran towards him.

Reaching one another he picked her off her feet and held her tightly swinging her around then finally dropping her back to her feet. Her loving giggle rippled out of her as she pulled her hair back behind her ear.

"Someone is happy to see me," she said, catching her breath.

"What's going on?" a strangled voice sounded in the vast expanse of blackness. The blackness was everywhere, like a smoke cloud seeping in from every angle.

"Someone, please help me!" The voice came again. It sounded like a boy's voice, raspy and pained but a boy's voice.

"It's my voice, I'm talking!"

The blackness continued.

The boy quickly realised this voice didn't echo, it was hollow, as if he was in a closed space, like a solid dungeon with no light, no sound.

"A dead room!" the boy shouted, the voice carrying nowhere.

A stab of pain hit his chest. The boy coiled over screaming as the pain gripped at his heart and lungs, as if they were being crushed by a tight grip, as fast as it was it disappeared.

The boy was left with a hollow scream as he breathed trying to catch his breath before another agonising clench began.

Shake off the pain.

He threw his eyes open again, his eyes darting left and right, searching for anything that wasn't black smoke. The smell of smoke slowly began to seep into his lungs. He coughed and gagged as he tried to find air.

Dazed and confused the boy let out a roar. All that came was a weak croak. "Who is doing this? Please release me!"

A voice called back, it was a low booming in the distance. "Not until you fulfill your task."

The boy had no recollection of a task.

The stab came again, like a thousand blades cutting at his chest, heart and lungs. He felt a warm liquid trickling down his chest.

"It's a dream, this has to be a dream," he groaned.

As the warm liquid began to pour down his chest he began to panic and his mind raced.

Blood, I can't breath, where am I? Dead room? It's a myth isn't it? Is this real? Stop the pain! Please stop, stop, stop. Stop the pain! Now! Blood Blood Blood!

"Please leave me alone!" he screamed.

The voice came again. "Not until you fulfill your task."

"What is the task? Tell me the task I will do as you say! Anything just stop the pain, let me out please, I beg of you give me the task! I shall fulfill I shall commit, I will do whatever you say!"

The face of an unpleasant disfigured creature, a ghoul, a face that looked to be melting away, the smell of charred and rotting flesh filled his nostrils, pale and green with red painted his face, an eye socket remained black with the other glazed over, he stared into the dead eyes as he realised what he stared at, a live corpse speaking to him with a mouth full of black teeth, it grinned as he spoke a disembodied terrifying cry.

"Kill Druenn Lightblaser!"

It lunged at him grasping for him, the boy backed away into the blackness as the creature lunged again. He screamed in terror as bursts of madness laughter left his body. He screamed, cried, roared, laughed and collapsed with a mighty jolt.

Rupert jolted upright on a table in a candle lit room.

Bookshelves and a hard cold floor, he knew this place very well, a fireplace in the corner. The large closed windows behind him running the width of the room, drapes pulled over as to stop the pure light from pouring in. The feeling to the air, he knew this place.

This is Terribor's room.

He wrapped his arms around himself and rocked back and forth, shaking off the shivering in the cold dense room. He tucked his head into his legs then stopped; pulling his hands away he felt the warm liquid on them and his chest.

Blood trickled down him.

His eyes welled with emotion as the fear gripped him and he cried out gripping his hands on his head.

"It was a dream! It was a dream! It was a dream."

Peering down at the torn tissues he searched for anything to patch the wound. Looking to the drapes he rolled himself off the desk and gripped the linen sheets.

In a desperate rush to stop the bleeding he ripped a strip of cloth from his grey shirt he could wrap around himself. The tear made an eerie echo in the silent spaces of the room.

Quickly wrapping the cloth round him he pulled it tightly and stifled a painful cry. Now heading for the door he dragged himself across the room, his body feeling drained and heavy with the loss of blood. Reaching the door he grasped the handle and turned, the door didn't move, breathing became harder as he realised what he most feared.

I'm locked in this nightmare! his mind screamed. *Find a way out quickly!*

Struggling to catch his breath with fear he rested a moment gripping the door, he began banging on the door.

"Someone help, please! I can't get out, someone!" His voice

was hollow and raspy, no one would be able to hear him.

Gripping his chest from another stab of pain he fell to his knees and began dragging his tired and weary body back across the room to the window.

I'll break that window if I have to. Pulling himself back onto his feet using the desk as support, he grasped the chair in front of it and slowly pulled it round to the window.

Grabbing his breath again he closed his eyes and took a few deep breaths, he felt another stab of pain.

"Ignore it," he panted, opening his eyes everything was a blur, he knew he didn't have much time before he would become unconscious. Knowing that the window was directly in front of him he grasped the chair and with the last of his strength he hauled it off the floor and launched the chair towards the window. Falling back Rupert watched the chair reach the glass then stop. He rubbed his blurry eyes and looked again, the chair still hovered in mid air before hitting the floor with a clonk, the sound of planks of wood hitting the floor. Turning back to the door, a blurry figure caped in black with his arm outstretched stepped into the room and closed it quickly behind him.

"What… who are you?" Rupert croaked as he tried pulling himself to his feet.

"Just think that you want to kill Druenn and the pain will be gone."

Rupert fought with the pain and watched the figure slowly pacing towards him. With a sudden jerk he was suspended in mid air, two rough hands held a strong grasp on his shoulders. Rupert attempted to thrash out of the man's grip but his body was too weak.

The voice came again. "Kill Druenn Lightblaser!"

TWENTY

Graduation

As the sun turned into evening and the colours of orange, yellow, and pink began to coat the sky like a blanket, music began to break out over the training grounds of Rienhold. The thick canvas tents overhead flapped in the cool breeze as people began flocking under them, tables ornately carved with young trainees battling one another.

Food on silver platters steaming and the aromas filled them. Hog roast, fruits, chicken, all beautifully decorated. The students flocked to the tables filling their stomachs. Conversation, laughter and dancing broke out and the party was in full swing.

The small groups that were graduating were pushed towards a podium on a stage at the far end of the furthest tent. Druenn, Emily, Rick wore the graduation cloaks covered in colours, navy blues, greys and burgundies striped and criss-crossed them.

Another boy and girl Druenn recognised by the podium, Precious, Emily's old friend, he didn't know why but they stopped talking to each other a few months before, girls baffled him.

I swear they are all crazy, one minute they want your help the next they scream at you and all but bite your head off for trying to help them, mental the lot of them.

Stealing a glance at Emily he continued the little discussion with himself.

Including her, what she sees in me God only knows.

He turned back to the other familiar face, he was a very attractive man with perfect features; he hadn't seen him much, he looked about seventeen, eighteen, but his name shot back.

"Kif… Kif Real right?" Druenn asked turning fully to him. Kif turned to Druenn, a smile appeared on his face.

"I am, and you're the famous descendant Druenn Lightblaser."

Instantly Druenn, Emily and Rick prepared for yet another DV fight, Druenn instinctively met the remark with his fight talk.

"And what's it to you?" he shot back snidely. Kif met his gaze, Druenn felt himself for the first time feel as if the stare Kif gave him had him cowering.

"I'm a big DV supporter and with good reason."

Druenn's expression changed to confusion. "Really? That's a new reply, most people are always looking for a fight, it gets annoying after a while."

Kif watched him for a moment as if contemplating whether to say something or not.

"Well that's why it's best to keep your identity to yourself." Then Kif gestured if to say like me.

"What are you trying to say Kif?" intrigue filling Druenn.

Has he got something to do with Divine Victory?

Druenn hadn't realised the old literacy teacher Mrs Sconetile calling names then the cheer of the audience as they collected their parchments and weapon of choice, the hand crafted sword, mace, axe, spear or bow and quiver. Druenn didn't need to think twice as to what weapon he wanted.

Taking a quick glance back at Kif before he made his way up onto the stage, Kif grabbed his shoulder and pulled him close.

"Meet me behind the tents after the ceremony.

Druenn silently nodded an unexpected race of adrenaline boiled up from the deeps.

What could he want to tell me?

With that Kif turned and walked onto the stage.

Druenn didn't hear the audience, not even Mrs Sconetile, he must have drowned it out in deep thought. He just watched the boy accept his parchment, shake her hand, turn and wave to the on looking students and exit off the opposite side of the stage.

"And last but not least I am proud to present to you all, Druenn Lightblaser!" Mrs Stonetile's arm flew out towards him and gestured him to join her on the podium. Druenn's feet subconsciously carried him onto the stage as the crowd roared explosively. He didn't see the audience but he did see Mrs Sconetile jump out of her skin when the crowd roared.

"Well done, my boy! Very well done," she said to him as she shook his hand and passed the parchment to him.

His mind still was focused on Kif until he held the parchment in his hand.

I've finished. I can go back to Pinevale and find my sister; I'm leaving tomorrow, without fail.

He stole a glance at Emily and his friends, Rick and the twins, in the crowd, Alex clapping ferociously with a large grin on his face, his broadsword mounted on his back. Obviously done a contract and returned for their graduation.

Guilt racked at Druenn's heart. *I don't want to leave without saying goodbye but it's the only way to get out of here without being guilt ridden into staying, I'm sorry my friends.* "Bastard!" a voice called from the crowd, an agonized cry. The crowd fell silent as the students searched where the yell came from.

"You Bastard!" it called again.

The students began to fan a path for the boy towards the stage, Druenn recognised him instantly.

Rupert.

Drenched in sweat, his sword in his hand, his eyes blood shot and blackened.

"You little shit, waltzing in here like some kind of celebrity, you DV scum!" Rupert spat.

Druenn drew his sword. "Have you come to finish some kind of unfinished buisness Rupert? You should have done this when I was ten, this is just suicide now. You have been brain washed by Terribor Strife!"

The crowd gasped in horror as the consequences of mentioning any ties with Terribor being evil and he would be expelled for abuse to a head teacher.

"No!" Druenn barked to the crowd. "I'm not afraid to say it and neither should any of you!" He pointed to the on looking students with mixed emotions on their faces.

"Shut your mouth, scum!" Rupert spat again. Druenn's teeth clenched, as the anger filled him igniting that strength deep within him. The Overdrive ability, enhancing his sense or awareness, accuracy and speed, that familiar feeling of feeling like a branch, placed under pressure and it will crack. *Pull yourself together, if I lose myself I could kill him and whether I hate him or not, I'm not a killer.*

Rick Diaz watched the crowd part in front of him as Rupert staggered past. Leaning over to Emily he whispered quietly into her ear.

"Look at Rupert." They both watched the boy staggering forward with one hand holding his sword the other tightly clenching his chest.

"He's not in control of his body, is he?" Emily replied in realisation.

Rick shook his head. "I detect foul play," Rick said, his voice drone looking on at Rupert then at Druenn on the podium. Rick listened to the raging Rupert growl uncontrollably.

"This place went downhill from the day you started here. Druenn leapt off the podium into the crowd. Emily and Rick ran to Druenn's side, even Kif and Alex.

"Back off, guys, this time it's just me and him."

They backed off.

"You're a damn fool, Druenn," Rupert croaked as he clutched his chest for a moment, then reached for his short sword in his other hand.

Druenn had reached his limit with Rupert; he needed to be taught a lesson, ever since that day six years ago at the lunch table, simply because of his second name, Rupert was willing to deem him as an enemy without a second thought.

"I'll finish you off like Thalandiul did with your mother, like the way your father was brutally strewn across Pinevale's streets.

Druenn heard a crack within his brain. Fury flooded through his body like a river bursting its banks. The sword that was in Druenn's hand was now clenched tightly causing it to shake with the strain.

"Shut your mouth!" Druenn roared, beginning to pace back and forth in front of Rupert like a caged lion awaiting his meal.

Rupert began to whisper mockingly. "I heard they both squealed like innocent children before meeting their impending death."

Druenn felt his body jolt violently, like a volcano about to erupt.

"You shut your mouth, Rupert!"

"Your parents' existence was pathetic," Rupert said taunting Druenn with an evil smile on his face.

The familiar crack within Druenn's brain shocked him again this time rippling through his body, everything slowed down as his mind became aware of everything, the teachers whispering, "We should break this fight up, Mr Lowpart."

The students also whispering amongst one another, "This will be like a clash of legends," and, "You better get back this will be a dangerous battle to get caught up in if we are too close."

Druenn's eyes began to glow a honey golden colour as he reached boiling point. He was in the state of mind known as the Overdrive, his stamina accelerated, his strength hardened. If someone was to throw a stone at him right now from a few feet away Druenn could dodge it simply by feeling and hearing the movement patterns in the air around him. He launched himself towards Rupert.

Rupert's eyes began to glow red as he launched himself towards the son of a DV member.

The teachers squawked and screamed, the students crowded round tightly, breaking out with renditions of "Fight, fight, fight!" and "Druenn, you can kick his ass, beat him down like fresh cut grass!"

Druenn thought about how much this boy had made living at Reinhold difficult over the years, the thoughts only intensified his hatred for Rupert.

I'm sick of him talking about my parents, my friends and me like we are dirt on the street; he's had this coming for a long time.

Blades met and an almighty crash of steel broke the steady sound of the students and the teachers trying to call the boys to stop the fight.

The battle between DV and COG had begun.

In the Dean's office, Warren scanned through the shelves of books looking for any book relating to COG members and leaders.

The Dean sat behind his desk sipping a freshly made batch of tea.

"Tea, Warren? This has to be one of my favourite brews," the Dean said, with a smile on his face and an eager tone to his voice.

"No thanks, maybe later, just looking for this book," Warren replied, clearly not phased by the question, his eyes between book to book as he steadily made his way around each shelf then climbing up a few steps on the ladder then if he had no luck progressing to the next one up.

The Dean shrugged and sipped his tea again letting out a small moan of satisfaction. Turning to the window behind him, he looked out over the grounds, looking to his right he could just make out the edge of the tents for the party. He smiled again, a large weight upon his shoulders felt like it was lifting.

Druenn has finally completed his time here. At least he'll be safe from Terribor.

The Dean's thoughts were interrupted as Warren called out in relief. "A-ha! I found it!" sliding back down the ladder he walked round the shelves and back towards the Dean's desk the book in his hands, the Dean studied the book. It was a hardback with a black and brown leather bound cover. Scanning through the pages. He flicked through them faster; stopping on a page he dumped the heavy hardback book on the desk with a thud. He bent over the table and pointed to a name.

The Dean studied the title:

Leaders of the Mystique Knights

Tharlandrial Rauhavoc	Grand Master
Tomarezz Hinkstith	*Leading Master*
Shorezz Tarrengar	*Sen Master*
Terribor Strife	*Battle Master*
Aroneth Grenth	*Duties Master*

Warren tapped at the name ferociously.

"He can't be trusted!" he pushed. The Dean turned to the book, and pulled it towards him for a closer inspection.

"Hmm…" the Dean started. "I agree we need to be careful but he hasn't harmed the students"

"He attacked Druenn the day he arrived, master. Remember? Right here in your office." The Dean pulled himself to his feet so he, like Warren, could look over the book.

"And also if this isn't enough." Warren quickly strode round the table to the Dean's top drawer in which he knew he kept all his latest newspapers. Opening the drawer he picked up the top paper looking instantly at the headline: 'An Unfortunate Turn of Events, Epsonstar's Death.' "Drykator Epsonstar, as you know, is the son of Durroc Epsonstar."

The Dean stroked his beard as he slowly nodded.

He claimed to see a man capped in black attack them.

"I don't mean to sound like I'm grasping at straws here, but I get the horrible feeling that's where Terribor went when he had his week off from work." Warren's voice was becoming more worried by the second, as if a serial killer had just been let loose in the school.

"Warren, I already believe he did it," the Dean replied,

remaining calm.

"Then, master, you must see…" Warren began pacing, walking back and forth.

"You must see that if he is going to attack it's going to be tonight. It's the last night he will have this chance; because of the festivities we will be weaker, less people looking."

The Dean's eyes widened with realization. *He could kill Druenn, tonight!*

"We need to stop him before he reaches him.

A guttural scream of agony ripped through the windows of the Dean's office. They both turned in unison towards the direction of the training grounds.

"Shit! Druenn!" Warren screamed. Warren darted out of the office and flew down the corridor. The Dean turned to the door then back to the window. Closing his eyes he reached for his cane propped up against the desk, grasping it he tapped the ground once, the smoke enveloped him. When he reemerged he was under the tents with the roaring students and the screaming teachers.

"Silence!" the Dean bellowed.

Silence instantly fell around the tents apart from one voice.

"I hate you!" the voice screeched like fingernails scraping down a chalkboard. A guttural choke. "I'll kill you! I will kill you!"

The Dean began pushing through the crowd of students looking on in horror. Reaching the centre of the group of people he stopped in his tracks.

By the divine! What happened?

TWENTY-ONE

The Time for Strife Is Now

Terribor listened to the commotion outside as he walked casually inside, heading for his office.

The wheels are in motion, steady as the commotion, begins to reek havoc on this seething notion, you people will perish and the heroes will fall, my turn as the master begins tomorrow at dawn, he sang to himself.

Reaching his office he walked over to his desk, the floorboards creaked under him. As he walked round to his chair he caressed the wood. *So many hours have gone by, so many years patiently waiting.* He sat down, holding himself upright grinning. Pulling his second drawer open he took out a piece of paper, reaching for his ink pot and quill he began writing his letter. *Grum GoG, it will be your turn to take the centre stage soon.*

After he had finished a small white pigeon, its eyes as black as night, flew in through the small open window in the corner of the room.

"To Ogor-Dab." He held the folded piece of paper above his head. The pigeon swooped down; plucking it out of his hand it flew back up and out the window.

He sneered at the closed door in front of him. Chuckling to himself he clicked his fingers creating electric sparks. He ran over his talents and making shapes with his fingers and hands.

"It's time."

The crowd opened just enough for the Dean flanked by Warren to walk to the front. The sight they saw took them by surprise. The wriggling boy on the floor screamed in agony, his face pale and his eyes bloodshot, sweat streaking marks down his face.

Druenn stood over the squirming Rupert his sword above his head ready to strike.

"I don't want to hurt you, Rupert. Don't force me to do this." Druenn's face was contorted with conflict.

His body was fighting back the Overdrive ability that was seething and coursing through his blood. His eyes sparked a crimson gold as he forced his anger down to stop himself from killing Rupert. Warren realised the conflict and instantly ran to his side, he placed himself behind Druenn and whispered into his left ear.

"You know you don't want to hurt him, it's not within your nature Druenn Lightblaser, you protect, you don't harm." Warren's voice was soothing but it did little to quell the bubbling sensation within him. Like a tidal wave crashing on an open bank, his anger swelled and grew searching for new thoughts to feed on. His attention fell from Rupert and a swell of anguish and betrayal swooped over and engulfed him, the thoughts of Warren screaming at him. His mind shot back.

"I said out!" Warren's voice roared at Druenn.

He turned to face Warren his sword lowered but his grip no softer.

"You! What right do you have to block me from my mother's old past!" he shot at him, taking two steps forward to be almost in Warren's face.

"Wh… What?" Warren stammered, his left eye flickering momentarily like a twitch. This came literally from out of the blue.

"You and my mother were a couple weren't you! You show too much emotion.

Warren's eyes blazed into his. Druenn heard a familiar voice inside his head.

Not here, Druenn. I shall tell you just shut up and calm down!

Druenn stepped back in shock from Warren's gaze,

"Breathe, Druenn. You can control this now."

Druenn began running the calming techniques that the Dean had shown him.

Emily and Rick broke through the crowd to Druenn's side.

Druenn had his eyes closed as he felt waves of relief crashing over him like water dowsing flames within him. He began thinking about things more rationally now.

Why did Rupert start a fight with me in the middle of our graduation?

He knew something was different about him, as if he wasn't in control of himself.

He opened his eyes and Warren was gone, turning he saw Rupert writhing whilst clutching his chest. Druenn had begun hating him since the incident on his first day, but even now watching this boy he felt pity for him.

This wasn't Rupert. *Or at least he's not in control.*

"It's not Rupert." Druenn spoke calmly now.

Warren nodded absently. Warren and another teacher, Mr Stone, were trying to lift him to carry him away but the boy wriggled and writhed and screamed.

"Something is definitely wrong," the Dean said quietly to Mr Stone.

"We'll get him to your office," Mr Stone replied.

The Dean's face contorted in fear then it was gone, he turned and faced the onlooking teachers and students. A large smile beamed on his old withered face.

"I thought this was a celebration!" the crowd roared and music began, the party continued with laughing shouting, singing and chanting.

Emily bounced on Druenn's back peering over his left shoulder. "Hey you," she said happily but with the hint of worry.

Druenn turned his gaze to her. "Hey you." He smiled a half hearted smile.

"You okay?" she continued.

Druenn nodded absent-minded.

Rick joined them both, passing Druenn his graduation weapon of choice, the bow and quiver with thirty steel arrows.

"What happened, Dru?" Rick asked.

"I really don't know, Rickarus," Druenn replied, now watching the Dean quickly making his way back towards the school. The Dean glanced back quickly his eyes finding Druenn's.

The Dean shook his head in disappointment turned and walked inside.

Druenn's heart dropped after seeing that.

What did I do? He attacked me, why would the Dean be angry with me?

"Come on, let's have some fun. Let's just put this behind us," Emily said, throwing her arms around both the boys as she led them towards the tables of food.

"Psst!" Druenn spun towards the sound of the noise, he saw Kif instantly just heading into the shadows outside the tents.

"Just a moment, you start without me. I won't be long," Druenn quickly explained as he darted in the direction of Kif. In the events that had just passed he forgot entirely about Kif Real meeting him behind the tents.

"But, Druenn, where are you going?" Emily asked. She was beginning to feel she was slowly being pushed out of Druenn's life ever since he learnt about his mother and Divine Victory.

And ever since that bloody Overdrive ability took him away from me too.

She pouted and turned to the food again leaning on Rick for comfort.

Kif watched the tent flap open for a moment letting a beam of light escape before a shadow appeared and met him outside then the beam of light was gone.

"What's wrong Kif?" Druenn started obviously wanting to get straight to the point.

Kif began biting his thumbnail as he swapped his weight between feet.

"I just wanted to ask you a favour really," he started; Druenn's feelings about this meeting were shrouded in mystery.

Kif looked Druenn in the eyes. "I am not Kif Real. My name is Reaflik Overa, I am Krona and Henrietta Overa's son, which means I am a descendant of Divine Victory."

It took a moment for it to sink in. Another descendant!

Druenn couldn't help but smile, a feeling of belonging came over him instantly.

"Wow, how have you kept it secret for so long?" Druenn asked, excitement in his voice.

Kif… Reaflik shrugged. "Just keep it to yourself then I don't get the divide that you had to endure."

He stared at Druenn a moment, with excitement in his eyes.

"I know you intend to leave tomorrow, I see the ambition in your eyes. I want to know if I can join you, I will follow for your reasons but mine are to find other descendants of Divine Victory, I know they exist" Druenn looked puzzled yet relieved also.

"I could do with the company, I wish to find my sister, she was…" An unexpected lump caught in Druenn's throat as he thought of his beautiful sister.

"She was taken… by bandits… when I was ten, chances are slim but…"

"You have to try, she's your sister, I understand completely," Reaflik replied.

Druenn wanted to change the subject off his sister before he'd start blubbering, the feelings were still to strong for Druenn to cope with. He thought of Reaflik's offer for wanting to join him.

"You say there are more descendants?"

Reaflik nodded. "In fact one was in the news only yesterday, did you know that Durroc Epsonstar was one of the only survivors from the original group? He was killed… murdered, leaving Drykator his son who is eighteen, so a little bit older than me and you but he seems to be staying in Cetni so that is where we need to go."

Reaflik was talking so fast with the excitement. *I would have never dreamed of beginning this quest, which could lead to beginning Divine Victory again*, he thought.

They began discussing their plans for leaving in the morning.

Emily listened quietly from the other side of the canvas. *Kif? A descendant? And Druenn is leaving with him? But we were going to join the arena together? He… lied to me?*

Tears welled in her eyes. She wiped them away ferociously, her heart throbbing. She felt lost. Her entire world had been turned upside down. The one person who would never hurt her had just ripped her heart out. The sound of joy and celebration roared around the tent, people eating with friends, drinking, girls and boys dancing in time with the music. Rick had just broke off dancing with a young blonde and began to finish his second few drops from his tankard of mead when he noticed Emily over by the edge of the tent, her shoulders jittering. His sense of celebration quickly evaporated.

"Emily? What's wrong?"

Emily saw Rick and broke down in floods of tears. Rick grabbed her and pulled her close.

"Druenn…" She tried to get the sentence out. "Druenn… lied… to us… both."

TWENTY-TWO

All Good Things Come to an End

In the Dean's dimly lit office were he and Warren – who was stood in the shadows, his arms folded staring at the boy on the desk.

Rupert writhed in pain screaming.

"I... must... I must kill him!"

Warren began pacing. "What do we do master?" his voice rattled, fear was creeping in now, fear for Rupert's life, for his own, even everyone in Rienhold.

"This is Terribor, isn't it?" he said, certain of his assumption.

The Dean raised his hand from the boy's forehead and looked at Warren, defeat written over his face, the boy still writhing in agony. "That's not Rupert in there," the Dean replied, sighing as he stepped back.

"And, yes, I would say this is one of Terribor's cantations"

"What can you do for Rupert, he's in pain," Warren replied pointing to the boy.

The Dean looked back for a moment then turned unable to look at the corpse on the desk still kicking in agony.

"I can't save him." A croak came out of the Dean, a tear welling in his eye.

"What?" Warren said incredulous.

Warren had been under the teaching of the Dean for over fifteen years, and not once had he come across a spell the Dean couldn't do.

"The venom runs too deep within him… he is lost."

"What now then?"

The Dean walked over to the far side of the room, reaching the far left he walked up against the wall, tracing his hand across the wooden wall paneling he cast a spell.

Warren watched his arms still folded. A bright lighted circle about the same size as the Dean began to glow. Warren blinked and shielded his eyes. When the Dean came into view again he held a long staff that spanned higher than him. Warren watched on in awe.

"We will need this for the job we have to do," the Dean's voice defiant with the task at hand.

"Is that the…" Warren started.

"Yes, Warren, the most dangerous staff in existence."

"The Harlequin Staff," Warren murmured. Warren had heard of this staff but only in legend.

This staff was supposedly able to create a continent used in the correct hands from nothing. And also what had created the swirling vortex off the coast of Ethalas, the maelstrom they called the curse after the last battle with the Meealduan staff, its brother. The staff was intricately designed with branches and leaves carved the length of the pole and at the tips of the staff the braches flaked out into a small blue pulsing box shape, which twisted into a triangle pyramid.

"We must kill Terribor before he begins another Mystique Knight cult." The Dean lowered his head in sorrow.

My plan to make him see the light has failed. He is pure evil.

He looked over at the writhing boy screaming again.

Warren stared at the Dean and gestured to Rupert. "We can't leave him like this, that's cruel."

The Dean flashed a beam of light from his fingers towards Rupert, instantly the boy went limp. Warren looked at Rupert and then back at the Dean confused.

"He's asleep, Warren, we must go now before he kills more of our students," the Dean croaked hurriedly.

Gripping the Harlequin staff to him he stepped out of his office towards Terribor's office. Warren at his side, he began flicking his fingers in different positions and gestures. The Dean knew he was readying his spells and cantations.

Warren felt a growing fear in his stomach.

Something isn't right, does he know this is coming? Focus Warren! Master will need your full potential he is old and won't have the strength to do this alone. I should have been able to finish this six years ago.

They reached Terribor's office and stopped.

"This is it, Warren. Be ready," the Dean said, his voice wavering with the same growing fear, Warren presumed. Clearing his throat he reached for the door knob, turned and threw the door open in a single motion.

Terribor stood from his desk and stuck his arm forward just as the Dean did, they both shouted in unison: "Bellostkrasees!"

The three men were launched into a spiral vortex of colour spinning and swirling round. Warren searched for signs of Terribor or the Dean trying desperately to find either one of them, purple smoke with green, black, orange, blue, turquoise, pink, grey. So many colours spun round them until he felt solid rock underneath him. As the colour dissipated he saw the Dean to his right just like he was before and Terribor a few feet in front staring at them. He had a staff of black smoke in his hands, Warren knew it was Thalandiul's staff.

"The Meealduan staff!" Warren called to the Dean

The Dean nodded, this staff was supposed to be the rival to the Harlequin staff, in dwarven he knew that Meealduan meant judgment and death.

Warren looked around him, the Dean said he was going to teleport them all to a safe location where they can do this battle away from the students but this was not where the Dean had planned. For a start the sky was purple and pulsating, the wind was unnaturally strong, a storm raged above them, the trees were twisted and broken, nothing grew on them, the brown trunks had a purple tint to them, the grass was grey. This place didn't look like Tharlian at all.

"Where are we?"

"We are between dimensions Warren, it would seem Terribor had the exact same plan as us, we have been teleported to a location where these two places exist in the same time and space, and it won't last long, see that?" he nodded to a black and white stream of lightning circling overhead.

"It would seem the fabric of time is ripping this world apart already," not once did the Dean take his eyes off Terribor who was striding back and forth proudly.

"So you knew all along it was me? Why waste your time on making me see differently you stupid old man!" Terribor sneered as Warren took a step forward. Anger was getting the better of Warren he clenched his fist. The Dean took his shoulder and shook his head.

"Together only." Warren resisted and took his present pose.

"You will pay for your crimes Terribor Strife third leader of The Mystique Knights cult," the Dean called out to him over the increasing wind.

Terribor's hand ignited in a ball of flames.

"You aren't leaving here alive either of you, I have already won!" he seethed.

The ball of flame hurtled towards the Dean. Warren blocked the flame with a barrier of wind, the flame was extinguished immediately.

The two figures instantly were locked in heavy combat, both striking different poses shouting different spells. Their hands ignitied in bursts of flames. Water streaked from Warren's fingers to douse the flames, wind blasts as they gushed over the flames. Lightning shot from the sky. Warren ducked and weaved through the blasts, judging the strikes quickly and calculating the next. Weaving through, he drew his sword igniting the blade with a thousand colours.

"Prenoxtar!" Warren roared and the colours blasted shards of glass with each strike against Terribor's flames.

The Dean watched Warren's graceful technique but he knew Terribor was toying with him. Taking a step closer he raised Harlequin high above his head and roared with a voice Warren and Terribor had never heard. The Staff launched the Dean into the air. Terribor copied and launched himself up with Meealduan.

Warren looked up feeling helpless.

Terribor watched the Dean, who began to spin the staff around him, sparks of lightning, earth, wind, water began to circle and pulsate like a flame losing control.

Terribor hovered high above the ground gripping the staff tightly. He launched himself forward, lightning crashes all around the two men.

The Dean swung the staff toward Terribor, a strong wind whirled until a tornado formed and encircled the pair, the two staffs began swinging in different directions as the staff's true potential began.

Warren gripped hold of the ground as a giant earthquake rippled under him. He held on to a clump of solid rock as earth began spiraling upward, the Dean fired rocks and boulders toward Terribor, they smashed against Terribor's shield of wind as though the Dean was throwing grass.

Terribor swung his staff forward and his left hand as well. A beam of blue ice streaked out toward the Dean and flames from his hand, the Dean forced the staff forward to hold back the two opposing forces. There was a shattering sound and the Dean fell from the sky. Warren by this point had pulled himself from the rubble of earth strewn across the ground and had spotted the falling Dean.

Master!

He threw his hand forward and caught the Dean by summoning winds to keep him in the air. The Dean hit the ground with a soft crash.

Terribor floated to the ground.

"No more games time to end you both," Terribor roared, a smile growing on his face. The Dean slowly pulled himself up off the floor.

"Crantomass!" Terribor bellowed.

His arms flung out towards the recovering Dean and a beam of dark purple and blue shot from both hands.

Warren fired a dark purple ball of flame. This ball was something he had never tried: The Force of Gravity. He forced the ball forward; it felt like he was throwing a rock half the size of him. He roared as he strained to throw it.

The dark ball hurtled towards the blazing beams of magic with tremendous speed. An almighty bright light exploded and forced everyone into the air.

Warren opened his eyes and searched for his master, the trees and grass were flattened, dead.

Terribor pulled himself up quickly. His eyes found Warren and he began spinning his arms and thrusting his arms forward, he bared his teeth and his black eyes wide. Fire and lightning began shooting from his hands again as Warren began blocking the oncoming blasts with shields of wind and water.

Reaching for his sword he had dropped he ran towards Terribor.

"Terribor!" he cried defiantly. "You will not kill my son!"

Terribor's eyes went wide in shock.

His sword flew out and he blocked Warren's. A momentary silence fell across the shattered landscape all that could be heard was the panting from Warren.

Warren's face was inches away from Terribor's as they both blocked swords.

"He's your son?" Terribor asked quietly, realisation just hitting him.

Then an evil menacing smile crept across his face, his smile looking abnormally long. "I'm going to enjoy this."

A burst of raw energy forced Warren back onto the floor. Terribor stepped over him his sword raised as Warren tried to back away.

Terribor's sword fell, but then stopped. He looked down the line and saw the Harlequin staff, looked up and saw the Dean, exhausted.

"Your... fight... is... with me," the Dean panted.

Warren backed off and pulled himself up.

The Dean turned to Warren. "Go, run. Get the students to

safety, I'll hold him in this realm."

A portal began to open behind Warren. He stared at the Dean incredulously.

"You can't do this alone!"

A shard of the purple sky fell and shattered on the ground nearby.

"The realm is breaking apart, Warren, just go!" the exhausted Dean's voice croaked.

The wind intensified and Warren's robes began flapping violently like a flag in a hurricane.

The Dean turned to Terribor and began conjuring another spell.

A flash flood of rain poured from the skies and his hand erupted in a torrent of raging water. Terribor parted the crashing waves that hurtled towards him.

The Dean knew he wasn't going home. Then something unexpected happened. A flash of colour appeared as Warren flew past him, using the wind to soar through the air.

"No, Warren!" he screeched his voice barely audible over the wind and rain.

"Leave now!"

Warren couldn't hear him. He had ignited a power he hadn't touched in fifteen years within him. As his eyes blazed golden from the overdrive coursing through his veins, time seemed to slow the rage he fed off fuelling the fires of his overdrive ability burned furiously within his heart.

Blasts of fire blazed from Warren's fingertips. Ten multiple blasts, Terribor struggled to compose himself. Using his shields he tried to hold back the blazing inferno now beginning to scorch his shields and his clothes. As the heat increased, Terribor started searching for options.

Warren stood incredulous that his fire inferno was holding him. He let out a grin as he saw Terribor fall to the ground with the strain, his shields wavering.

"Master, we have him!"

The Dean began to smile as he prepared to conjure a spell, which would encase Terribor in iron chains. He spotted the glow radiating from Terribor too late.

The Dean called out to Warren, "Get back!"

The air began to feel thin as he felt a thickening pressure that flew towards Terribor. A bright light streaked across the sky then a blast of energy sent the Dean and Warren somersaulting through the air. They hit the ground hard. Warren struggled to get to his feet, his vision blurry.

He watched a black figure slowly walking towards him. He heard the sound of footsteps behind him. From the step… step… step… step… step… step … pattern he could tell the Dean was limping.

"We finish… this… now," the Dean struggled to say.

Warren gripped the dirt hard as he pulled himself onto his knees. The Dean stood over him now. Warren quickly tried to catch his breath. The sound of lightning building and thunder began crashing in front of him.

"It is time for you to go," the Dean said quietly, remorsefully.

Warren craned his head to see the Dean staring at Terribor. He tried to speak but no words followed.

Why couldn't I speak? What is happening? How have things come to this?

"It has been an honour training you, Warren, but now our paths must separate."

Warren was mortified. He understood what he was going to do. Stealing a glance behind him he saw a portal open up. Shaking his head he looked up at the Dean.

The Dean looked down at him with a poor attempt of a smile.

"Take care of my grandson." And with that Warren was thrown into the air by an invisible force, like gravity was sucking him towards the portal.

"No! Master!" Warren managed which was no more than a terrified screech.

He watched the Dean thrust his staff forward as did Terribor.

An almighty blast exploded. The blast creeping toward the Dean, black smoke engulfed Warren as he slipped through the portal.

The blast was unbearably strong, the Dean fought it back as much as he could but did not have the energy to repel it. The blast ripped through his flesh, flames engulfed his hand. The burning grew and he felt his arm disintegrating. As the Dean endured his last torturous moments he thought of the only people who could stop this madness.

This is it. Good luck, Druenn.

His right arm flew out to protect him and the burning began again as the blast evaporated his arm. A cool feeling rippled through his chest, then an agonising explosion ignited within him like nothing he had ever felt. His robe ignited in flames, he looked down at his naked body, watching his clothes burn away, leaving his red flesh to blister and peel as the skin boiled then blackness engulfed him.

Terribor watched the beam of flames explode in front of him. The Dean erupted into ashes.

A thousand black flakes floated from the sky as Terribor watched the world crack and crumble above him. He smiled, looking down at the small pile of ash on the ground.

TWENTY-THREE

The Truth

Warren Anguish scrambled through the dormitories searching for Druenn. His robes were torn and blackened, sweat beading down his forehead pouring down his face.

Running past students smiling and laughing, heading back to their rooms after the party, he saw a couple of girls heading up to bed.

"Girls, have you seen Druenn?"

"No, sorry, not since that fight earlier."

He ran on asking anyone he could find. The one time he needs to find him no one has seen him.

Heading down to the training grounds where the party had taken place he searched, his eyes looking for any signs of him.

Come on, damn it! Show yourself!

Only a few people were left, tidying the areas and musicians packing the instruments away. He ran back to the dorm rooms.

Druenn left Reaflik's dorm room to head back to his own. Everything was different now, he wasn't alone, by one shocking moment he now felt excited and compelled to go with Reaflik to Cetni to find Drykator and protect the king.

I can do that, he thought to himself, an excited one-sided smile unable to be moved off his face.

Divine Victory and follow in my mother's footsteps.

Unexpectedly he heard his father's dying wishes.

"I can't do this on my own, I need you to guide me father!" Thomas stretched his other hand out to him as if to drop something into Druenn's hand. His mind reeled back six years.

I was only ten; I had no knowledge on how to protect them all.

He remembered his father saying those words that had led him to this one moment in time. "Remember me and fulfill your mother's legacy."

Now he was doing just that. *My mother died protecting the king and she has become a hero of legend, I shall keep her spirit and her legend alive. I am The Saviour Reborn.*

Warren ran down the corridor, he spotted Druenn and launched himself at him.

Druenn smiled. "Warren, I'm sorry about earlier, I still need to learn how to control it. I'm getting there."

"We have to leave now!" Warren said hurriedly.

"What... what happened?"

Warren grabbed Druenn by the shoulder and tugged him down the corridor with him.

"You are in mortal danger we need to leave this place at once".

Druenn pulled and tugged on Warren's tight grip. "No, wait. Tell me what is wrong?" Druenn was beginning to feel worried.

"Is it about Rupert? I have no idea what has happened to him. All I know is it's not him any more, he isn't himself."

Warren was now getting agitated with Druenn's constant talking. "Shut up...just shut up and come with me."

Druenn pulled hard and broke free from Warren's grasp. "No Warren, you tell me what's going on. I'm getting sick of you talking in riddles and saying I'll tell you later and when you're old enough. I want to know!"

Warren began to panic his eyes darting in different directions.

He'll be here soon.

He calmly replied in hushed tones, "Druenn, if there is a moment in your life when you had to trust me now is the t—"

"You told me that before! Warren, I now want a straight answer." Druenn began raising his voice the more irritated he became.

Warren gritted his teeth and watched a student's head poke around a doorway then, after realising it was Warren and Druenn, disappeared out of sight again.

He was fuming, Druenn always had to challenge him on everything.

"Now isn't the time for your little moments, Druenn!" he snapped.

"He killed him, Warren," Druenn said, scratching his forehead.

"Oh, by the Divine, he is dead," Warren said, shock freezing his body to the spot.

Druenn watched him anxiously. "What do you mean? Who?"

Warren felt a sudden surge of terror hit him like a horse and carriage, gripping Druenn's shirt he pulled him along the corridor.

"We must leave this place at once, I'll explain on the way as soon as we are out of these gates."

Once again Druenn pulled on Warren. "No, I am not your puppet any more, Warren. I have graduated, you can't control me any longer!"

Warren double backed and walked up to Druenn until his face was inches from Druenn's.

"Is that how you see it, I was controlling you? That I was

somehow manipulating you?"

"What I am saying Warren is that was exactly what you were doing!"

Warren felt a stab of pain in his chest. *The ungrateful brat! How can he think I was controlling him?*

Warren bared his teeth again as he grabbed Druenn's wrist and tugged again. "You're coming with me," he seethed.

Druenn pulled but couldn't break free, he swayed his arm to and fro whilst grunting words as he swung. Finally he broke free with a mighty swing, his hand hit the wall behind him, a shot of pain ricocheted through his arm as a click rippled down the echoic hall.

"No! You can't tell me what to do. You're not my father!"

"That's just it – I am your father!" Warren erupted, the echo carrying the length of the tight corridor.

Now all the heads of the students poked out from their rooms down the long expanse.

Druenn was numb as he blankly stared at Warren. Warren slumped his head in defeat as if a weight had been taken off his shoulder and a heavier one had replaced it.

"My… fath…" Druenn shook his head absently, his eyes unable to focus, his thoughts unable to process.

"Yes, that is why I showed emotion in the lesson… towards your mother," he breathed slowly and carefully.

"I was in love with your mother, Druenn."

Druenn scrutinized the floor. He felt that the puzzle he had been piecing together for six years had just been smashed beyond repair.

Nothing makes sense. How could he *be my father? Thomas was my father, the man that died in Pinevale.*

He cupped his hand to his ear as sounds and visions of the past blasted into his thoughts. His thoughts gazed over holding his father dying in his arms.

No… That man dying in my arms.

All those years with *a stranger? Who was he?*

"Follow your mother's legacy," he heard Thomas say.

"My little Druenn," more words spewed out. Thoughts of Warren collecting him, the training, the arrow fired, the bullseye, the arrow fired the sound of gurgling and choking as the bandit chocked and spluttered on his own blood.

Blood made because of me, he thought. Reason seemed pointless. This was a mighty deception. *Who actually am I?* His head began to ache.

Warren's voice began to echo from the edges of his thoughts. His heart raced now, his breathing quickened, his vision blurred.

"Druenn, we still need to go." Warren reached out his hand.

Druenn looked at the hand, the blackened hand with a cloth wrapped around the palm was shaking. He recoiled from it backing himself up. His face began to turn to distress; he looked like he was going to cry. His voice was weak with emotion. "Druenn, please, don't do this, not to me, you know me, nothing has to change I promise." He choked on the last word, tears beginning to fall as he watched his own son backing up slowly against the wall terrified of him.

Druenn's whimper only fueled his agonising pain.

"Why…" Druenn dabbed at his tears, only wanting to run but he was numb, he felt dead inside. "Why…" his voice croaked.

Warren took a step forward. Druenn jumped and backed up a further three spaces. Warren searched for an answer. "You were going through so much I knew it would destroy you… I…"

Druenn's dismay brought on a stab of anger. "Six years you

had," Druenn forced out a guttural growl.

"I know… I tried. I really did." He took another step and Druenn turned and ran, he didn't care where or why he was running, he didn't understand anything at all so he ran.

Warren fell to his knees as his son disappeared round the corner at the end of the corridor, his footsteps fading into silence.

Warren gripped his chest. He felt sick.

Druenn dashed down another corridor, his vision blurred from the tears, a sick-churning feeling stopped him in his tracks. He began to vomit. Falling to the ground he crouched and spluttered, an upwelling feeling he hadn't felt since his father died.

Thomas brought me up; he's my real father.

His mind wandered back to his father, the blooded fork mark on his body. Druenn vomited again as an agonising scream ripped through his chest and out his mouth.

The students around Reinhold heard an almighty screech, the sound someone would make if being slowly tortured.

Druenn teetered on his knees as his vision began to darken. An overwhelming blackness encased the boy. He fell and he felt nothing, thoughts, feelings, and memories faded. *Peace? No, too much.*

Warren pulled himself off the stone floor and punched the air in front of him, a portal opened.

"I'm sorry, Druenn… I'm sorry for everything," he sobbed, and stumbled into the portal.

Terribor Strife burst around the corner and saw Warren enter a portal and instantly the portal shimmered out of existence.

He cursed his misfortune.

At least Reinhold is mine.

TWENTY-FOUR

The Contract

Druenn awoke slowly, the memories of last night hadn't returned to him yet. Still half asleep he searched his room, he saw the drapes to Emily's side of the room still and no sound from the other side.

In the distance a bell tolled, it was the bell for classes.

"You're finally awake, get up and get ready." The voice was familiar but, at the same time, whoever it was they didn't sound happy. He tried to process this whilst searching the direction from which the voice came, before he got a glimpse of the person he felt a thud hit him in the face, they were soft enough to be his clothes. He pulled his brown leather trousers from his face as he saw a leg disappear around the edge of the door.

Emily? he thought.

He pulled on his linen shirt as he exited his room. There was an unusual atmosphere this morning; a large crowd of students all pushed and shoved through, there was a sense of urgency about them.

"Hey, Ronin," Druenn called to a small boy with long, brown hair.

The boy turned and saw him.

"Where's everyone going?" Druenn called again.

"Everyone has been told to head for the assembly room, called the whole of Reinhold."

A bell continued to toll overhead. Confusion settled in, he followed the crowd still not fully awake. They all filed into the assembly room.

"Form lines!" Terribor's voice roared and echoed around the room.

The younger students jumped and immediately filed in to their classroom lines as they would for a fire drill.

Druenn casually took his place in line with his class, he noticed a few boys took their place in the likes of the Divine Victory class.

Druenn watched Alex, the twins Sam and Bram, Rick and Emily. Druenn searched for Reaflik to join them, he didn't. Druenn was disappointed. Reaflik watched Druenn; he gestured to join them. Druenn's smirk was unmistakable when they both decided to defy Terribor.

They both walked over to the line. By this point everyone was in line. Druenn literally must have been in with the final group.

Terribor spotted them and his expression changed to incredulity. "Where are you two going?"

"To our line," Reaflik grinned whilst pointing to the line.

"What class is that?"

"Warren's," Druenn replied.

"History of Divine Victory to be precise," Alex chimed.

Terribor knew Alex had graduated and could not fathom as to why he formed in line with these degenerates.

Swallowing hard he pulled his attention away.

They'll be dead soon anyway.

He turned to the onlooking students and the teachers around the edge of the room. Silence fell around the room.

The silence was eerie, Emily felt she was waiting for someone to drop from the gallows. She turned and spotted Druenn watching her; he smiled; she sneered and turned away.

The shock hit Druenn like a boulder. *What did I do? Oh shit!* It clicked. *She might have heard about us leaving.*

Terribor cleared his throat and began his speech. "Last night it was brought to my attention that…" He paused a moment observing the faces of the students. "The Dean of Reinhold passed away last night."

Gasps of shock rippled around the room. Druenn felt a knot catch in his throat, he couldn't breathe momentarily, and he took short breaths as he tried to process the devastating news.

"Silence!" Terribor growled, the students fell silent once more.

"Also Warren seems to have disappeared," Terribor continued.

Druenn's eyes shot up at Terribor in shock as realisation hit him like a tidal wave, last night's events came flooding back.

Warren's my father! Druenn gripped his head with both hands as if he had a bad headache.

"What's wrong, Dru?" Reaflik whispered, Emily obviously hearing Reaflik turned, her face clouded with concern, but forced herself to look back at Terribor.

Druenn realised he was still in the hall with a few people including Reaflik watching him confused on his reaction. Composing himself and acting like nothing had happened he shrugged Reaflik's comment aside.

"I'm fine," he said, forcing his feelings inside again.

Stop showing your true feelings so openly you idiot! He scorned himself whilst pinching his right leg until he could feel the searing pain. *Nothing in comparison to what I have had to endure.*

Terribor continued. "So with no other higher ranking members from this day forth I shall continue to run Reinhold."

About half the room erupted in cheers and applause, the other half stared in disbelief. One student yelled out to them, she was dark skinned and must have been a year below the graduates.

"Do you have any respect? The Dean just died for the Divine's sake!"

The other side giggled and made rude comments and gestures.

She stepped back in frustration.

"Settle down," Terribor coaxed raising his hands up and gesturing for them to be quiet.

Druenn just stared in disbelief and shook his head, too angry and frustrated to react and watched things to go from bad to worse.

The students settled and Terribor began again. "I have a contract for the entire school.

Another cheer went up

"You can earn yourselves, two thousand gold pieces, every one of you." He pointed around the room. "For this one contract."

"What do we have to do?" came a low rumbling voice echoed from the back of the hall.

Skipping straight to the point Terribor excitedly began retrieving maps from a large basket on the edge of the hall. Placing them up along the wall behind him Terribor explained what the contract was.

"We all shall march out of Reinhold together west towards the small village of Harash then turn north towards the Ruis Thillis Mountains until we reach camp Swiftrunner where we have been asked by our contractor to kill all the rogues and traitors to the kingdom there. March home and claim your two thousand gold pieces, who will join me?" Terribor encouraged.

Druenn listened to students cheer with excitement, even the students that were ten, eleven, twelve years old have been asked to go on this contract as well. Druenn knew that wasn't right.

No child that young should witness death.

His thoughts flashed upon the Dean and the last look he had given Druenn, that scornful look. He shuddered from the thought, his thoughts turned to how the Dean died.

He felt a tap on his shoulder.

"He did it didn't he," Reaflik whispered, not being a question but a statement, he knew it too. Druenn nodded absently. *He did, he's evil, and he's picking off all the good left in this world.*

A deepening hatred boiled and swelled like a river beginning to break its banks.

This battle between good and evil has been hidden from me for too long, I understand now. It's up to me to make a difference, I must protect the ones I love.

His thoughts left the Dean. If he was Warren's son, it didn't matter. Druenn's eyes gazed over his line, Alex, Sam, Bram, Rick, and Emily. It's his duty to protect them.

Reaflik tapped his shoulder again. "So what do we do? He'll know if we don't go tomorrow wont he?"

Rick kept his eyes away from Druenn and looked only at Reaflik. "We all need to leave as early as possible tomorrow so we don't get dragged into this."

Bram piped up and joined in. "Surely there won't be a pay out of two thousand gold pieces per person will there?"

Druenn shook his head.

"That sounds like a way to lure you in, we need to talk about this together elsewhere not h—" Terribor stopped talking and looked directly at Druenn. "If you lot feel so free to talk over me you can tell me all about it in my office after this assembly. Go now," he gestured to the students to leave and fixed them with a glare that could have killed, Druenn was sure.

They all looked at one another, rolling their eyes and sighing as they strolled out. As soon as they were out of the room and doors closed behind them Alex turned to the group as they walked.

"Okay, guys, go get all their weapons and be back as fast as you can, go!"

"Okay, on it!" Bram and Sam began running down a side passage to the dorms.

"I can't believe the Dean is dead." Emily walked ahead, next to Alex, flanked by Rick then Druenn with Reaflik just behind.

It was annoying Druenn Emily was being like this.

Oh, Emily, why act like this now when we need to be a unit.

His heart felt heavy, as if he felt constantly sick, an endless feeling of worry, or nerves, he couldn't be sure, all he knew was he hated that feeling and had to sort it out as fast as he could.

"Emily?" Druenn tried to say with interest but he knew it sounded weak and pathetic. She didn't even react, just carried on walking by Alex. Druenn rolled his eyes knowing why.

You're so pathetic Druenn, be a man, for the damn divine grow up and talk to her like normal, you don't know why she is mad at you anyway.

He tried again. "Hey, Em, you got to know about this."

No reaction.

Druenn gritted his teeth, and clenched his fists in frustration. Reaflik let out a stifled giggle.

Druenn turned and gestured as to say 'shut up or I'll smack you'.

He grinned again and held his hands up, obviously saying 'all right, calm down'.

Looking ahead he could see they had almost arrived at Terribor's office. His heart in his throat he made one last ditch attempt, swallowing hard, he gestured for everyone to go in.

"Go on, guys, I'll see you in there." He grabbed Emily by the arm before she could go in then closed the door in front of her.

"What's going on, Em?" Druenn asked

She folded her arms and gave him an aggravated look of disapproval. "You know what!" she fired back, licking her top lip as her eyes scanned Druenn and making him feel as if she'd pounce at any moment.

"I think I do. Just hear me out, okay, please."

"Okay. Talk," she replied bluntly.

He'd never seen Emily without amusement on her face, it was as if the life had been sucked out of her. The world was a very dull place without her.

"Okay, Kif is a—"

"Member of DV. I know, I heard."

So she did hear it, he thought.

"And you're upset because I was supposed to come with you to the arena in Cetni."

She scowled at him.

"You got it in one," she replied sarcastically.

Druenn recoiled; he hated sarcasm directed at him, it was like having an arrow stuck through him. He forced the comment aside and continued. "Listen, I want all of us to come. You can go to the arena and to be honest when we have done whatever Reaflik wants to do, which I believe is to see the King, I will join you so I will be running, like, a day later but I still want to join the Arena with you. We have planned it for so long."

Emily stared at him blankly, then she looked as if she was considering it.

"I am sorry, Emily. I never meant to hurt you." Druenn was starting to feel lost without Emily's smile. He wasn't used to this, he felt off balance and uneasy, but then again it could be the situation as well.

"I just want to see you smile again." Druenn gave a weak smile.

Emily's anger seemed to disappear ever so slightly but he knew it would take a lot more before he'd be forgiven.

Turning on her heels, he gestured for them both to join the rest of the group inside Terribor's office.

Sam and Bram sprinted back towards Terribor's office both praying they'd get back before Terribor. While the two of them juggled five swords and three bows with the quivers slung over their shoulders they burst through the door. Breathless, they quickly found the owners to the weapons.

Druenn loved his newly acquired bow from the previous day. The hickory bow's grip had been designed with finger grooves, the bow's upper and lower limbs curved back then sharply arched over on itself before the string groove making a very stretched M shape, his rounded leather quiver was designed with a pattern of silver leaves that continued the length of the quiver.

Alex turned to the group. "Okay, we have to pray this works."

The others were confused why Alex sent for their weapons.

"We need to threaten him if we stand a chance on avoiding this contract tomorrow agreed?"

The group nodded still very perplexed by this sudden plan. Emily stood with her sword in her hands awkwardly.

What makes him think we could do this? I mean… he killed the Dean and drove Warren away, she thought, feeling a rising flutter in the pit of her stomach. Something bad was going to happen.

"Emm… I don't think this is the best idea." Druenn couldn't help but agree with her. He nodded and continued. "She is right, I mean, look at the Dean…"

Alex turned towards Druenn; he smiled and walked towards him.

"Don't worry, Dru," he grinned and punched an encouraging punch on Druenn's right bicep, the sort of punch you would if to say man up.

Druenn didn't want to admit it but Alex hit him hard, right on the muscle, he flexed his arm and winced from the pain. *Bloody good going, Alex. Smack my drawing arm.*

He let out a quiet bellow of laughter, even Emily giggled. That smile he hadn't seen in a few days, he had missed that so much.

"Sorry, Dru, forgot you're still a weakling," he teased shooting a cheeky wink.

"You're our best hope, you know that, right?" he smiled and began to chuckle again.

Druenn couldn't help but giggle himself and rubbed his arm ferociously.

The sound of students flying down the hall and past the door sent the group wheeling. The assembly had obviously finished.

Alex took the front closest to the door flanked by Rick, his sword in front of him, Druenn to the left with an arrow in his hand preparing to knock, Emily behind him, and behind Rick was Reaflik either side the twins.

The sound of students faded and a slow knock, knock, knock on the floor just a few paces away from the door.

"Be ready, guys," Alex said calm evaporating from his voice and nerves entering his throat.

A quiet voice on the opposite side of the door said a word none of them had heard before. "Wedthorin."

An unusual rubbing noise squeaked and rippled overhead

working its way invisibly down towards the floor.

The door flung open and Terribor walked through, the door slammed immediately shut behind him. In an instant Reaflik, Emily and the twins flew into the air against the window Alex turned on Rick and slashed his sword, Rick's eyes grew wide in the shock. He blocked and weaved from Alex's blows, Druenn was stunned with what seemed an even battle with Terribor to now only him and Terribor. Druenn raised his arrow to Terribor as he slowly raised his sword. Druenn forced his right arm to pull the string back but he couldn't, the pain that seethed through his bicep refused to cooperate with him. His memory instantly kicked in.

Alex planned this! His mind played back the images of Alex playfully punching his arm. *He immobilized me!*

Reaflik began to run to Druenn's aid as he slowly backed up in defeat. Launching himself toward the monster he was met by another's blade. Reaflik looked over to see Alex grinning intently at him as he began slashing his new target. Rick composed himself and began running towards Terribor. The door flew open and Rick's brother appeared from round the corner in his familiar blue garb.

"Joe?" Rick said stopping in his tracks as he watched his brother slam the door shut as he raised his sword to fight his own brother.

Rick shook his head in horror.

My own brother has been corrupted by this sick twisted man! Druenn realised it was up to him as he took another step back he analyzed his situation.

Okay Rick in combat, Reaflik in combat, twins, one unconscious on the floor the other pinned to the window and so is... Emily!

He found his flame to fuel the fire to crack the overdrive.

Anger – no, hate – coursed through his veins, the familiar crack within his brain snapped and his eyes ignited the gold colour. He felt nothing but hate burning him, no pain, no feeling of weakness just revenge.

He jumped onto the desk avoiding a slash from Terribor, he knocked an arrow.

Target engaged, fire!

The arrow flew through the air and caught Terribor before he could react.

His shoulder cracked and blood flowed. He screeched, more with shock he had been hit. Without a thought he pulled it out, wincing. He turned to Druenn again, igniting a ball of flame, his sword igniting with it, he slashed again.

Druenn ducked and weaved finding his sword he threw his bow on his back and drew the sword. By this point Rick and Reaflik had been pushed back and were now protecting the other three, Joe and Alex left their targets and joined Terribor forming a wall around Druenn.

"We finish him now," Terribor said.

Alex took a step forward swinging his sword around him.

"I would gladly master, so it's Divine Victory you want to start Druenn huh? You and Reaflik want to restart that ridiculous group? Yeah we knew about your plans, why choose now to start this pathetic cause?"

Druenn let out a low growl as the hatred had reached boiling point, the point where he would be told by Warren to calm down. This was the boiling point where the hatred would eat him alive and drive him mad. Druenn didn't care, he analyzed the people in front of him. Terribor the man, who would and will try and kill the king, killed thousands of innocent people including the Dean, Durroc Epsonstar, maybe even his father, Warren, Joe, he remembered on the archery range he stormed away because of him, hated his very existence and Alex, a betrayer, a good friend for so many years and now decides to try and kill these good people behind him.

"We will never let you start Divine Victory, you die here!" Alex seethed.

Druenn gritted his teeth. "I'll destroy you, I'll just have to destroy you, all of you people who would do things like this."

He ignited in one movement he flew at Alex his blade flowing gracefully hitting flesh and blade.

"I'll eliminate you all by myself!" he roared defiant and strong.

Emily felt a chill creep down her spine, she guessed the rest did too.

Druenn's movements were impossible to follow, he met Alex's flesh over and over, Joe joined in, Druenn matched it kicking up a sword that was on the floor, slicing and weaving with both blades. He danced, a famous stance, the outnumbered mouse never surrenders. Terribor's blade also joined the dance, three blades flew around him, he met each one with incredible force and counterattack resulting in another horrible gash for Alex and Joe. Terribor pushed the two boys in front of him. The blades swung, their very existence teetered on the edge of life and death, until Druenn sliced Joe across the cheek. Joe instinctively recoiled out of combat to assess his damage, in that moment he watched on as Druenn's blade blocked Alex and the second slid through Alex's chest. Alex's eyes bulged, a second later Druenn had spun around, the sword sliding out of his chest and through his throat. The fight paused as Druenn realised what he'd done.

A guttural gurgle came from Alex as he fell to his knees clutching his throat suffocating, blood gushed from the gaping wound, he was drowning. Panic filled Alex's thoughts.

Oh no, by the Divine, no! I'm drowning, I can't breathe, please let me breathe!

Emily screamed as her eyes filled with tears for her good friend, he may have turned but he was still her friend.

Joe launched himself towards Druenn roaring at him for the loss of his friend. Druenn spotted the blade flying towards him, he spun out of the way; everything seemed to slow down. Joe buckled as he stumbled from Druenn's quick escape. Before he could recover, he felt two sharp punches through his back. He knew from that moment it was all over, he looked down at his chest and saw the two ends of Druenn's blades coated in his blood. Joe felt sick, he felt numb. He knew he shouldn't have been so foolish.

In the corners of his memory he heard a voice. An agonized screech that chilled him to the core, he knew that voice well. *Rickarus!* He knew he had failed him, he knew then he had picked the wrong side, he got sucked in, *peer pressure*, he didn't really want to be on that side, he just got sucked in and as a result he was going to die.

Rick ran to his brother, Druenn pulled the swords out, Rick held his brother, tears streaking down his face.

He wiped the blood out of Joe's face and around his lips.

"Joe… I'm so sorry!" Rick tried to manage forcing the lump in his throat down only making him sound choked and weak; he knew he didn't have long to talk to his brother.

Joe looked up at his brother, the one person he always looked up to. "I'm sorry, Rick, I shouldn't have got…"

He winced from the pain, his eyes beginning to droop. "I got carried away… you know?"

Rick nodded unable to speak, he held his brother close to him.

"You're the only family I have left, I love you!" Rick forced out before his closest friend left to join his mother and father.

Joe let a smile escape him whilst looking into his brother's watery eyes. "Don't cry for me, brother… we'll meet again soon," Rick sniffed and nodded then hugged his brother tightly. Joe arched his back and went limp as he exhaled for the last time.

Rick didn't loosen his grip. His body jerked violently. "No… Joe… No!" he sobbed.

Terribor walked over to Druenn, who was fixed to the floor, in stunned silence.

I killed two innocent people.

Druenn saw the blood over his hand and sword; he recoiled and dropped the sword to the ground. It hit the ground with a clatter.

What have I done?

"See what you do, Druenn?" Terribor whispered over his shoulder.

"You kill. You were raised for one purpose, to kill."

Druenn's breathing quickened in realisation. *I'm a born killer, I'm a monster!*

Reaflik drew his sword once more to face Terribor. "Don't you dare poison his mind!" he said defiantly.

Bram and Sam were pulling themselves up, and they picked up their bows and knocked an arrow to prepare to fire.

Emily scrambled over to Rick who was still clutching at Joe unable to comprehend his brother was killed by his best friend.

Druenn fell to his knees. His eyes began to well with regret for his murderous acts. He shivered, as he began to grip himself tightly, curling into a ball.

His memories began to flood in, his father… the man… Thomas, he didn't know any more. His sister, thoughts of how she was carried away, what could have happened to her, his mother burning. Rupert writhing in agony, the Dean dead, Warren…*father?* Missing or dead and now Alex and Joe their bodies strewn across Terribor's office room drenched in their own blood.

Because of me, all of this because of me. I'm better off dead.

He felt alone and lost like he did as his father passed away in his arms, *he is my father because he is the one who raised me.*

Reaflik began to slash wildly at Terribor. Terribor toyed with him, his fighting skills were nothing in comparison with Druenn's, not enough anger to land a blow strong enough.

He clings on to hope and willpower.

Arrows flew from the twins, Terribor danced through them like trying to shoot at a flag in a gale.

Emily held Rick for comfort, she stole a glimpse at Druenn on the floor frozen, and unable to understand why this had happened.

He needs me she thought, *my anger with him can wait, he needs me.*

She crawled over to him, taking his face in her palm so he'd look at her. Even she could see he looked terrified, his eyes were wide with shock, red and watery from the tears.

His heart bleeds for those he hurts in any way.

"Druenn," she whispered to him a smile on her face.

"Look at me, honey, please… look at me."

Druenn slowed his panting as his eyes met hers. He saw the familiar twinkle in her green and blue eyes. "I believe in you, you did what you had to do, we need you." His eyes flittered across Reaflik struggling to ward off Terribor's attacks, Rick mortified and crying still holding his brothers hand. The twins he couldn't see because they were behind the desk. He looked back at Emily.

"I need you," she said with that special look of hope she always wears when Druenn is in combat.

In an instant he composed himself, his beautiful sky blue eyes flashed and clouded until the gold returned to them.

She crawled several paces back. "Do what you need to do."

Druenn bared his teeth and turned to the man of pure evil, his memories flashed more clearly now, the Dean, his father, Warren, Alex, Joe and Rupert.

It's because of him! He's the reason, I swear from this day on I shall eradicate evil from the kingdom, I swear it!

He gripped his sword and leapt to his feet.

Reaflik felt his grip on his sword loosen; another slash later and the sword fell out of his hand. He saw Terribor's sword swing back around. Druenn blocked the attack and pushed Reaflik back to protect another flurry if it came.

"Your fight is with me Terribor Strife, not these innocent students."

"Not with you, Druenn." His gaze turned to Emily. "With her!"

Druenn felt a blast of wind smash into him, he felt as if he had been hit by a boulder, him, Reaflik and the twins fell against the window.

They watched helplessly as Emily floated through the air towards Terribor's outstretched hand. Her neck landed into his grasp.

Druenn pulled off his bow and knocked an arrow with a perfect aim for Terribor's head. Druenn instantly became weak with panic as he realised his friends were quickly being picked off, he knew that Rick couldn't fight in his state, Reaflik was exhausted and fatigued, so too were the twins, no one was any use to him, and now he had Emily.

"If you hurt her…" Druenn gasped for air as if he had been punched in the gut.

"You'll do what? Fire? I doubt that entirely." He held a dagger to Emily's throat.

"Druenn, kill him!" Druenn paused taking dead aim, deciding his next move.

"Lower your weapon and she lives!"

Druenn did so.

"That's a good boy," Terribor mocked.

Druenn watched Terribor carefully.

"I know you all intended to leave before tomorrow's contract let's just say this will help you reconsider."

Rick, still holding his brother's hand, looked up at Terribor, rage filling his gaze. Reaflik and the twins panted watching intently, Druenn took a step forward.

"What makes you think we would go on this contract?" Druenn asked, keeping his voice steady. *Stay calm and keep him talking, distract him from the option of killing Emily.*

"You all go on this quest, or Emily dies. She will be released when you arrive at the site. Deal?" Emily wriggled but couldn't break free from Terribor's strong grip, she felt as if she was caught in a vice with no escape.

"Please, don't do this, Druenn." More tears filled her eyes. "I don't want to lose any of you."

Druenn winced inwardly at the last comment as it stabbed at his chest.

I don't want to lose you, Em.

"Deal? Druenn, it's now or she dies," in a panic Druenn nodded his head, his chest throbbed for the amount of people in pain right now, so many things had gone wrong with in the space of one day.

"Deal." Druenn gritted his teeth again whilst he spoke.

This isn't right, Rick lost his brother and Emily and I have lost Emily, The Dean and Warren, we all lost Alex. So many hearts bleed today.

"Good, then I will see you tomorrow ready for the march up to the camp," and with that Terribor with Emily disappeared out of the door.

Druenn breathed heavily trying to slow down his heart racing, he turned to assess the damage done.

Reaflik held his side, blood trickled down his fingers. Reaflik spotted Druenn's gaze.

"It's all right, nothing some linen won't look after, he just caught me."

The twins tended to each other's wounds, Sam had a nasty cut on his forehead and Bram had taken a shard of glass to his left thigh.

His gaze turned to Alex on the floor, his eyes already glazing over. Hands on his hips he shook his head in frustration.

Why Alex? You've been such a loyal friend. You fooled everyone.

He couldn't help not feeling the sympathy he knew he should but that was because his mind was in so many different directions.

He turned to Joseph, still on the floor, tracing up from his feet, legs, body then Rick knelt on the floor next to his brother, holding his face he wiped another tear away.

"This would have never happened if I didn't get caught up in your life, Druenn."

Druenn stood and listened to what Rick had to say, he agreed but it hurt so much more to hear it coming from his friend.

"Rick, I…"

Rick rose to his feet and gestured for Druenn to be silent.

"No, I don't want to hear it, you killed my brother! And then you get Emily taken from us, just after breaking her heart because you want to go off playing heroes with your new friend." Rick waved his arms in the air then punched the desk in frustration after letting out a mighty cry for his loss.

"Get your thick heads out of the clouds you stupid immature children!" Rick roared at Druenn and Reaflik.

"Rick!" Druenn tried again.

"No. Forget it, I'm done, im washing my hands off of you. I'll get Emily back and leave myself, the both of us and we are going to Cetni to the arena. Have a great life, Druenn," Rick spat as he stormed out.

Druenn watched the door slam behind him, leaving him clutching his hair.

Why is everything going wrong? What is happening?

Terribor looked up at Emily suspended from the Dean's office ceiling, bound and gagged. Tears dripped down into a large goblet placed directly where the tears fell.

Terribor sat in the Dean's seat, stroking his black hair and grinning. "Everything is going according to plan."

TWENTY-FIVE

Shreftwood Swiftrunner

Warren Anguish stumbled through the forest far north of Tharlian. He had begun climbing the steady incline towards Camp Swiftrunner for half a day now and he stared up into the dark trees of the forest. Up here the lush green grass danced in the breeze and the trees swayed along with it. He was exhausted mentally and physically, he just wanted to be in bed and sleep but he knew he had more important things to attend to.

Warren had done this before several times. He knew better than to just aimlessly wander through Ranger territory, which could result in instant death.

He raised his hands high above his head and spoke loudly to the forest. "I come alone, I am armed but no intention in using them. My name is Warren Anguish ex-member of Divine Victory Second Division, I wish to speak to your master, Shreftwood Swiftrunner."

There was a moment of silence then a soft thud like a branch had hit the leafy ground. A figure drifted towards him, the cloak disguised them so well it was common to not know you were being attacked before a ranger was a foot away from you.

"Anguish? Is that you, my old friend? It's been a while," a young friendly voice answered.

Warren knew it well, the perfect diction and sweet flowing

words told him instantly that it was an elf to start, as the figure came into view and lowered his lush fern green hood and saw the long flowing hair, the pale complexion and bright purple eyes Warren knew instantly, a large smile streaked across his face.

"Gravland Petture!" a bellow of laughter broke through Warren's mouth, he clapped his hands in joy, Gravland gazed at Warren a smile across his face. Gravland was around about the same age as Warren – early thirties, his long brown hair with small braids on the left side of his forehead.

His leaf green linen shirt was designed without sleeves and his brown leather trousers were scuffed. His leaf green cloak and hood was the main feature about his outfit, it was the rangers way of disappearing into the shadows of the forest.

He was lean but well built, obviously undergone hard training with his bow and arrows.

"I thought you were dead!"

"I was," the perfect melodic voice continued. He stroked back a lock of hair behind his pointed ear, he planted his bow into the loose undergrowth, and lent on it.

Seeing Gravland had lowered his weapon' three other soft thuds hit the ground and gracefully glided toward them, they positioned themselves perfectly in line with each other to create a triangle, Gravland being at the front.

Warren remembered Gravland when he joined Divine Victory, he was nineteen when he first joined, a very enthusiastic boy, sometimes over the top and got him into trouble but now Warren could see he had matured, the camp of Swiftrunner had done him some good.

Master Shreftwood is legend of his time and an incredible master, what id give to study under his guidance.

"How did you survive, I saw... You were killed, in the tower of Valmorgen, the day we killed the Queen Morrandier. Gravland's eyes dropped to the ground his face contorted with pain.

"I thought I was also." His face perked up as he continued. "Shreftwood came to the tower later on that very day to ensure there were no survivors of Divine Victory. He found me and nursed me back to health here." He raised his arms in gesture to the surroundings.

"Hello, Warren. Oh, it has been such a long time," a high soprano voice whisked through the soft breeze, this voice was beautiful. It was like music to the ears. Warren also knew who this was.

It's Shreftwood's sweetheart.

He turned his gaze toward the direction of the voice, his gaze reached a beautiful woman behind him. Her outfit looked more ready for battle, she wore grey knee long boots, leather trousers that clung tightly to her thighs. Her light brown shirt fitted snuggly round her chest and tucked under her belt round her waist, over the top she wore a basic light plate of chest of armour, wrapped around her neck was a long draping crimson coloured cloak, her quiver protruding from underneath. A short sword at her waist, she held her hands on her hips as if posing for him. Her long black hair danced in the sweet breeze, her eyes glowed like sapphires; they burnt holes through Warren. She could always tell when he was lying or understanding a situation before Warren could say a word, she was an incredible woman for reading people's thoughts.

"Lengolassa, how good it is to see you." He embraced her, he had missed these people, she didn't join Divine Victory but she stood alongside fighting from the sidelines. Warren couldn't lie he hadn't seen a female fighter as good as her, not even Sarah could compare to her; she could fight with a sword and in the blink of an eye switch to her bow and arrow and already have three enemies dead.

"I heard you want to see Shreftwood?"

"I do very much so, it is extremely important and I'd appreciate you two being there too."

"What seems to be the problem?" Gravland asked, turning back the way the rangers had come. Using his long bow as a walking stick he walked side by side with Warren, Lengolassa on the opposite side. The three rangers that accompanied them formed a triangle behind them, an arrow knocked as they probed the trees for any enemies.

Reaching the camp Warren was astounded at the progress they had made since he was last there. Giving Warren a pat on the back Gravland smiled widely and looked out over their land.

"Warren, welcome to Camp Swiftrunner."

Warren stared over the large wooden houses within the trees with rope bridges going between them. He saw a water mill carrying water from a stream nearby, the houses on the ground built to the elvian tradition, blue tiled roofs which glided down the length of the houses until reaching the ground themselves.

Warren walked with his two friends through the camp. He knew this wasn't a camp any more, this was a fully functioning village. A small fishmonger, butchers selling their goods called to potential customers as they walked through. He could hear in the distance a large two storey building with loud talking and laughter. He had no doubt that what he could hear in this building must have been a gambling hall. Elves were famous for their love to gamble.

They reached a point where the forest immediately stopped and

Warren could see there was a large circle on which there was one large two storey building; outside he saw people all with wooden swords in their hands following in unison what must have been a lesson, teaching them discipline in combat. He saw children as young as seven or eight also joining in.

I guess you can never be too young to learn how to protect your family, Warren found himself thinking. His mind reeled back to last night when he watched his son run from him in the hall. His heart felt it was trying to jump out of his throat, he felt that sick feeling he had felt the day before, what was it that really stabbed at his emotion?

Guilt? Knowing my son hates me? That I failed the Dean and Druenn? His subconscious happily agreed. *You messed up so badly this time Warren, and now everyone you knew down there will pay for your idiocy.*

By the time he had fallen out of his daydream Lengolassa had disappeared behind a curtain that served as the entrance of the large building.

Gravland bounced on his feet in line with Warren. Warren eyed him, Gravland had a grin on his face and gestured to watch who was coming.

As movement was heard from behind the curtain Gravland leaned in and whispered something into Warren's ear.

"Oh, by the way, guess who else survived thanks to Shreftwood's quick thinking?"

Warren wheeled in shock and excitement. "Who?"

The curtain moved aside and Lengolassa stepped out to hold it open for two shadowed figures now making their way out.

First Shreftwood walked out, his peaceful eyes meeting Warren's, his smile radiated a safe aura, it always did. He wore pale grey knee length boots and his brown leather trousers. He could see they had chainmail and fur within sections of them. He wore a tabard of the guild of rangers, a burgundy base and golden bow with trees in the background. The main feature for Shreftwood was the large shoulder pads he carried, grey leather with what looked like dragon scales plated over the top. His brown shaggy hair looked like it had been recently washed.

Warren met his gaze again and a wave of relief rested on Warren's shoulders.

"Oh, Warren Anguish what an honour it is to see you again," Shreftwood said, his voice smooth and calm, a slight hint of an Ethalas accent still present in his voice. He stepped forward and took Warren's hand and patted his shoulder.

Before Warren could speak the second figure had appeared in the doorway. A deep rumble of a voice burst out.

"Warren Anguish, it's so good to see you!" A bulky man strode out to place himself next to Shreftwood.

"By the Divine, Krona!" Warren said. Krona was heavily built with muscle, he carried a large shield on his back. He wore bulky brown boots which looked too heavy to wear, his greaves were no different, dark grey plated greaves and chest piece, he too wore the guilds tabard along with his shoulder pads what looked like the horns of a large ram placed back to front, they curled round to meet and mounted on the horns were two large slabs of metal. That's the only way Warren could describe it, two slabs of metal. They didn't look odd, just heavy.

"I had no idea you had survived too Krona."

"Well I'm afraid we are all that's left of our little group." His eyes touched on Gravland, Shreftwood and Warren, he let out an exasperated sigh and placed his knuckles on his waist.

"The things we could have done, had things turned out differently."

Warren nodded absently, his mind wandering back to happier days, days shared with a team of friends that he'd grown very fond of. Sarah drifted into his memory and his heart throbbed.

I miss her so much, he thought, what he would do to be with her right now, to be near her, to be holding her, to be loving her.

Shreftwood's calm articulated voice began to grow louder as Warren slowly began sensing the conversation around him.

"So you have some news to discuss with us, Warren? Warren?"

Warren reeled back to the present. Quickly shaking his head he followed Shreftwood back into his building. The long room was bright; the horizontal patterned wood had been painted in an array of colour, the wooden walls red with black and white patterns that Warren knew told stories but did not understand them.

The room had a large open window space that stretched the length of the far back wall, the wooden floor covered with hand-woven carpets, patterns such as the Cetni white tiger with the blazing blue eyes.

A small table that must have only reached up to Warren's ankles looked like it could only fit six people round it, there were small red cushions marking the seating. Shreftwood knelt down on one at the far end of the table Krona following to the cushion on his right, Lengolassa on his left and Gravland next to Lengolassa. Shreftwood gestured to take a seat at the opposite end of the table to him. All four of the group placed their hands on their knees with their backs straight.

Warren copied out of politeness.

"Straight down to business," Shreftwood said, clicking his fingers he looked towards the doorway where two young boys dashed in.

"Tea please boys," the two boys bowed politely and scampered off to make tea. Warren watched the two children dart round a corner the far end of the room.

He lay his hands face down and spread his fingers wide then tightened his grip. Shreftwood scrutinized his pained expression.

"We have a problem in Reinhold" Krona leaned forward waiting impatiently. "The Dean is dead."

Shreftwood's expression dropped mournfully. He knew the Dean well. He had served with him briefly in Divine Victory as he taught the first generation humility and inner peace.

"Oh no, that is a sh—"

"Terribor killed him." Krona leapt to his feet, Lengolassa also, Gravland and Shreftwood lent forward, concern clouding everyone.

"What?" Krona's deep rumble of a voice barked.

Warren's head dropped in dismay. "He had turned a student against Druenn."

"Druenn!" Shreftwood said, his concern deepening. "Your son?"

Warren nodded. In a panic he explained the story on how Rupert had been corrupted, the Dean's untimely demise and finally Druenn and Warren's relationship breaking on learning the truth that Warren was his father.

"And now I fear Terribor is planning to kill all the students in Rienhold"

Krona was now stood pacing listening intently as he stroked his brown stubble. "How does he intend to do this?"

Warren shook his head in thought back to when he broke in to Terribor's office the night before.

"I found documents, nothing that seemed important at the time, had I known this I would have reacted sooner."

He breathed slowly then continued, "I found a contract on his desk signed under the name Tomarezz Hinkstit."

Looking at the group's faces he knew they all knew that he was talking about one of the high leaders within The Mystique Knights.

"This contract had a reward of twenty-five hundred thousand, seven hundred and ninety-three gold pieces which works out about two thousand gold pieces each. The contract entailed marching north," he breathed again. "To Camp Swiftrunner and kill everyone on site, including a map of the fastest route from Reinhold to here."

The group's bewildered expression only deepened Warren's fears.

Shreftwood's eyes bored into Warren's, his features calm and ready for what needed to be done, another wave of calm washed over Warren's fears.

"How long do we have?" he asked, his voice demanding.

"They will be here by nightfall tomorrow."

In one swift move Shreftwood kicked into action, standing he began pointing at the group. "We all have to get to Terribor before he starts recruiting. He'll have the students gone and will instantly be able to start the new Mystique Knights in Reinhold. Gravland I need your best and sharpest shots on target so no misses. Krona, I'll need you to keep his *full* attention on you, don't give him a second to look elsewhere for targets."

Tightening his straps on his shield Krona unsheathed his sword and ran his finger across the blade. "Easily done, sir."

"Lengolassa, my love, I'll need you on this one, I'll need you to deliver as many blows on him as possible, back stabs etc on his back so you'll need to get up close and quietly."

She nodded in awe with her love.

"Warren!"

Warren looked up at him awestruck, only feeling inspiration for Shreftwood.

The way he fluidly takes charge with no fears for him only protecting the group.

"Warren, you're on crowd control, it's your job to ensure no stray blasts of anything he creates gets past Krona."

"I'll do my best, sir" Warren's rattled voice came out weaker than he expected.

This is it, the final stand of Divine Victory. A feeling of pride touched his very soul but it was quickly sucked up remembering the strength of Terribor and... *the staff!*

His eyes widened, Shreftwood locked on again. "Warren, what else?"

"The staff," he choked. "He has Meealduan."

Shreftwood's expression didn't change except for a small smirk in the corner of his mouth. "Then we will need to be faster."

Krona turned for the door, the children arrived with the tea. Krona ruffled one of the children's hair and took a small cup from the tray they held up.

Warren rose to his feet. "We are going now?" he asked, his thoughts scattered and unable to comprehend the speed at which these people were working.

"No time like the present," Krona declared, turning to look back at Warren.

Warren shook his head and pulled his robe tightly around him.

Gravland took Warren by the shoulder, with one arm outstretched he gestured toward a door adjacent to the table.

"This way, we'll get you kitted up."

Krona followed Shreftwood outside. Passing the students

outside he headed for their master.

"Mistfear!" Shreftwood called.

A long white haired elf with a scar across his right eye looked up from his students and began gracefully gliding towards them.

"Sir?" he said, his voice hard and gruff. He was a young elf of forty-three but he had seen his fair share of war, in fact enough war for twenty people. Luchance Mistfear was a renowned leader of war famous for his leadership and relentless war strategies.

Shreftwood placed a hand on his friend's shoulder. Mistfear waited intently, stealing a glance at Krona who was arranging his helmet.

"Listen carefully, I need you to take care of camp Swiftrunner whilst we are gone."

"Sir?" he nodded but confusion in his voice.

"Terribor Strife is starting the Mystic Knights, we need to stop him before this gets out of hand, I'm taking what DV members we have left to end his tyranny."

"I understand, sir, I shall continue training as I should."

"No, Luchance. I need you to be ready."

"Ready, sir?" Shreftwood took a long breath.

"An army marches for camp Swiftrunner."

Mistfear's eyebrow twitched. "Then surely you should stay here?"

"No this must be ended tonight," Krona chimed in.

Mistfear nodded. "I shall ensure my men are set for battle."

"No, Luchance, there will be no war. These are children, students from Rienhold, they don't realise what they are getting themselves into, threaten them and make them see reason, I know you can do this, send them back."

Mistfear looked torn. "But if they threaten our civilization we should at…"

"No, Luchance." Shreftwood's voice was stern now. "Don't hurt any of them, we must go."

Lengolassa arrived with five horses in tow all great white geldings.

Warren stepped out of the building with Gravland both fully dressed for battle. Warren kept his robe only now over the top, one large leather shoulder pad strapped to his left shoulder, chainmail round his chest and a sword by his hip and a smaller sword on his back. Tightening his greaves he took the reins from the closest horse and pulled himself on.

This is it, time to shine, Warren, or we all face certain doom.

Shreftwood turned to his group. His face hard as rock, he looked at each member. *I hope we are ready for this.*

"DV members, we must reform for a final duty to protect the King and our people!" he called.

"For the future of Cetni!"

Krona chuckled. *Here we go again.*

Mistfear watched the greatest fighters disappear into the trees. He turned to his pupils. Anger gripped him.

They think they can waltz up here and take our land? Who cares what Shreftwood says? This is for our people.

Watching the children practice their routine fighting stances, he called for the elder rangers around the camp.

He eyed them, all eager and ready to stare death in the face. "Prepare for battle!" he called, and the group bowed.

TWENTY-SIX

The Price We Must Pay

Druenn sat on his bed, his fingers clamped together, his feelings were scattered, defeat, remorse, regret.

Reaflik sat beside him. "So... what now?"

Druenn ran his fingers through his growing hair. "I don't know, Flick, I just don't." He buried his head in his hands. He felt a tear well in his eye.

Who was his father? Why did Terribor kill the Dean, he knew. He did, no other explanation.

Emily taken by Terribor and will not be harmed as long as they go to war up north.

Rick his best friend hated him for killing his brother. He had killed two people, students at the school.

"Come on, Druenn, we need to get Emily back." Reaflik coxed, trying desperately to infuse some determination in his beaten friend.

"I don't know how, it's Terribor, he's executed this plan so perfectly. My guess is the only way will be when they release her when we get there, then we run, that's all I can think of."

Reaflik jumped to his feet and walked over to the bookshelves, leaning up against them he thought carefully.

"He will be expecting us won't he, he knows someone like you wouldn't give up on Emily so easily."

Druenn's head looked up. "So we call his bluff, we just have to hope he doesn't harm her in the meantime."

"It's a risky gamble, Druenn. Do you really feel that's wise?"

"I honestly can't think of another way, she must be locked up in his office and he will be waiting." A stab of emotion coursed through him as his heart went out thinking of Emily in pain.

Now standing, unable to contain his growing apprehension. "We need to train."

"What?" Reaflik crossed his arms confused why Druenn would choose to train.

"But… Emily needs us."

"And she'll need us to get her out of battle tomorrow, we need to train to ensure we don't miss any enemies as we escape together."

A knock on the door caused the two boys to turn in unison. Bram followed by Sam stood peeking round the side of the door. "We both heard your plans on running as we begin the fight. Do you mean that? Flee from the battle?"

Reaflik nodded, his face stern.

"Druenn thinks we need to practice retreating."

The twins looked at each other then returned to Reaflik. "That's what we hoped, we need the practice too."

TWENTY-SEVEN

I Know Druenn Lightblaser

Over the great capital city Cetni, Drykator walked towards the Mages University.

The rain beat down on his thin shirt. Small puddles gathered together breaking the banks between the cobbles and grouping together like a gathering army of water.

Stepping up to the large doors a guard to his right looked at him only wearing his civilian clothes, brown boots, brown trousers and red-laced shirt and red cloak, his sword at his side.

"Drykator?" the old guard asked, his voice struggling to speak over the pouring rain. "What brings you to the mages?"

Drykator watched the old man, his long greasy grey, shaggy hair draped over his face, his eyes sunken and his thin skin making it impossible to miss his pale cheekbones.

"Good afternoon, Brently. I hope to find someone who knows a certain person," he called wrapping his cloak round him and spitting the pouring water from his face out of his mouth.

"Ahh right." Brently nodded, understanding not to ask questions. He had learnt to stay out of Divine Victory's buisness in the past.

Even though Drykator wasn't a member he knew his intention was to restart the group.

He rapped on the door with three soft taps, a bang, then a further five taps. The doors slowly creaked open. Drykator stared into the well-lit circular room.

"Where's that Drago Character, he not with you? I noticed he seems to travel with you a lot these days?" Brently asked as Drykator began to move.

Drykator stole a last glance at the old man. "He's in the tavern again," he said quietly with the hint of frustration.

Once again, Brently nodded.

Drykator walked into the oval room. The marble floor was brightly coloured with a rainbow running a ring round the edge, a blue pillar following inward to a large star with seven points all representing the colours of magic:

Earth, Air, Fire, Water, Gravity, Life and Death.

Pillars surrounded the room. Circling above the pillars stained glass windows with images Drykator couldn't make out, they were too high to see. To the right beyond the pillars was a desk he guessed was the reception.

A soft pat of shoes patted across the marble floor towards him. Looking in the direction of the footsteps he spotted a long flowing white silk dress, tied at the waist with a thin white rope. Her hips swung side to side so elegantly.

His eyes rose to her face. She was beautiful; her grey eyes were dazzling as she watched Drykator standing in the centre of the room.

"Hello." A sweet chirpy voice resonated out of her in her light soprano voice.

"My name is Nathuni Alstar, is there anything I can assist you with?"

Drykator collected himself and nodded. "There is, I am looking for someone, someone specific and need to know if anyone knows who he is."

The young girl cocked her head to one side and looked at Drykator with intrigue. "Well... maybe I could help." Her voice was so soft and melodic he loved listening to her.

"Oh... Okay," Drykator said, taken aback. "Do you know Druenn Lightblaser?"

She puzzled it over for a moment, her eyes returned to him with a small smile. "No... I haven't."

Drykator's heart sank. Sighing he turned to look around the room. "Is there anyone else I can ask?"

"One moment, please," she replied, that sweet voice dancing through Drykator's thoughts.

Nathuni turned to two older women just as beautiful but mature and wiser looking.

"Lady Aylianna, Lady Nariel, may I please speak with you?"

The two women walked over to join Nathuni. "What seems to be the problem, young one?" the tall dark haired woman asked.

"This gentleman is searching for a man called Druenn Lightblaser, does that sound familiar to you?"

The two women pondered the name over and then turned their gaze to Drykator. "We are not accustomed to that name but we shall consult our high majy for you."

Drykator quickly broke in only wanting to deal with his father's last wish himself.

"With all due respect I would like to talk to the mage myself". Drykator wasn't sure what a Majy was but he thought it must be their master.

The two women bowed to him and turned to Nathuni.

"Youngling, go ask for Lady O'Skreeva."

"Yes, my elder." She bowed to the three of them then turned and scurried away.

Drykator continued to study the room around him, the two women eyed him, swinging back and to on his toes to heel he made a small awkward smile and continued to look around.

"Aah, Mister Epsonstar," a croaky voice resonated around the oval room.

He turned to a woman appearing from the shadows behind Aylianna and Nariel. Her violet robe elegantly danced across the floor followed by the soft pit pat of her soft lace sandals.

"How may the University of Mages assist you? You may leave now girls" without glancing at her students she gestured for them to leave, the two women bowed and left. Nathuni stood at O'Skreeva's side. She looked down at her young sixteen-year-old student.

My little Nathuni, how you have grown from when we first met.

Keeping her voice strong and authoritative she looked at Nathuni. "You too, youngling."

"Yes, Mother." She turned and left.

Drykator gestured the question, is she your daughter? He could see Miss O'Skreeva was well into her sixties, her features were withered and pale.

"She's not my daughter, I found her when she was ten years old. I took her in and raised her as my own."

"Where was she?" Drykator asked.

"It was part of the bandit situation six years ago, shall we take a walk?"

O'Skreeva began to walk alongside Drykator as they made their way through the university.

"First of all I'd like to apologise for your loss," O'Skreeva said.

Drykator nodded. "Thank you, he is at peace now."

Leaving the oval room they ascended down into a corridor leading towards the courtyard gardens.

"Those bandits are still out there you know? They destroyed another village, Rudor has become the latest victim to their plight, I oversaw the recovery of the survivors last night."

"How many made it out?" O'Skreeva asked her voice becoming somber.

"Five out of a village of fifty-two, all adults, no children survived."

"Are you saying they are targeting the children?" O'Skreeva continued concern growing for the bandit situation.

Their twisted evil has gone on far too long, she thought.

They passed a class of students studying battle techniques. Drykator paused to watch.

"Battle Mages! O'Skreeva exclaimed.

"They are magnificent," Drykator replied in awe.

Two students were stood in the centre of the room, a man carried a staff and the other was a girl, no more than fifteen, twitched and caressed her hands. The male thrust his staff forward screaming in a beastly voice causing Drykator to jump.

"Reechor Stendar!"

A beam of golden light and electric bolts blasted out of his staff. The bolts hurtled towards the young girl.

Pushing her arms forward gracefully Drykator watched a ball of water appear from nothing. The ball twisted into the shape of a shield.

The blast hit the wall of water, the water ignited in a explosion of waves as the electricity conducted the water, the water evaporated and left the girl holding a pulsating ball of electricity that she launched back at the man, unable to find a spell fast enough the man flew off the ground into the back wall.

"And that's why students you do not always need a weapon to fight your battles just this." The teacher tapped on her temple. "This will save you far more than any weapon."

Drykator and O'Skreeva continued on out into the courtyard where a few students were reading on small benches or practicing spells.

"I think the bandits are searching for someone, it actually coincides who I'm looking for" Drykator continued.

I'm starting to wonder if anyone knows this person.

"Aah, yes, Nathuni mentioned your searching for someone."

Placing his hands behind his back he continued, "I'm looking for a man called Druenn Lightblaser, do you know who he is?"

"Druenn. Wow!" Her eyes opened wide with surprise.

It does make sense though, he is searching for descendants.

"Yes, I do," she said slowly.

Drykator's eyes shot up. "You do?" He felt dumbfounded.

I've found him, I have actually found him!

"Where is he? I must find him!" he said in haste. "There's no time to delay!"

"The last time I saw him was six years ago, Mister Epsonstar. I do not know if he will still be there," O'Skreeva explained.

"I've got to try," Drykator replied.

"The last time I saw him he was on his way with Warren Anguish to Rienhold."

"Rienhold!" He knew all about Rienhold, when he was younger he would argue regularly with his father for permission to study there.

"If you are going to go I know a guide in the city that will take you."

"Thank you for your help, Miss O'Skreeva."

Later that evening Drykator stepped back into the Dragon's Demise Tavern. Searching the room he saw Drago in the far corner a bar maid sitting on his lap. Gulping down the last of another pint he pulled the barmaid's lips to his, letting out a yelp.

"I'm on a roll!" as yet another man banged his fists against the table and pulled himself from the table, the man stomped past Drykator muttering to himself.

"Stupid dragonslayer, who does he think he is? Stealing all my money, what is the wife going to say now."

Drykator could not understand Drago.

All that talent and he just wastes it on drinking, gambling and women, I'm not letting him waste it any more.

He stormed over to the table and pulled him up by his collar, the barmaid scampered back to the bar. The music stopped and everyone turned to Drykator and Drago.

"Get off, you fool, can't you see I'm winning?" Drago bellowed as his eyes darted round the room only wanting to run from their gaze.

"No, you child!" Drykator replied anger welling in him. "I want to show these people how much of a coward you are, you claim to be a hero! Then show it!"

"I killed a dragon no more than…"

"What's heroic about killing a creature that forged the world, being a hero is about loyalty, honor, protecting the weak."

Cheers went up from around the room.

Dropping Drago to the floor he watched the boy scramble about on the floor before pulling himself up drawing his Dragon blade.

"Raising your weapon to me isn't heroic, you don't have a clue do you!"

Walking away from Drago he listened to the cheers as the people began to chant a familiar song.

Epsonstar for the free, Epsonstar freed you and me, let Epsonstar come and save us all, let his son hold us strong and never fall.

Drago brushed himself off and quickly collected his money before packing his lute away.

Drykator searched the room then called out. "I was told by Sadia O'Skreeva that someone here can take me to Rienhold!"

The people went back to their drinks and conversations, a hand raised in the centre of the room.

"That would be me, sir."

Drykator walked up to the man, he looked like he was in his late thirties, maybe very early forties.

"You can take me?" he asked eager to get going.

Drago watched him carefully standing by his table.

Coward? We'll see who the coward is' I'll show him what it means to be Drago Dragonslayer!

"Yeah, I used to work at Rienhold… Well before it was taken over by their new leader," the man continued.

"What happened?"

The man explained roughly what had happened earlier that week. "Terribor Strife his name is, the teachers got suspicious he was killing everyone off when the Dean turned up dead and then three teachers died that night. He's sending all the students to their deaths tomorrow, the bastard!" He took a large swig of his wine. Wiping his face he looked overcome. "There was nothing I could do. I was just the gatekeeper." Throwing his arm out he took Drykator's hand.

"Name's Dontain, I'll be honored to take you there."

"Thank you, Dontain. I do appreciate this."

"I hope you don't mind my asking but why do you want to go?"

Drykator felt a stab of fear as he recalled on what Dontain had just said.

He's sending all the students to their death's tomorrow!

"I'm looking for Druenn Lightblaser."

Dontain's eyes widened in fear as he reached for his spear lying on the chair next to him. "We better get moving then."

Lighting a torch, Drykator mounted Runner, he whinnied and reared before galloping into the dying sky.

Drago mounted Strike, his white stallion.

A coward? A coward? The divine burn him, me. A coward? I'll show him! he thought as he watched Cetni float into the distance as he charged after Dontain and Drykator. *Let's see if this Druenn Lightblaser is worth all of this trouble.*

In the University of Mages, Nathuni stared out of the window as the rainclouds began to disperse above the the city walls.

Druenn Lightblaser. I wonder what kind of man he is. Sounds like an exciting person. I wonder what he does?

A young girl walked gracefully behind her. Nathuni watched her arrive. She was new in the university; she had arrived from Rienhold a few days earlier.

"Is everything all right?" she asked.

"Oh, Shiele, I was just wondering what kind of person Druenn

Lightblaser was, a man came looking for him earlier."

"Druenn Lightblaser? I knew him, he was in Rienhold with me!" she replied excitedly.

"Seriously?" Nathuni replied only wanting to know more.

"He sounds fascinating. Please tell me more about him."

Shiele began her story about the boy called Druenn Lightblaser.

Terribor watched the sun disappearing over the horizon. He cackled quietly, pouring himself a goblet of wine as he placed himself regally on the Dean's chair.

He took a sip.

"Druenn and all of your little companions, it's time for you to die!"

TWENTY-EIGHT

We March To Our Graves

"Get up, you maggots!" someone shouted, his voice sounding rough and croaky.

Druenn woke up with a start as he felt his body fall helplessly out of his bed tumbling on to the floor. His eyes shot open.

Two students he barely knew only by the fact that they were prefects of Terribor supporters towered over him. Reaflik decided to stay with Druenn that night and now they were both laying on the floor in the dim light of the two torches the prefects were holding, they heard a muffled voice coming past the doorway, their eyes darted towards the direction of the door to see Emily and Rick bound and two more prefects dragging them past.

Druenn turned back to Reaflik, his heart pounded with trepidation, he looked towards the window, it was still dark, the stars and moon disappearing behind a dark cloud; the cloud looked down at Druenn mockingly. He could see the same look on Reaflik's face as the torch passed him.

His face quickly changed to a wince, he grunted. Druenn instantly feared for his new friend. He quickly realised the reason for his friend's sudden pain.

As Druenn watched Reaflik recoil from the blow a stab of pain raced through Druenn's chest, he winced as the wind left his body he saw the foot retract from the prefect.

"Get to your feet, scum!" the voice squawked again. The two boys were hoisted up onto their feet like two ragdolls at the mercy of their masters.

"It's not even morning yet," Druenn's rattled voice said, his eyes searching for Reaflik but he had already been hoisted up and dragged out of the room.

Still rattled and dazed from his sudden awakening he was struggling to process all this information.

We can't leave now my plan isn't set! he screamed inside, thinking of Emily and Rick. He knew he needed to save them now.

His mind reeling for a solution he realised a simple plan that would help him escape the clutches of this prefect.

Stamping on the prefect's foot, his grip loosened as he howled in pain.

Druenn shrugged him and pushed him to the floor, grabbing his green leather shirt and slinging his bow and quiver on and finally reaching for his sword he wrapped the belt round his waist.

Stepping out of the room he quickly caught up to Reaflik's restrainer. Before he could reach him Druenn felt a pain in his back and then two clamps like vices as two prefects grabbed his arms and dragged him out into the courtyard.

Druenn was not prepared to see what was waiting in the courtyard. He began to panic as all his plans and solutions were slipping away like dust floating away in the wind. He knew now that none of his friends would live to see the sun go down that evening including Druenn.

We are going to die.

In front of him was the entire school. The whole of Rienhold had been pulled out. Formed in lines with their classmates including

334

the new recruits. Druenn's heart went out to the little ten-year-olds.

What madness is this Terribor? Druenn thought, his hatred only deepening for the man. Torches encircled the army of students that were the Terribor supporters including his prefects all stood with crossbows facing towards the students. Anyone who shared an opinion of Divine Victory or chose not to was sentenced to his or her deaths.

"My friends!" Terribor called from the front of the crowd. "This is a glorious morning, you go to certain victory and riches today!"

The crowd roared.

Druenn fell to the floor as the prefects dropped him into the crowd. He scrambled to his feet to see Emily standing beside him. Rick and Reaflik also stood by her. Even the twins were there, holding their weapons ready. Druenn instinctively went to hug Emily before she pushed him back along with a slap across his cheek, his cheek burned as he watched Emily refusing to flinch. She began to whisper. "Why didn't you come for me?" Her eyes welled to this betrayal.

"Emily," Druenn started, confident that his decision was the correct one. "I would have done anything you know that, but I knew I'd end up like Rick."

Rick thought for a moment feeling his head where dried blood that had been trickling down his forehead earlier and he remembered hanging suspended with Emily from the Dean's office ceiling.

"What's the plan now?" Bram asked, his eyes darting around the excited crowd.

Druenn had no ideas left.

Forcing his fears down he stayed composed and strong for his friends, stealing a glance at Emily and Rick, his two best friends both wanting to be anywhere away from him. He watched Emily for a moment, her face was unreadable. He remembered not too long ago he could read her like a book.

Oh, I miss her hugs, I'd give anything to know how she feels.

"I know what you're thinking," Emily began. "I'm thinking where has my Druenn gone? You are not the Druenn I love!"

Her words hit Druenn like an arrow to his heart, he felt an unsettled sick feeling in the pit of his stomach.

"Go to war!" Terribor roared his voice echoing into the darkness of the far edges of the courtyard.

The crowd began to march, the prefects ensured they were marching alongside them and were barged and pushed until they joined the army that was marching from Rienhold.

Druenn's emotions were scattered, he felt mentally drained from the mixed emotions of the last few days.

And now I've lost Emily. We march to our doom.

He watched the edges of the horizon begin to turn a beautiful sea blue, across the dark silhouetted trees and a windmill far off in the distance.

Epilogue

Shreftwood Swiftrunner, Krona Overa, Warren Anguish, Lengolassa Beechwood and Gravland Petture stared down the long road towards Rienhold. The sun was just peaking over a large cliff to their left across the long plains of fields and streams, casting a beautiful ting of yellow and pink on the grass.

Shreftwood stepped forward a pace in front of the group. "Be on your guard my friends. He will have an army in there." He nodded in the direction of Rienhold.

"But the students have already left for Camp Swiftrunner," Krona said, tightening his shield's strap around his wrist.

Shreftwood did the same only with his bow. Taking a small, triangular hand guard that worked as a small hand sized shield from his belt he clipped it to his phoenix-crested bow.

"It won't be the students, Krona," he replied, sounding sombre.

Warren looked over at Shreftwood, his expression was strong but he could see he knew this was a battle they couldn't win.

But we are Divine Victory surely we can win this. He couldn't take us all... could he?

Warren heard Shreftwood's voice in his head repeating those words.

It won't be the students. He will have an army in there. He couldn't have had members elsewhere.

"Time to face him, this new Black Betrayer."

Warren walked with his good friends towards Rienhold. He felt

337

the same trepidation for the battle ahead but the same pride standing side by side with Divine Victory. He missed his days with them, the fun he had as well as the pride and respect. *And the gold was better.*

The gates were damaged and swung freely in the wind. Entering Rienhold they searched the long hall, darkness, empty, deserted.

The wind blew softly through the space giving the impression that the building was breathing.

Lighting a torch they walked down the dark corridor, their steps echoing back and forth.

Warren looked around horrified; this once precious school was destroyed. Parchments floated across the corridors, upturned tables and desks lay strewn across the classrooms.

"Let's head for Terribor's office," Shreftwood said, searching for the route. Warren took the lead and guided them into the mess hall which used to be the where the students had their dinners. But instead of being rows of tables and benches there was a single wooden throne in the centre.

The group stopped as they spotted a silhouette slouched in the chair. A soft tap could be heard as the shadow tapped his finger against the arm of the throne.

"I thought you'd bring the rest of you, Krona, Gravland, nice to see you survived," the shadow murmured.

Shreftwood stepped forward. "You will pay for your crimes, Terribor Strife!"

Terribor stood from his throne and clicked his fingers. More silhouettes began appearing round the edges of the room.

"Will I, Shreftwood Swiftrunner? Or will you!"

To Be Continued…